QUEENIE
& THE
KRAKENS
THE KRAKENS MOTORCYCLE CLUB

INTERNATIONAL BESTSELLING AUTHOR
ALEERA ANAYA CERES

Cover design and typography image by: Moorbooks Designs

Kraken MC logo by: Moorbooks Designs

Edited by: Lisa Nieves-Taylor

To Crystal and Kathryn.
Thanks for putting me in a chokehold and making me finish this story.
"Because we need more mermen bikers."
I love you.

Author's Note

Queenie & the Krakens is a Reverse Harem, Why Choose standalone that contains content not suitable for readers under 18. Inside you will find MM, MMF, and MFM pairings, explicit scenes. **For a detailed list of a Trigger and Content Warnings**, please visit my website.

NAOMI

There are three integral rules I like to live my life by.
   1. Don't follow stupid people.
   2. Don't get involved with pricks.
   3. Don't go to the other side of town.

Funny how within the span of a single night I've managed to break all three.

I guess I should give some backstory on this, huh?

I mean, the rules themselves seem pretty self-explanatory. Following stupid is just plain stupid. That saying comes to mind: "If your friend jumps off a bridge, would *you*?" The answer is *hell fucking nah*. I'll watch your destruction from my safety net, far, far the fuck away where you can't pull me down to my death alongside you.

Then there's the prick thing. You'd have that rule too if you spent your whole life watching your mother get used and discarded by the same type of asshole time and time again. Seeing her spirit broken down, hearing the tears every fucking night? Yeah, I was over it by the time I turned twelve—when I vowed I'd never be someone's scraps, whore, or doormat.

As for the other side of town?

That's motorcycle club territory.

Everyone fucking knows the docks are ruled by the criminal underbelly of our little seaside town. If you want to go there for a gritty bar fight, to slum it with druggies and leather-clad assholes who will forget your name the moment you say it? That's where you go.

It's where I avoid.

It's where I currently find myself, backed into a corner as some sleaze looms over me, caging my body in with tattooed arms. I can smell the stench of booze and weed on the prick's breath, bloodshot eyes raking over my figure appreciatively.

Which brings me back to how I ended up breaking three of my most important rules in one night.

See, I never would have come here on my own. No way, no how. But it's not my fault. Sure, I'm the stupid that followed another stupid here, but I only did it to stop her from doing something stupid. You get?

See, Lourdes is my best friend. She's also heartbroken and drunk, which don't make for a good combination. In her attempt to get over her prick of an ex, she wanted to slum it. Make him jealous. Have crazy, hardcore sex with a sleazebag from the other side.

That'll teach the stuffy, missionary-only suit.

And I, being the good friend that I am, couldn't let her walk into the mouth of the shark alone.

Literally, the name of the bar is Shark Mouth, and as far as I can tell, it's neutral territory. See, I may not know much about the supernatural wars, but I know the island is split into territories, ruled by motorcycle clubs, mafia, and drug lords.

Yup, it's a kingdom of supernatural shit heads.

Vampires, shifters, and demons, *oh my*. These are creatures that live here in abundance, but none more dangerous than the leather-wearing bikers of the Caribbean Sea.

One wouldn't usually find mermen and bikers in the same sentence, but this town is full of weird shit.

My eyes flick over the leather cut and patches. The Rogue Wave MC. Their logo is a wave of red that I think is meant to be blood. The word 'Secretary' is slapped against his shoulder, so that must mean he's important in his little circle of bike rider delinquents.

He leans down, his damp hair brushing my forehead, making me shiver. Not in a good way. It's in one of those 'I see a spider crawling across my desk' type of shivers that makes me want to set the whole fucking house on fire, homelessness be damned.

"Where have you been all my life?"

QUEENIE AND THE KRAKENS

Ah, fuck this.

Is he fucking serious?

Where the fuck is Lourdes? I was following her to the bathroom as she elbowed her way through the crowd, only to be cornered by Mr. Shitty Pick-up Lines here.

And he's pressing *closer*. Yeah, this is a big no for me.

Without answering, I duck, darting beneath his arm and start to stride quickly away. Because I really, really don't need this shit.

I realize my fuck-up as soon as I take two steps away. I gave my back to my enemy, a fucking merman, who is as dangerous as a shark.

A hand clamps around the ends of my waist-length braids and pulls, yanking me backwards. I cry out as pain splinters through my skull, my feet stumbling against the slippery ground. A strong arm wraps around my waist and pulls me close. I struggle on instinct, using my elbows to strike against the body that keeps me captive.

"Let go of me!"

"Play nice and I'll be nice, you little bitch," he snarls against my neck.

Fuck fuck fuck fuckity fuck.

This is why I didn't want to come.

I bring my knee up and slam my heel down on his foot. He howls and I thank the high-heeled shoe gods as his hold on me slips. An elbow to the gut and I whirl away from him, watching cautiously as he hops on one foot.

The sight would be comical if I weren't so fucking terrified.

"You little slut!"

My heart pounds up to my throat at the sudden menace in those eyes. I'm fucked and I know it. He knows it. And God certainly knows it.

Goodbye, world. I'm about to be merman meat.

But that's when I feel a presence at my back, looming and as equally dangerous as the dude in front of me. In an instant, I know I'm surrounded, and fear is a prominent thing that slides down my spine and makes me tremble.

"Fuck off, Jet," the voice behind me growls.

Fucking. Growls.

Like an animal.

It's a deep, gravelly voice and the back of my neck itches, urging me to turn and catch a glimpse at the face to match the sound. I don't, though. Fear leaves me petrified in place as the man in front of me, Jet, snarls a feral sound at the man behind me.

"Mind your business, Scorp. The little lady here is with me."

"Um, fuck no, I'm not." His glare at my words looks like it could kill me on the spot. I don't cringe away from it but meet it with a deadly look of my own. "In case that wasn't clear when I walked away from you, asshole."

Probably not a good idea to mouth off to a biker. Shit, I've broken every other rule, what's one more thing to top the cherry off on this night?

While his eyes narrow, there's a rumbling laugh from the man behind me. I hate how that laugh travels down my body like a blanket of warmth. Fuck no.

"You heard her. Fuck off."

Tension cackles between the two and it seems like there's something deeper here. Some secret war I'm not picking up on and makes me uncomfortable. And just like that, it ends with Jet narrowing his eyes on me, a slow-curling smile twisting his lips.

"I'll be seeing you, little girl." And then he shoves past us, leaving behind a bitter taste on my body, my soul.

"Motherfucker," I groan.

Again, the stranger behind me laughs and I jolt away, realizing just how close he is. I turn, ready to bring my heeled shoe up to slam into his balls and micropeen, but I stop the moment I see his smile.

That is a smile of the heavens. The smile that wet dreams are made of. A mouth made for kissing, made for a good oral session. Fuck, it's a smile that makes me wet.

Have you ever seen a man's mouth up close and thought, damn, I'd make him live between my legs? Or, man, he looks like he'd be a great lay? Yeah, that's kind of what rushes through my brain when I see this guy.

I press my thighs together to ease the rush of desire flooding through me.

Okay, so desire might go hand in hand with stupidity. I stave it off and stiffen, hardening my resolve as I face off against the man.

Beautiful honey eyes take me in from behind dark, lowered lashes. His skin is smooth, brown, and muscled. He might be wearing a hoodie but fuck if it does anything to hide what I instinctively know is underneath. Dark jeans press against tall, thick legs that are spread apart, and leather combat boots are laced on his feet. A quick glance beneath the waist tells me that, unless home slice here shoved a prize-worthy eggplant into his boxers, then he definitely does *not* have a micropenis. Erm, not that I care.

Tattoos are spread along his neck, twining up against his dark skin. Barbed spikes decorate the outer edge of his eye in black and red, but it only deepens his criminal appeal. I hate how I find him attractive.

"You okay, pet?" There he goes again, using that perfectly deep voice that sounds like chocolate and sin.

His dark, damp hair is twisted into thin braids around his head, a single one bouncing against his forehead.

"Fine," I grind out, closing my hands into fists.

He smells like salt and summer breeze and something richer, and I can make out the cutting lines of closed gills on the side of his neck.

Merman.

Contrary to old lore, mermen and mermaids can walk on land just as easily as they swim in the water. Which make them dangerous, considering they ride on land and sea—and rule both with an iron fist. And I'm not dumb. He might not be wearing a cut, but the scent of leather clings to him just as much as the salt does, and it doesn't take a genius to equate a merman shifter to a motorcycle club.

A rival to Jet, perhaps?

It doesn't matter. I want nothing to do with either of them.

"I'm Scorpion." He holds his hand out for me to shake and my gaze is riveted on it, knowing if I shake it, he can squeeze, pull me towards him, get just as handsy as the other bastard was.

No thanks.

"Cool."

He leaves his hand extended. "Not gonna tell me your name, pet?"

I almost choke. Telling him my name could be dangerous. For the both of us.

"Alright." He lowers his hand, but that seductive smile doesn't unfurl. "Can I buy you a drink?"

My breath leaves me in a shudder. "No. I'm leaving."

His cool eyes assess me, searching for a lie, no doubt. "Want a ride?"

The words seem to be laced with double meaning. He says the word 'ride' too suggestively, and fuck if that doesn't make me feel things I shouldn't even be contemplating.

"No."

"Alright. I can take a hint."

The pulsing beat of music in the bar strums a relentless rhythm straight to my core. Over and over, it pounds with desire all because of a fucking look.

"Well..." I gesture through the air. "Thanks?"

He smirks but doesn't move. Like he's leaving the running away to me. And maybe it's a testament to my cowardice that I walk away first, his chuckle trailing after me even over the abundance of noise in the place.

I let the crowd swallow me up and I elbow my way to the bathroom in time to catch Lourdes stumbling out on wobbly legs. One look at her and my stiffness melts. Tear marks and mascara track down her cheeks, and her eyes are puffy and swollen.

"Honey..."

The sound of my voice has her breaking down and throwing her arms around me. Her sobs drown out against the material of my blouse. My hand pats her curls down and the other rubs comforting circles against her back.

"Let's go home, babe." She lets me guide her out of the bar and into a cab. It drives us across the island. We leave behind the slums on this side of the island, only to come to the slightly richer suburban area along the coast.

Lourdes and I are by no means rich, and I probably sound like a snob with my distaste for the other side. Truly, it's not the slums I'm averse to, but the criminal activity. We can say I've had issues with that kind of life before.

Never again.

So, when the cab pulls to a stop in front of a modest, sea-side house that Lourdes and I share, I pay and help her climb out and up to the front door. Inside the safety of our own place, I can relax as I lead her upstairs to her room.

She lays against her plush covers, taking in a shuddering breath. "I'm sorry," she whispers. "We shouldn't have gone there. I'm so pathetic, I couldn't even—"

"Ssh, babe, you aren't pathetic."

She purses her lips incredulously then squeezes her eyes shut. "I love him."

"I know."

I hate seeing her like this. I hate the memories it brings up of my mom. Her revolving door of men that chipped away her soul, stealing piece after piece until she was left more broken than put together. Leaving me to try and fix her. But the one thing people don't tell you about broken hearts is that it's like shattered glass with missing pieces. You can cram broken edges together all you want, but they never fit the same.

She falls asleep as soon as the words leave my lips, making me wonder if she'd even heard them at all. It doesn't matter. She's strong. She'll heal. I'll make sure I help her like I was never able to help my own mother. Pulling the blanket around her body, I tread to my own room and peek out my window and to the front yard.

The moon is high in the sky and sends silver light shining against the street. I let the curtain fall closed, and as soon as it does, I hear it.

The revving of a motorcycle, shooting off into the distance.

NAOMI

I kill the engine and wait for the boat to still before sorting through my supplies. I always like to double—sometimes triple—check to make sure I have everything I need before going on a dive. Camera, water samplers, bucket, net...

I sigh as I go through the motions, pissed because I'm not even supposed to be fucking working today. Unfortunately, one of the college kids interning at the lab fucked up and *spilled* an important water sample we needed for the testing we've been working on for months. Months of hard work fucked because some idiot with trembling hands spilt water like it was beer at a bar. *Oopsie*, my ass.

Because we have low tolerance for bullshit like that, we kicked his ass to the curb. Hence why I'm a few miles outside of Santo Domingo in the middle of the Caribbean Sea, going through my supplies and cursing the ever-living shit out of Mr. Slippery Hands.

With everything in place, I start to strip down out of my jean shorts and top. As I start to shimmy out of my swimsuit bottoms, my phone rings. I ignore it, letting it go to voicemail. It stops, but just as quickly picks up again.

Grumbling, I grab it and wince at the I.D. before answering. "Hey, Julio."

"What the fuck, kid?" his grumbling voice replies. "We had a deal."

"I'm working."

"It's your day off."

Yeah, no shit.

"Some dumbass at the lab ruined all our fucking samples so I have to get new ones."

He grumbles in response, like he doesn't quite believe me. "We had a deal."

I roll my eyes. As if I could ever forget the deal. The deal that says when he calls, I answer no matter where I am or what I'm doing. Not answering means havoc for the both of us. Grumpy ass bastard.

"Yeah, yeah, well, I have to get back to work. I want to go home."

"News says a hurricane is coming."

I look up at the sky. It's bright, but that can change in an instant. I've learned not to trust what I see; the ocean is so volatile. "I'll be careful," I assure him.

"Call you to check in tomorrow, kid."

I don't say goodbye. I just hang up. A twinge of guilt niggles through my chest at the action, but I shove it aside. Our whole relationship is based off not caring too much about one another. Or at least, pretending that we don't. And hell, it works.

Shaking those thoughts off, I finish stripping until I'm naked. Picking up my water samplers in one hand and hanging the camera around my neck with the other, I walk to the edge of my little boat, take a breath, and dive in.

The water is just the right temperature against the warmth of my body, and it envelops me the moment I sink beneath the surface and kick my legs. I hold my breath for as long as I can before instinct and years of evolution take over.

My body morphs, changes, *shifts* until the lines marring my neck open, pulling water in and I'm breathing salt water into gills. My fingers and feet grow webbing between fingers and toes. Scales scatter along my body, hardening against my flesh, becoming a part of me. Even my eyes morph into something *other*. Pupils dilate to impossible proportions, so the sting of salt doesn't burn.

Kicking my webbed feet, I propel myself deeper into the water. In order for the samples to work I need to go to the deeper depths since studying shallow water isn't the same. The deeper part of this ocean is a maze of beautiful coral reefs in an array of bright colors. Fish ignore me as they dart in and out of their anemone homes, the light piercing the surface catching against bright scales that mimic my own.

I love the ocean. It's probably the one thing I inherited from my father that I'll always accept. We both have an innate love for the water. I weave my way through coral branches and seaweed, swimming leisurely until I reach the drop off that leads into deeper, darker depths. The dangerous depths.

This dive isn't usually supposed to be done alone, but the lab is on a time crunch and need their samples *now*. No one else was available, and I don't mind. I grew up in the ocean. I'm as familiar with the touch of these waves as the lines against my palms or the light trailing of scars along my brown skin.

Down deeper on this part of the sea, the evidence of a storm's destruction lays. Ships broken into scraps of twisted metal, long lost statues and treasures are buried in the sand, creating a small underwater city. Everything is covered in algae and barnacles, and I can't help but think it all looks like it's part of a story book.

I adjust the camera strap around my neck and start recording. It's required we always document our recollection of data for future references in the lab, so this camera is state of the art, expensive, and high quality. I make sure it's recording as I make my descent into the city below.

There's always a certain mystery about this place that I love. The water hums and groans as the waves push at metal walls, giving the place an almost mystical feel. Everything about it is alluring, from the ripped metal to the rotting bones of people trapped beneath the wreckage.

People don't tend to come to this site because they fear it's haunted. That logic doesn't make sense to me. In a world where vampires, shifters, demons, witches, and warlocks exist, they're afraid of ghosts?

Everyone is something in this world, and some things I fear more than the wails of those drowned at sea.

I find a nice little spot to fill my water samples and set my device down. It's state of the art and fills on its own. I make sure to record everything I do with the camera around my neck; the device displays the time and temperature of the water as it records.

Once I have everything I need, I pick up my water samples, but something stops me. A humming, heavy vibration through the water.

I'm smart enough and experienced enough by now to know how to differentiate the feel in the water. I can tell when there are sharks or other predators. This feels... different, and I'm not quite sure what it is. Then I hear the humming of voices that reach me like sonar.

People assume merpeople speaking underwater is garbled noise, but it isn't. There's a certain music to be heard, melodies in everything that happens that can't be heard above the surface.

Now, I'm not a curious person by nature. Which sounds stupid, considering I'm a Marine Biologist. The ocean intrigues me and so do its creatures, and I want to make it a better living place. For years, contamination has affected the ocean. Not just the animals, but their habitats, mating cycles, and even us mer shifters.

I'm altruistic in this sense, because half of me belongs here in the water, and it breaks my heart to see it so tarnished.

Anyway, I'm the least curious person I know. On the other end, Lourdes is the most curious person I know. I can walk by a fight and ignore it without turning to catch a glimpse of the faces throwing fists. I can pass by a crash and step over blood and bone on a sidewalk.

I don't give a shit. Not my life, not my problem. I've tried to harden myself as much as possible in this life, but if you were me, you'd understand why.

So, as I drift slowly towards the noises, I tell myself it's for studious purposes. Because whatever creature is here right now is part of my investigation. Whatever creature is here could help me in my studies to discover why the fish are dispersing to other waters, if predators have drifted off their usual course and have taken life in the Caribbean.

It's the only reason I weave my way through the sunken ship, past metal walls and into the quiet, eeriness of the place. I'm all but holding in watery breaths, the camera capturing every little moment before me.

The sounds grow louder, the water pulsing around me in gentle, stirring pressure. I approach with caution, pressing my back against a wall while my webbed feet keep me upright. Voices reach my ears, the melody of them harsh and biting. Something about them makes me feel a sudden clamp of unease. For a moment, I want to swim away. This is obviously not an animal, because animals do not talk.

I close my eyes as fear suddenly grips me in a tight fist. I don't know why. Call it instinct. I almost scoff. Where the fuck was my instinct when I was swimming down here? It's like it flew straight out my asshole in a massive shit.

Ugh, okay, not a pretty picture.

The voices grow in volume, and my nails scrape against algae. I grit my teeth, wanting to swim away, but something keeps me frozen. It's *not* curiosity. No way. And whatever is going on here I could give two fucks about.

So why am I turning?

Don't turn, Naomi, don't you fucking do it... What are you doing? Fuck!

I can't stop myself. Like an addict hitting up his next fix, I'm obsessed with knowing what's on the other side of this wall. I can't stop the movements of my body. Like I have no control whatsoever of my own limbs as I chance a peek around the corner, holding my camera tightly between my hands to capture everything.

I regret it immediately.

Many things happen at once as I catch a glimpse on the other side.

First, my brain registers what the fuck is happening. It registers the mermen, counting four of them. It registers their cuts, black leather that presses tight against the expanse of their scaled bodies, and the red symbol etched on the back that I recognize. I notice everything, my mind capturing the scene before me like snapping pictures in quick successions from a phone, one right after the other, each detail more prominent than the last.

Like the chest at their fins opened and filled with jewels, golden coins, rubies, crowns...

Like the merman two of them are holding down while the third plunges a knife into his chest.

Blood plumes through the water like smoke from a campfire. Red, like the symbols on their backs.

My gasp threatens to tear out of me unbidden, but I bite down hard on my tongue. Nausea roils inside of me at what I just witnessed, and I must make some noise despite it because three heads jerk in my direction as the knife comes out of the now limp body.

It's like the silence before a collision where we all float there, frozen, like we're all trying to process the situation and each other just before everything is plunged into chaos.

I'm the first to move.

I turn, swimming away. I've never moved my sea legs so fast before in my life. Their shouting reaches me, nipping at my fins like I'm being chased by sharks. But this is much worse. At least sharks kill because they have to. Because they're hungry.

These mermen will kill me for fun.

"Take care of the bitch!" The shout follows me as I turn sharply at a corner and my breath catches until I want to choke.

My body collides against metal walls, and I use my palms against them to give me a pushing chance of momentum as I speed through the water and make it out of the boat. They're fast, and in open water I have nowhere to hide. My chest heaves with every breath I take, my heart demanding to cave through my ribs. The waters around me are lapping violently, jerking me from side to side. I push through it, speeding up towards my boat. It's a bad idea, I know it's a bad idea, but I have nowhere else to go.

Curses and shouts reach me just as I breach the surface. My hands scramble for the side of my boat and in my panic, I'm barely aware of the storm raging overhead. The boat tilts with my weight, my fingers grasping aimlessly. I haul myself to the side, hanging half in, my legs dangling out. My arms scramble for the ground, reaching for my cellphone. I grab it in my fingers right before I'm yanked back down below.

I'm whirled around, grasped in an angry grip. I catch a flash of angry eyes, pupils blown wide, and a single scar cutting through a tan face.

I fight, flailing my limbs with all my might, using maneuvers I never thought I'd have to use. I may hate Julio, but at least he taught me this. Because he'd known one day I'd need it to survive.

"Bein' a bitch is hard," he'd said gruffly while leveling me with his gaze. I'd glowered at him, offended at the term he'd so nonchalantly used against me. "Gotta learn to defend yourself."

My hands close into fists, one wrapping tightly around my waterproof phone, the other closing into my palm. I strike, my movements quick and deadly just like he taught me. Jabs against the gills, the sides, the inner thighs, the jugular.

He jerks back in surprise, trying to catch his breath while I know his body is screaming in pain. I don't bother to wait for him to recover. I swim away from my boat, dreading leaving it behind but knowing I have no other choice. There's no way I'll get it in time. My fingers fumble with my phone, holding onto it for dear life as I speed through the storming waters. I try to unlock it blindly, but my hands are shaking too badly. The waves and current lap like an angry, avenging god, pushing me back towards death, but I refuse to give in.

I am not going to fucking *die*.

But the hurricane is relentless. My sea legs tangle and I spin back, landing hard against my attacker's chest. He grunts, my head bangs against him, rendering me dizzy. His fingers grip my hair and pulls and as I cry out, my elbow jerks back to hit him in the side hard. He grunts and then I feel it.

The swipe of steel against my skin. The crash of a fist against my temple.

Adrenaline and surprise have me jerking away, and this time he lets me go. I'm gasping on tumultuous waters, and I don't need to look down to know I'm injured. That he fucking stabbed me. Combined with the blow to the head, my whole body suddenly feels weighted like an anchor.

My eyelids grow heavy, my body numbing. My fingers open and the phone slips from my grasp. I try to reach for it, but it's already sinking, and I'm drifting.

My attacker reaches for me, getting closer. I don't want to look as his hands press into my body, so I stare up at the surface in time to see a streak of lightning crack along the sky.

In time to see a wave cresting.

In time for it to crash and rip me away from the merman just before it tosses me into the maelstrom.

— ℓℓ —

I drift in and out of consciousness, my fingers twitching, my legs flailing. I try to open my eyes, try to swim for the surface to catch a glimmer of sunlight, but the storm still wages on. It sounds like the crescendo of a cymbal crashing over and over again, even in the deep. My vision blurs and I somehow manage to get a glimpse of tossing waves and the shadow of something dangerous within.

The cackles reach my ear like the sound of a devil screaming with delight. The shadow looms closer. I try to swim away from it, but it's too hard. It approaches, given form in the darkness. Chrome and hydraulic steel that's as familiar to me as my own name tear through the water like a zipping current, cresting with the wave. I catch a single glimpse of the merman riding the bike. I think he notices me, because he slows his speed, but it's too little too late before it smashes against my body.

Then all I know is the darkness.

BOX

I fucking love hurricanes, and I'm not a motherfucker who loves easily. But *this*? The lightning flaring down from the sky? The boom of thunder? The rising waves crashing and converging against one another?

Perfect weather for riding, if I do say so myself. And I do.

My brothers think I'm psycho, fucked in the head, but I don't give a single fuck. There's something liberating about riding with the water, controlling my fat boy as it sails and glides like a fucking sea horse.

I can't remember a time when I didn't ride. A love for this life is the only worthwhile thing my old man ever left me right before he split, leaving my ass all alone in the world. The joy of adrenaline, a life of danger, pussy, and brotherhood is all I'll ever need. When I moved from Australia to the Caribbean, it was to leave everything I knew behind me and start fresh. It wasn't long before I gravitated towards the criminal parts of the island because it's all I've ever known.

I don't regret a fucking bit of it.

There's no place I'd rather be than in the Kraken Motorcycle Club, living life like a fucking king. Others tremble when our names are mentioned. Our enemies fear us as much as they respect us.

Especially me.

As the enforcer, it's my duty to punish those who try to fuck us over and honestly, this level of craziness is in my job description.

How do I expect people to fear me if I don't give them a reason to? I can stare down the barrel of a gun without blinking and with a smile twisting my face. I won't be respected if I don't do *this*, too.

I'm a fearless motherfucker precisely because of this. Because what are a few bullets whizzing by me compared to lightning striking the surface of the pissed off ocean? What are mere men compared to the wrath of the gods?

Absolutely fucking nothing.

I rev the engine, my gills taking in water, my thighs straddling my fat boy as I dive with the rising wave, screaming as I go down.

The darkness of the ocean clears up for a single second as a flash of lightning strikes again, illuminating the water in front of me just in time to see a body amongst the waves.

"Fuck!"

I slow my pace, but it's too late. I'm already too fucking close. The body hits the side of my bike and sends me careening. My grip on the handlebars tightens, trying to gain control once again. I teeter, then straighten, steering back in time to see the body sinking.

"Fucking shit."

I speed up, stopping shy of the body before I jump off my bike and swim down. The rapid currents try to yank it away, but I'm faster, grabbing a wrist and pulling it towards me. A soft, feminine figure hits mine, and I hold her with a gentle care that surprises me.

Well, fuckin' shit.

Blood plumes out of her temple in skinny wisps, and a goose egg is already forming on her skin. After taking a quick inventory of her injuries, I notice she's got a laceration on her side. I'm familiar enough with violence to know what a stab wound looks like. Just like I know the sudden paling of her light brown skin isn't normal because she's dying.

"No the fuck you don't." I haul her into my arms and kick my sea legs to my revving bike. I may be an asshole, but I'm not letting her die, especially not after she hit the side of my bike. That's bad for business. If I was to leave her and she washed up on shore, dead, the evidence of my bike against her skull would be enough to send the feds straight into Kraken territory.

That's a mess we don't need. Not with everything else going on and the wars we have waged with other local MCs.

With a few difficult maneuverings, I'm able to haul her onto the bike in front of me, placing her in a position so she doesn't fall off. Her thighs straddling the bike, but facing me, our chests pressed together, the bite of a camera hanging around her neck digging between us. Before I cradle her head to the crook where my neck meets my shoulder, I notice how fucking pretty she is.

Long, thin braids spiral like snakes around her bare shoulders. I push them away and hold them back tightly in my fist with one hand, starting my bike with the other. The vibration of my bike pushes our bodies closer together and I hold my breath for a second, willing my dick not to stir to life at her proximity.

I'm not going to take advantage of her, but I'm not blind, either. I certainly noticed her body, how could I not? She's naked, bright teal and gold scales expanding all over her body, covering all the sexy bits, though not hiding the fullness of her breasts, either.

Trying to keep my thoughts to myself, I finally steer my bike over another rising wave and let the wind push us away from the deep depths of the Caribbean and towards the shore.

SCORPION

The merciless winds whip ice cold sheets of rain against my body, tearing at the lapels of my cut. Lightning strikes, brightening the ever-darkening sky in brief flashes. Waves lap up against the shore, pushing into our bungalows.

I'm not worried about the houses. We've lived through hurricanes and have rebuilt our compound from the ground up many times before. Hell, it's not even an issue about the flooding when we can all fucking breathe underwater.

The issue here is that Box, that crazy motherfucker, is out joyriding in the ocean again.

Asshole knows how I feel about that shit. I'm only twenty-nine and I feel like I'm constantly babysitting both his ass and Slug's. Thankfully, Slug doesn't have as much of a death wish as Box does and doesn't risk breaking his own fucking neck while riding in a storm.

At least Slug is off doing his own dumbass thing *inside the compound.*

Meanwhile I'm stuck out in this stupid fucking storm waiting for Box to get back, like a parent waiting for a sneaking teenager to come home. This shouldn't even be my fucking job. Unfortunately, Rock sent *me* out here to give him a stern talking to when he deigns to show up.

The growling sound of a bike screams over the storm and I scowl, watching as a wave rises high and just as it comes slamming down, a bike rips through the water, sloping up the sand. Box pulls to a stop near me, sending a spray of sand and water against me that I barely feel.

Can't feel jack shit in this cold.

But I might be hyper focused on what Box is carrying in his arms, or rather who.

He hops expertly from his bike, pulling with him the limp body of a naked female. I watch, mouth hanging open as he cradles her against his chest, her legs and upper body hooked over his arms. At first, all I see are her braids, dangling between them.

"What the fuck, Box?" my voice screams over the shrieking wind. But then he steps closer and I see her face, and I feel like I've been punched in the gut. The curve of those high cheekbones, that long slender neck and lithe body...

I *know* her.

"What the fuck did you do?" I demand. The anger that slices through my body like a knife is so sudden it's surprising. I've never gone toe-to-toe with my MC brothers before. I've never felt such a blinding rage like the one that suddenly flows through me, either. Not the kind that makes me want to dart forward and wrap my fingers around the blond's stupid tatted neck and squeeze the life out of him.

"Bitch randomly appeared in front of my bike," he supplies coolly, the usual shit-eating smirk he wears twisting wider until he looks manic. The asshole relishes in it. He wears his own special brand of psychotic like the jewelry gleaming against his ears, nose, and lip. As if all that metal piercing through his flesh isn't enough, his face is twined with tattoos. He looks like everything the rumors of the island make us out to be.

Criminals.

I mean, we *are*, but that's beside the point.

He steps around me like I'm a fucking piece of furniture and not his VP, who has been standing out here for fucking hours in the cold, waiting for his dumb ass to get back. I turn, watching the brisk steps he takes up the small slope of sand and to the large bungalow that serves as the Kraken MC's clubhouse.

"And you decided to fucking kidnap her?" I rush to catch up to him. He shoulders his way inside the clubhouse.

"Stitch! Rock! Where the fuck are you cunts?" he calls out, ignoring my question entirely.

Asshole.

"Box..."

"Rock! Get your old ass out here!"

His hollering has garnered the attention of everyone here. The club honeys and my brothers pause what they're doing to gape. I barely resist the urge to snap at them as Box's stomping shakes the wood at our feet.

"Rock! You fuckin' cunt, we got ourselves a situation, eh."

When Rock pushes open the door to his office, the frame rattles. Great. He is not happy. His gray eyes flick over Box, and whatever he's about to say dies when he catches sight of the female in his arms. His mouth closes, opens.

I don't think I've ever seen my Pres speechless before.

"The fuck is this shit?"

"Get your supplies. She was stabbed."

The breath leaves me, and I'm struck stupid the second time today. I look down at her again, following as Box shoulders his way into Rock's office and sets her down on a plush leather couch in the corner. As soon as he releases her, I can make out the wound on her side and something inside me seems to snap.

I remember eyeing her from across the bar at Shark Mouth. How there'd been a look of defiance and exasperation as Jet pressed close to her, rather than fear like any other female would have displayed.

Jet's a fucking asshole, and I shouldn't have gotten involved. But when I saw his hands wrap around the ends of her braids and tug, I saw red. I don't want to contemplate why. I've never felt possessive over a bitch before, but the truth is, I was intrigued by her.

She looked unaffected standing in that shitty place, a place we convene to with other clubs because it's neutral ground. I'd wanted to make my move, but she shut me down too quickly before I even could. Fuck, she'd sneered at me as if I was no better than Jet.

I wonder if I'd been in my cut, what she would have thought of me then.

The pretty thing couldn't have hidden the desire glaring in her eyes when they traveled to rest on my dick, which had pressed tightly against the confines of my jeans. But as quickly as she admired it, she shut down, brushing me off and walking away.

Okay, I might have watched her swaying ass in those tight little jeans as she left, the urge to palm the globes in my palms strong. That had been my last glimpse of her; her ass swinging as she was swallowed up by the crowd.

I'm hauled back to the present as Rock begins to work, his big, rough hands quick and efficient. You wouldn't think by looking at him, due to his rough appearance, but he'd been an army medic. He snaps latex gloves onto his fingers and works at checking the wound to sew it closed.

"Storm was tossing her around like a foockin' rag doll, mate," Box says, emphasizing his point by flailing his hands through the air. "Didn't see her till it was too late. Tried to slow down, but she crashed into the side of my bike. Couldn't leave her there."

"The wound is clean, didn't hit any major arteries," Rock supplies, his sharp gaze quick as it trails over her naked body, stopping a single second on the camera she's wearing like a necklace around her neck.

"Wonder who the fuck tried to off her." Box whistles low. "Face like that seems too pretty to off."

I agreed. But that feeling low in my gut unfurls, becoming an almost instinct that has me blurting out, "The Rogue Waves."

Rock pauses what he's doing for a brief second. Stoic as he starts sewing her up, he asks, "You sure about that?"

"She was at Shark Mouth last night. I saw her reject Jet."

Shit. Had Jet followed her out? Had something happened last night? I should have followed her myself, made sure she was okay after that encounter. Fuck, why didn't I think?

"I don't blame her. Has the face of an overused asshole, that one." Box chuckles.

"Do you really think rejecting him is enough to warrant this?" Rock doesn't have to gesture at the wound. It might be a clean stab wound, but the cleanest fuckers can still have the dirtiest intent.

For the first time since Box laid her down, I bring their attention to the camera around her neck. "Maybe that can tell us something."

"Maybe," Rock hums his agreement. "But first, let's get her fixed up so we know what the fuck we're dealing with."

My jaw clenches and my hands roll into fists. I take a breath as I watch Rock work, knowing that she's in great hands. Once he's finished, and we set her up in Rock's room, I know now it's just waiting game, because the lens of the camera is fucking *broken* and can't tell us shit.

We have to wait for her to wake up so she can tell us exactly what happened and who stabbed her.

So I can wrap my fingers around their fucking throats and make them pay.

NAOMI

P ain bursts all at once. Consciousness isn't slow coming; it's a collision, a pounding. It's muffled voices behind closed doors that seem like they're screaming, and dim lighting that feels all too florescent for my weak eyes.

A gasp tears against my throat and my mind is so confused, it's giving mixed signals to my body, making it think I'm choking down water instead of air. Fuck, it *hurts.* The gills on the side of my neck open and close, breaking off my airway while simultaneously choking as it begs for water.

When I finally have my shifting body under control and I realize I'm on land—not just on land, but in an actual bed—I'm able to quickly assess my situation.

This isn't like those fictional books Lourdes likes so much. I'm not disoriented, my memories aren't slowly coming back to me. Nope. I remember exactly what the fuck happened, and I am pissed off about it, too. So pissed, I swear I can cut a bitch.

Which is precisely what I plan to do.

I sit up on whoever's bed I'm lying in, one that smells like rich tobacco and leather with the undertone of something dark and sweet like caramel, and sweep my gaze around the room. I'm alone, thankfully. There aren't enough things out in the open of this dim room to let me know much about who inhabits it, other than they're too clean and like to smoke.

Throwing my legs over the side of the bed, I wince as my side pulls and my whole body screams in protest.

Fucking bikers and their fucking knives and bikes.

My teeth grit as my toes touch the floor, and I can't contain my brief wince of pain. I look down at myself to find that I'm naked, finding my wound bound with a bit of gauze and tape. Giving an experimental twist of my body, I grunt again. It's certainly uncomfortable, but I've dealt with worse pain than this. It's only that thought that has me moving, searching quietly through the room for a weapon. I open drawers but find nothing other than neatly folded t-shirts and boxers in varying shades of black, gray, and white.

I decide to steal one of the shirts, considering I'm naked, and slip the material over my arms, hissing out a breath. The black t-shirt is large enough to cover my private bits, but I don't bother with pulling on the boxers. One look at the waistline and I know they'll just fall off me no matter how many times I fold them.

I keep searching, frustration growing by the second. I almost think it's hopeless until I reach inside of a big boot and procure an army knife out of one of them. Ha!

Thanks for the tip, Julio. He always used to hide shit inside his shoes, too.

With firm hands, I flip it open and grasp it in front of me, just like he taught me.

I don't know where I am. I'm naked and injured, so these things make me vulnerable. What they probably aren't expecting is that I know how to work a knife, I know how to defend myself, and I have the fucking determination to get out of here. And send them all to hell while I'm at it.

Tip-toeing my way to the door, I crack it open the slightest fraction and press my ear to the crevice. I hear a muffled voice from somewhere but can't make out any more than one out in the open.

Not leaving anyone behind to guard me? That's their fucking mistake.

Confident in my abilities, I ease my way down the hall. There are rooms on either side of me, all of them firmly closed. Sounds come from them which I'd rather not contemplate, but they give me a boost of energy, knowing whoever is behind those doors will be kept busy as long as they aren't a two-pump chump. I make it to the end of the hall to a very large open floorplan. I recognize the place for what it is immediately.

Bungalows are traditionally small, but this one has obviously been renovated to fit a decent amount of people. The windows are open, letting in a chilly sea breeze. A pool table sits in the center of the place; there's a large flat screen, worn leather couches, and the open floor plan is to my right. The left side veers off into a dining room with a long old table and chairs, and a kitchen from where the voice is coming from.

I tip-toe towards that voice.

I know I should run, but I have no idea if there's anyone keeping watch outside. No, my best bet is to incapacitate one of my captors and figure out where the fuck I am.

As I approach, the voice grows louder and louder.

"...touch that dangly thing that's strung in the back of my throat..."

The loud, belching song lyrics startle me enough to have my feet nearly slipping. My eyes widen and I watch, trying to keep my surprised fascination at bay while I observe the creature in the kitchen sing and dance around pans of food.

"I said WAP, WAP. Uh—uh—uh." He stops shaking salt into a pan, bends, and starts...

Yeah.

My captor is fucking twerking.

He's pretty good at it, too. I can appreciate the subtle art form of his moves, despite the circumstances. The jeans he's wearing hug his thick body like a second skin and his ass jiggles with each pop of his waist.

I blink, willing myself to stay focused as I approach. The army knife is high over my head, and I bring it cresting down with a cry just as my attacker turns.

The blade snags against the leather of his cut.

Wide eyes stare at me. "Oh, shi—" He yanks his earphones out. "Wai—" But I'm already diving forward, aiming for his gut. "Oh, fuck!" He dodges and my feet slip against the wet floor, which I hadn't noticed before now. I start to fall backwards but gain my footing.

Fuck.

I've lost the element of surprise, and my chance to take him down has gone. I turn and flee, my legs pumping beneath me.

"Hey! Wait!" he calls after me, but I can't stop. Freedom is too fucking close.

The door looks so close but also somehow miles away. That's just the adrenaline talking, though. Still, it feels like it takes forever for me to reach it. I'm a few steps away when it bursts open to reveal a massive man framing the entire doorway. Reeling back, heart tightly lodged in my throat, I try to turn in my panic, unaware of what to do now. All I know is that I need to escape. I need to get *away*.

Arms encircle me from behind, wrapping around my waist. Not tight enough to keep me tethered, so I whirl, the knife in my hand raised and prepared to fight. A hand catches my wrist, stopping the weapon's trajectory. I start fighting, my naked legs kicking out, my eyes darting blindly around the room for an out.

"Calm the fuck down!"

My head rattles as my captor shakes me. The brusque movement clears my mind, making me see straight. Trying not to tremble, I freeze and look up into the honey eyes of one of my captors.

"You!" I gasp.

I'd recognize him anywhere. Which is probably pathetic considering we've only had one interaction in a crowded, dimly lit bar, but my treacherous body remembers. It buzzes, and it feels like every nerve ending has been shot with an electrical wire. My naked thighs rub together involuntarily as liquid desire accumulates right at my pussy.

His features are clearer in the sharp light of day, and it enhances his beauty. He's out of the dingy hoody he was in the last time I laid eyes on him. Given all that's happened, it doesn't feel like that only happened mere days ago. Today, he's wearing a leather cut, with words stamped on either shoulder.

Kraken MC

Vice President.

Scorpion.

Anger is so sudden, it squelches any desire his hot body might have had me feeling.

"You son of a bitch!"

I attack, my knee flying up to hit him between his legs. His grunt lets me know it hurt. His hands slacken their hold enough for me to wrench away. My arm swings with all my might. At this point I think the only thing fueling my movements is adrenaline, because I feel a tug of pain at my stab wound that should cripple me, but it doesn't.

Just like the blow meant for Scorpion doesn't reach him either.

I'm hauled backwards, the knife sent flying from my grip. This time, I'm wrapped in an unyielding grip that tightens, preventing me from flailing like I want to.

But fuck if I don't try until I'm wheezing.

"What the fuck is going on in here?!" The thunderous boom of a voice cuts through my screeching cries. The hands holding me tighten around my ribs, cutting my airway short until I'm gasping in heavy pants, my lungs desperate for air.

A crowd has formed in the opened space of the bungalow, which I didn't notice in the chaos I caused. I barely notice the men and scantily clad women now. Not past Scorpion in front of me, heaving on the floor and struggling to stand. Certainly not past the sudden appearance of the glaring man.

His eyes are narrowed from beneath thick brows, bulging, tattooed arms crossed against a massive expanse of chest, and the thin line of his lips are pursed in disapproval under a thick pepper colored beard. I don't let myself observe his features too closely. I can't see past the words stamped on his cut.

Kraken MC.

President.

Rock.

He takes one look at me, but that hard expression doesn't soften against my own of defiance. His eyes flick to the person behind me. "Take her to my office," he orders in a voice that reminds me of musk and tobacco, like smoke curling through air. I know immediately that the room I was in is his. "We need to talk."

NAOMI

The inside of the president's office is as pristine as his room. With not a single thing out of place or even a speck of dust on the surface, I can tell what type of merman he is just by being in here. The kind who likes order, who likes to be in control to the point of being brutally commanding.

Whatever creature was behind me during the... altercation... carried my body, limp legs swaying just above the floor beneath me, and deposited me onto a plush leather couch in the office. When he moved away, it gave me a chance to stare at my captors.

Three of them in one room is overwhelming, their presence enough to threaten to choke me. I keep my cool as I analyze them from head to toe.

Scorpion, the Vice President, I've already met. I ignore his heated glares and the way he cups his injured dick in his palm. I don't want to feel guilty about harming the prized eggplant, so I focus on the other two males in my presence.

The President. *Rock.*

I study him first since I didn't get a chance to out there in front of everyone else before I was lugged in here like a sack of potatoes.

He's older than Scorpion, late forties or early fifties, I'd guess. The sign of his age lives in his dark hair and beard, both which are peppered through with gray and white. The surly pull of his dark eyebrows over eyes like steel and the thin press of his mouth as he watches me is... appealing.

For an older man, he's, well, he's attractive as fuck. Despite the situation, I can admit that about him. His burly, tattooed body, clad in dark jeans, a t-shirt, and his cut, sits behind his cherry wood desk. Even with the distance between us, his smoky, rich scent surrounds the whole office. My breath comes out in short spurts as I struggle not to inhale the intoxicating scent of him while at the same time struggling with the pull of my injury.

The third man in the room, the creature who grabbed me from behind, is another older male who looks equally surly at the president, if not more so. His long black hair all but covers his face in silky strands, nearly hiding his pretty, slanted eyes. I can't see much of his features behind the hair, other than the defiant tilt of his mouth. So, I focus on what I can see. His cut.

Kraken MC.

Secretary.

Delfin.

"Your name is Dolphin?" I snort, not meaning for the words or the sound to come out of my mouth at all. I can feel his glare at my mocking, but I just force a smirk to my own lips.

If I'm going to die anyway, I might as well piss them off on my way to hell.

"Let's just cut to the chase," the president barks.

I sneer at him. "Yes, let's talk about the fact that you *kidnapped* me, shall we?"

Scorpion makes a strangled sound. My eyes flick to his for a brief second and I note the pleading panic in his gaze as he looks at me. I refuse to contemplate what it could mean and turn away, glaring at the president again.

"Seems to me like you're confused, baby doll. You see, it was our brother Box who found you in that storm. If he hadn't brought you here, you'd be fuckin' dead."

My eyes roll so hard and so fast to the back of my head, I swear I can see my fucking brains. I hold up a single finger. "First of all, don't call me 'baby doll'. Got that, Daddy Kraken?" His incredulous look almost makes me want to howl with laughter. I hold up a second finger. "Secondly, your brother *Box* didn't do jack shit except ram into me with his ugly ass bike. So, try to condescend to me one more fucking time. You won't like it when your balls end up stuck to your throat after I kick them. Just ask eggplant dick over here." I point to Scorpion without meeting his expression, but I can imagine it well enough.

"The fuck did you just call me?" The president's eyes are wide with disbelief. I don't blame him. I know his type. Their heads are so far up their asses, they can't fathom how someone can talk back to them the way I am.

"Daddy Kraken," I repeat slowly, my smile in place. "You're the president of this MC. That means you're their *daddy*."

His knuckles slam down against the surface of his desk, and he uses that to push himself up to a standing position. The rage he emits is akin to a storm. It swirls around me like rapid winds. Not magic, but an anger so potent, I can feel it as if it *were*. He looms taller, and I'm sure I should be intimidated by his sheer size.

For a moment, I'm dizzy and weak against him, both physically and emotionally, but I dispel that notion quickly enough.

"That storm whipped you around like a fucking doll," he growls, his anger bursting through his words. "He saved you from a fucking hurricane, brought you to our compound with a stab wound that *we* stitched up. The way I see it, we saved your fucking life, baby doll. Yet you dare to disrespect me in my own fucking club? That shit doesn't fly here."

His intimidation tactic does *nothing* for me. I don't flinch or cower in fear like he expects me to. I meet him, gaze for gaze.

"Now, we have a few questions for you. Like, who the fuck you are and who the fuck is trying to kill you?"

They don't know who I am, and I don't mean for them to find out. I don't want to have anything more to do with these people than is wise, so I stand up, startling Scorpion and making Delfin tense like he's ready to lunge and tackle me. I take a step forward, my bare thighs sliding together, making me realize the vulnerable position I'm in.

Being vulnerable doesn't mean I'm scared, though. Even if I was, I certainly wouldn't show them just how much. Yes, I'm nervous about where I'm at, about who is surrounding me, but if there's one thing Julio has taught me it's to not show fear.

Even when the odds are against me.

I stop shy at the edge of the desk, slapping my own palms down against it, leaning forward so our faces are just inches apart. The t-shirt that smells like him rides above my ass, and if there were anyone behind me, they'd be able to see every inch.

I inhale the rich scent of him. It surrounded me before, but this close I can nearly taste the tobacco on his breath. Swiping my tongue across my bottom lip, as if I could capture the lingering taste and hold it inside, has his pupils flaring wide.

I tilt my head up. "Fuck off," I whisper. He jolts at the words, and I bite back my laughter. "I don't have to tell you shit. In fact, this is where our crossed paths end. So, thanks for your help, and make sure you tell Box I said thanks as well, but I'm fucking out."

I turn to do just that. To leave and flip them the finger on my way out, but my legs stumble and a sharp pain tugs at my side, one I've tried ignoring up until now. Blinking down at the gray shirt I'm in, I notice the spreading smear of blood against it, right where my stab wound is.

The goodbye I was about to utter dies on my fucking mouth as I go tumbling towards the ground at the sight of blood and the sudden shock of agony that jolts through my body and pulses at my head.

"Ah, shit."

Those are my last words as I hit the floor, and then it's lights out for me.

NAOMI

I wake up again feeling disoriented. The sensation lasts about a few seconds before I jolt up, a low hiss pushing past my clenched teeth at the pain. I know without looking that I'm back where I was when I previously awoke, if the heady scent swirling around me is anything to go by. Just like I know instinctively that I'm not alone.

I don't look up to meet anyone's eyes. Instead, I gingerly reach for the hem of my borrowed shirt and lift it up, as if focusing on something else can hide my humiliating descent to the floor, or the memory of it, at least. The wound at my side is no longer bleeding and looks freshly stitched. I probably pulled it in the altercation earlier.

Finally, my gaze flicks up to find both Scorpion and the president standing vigil over me.

My face heats and I'm glad my cheeks don't darken so they can't see the evidence of how embarrassed I am. Seriously, that would have been such an amazing exit had I not fucking passed out. I could have been at home by now, tucked safely in my bed. Maybe I would have asked Lourdes for a hug as I worked through this crazy fucking experience over a tub of ice cream. I would have called—

"Shit!" I drop the hem of the shirt and look around as the thought suddenly slams into me. There are no windows in this room, so I can't make out if it's day or night. I have no idea how much time has passed at all. "Shit, shit, shit, *shit*!" I look up at Scorpion and his president, and I know I can't keep the panic from my features. It seems to startle Scorpion, but the president is unmovable. "How long has it been?" I ask.

"Since... what?" Scorpion's honey-colored eyes assess me slowly.

"Since Box found me? *How long has it been?*"

"A whole twenty-four hours, I think."

"Fuck, fuck, *fuck!*" I toss my legs over the side of the bed and stand. I'm careful not to pull my wound this time, but I still move with a quick urgency, crossing the space between us so I can grip the front of the president's cut. "I need a phone," I demand. "Now!"

His eyebrows raise a fraction before his meaty hands grab my much smaller wrists and shove me off him lightly. "I don't have to give you shit," he says. I don't mistake the twinkle in his eyes for what this really is. Satisfaction.

My, how the tables have turned.

And he's enjoying every fucking bit of it.

But I don't have time for these fucking games. I need a phone. I need to make a call, or it will end very badly for everyone involved.

I may be a crass bitch towards them, but I know what they say is true. One of their own helped me; he brought me back here after I was attacked by the Rogue Wave asshole and patched me up. I may hate what they stand for, but they *did* save my life, apparently. Maybe I *should* be grateful.

Which means I need to make this fucking call.

"Please." My voice cracks on the word, and the fact that I'm begging seems to finally surprise the president, because the tough façade breaks a fraction. He doesn't seem nearly as gruff as he'd like me to believe when he's staring at me like that. It's there and gone in a flash. Like I'm someone he wants to take care of. "I will give you whatever information you want about what happened. I'll tell you my name, who stabbed me, but let me make a call."

He looks me over, probably wondering if I'm going to call the cops. If he believes for a second that that's who I'm calling, he won't let me near a phone. I don't want him to know who it really is, but I give in an inch.

"You can monitor the call if you want. Just... please..."

His expression doesn't soften but his shoulders do. "Fine," he concedes. "In my office. Now."

36

My shoulder blades itch as the president's stare pierces me. It's a stare I feel through my blood, down to the marrow of my bones. It's impactful, makes me feel like I'm being touched when his hands are nowhere near me.

Even though my back is turned, his gaze doesn't leave me, doesn't travel down to stare at my bare ass either. His focus is sharp, undistracted, as my fingers tremble while I dial a number from a burner phone in his office.

It rings and rings. Usually, my calls are answered within the first ring in those moments I deign to call him. But I'm calling from an unknown number. He's probably flipping his screen the bird right now.

But then he answers, and the breath is expelled from my very lungs.

"It's me," I say by way of greeting.

He's quiet on the other end, but I can hear other sounds. Loud rumblings and cursing and... are those *gunshots*?

"What the fuck, kid?" He doesn't yell, but he doesn't need to. He never did. I can imagine the stern expression on the other end of the line, but instead of making me feel chastised, it just pisses me the fuck off. "I've been callin'."

"I lost my phone." It's not an outright lie, but I don't want him to know the truth. I don't want to face that *I told you so* or the wrath that comes with it. I'm not sure anyone deserves that. There's also a part of me that doesn't want him coming down here and fucking up my life like I know he's bound to do.

"We had a fucking deal."

"I call, you answer. No matter what the fuck you're doin' or who the fuck you're with, you answer. Don't and you won't like the consequences."

"I said I lost my fucking phone."

The rumbling on the other end stops. For a heartbeat or two there's nothing but silence, then his growl cuts through and nearly shatters my ear drum. I swallow, for the first time feeling a bit of fear.

"We're a few hours out."

My eyes close and I wish I could thunk my head against the surface of the desk. The first time I woke up, I should have called him straight away. I'd been too pumped on adrenaline to do it.

"Go home," I whisper. "I'm fine." And I hope he can't hear through the lie.

"Buy a new phone," he orders.

"First thing tomorrow."

"Call me right away."

"I will."

"If you don't—"

"I won't like it. I fucking know that."

He grunts. "Do it, kid."

I hang up before he can say another word.

Setting the phone back down on the desk, I make sure to take a deep breath. I roll my shoulders to ease the tension that accumulated there, but it's pretty useless. I'm wound so tightly I feel like my soul will jump straight out of my body at any given moment.

I turn slowly, meeting the president's keen gaze. He doesn't question what I'm sure must have been a strange-sounding phone call from his end, but his gaze does pierce me in places I never knew existed.

Trying to make levity of the situation, I clap my hands together. "So, Daddy Kraken, what do you want to know?"

ROCK

I've seen and heard a lot of crazy shit in my life. Literally, I thought I'd seen it all. I've traveled the world, I've killed out of duty, murdered to protect. I've healed the wounded, watched them die, and felt my own life start to slip away more often than I'd like. I've battled monsters and supernaturals and humans.

And through all that fucking time of sweat, blood, tears, through all the bodies of the dead I've waded through and all the souls that stain my hands, I have never seen someone like her.

I joined the army straight out of high school and spent a good chunk of my life there. Whores, exotic dancers, mothers, bakers, nurturers, witches, vampires... I've met an array of women throughout my lifetime. Unlike some of my club brothers, I've traveled the world and seen wonders some of them could never even imagine.

After I came back and settled into my role with the Kraken Motorcycle Club, I'd already garnered a reputation as a ruthless son of a bitch. My name was given to me in the army. Rock, because I'm un-fucking-moveable. You'd be too if you've witnessed half the shit I have. My training was exactly what I needed to climb the ranks and become president of this MC. I helped us become one of the most feared clubs in the Caribbean. Grown ass men have literally *trembled* at the sight of my scowl.

And this woman stares at me fearlessly. She undermines my orders, disrespects me in front of my men, she calls me fucking *Daddy*

Kraken.

I'll never admit it aloud, but she's fascinating.

And fuck if the condescending word 'daddy' doesn't get me hard as steel as it leaves her pretty little lips.

I stare at her long and hard. I know it makes her want to fidget, but she obviously has a strong will. I recognize the strength in her as something to be admired. Just like I recognize there's something that makes her wary of us. Not just because we're an MC, not just because of the circumstances she finds herself in. There's more to it than that.

Starting with that cryptic fucking phone call.

I never would have left her alone to call the cops or anyone who could mean harm for the Krakens over a misunderstanding. Between her annoyed reassurances, I also caught the notes of relief. I want to ask about it, but there are more important things than her calling a friend to let them know she's okay.

"What's your name, baby doll?" I ask her.

Her nose scrunches at the nickname I benedict her with. I like the annoyed expression on her face even more than I like her fire, I think. Makes me want to bend her over my desk and plow into her from behind. Call me daddy then. I dare you.

Christ. I force myself to get a grip. She's half my fucking age. Not that I think it matters much. A lot of the club honeys are way younger than me and I've fucked them all.

"Naomi," she supplies, leaning back against my desk, crossing one naked leg over the other. She's not shy about her own nudity, but she's not exactly teasing me with it either. More like, she doesn't even realize she's naked. Or if she does, she doesn't care because she doesn't see me as a threat.

Damn fucking lowering, that thought.

Not that I'd ever take advantage of her. We aren't that kind of a club, and I'd fuck up anyone in the brotherhood if they ever hurt a woman that way—if Slug doesn't get to them first. But that blasé attitude of hers in my presence only reminds me that I'm getting in years. Now, I just feel old as shit.

"You got a last name, baby doll?"

"Queen."

I smirk. Seems fitting somehow. "Alright Naomi Queen. So, tell me, what happened to you?"

"I was getting water samples for the lab. I'm a Marine Biologist," she explains after I quirk my eyebrows.

The words are said with pride and just a bit of daring. Like maybe she's waiting for me to contradict her or say something stupid. I don't. I can tell just by looking at her that her intelligence surpasses mine completely and she fucking knows it. I wonder how often she's had to deal with people belittling her for that career or making smart-ass comments. Well, she won't be getting them from me in that regard.

"I heard noises and went to investigate in the abandoned ship off the coast of Santo Domingo." She pauses, tilting her head to the side. Her eyes close and her lips press together. I know she's remembering the events and I can't help but feel awed by her.

I've seen seasoned warriors take blows to the head and knife wounds lighter than hers and tremble when they recount the events. She says everything with a silent fury, and I admire her spunk.

"There were four mermen." Her eyes open. I didn't notice before, but they're dark brown, blown nearly black. "Two of them held one down, while the third stabbed him..."

I tense.

Now, here's the thing... I don't give a fuck about other MCs in the area, so long as they don't fuck with me. They can do whatever they want in their own twisted ranks, like stab each other in abandoned boats. The issue with this is, the Krakens have been at war with the Rogue Waves for a while now. With the hurricane coming in, not all my men have been accounted for at the compound.

That makes me nervous.

"Who were the men, baby doll?" My voice lowers, and I don't just utter that nickname for teasing now. "Were they wearin' cuts?" I press a finger to my shoulder, over the stitched words *Kraken MC* and the depiction of the ancient beast on my breast.

She takes a breath. "Yes."

This time, I push away from my office door and prowl towards her. She doesn't flinch back, but lets me advance, even though there's a wariness in her expression. It's given away in the tight press of her lips and the slight ticking of her jaw.

I don't stop moving until we're touching. Until my jean-clad thighs are pressed tightly against her naked ones. This proximity feels like a threat, as it should. No, I'm not going to threaten her, but she'd be smart to fear my wrath right now.

"What cuts were they wearin'? Do you remember?"

She hesitates for a fraction of a second, and that's all it takes for my impatience to spike. I grab her arm, squeezing. I keep it light, not hard enough to hurt, but hard enough to send a message.

"The name on their fuckin' cuts, baby doll," I warn. "And don't lie to me."

She tries to jerk away from me, but my grip against her is adamant. Her long, thin braids have fallen, curtaining her banged up face. She tosses them aside with one hand, glaring up at me. "The Rogue Waves," she spits out.

I let her go and step back, a million curses burning against the tip of my tongue. I mentally go through everyone who presented themselves at the compound. A few of my men are missing. Box— the crazy fucker had left shortly after bringing her—Lilo, Wire, and Raze.

"Did you see who they stabbed?" Maybe it's not one of my own men. In fact, I'm hoping they are killing each other off. But a bad feeling twists in my gut and intensifies. It's never a good sign. Especially not with the rising tensions we've been having with the other local MCs. Especially not when I'd sent my men out to patrol land and sea before the storm hit.

She blinks, twisting her braids together. "It—it happened so fast, but..." Her fingers sweep along her neckline, reaching for something that isn't there. "My camera—"

"Box found you with it hanging around your neck. The screen was busted."

"I caught it on video. Even with the screen busted, you can find it on the hard drive."

I nod once. "Good. Wire is our tech guy; I'll have him do that immediately." If he isn't at the bottom of the fucking sea with a knife in his gut.

The thought grips me and I let out a low curse.

"What else happened?"

She smiles ruefully and gestures at her side where the wound is and again at her face where a knot formed against her forehead.

"What do you think happened? They heard me. One of them chased me and left me with a little parting gift before the hurricane swept me away." She turns her head away and I make out her hard swallow. "The storm saved my life."

There's an urge in me to cradle her cheek in my palm and offer her whatever comfort I can. The fuck's wrong with me? I push away from her and gather my thoughts.

I need to call Church. I need to get my fucking men together *now* and do a head count.

I pull out my regular phone from my back pocket and send out a mass text, calling for Church. When I pocket it again, I look at Naomi. There's also the little matter of dealing with her. If what she says is true—and we'll find the truth out after pulling the footage from the camera—then her life is in danger.

She might not know it, but if she was a witness and got away from them, they aren't going to stop until they find her. And when they do, I hate to think what they'll do to her.

I shouldn't care about some bitch who was in the wrong place at the wrong time, but she might very well have witnessed the death of one of my club brothers. I can't let her leave here to be drowned by them.

I have to protect her.

The *Krakens* have to protect her.

Even if she tells us to fuck off.

"You can take my room," I tell her slowly. Her expression goes from soft, to confused, to rebellious in an instant.

"I think you must be confused, Daddy Kraken. I'm not staying here."

"The Rogue Waves could be out there looking for you. I can't in good conscious send you to your death."

"Aw, a biker with a conscious," she mocks with an eye roll. "Listen, I can take care of myself."

My eyes rove over the bump on her head, down to the stab wound like I can see it beneath her t-shirt. "Evidently not." My eyes go back to hers.

She growls and pushes off the desk. "Those assholes probably think I'm dead. Besides, they can't possibly know where I live, and I won't be caught dead on their side of the island. So, no offense, but getting hauled into the middle of whatever war you have going on won't keep me safe. I'm going home."

No one ever dares to disobey my orders. In fact, it pisses me off when they do. There's the beginning of anger stirring in my belly, but it toes the line of desire too. It's a dangerous feeling, one I need to remind myself to keep in check. Because as dangerous as this is, feeling anything for a woman half my age, one like her especially, could be catastrophic.

"I don't think I made myself clear. You will not leave this compound. I need you alive."

She explodes. Laughter shakes her frame, and she starts to walk past me, bumping her shoulder against mine in a show of force. She makes her way to the door. Her hand comes down against the knob, and my body moves as it opens.

Slapping a palm against the surface, I close it. We're too close. I'm inhaling her sharp scent of salt and berries and something infinitely softer and smoother beneath that. Her head grazes the tip of my beard and I press closer to her, my chest enveloping the expanse of her backside. Even with barriers of clothing, I feel every inch of her heat, just like I'm sure she can feel every solid inch of my dick against her lower back.

"Let go of me."

I swear I hear the hint of breathlessness in her tone, and fuck if I don't want to bottle up that sound for myself. The soundtrack to my jacking off later, is what I'll label it.

"No," I tell her, my voice equally rough. "You aren't leaving."

Her body tenses while curling back into me at the same time. I wonder what she's fighting, if she's fighting a desire, the same kind I feel.

"I'm not staying here," she says again, more firmly.

"You are, baby doll." I press her against the door with my body. "You're staying here, and your fate will be decided in Church, once I bring this up with the others."

"You son of a bitch whore!"

I'm expecting her to try and whirl to kick out at me. So, when she makes a move, I already have her wrists captured and pinned above the door. Her struggles against me do little more than press her ass against my cock. I press her body tighter against the frame.

"I would be careful how you speak to me, if I were you," I warn darkly. "I'm not some regular John off the street. I'm the president of the Kraken MC, and I'll have your respect."

"Or what?" she hisses, her words all but muffled against the wood. "Are you going to kill me? Torture me?" Then, she presses her ass against my hard dick. "Fuck me?"

The words are a taunt, almost daring, but I can hear the underlying hint of fear in them. She may talk tough, but deep down she is afraid of what we plan on doing to her. It's why she's trying to run away from here as fast as she possibly can. But I can't let that happen.

"No, baby doll." I loosen my hold, pulling one hand away but still gripping both of her wrists. I reach into the back of my jean pocket, touching for cold metal. "Not going to fuck you." I bring the cuffs up and quickly slap them around her wrists. "Just going to keep you safe."

Her whole body jolts with surprise at what I just did and how quickly I seemed to manage it. I step away just as she whirls, her shackled fists aimed straight at me. She doesn't reach me, though. I'm already shoving her back and opening the door at the same time. She nearly falls through with a cry.

Explicit curses start falling from her lips that would make men in the army blush. It gets the attention of everyone in the compound, and I'm starting to get pissed enough that I shove her shoulders and watch as she falls onto an awaiting prospect.

"Get her to my room and don't let her out of your fucking sight," I growl. Then I sweep my gaze around at everyone watching on. "Is this a fucking movie? Fuck off! The rest of you, time for Church!"

—— *ele* ——

"Is this about that pretty little piece Box fished out of the ocean?" Cook asks with a low whistle. His eyes flicker to the back of his head a moment as he hums contentedly. "She's a beauty. Got the slip on Slug and Scorpion."

Scorpion flips Cook the finger. "Fuck off. She caught me off guard."

"Well placed blow to the dick, that was," Cook barks a laugh. "I'd pay good money for her to kick *me* in the dick."

Slug chuckles quietly, not at all bothered by the teasing he's endured to be caught in a vulnerable position by the woman. Then again, very little ever seems to bother Slug. His heart is as big as his stomach sometimes and he's not one to hold a grudge.

Scorpion, on the other hand, looks pissed. He hasn't stopped cupping his dick since she delivered the blow.

"I'd ice it if I were you," Cook supplies. "Got some frozen peas in the kitchen."

Before Scorpion can start an argument that will last for hours, I bark, "Enough!"

It slices through, silencing them all.

"Cut the shit, all of you. Who the fuck is missing?"

Heads turn in the room we use to hold Church, taking inventory of everyone present.

"Box is missing," Scorpio says. "So is Raze."

"Fuckin' shit. Where the fuck are they?" My gut twists just thinking of what could have happened to either of them. Especially Raze. My instincts are screaming at me, like deep down I already know what's coming.

"Box is on his way," Slug says, hanging up his phone.

I nod. Box and Slug are tight, so if anyone knows, it's him. Besides, it wouldn't make sense if it were him the Rogue Waves stabbed, considering he's the one who found Naomi in the first place.

"Raze's phone keeps going to voicemail."

I run a hand over my face.

"Pres, what's going on? *Is* it about that woman?" This comes from Wire, who arrived ten minutes after I called Church. He's always been the more serious of the bunch. Big glasses perch on the end of his nose and he slides them up with his middle finger as those curious, intelligent eyes start to read between the lines.

"Her name is Naomi Queen," I start by saying. "She's a marine biologist who was caught at the wrong place at the wrong time." I nod at Scorpion. As my VP, he's usually in tune with my moods and gestures, and we can communicate without ever speaking a word.

"I met her two days ago at Shark Mouth. She caught the attention of Jet."

Cook whistles. "Jet, the Rogue Waves' Secretary?"

Scorpion's jaw clenches. "The one and only. He got pretty handsy with her, pulled on her braids and shit. Wouldn't take no for an answer so I stepped in and told him to fuck off."

"I bet he didn't like that." Slug's face darkens. It's one of the only times we've ever really glimpsed another part of him. When women, children, or animals are hurt, it's like there's a beast that awakens inside him and nothing can stop him when he's on a path of destruction.

Scary shit.

"He didn't. I tried to talk to her then, but she shut me down and left." Scorp shrugs. "Next thing I know, Box is bringing her in."

"She was collecting water samples." It's my turn to speak, to fill in the blanks she'd given me. "Says she heard noise. Went to check it out and witnessed three Rogue Wave assholes killing someone."

I'm greeted with silence and shock until Wire deigns to break it. "One of their own?" He sounds both hopeful and skeptical.

"She doesn't know. Says she got it on camera, but it's broken."

Wire flexes his fingers, already tapping into his brilliant mode. "No problem. I can probably save the hard drive and recover the images."

"Yeah, that's what she said."

"Fuck..." Cook says, as if suddenly realizing the gravity of the situation. "You don't think it's Raze, do you?"

"I don't fucking know if it's Raze or not. That's why we need to keep trying to contact him and recover that footage. The hurricane is passing, so I want you all to split off into groups out there and look for Raze. Call him, ask around, but do it discreetly. Wire, you recover the footage so we can see exactly what the woman witnessed. Slug, you're on guard duty."

"Wait, pres, what do you mean guard duty?" Lilo asks, scratching at his dreadlocked mane. "Are you keeping the bitch here?"

"You saw what the Rogue Waves did to her. Gave her a concussion and stabbed her just before she got pummeled by Box's bike. If they even catch a whiff that she's alive, they're gonna come after her. She might have been the last one to see one of our brothers alive." My gut says the words are true, even though they taste vile against my tongue. "She's a witness, and because of that she is now under our protection until we get this shit solved. So, she can't leave this compound."

"But why Slug?" Cook asks. I detect a hint of a pout in his voice and shoot a glare his way.

"Because Slug is the only bastard here I trust to not actively try to dip his dick into her."

"Aw, pres..."

"Enough! You aren't allowed to fucking touch her. She's under our protection. She isn't going to appreciate it, so I expect escape attempts. Keep your fucking eyes opened and don't fall for her shit. Now hurry the fuck up. We've all got shit to do."

NAOMI

M y wrists rub raw against the metal band of cuffs. I've been at it for what feels like hours and have done nothing except irritate my skin and pull at the wound at my side. My energy starts waning after so long and I realize just how truly tired I am. Tired, pissed, and hungry don't make for the best combination in a woman. It makes us dangerous. Lethal. I've never committed murder, but the current state of my empty stomach has me contemplating it.

I wonder if it'll be bad for me to wrap my bound wrists around the prospect's neck.

When Daddy Kraken shoved me against this asshole, he all but dragged me kicking and screaming into the familiar tobacco-scented room. He tossed me onto the bed with a growl, his lecherous gaze roving over my bare legs. I had to cross them because his eyes zeroed in on my pussy before he emitted a hungry growl.

Fucking asshole.

He hasn't stopped staring at me since, and just quirks up his lips in amusement at the sight of me trying to break free from the cuffs. Which goes to show just how tired I truly am. Julio taught me a thing or two about cuffs. I should be able to get out of these and shove them up the prospect's ass on my way out. Instead, I'm feeling lethargic and frustrated.

Oh, the agony of being hangry.

I stop struggling to catch my breath and look at the prospect. He looks like he belongs under a bridge, scaring children for scraps and crumbs. Stringy hair is pulled back with a strip of leather, and as he smiles, I catch the glint of silver teeth.

His cut isn't as lavishly decorated as the other ones I've seen. There's the Kraken MC insignia, tentacles tearing through the water. There's no name embroidered, either. Just the word 'Prospect'.

"So, prospect." I get comfortable against the bed, uncrossing my legs. His eyes go straight to the spot between my thighs like I predicted they would. I'm giving him the illusion of comfort, pretending to be harmless while I gather my wits because I am anything but. "How does it feel like to be everyone's bitch?"

His head jerks back at my statement, the lecherous expression he was wearing morphing into something different. "The fuck did you just say to me, bitch?"

I smirk knowingly. It's so easy to rattle men sometimes. Their egos are more fragile than glass.

"I'm curious. Do your duties include getting to your knees and sucking dick, or do you have to wipe Daddy Kraken's ass every time he takes a shit?"

"Watch your mouth, bitch."

"Aw, hey I get it. Not easy being everybody else's fuck boy, is it? I just have a question... do they lube you up before bending you over or do you take Kraken cock raw?"

He lunges for me, just like I thought he would. I'm ready for him and when he's within striking distance, my feet lash out, hitting him against his nose. The satisfying crunch of it makes me cackle while he rears back with a curse. "You broke my fucking nose!"

Blood pools down to his mouth and neckline as he cups his nose, crying out as the pain overtakes him.

I feel satisfied enough with that result. If they thought I was going to be a meek little captive, then they can go fuck themselves. Protection, my ass. I know I'm going to be little more than a prisoner here. But I refuse to act like one. I refuse to take this bending over like this prospect here does.

"You fucking bitch!"

"I'm sorry, what did you say? I couldn't hear you over the sound of your whining."

He growls and goes to lunge for me again, but the door to the room opens and in walks an *actual* member of the club. He's my twerking captor from the kitchen.

He stops and stares from me to the prospect, the jovial demeanor about him shifting into something different, almost savage. I barely blink and he's rushing for the prospect, his fist connecting to his face in a blow so powerful, it knocks him on his ass within seconds. The prospect doesn't get back up again.

The twerking man bends in silence and picks the prospect up by the feet, dragging him out of the room and tossing him into the hall like he's a sack of garbage.

It's an amusing sight.

Amusing and fucking terrifying, to think he has enough power in a single, well-placed blow.

As soon as the door is closed again, he turns to me, but the murderous expression is long gone. I'd almost think he didn't just knock out a full-grown man with one punch. He wears a jovial expression, one that doesn't seem to fit on a biker, or at least, what I know of them.

Thick blonde hair is in messy curls atop his head, and his rounded jawline is covered in a darker beard. His smile is so wide and infectious that I just know is real and not a façade. He's thick. I noticed that before in the kitchen when he was popping his ass out like a seasoned stripper.

I hate how fucking good-looking he is, to be honest.

"Sorry about that," he says. There's a kind of happy lilt to his voice. It amazes me, really. If o to 100 had a definition, it would be him. "How are you feeling?" He keeps his distance and, unlike the prospect, his eyes don't travel below my neck.

That alone immediately gains my respect.

"Oh, you know, doing swell. I'm cuffed in a room that smells like cigarettes, naked from the waist down, starving, and am stitched up like Frankenstein. Can't complain."

He blinks slowly, like my words startle him. Then he tosses his head back and laughs. A true belly laugh. For some reason, the sound has my own lips quirking up in a smile.

"Well, I can't do anything about the smell, but I can do something about the rest of that." He approaches slowly, pulling a key out of his pocket as he goes. I almost sag into the mattress in relief as he grabs my wrists and undoes the cuffs then tosses them on the dresser. "Also, you mean the monster."

"What?" I rub my wrists.

"You said you're stitched like Frankenstein, but Frankenstein is the doctor who created the monster. The monster didn't actually have a name."

"You know this because..."

For a moment his cheeks pinken with a hint of bashfulness. "I read the book."

Oh, be still my stupid fucking heart.

I hate bikers and criminals, but the man fucking *reads*. How can I hate a man who reads? Seriously, men who can appreciate a good book is an aphrodisiac to us women. It shows a level of intellect we find fascinating. As for me? Makes my pussy wet. He can open my legs like the pages of a book and study me any day, if you know what I mean.

Insert eyebrow waggle.

I realize I'm staring, and I probably look a little dumb. I just can't believe he's actually read a book. Not that he looks dumb... okay, maybe I'm stereotyping him, especially after that twerking scene in the kitchen.

"You mean to tell me, you've read Frankenstein? What, like for fun?"

He rubs at the back of his neck. "Yeah. Mary Shelley is one of my favorite authors. She practically invented the horror and sci-fi genres."

My eyes narrow on him. "Prove it."

"What?"

"What's your favorite line from the book?"

"You're serious?"

"Like a heart attack."

He cocks his head to the side and observes me for a moment before he smirks. "*'There is something at work in my soul, which I do not understand.'*"

My feet touch the floor and I step closer to him. My finger pokes his shoulder. He's a head taller than me but it doesn't feel towering or suffocating. I poke him again in the other shoulder, right over his designation, then against his road name.

Sgt. At Arms.

Slug.

"Um..."

"I'm just making sure you're real," I tell him. "A man who reads and quotes passages from memory is like a fucking unicorn."

His laugh is a delightful sound. "Wait until you hear me quote Jane Eyre."

I press my hands against my chest. "Be still my heart, I don't think I could take it."

"You like books, then?" His bright green eyes are alight and for a moment, I find myself lost in them before I realize he asked me a question.

"Oh, not at all. I'll read biology and science books. Anything else is frivolous and unamusing."

"That's a shame. I thought I'd finally found someone I could buddy read with."

"Sorry to disappoint you, Slugger."

He pats me on my shoulder, the touch filled with a bit of reverence. I like that. I like *him,* and it didn't take but two minutes for me to find that out. There are some people you just vibe with, regardless of who or what they are. Slug is one of those people.

"That's okay, Queenie. Now, let me find you some pants and get some food in you." He turns away from me and towards the door before I can acknowledge the nickname he's just given me. A play on my last name. Queenie. No one's ever given me a nickname before. I don't count the infuriating growl of the word 'kid' to be one.

I find that I like this one.

I like it a lot.

I follow him as he holds the door open for me and leads me down the hallway. There's no longer a sign of the prospect, at least. Maybe he got taken out to the dumpster where he belongs, because I doubt he woke up on his own that fast after that blow. Slug stops in front of a room and raps his knuckles across it.

It's answered by a beautiful woman with ebony skin and tight curls. She's wearing a tight top and a short skirt, which I eye warily. Bright red lipstick is like a neon sign that makes me zoom in on those perfectly shaped lips.

"Slug!" she greets him warmly, her voice like melted butter. "What can I do for you?"

"Hey, Sugar. Was wondering if Queenie could borrow some pants from you."

The woman, Sugar, flicks her eyes to me. I wait for the hatefulness, the spite that I know usually accompanies women in MCs, but it doesn't come. Her dark eyes seem to warm with empathy and her smile widens. She pushes open her door and beckons me inside.

"We look like we're about the same size," she chats. "Want a skirt or pants?"

"Pants, please."

I take in her room and the burst of colors and textures and scents. Everything in here is just a little bit brighter. Fabric appears to have exploded around the place, and litters almost every available surface. She steps over her strewn clothes and into a closet, whipping out something black and leathery and tosses it to me.

"Those should fit you." She takes in my long legs. "Might be a little loose in the ass, though."

Not bothering to ask to borrow a pair of panties—ew—I snicker as I bend and push one leg into the tight leather, then the other. I don't really care that Slug is behind me, probably watching me bend over. My own nudity has never bothered me before and I'm not going to get shy about it now just because he's in the room. I pull them over my ass and, sure enough, they're a bit loose but at least they don't completely sag.

"Thanks," I offer with a genuine smile, which she returns.

Usually, I'm good at gauging whether or not people are completely shitty. It's a gift; what can I say? She's decent. Something about her quick smile and sharp gaze reminds me a little bit of Lourdes, and I find that comforting.

"I don't suppose you have any shoes?"

She turns and rummages through her mess of attire and emerges with flats, tossing them in my direction. "See if these fit."

They're a little big, but it's better than walking on germ-infested floors of a motorcycle compound. That's just asking for all sorts of venereal diseases.

"You're awesome, as always, Sugar." Slug holds the door open for me, gesturing at me to follow him out in the hall.

"Anything for you, Sluggy."

"Thanks for the clothes."

Sugar salutes goodbye and I shuffle out awkwardly after Slug.

A part of me would have liked to chat with Sugar a bit more. She has one of those intriguing presences that fill me with curiosity. Is she a club whore? An old lady? She didn't act like one, all spiteful and bitchy.

Instead of leading me back to the room, Slug leads me to the kitchen.

"Now," he begins. "Let's see what we can do about your empty stomach." He pats the edge of the counter. "Sit right here and let Slug take care of you."

Chuckling, I do as he says, finding it easy to follow orders because he's so likeable. My legs sway beneath me and I watch him get to work, turning on the fire to heat up the food. He hums while he works, pulling out plates and spoons. Soon, the space is being filled with the delicious scents of spices and seafood.

My stomach gives a rumble. "That smells so good..."

Slug pulls the top off the pan to reveal the food underneath. "Can't go wrong with paella," he says, ladling both bowls with food. He hands me mine and I take it gratefully, humming as that first warm bite hits my tongue.

"Oh my god..." I moan around a mouthful. "Fuck me, Slug. This tastes delicious."

He smirks around his own spoonful. "You think so? Cook usually makes the meals around here, but I had a craving..."

I quickly dig in, taking huge bites, one after the other, until I'm all but licking the bowl clean and demanding more.

"A woman with an appetite." Slug hums as he heaps more into my bowl. "You're stealing my heart."

"You stole mine first when you quoted Frankenstein and then fed me." I point my spoon at him. "You, Slug, are my new favorite person in the world."

"Aw, thanks Queenie."

We eat the rest in silence. When I'm finished, I observe Slug while he eats. He enjoys the food as much as I do, humming and bobbing up and down on his feet as he does. The best part about it? He doesn't even realize he's doing it. There's something tranquil about the moment, and something about him that makes all my tough edges soften.

"Hey, Slug?"

He looks up before he gets a chance to start licking his plate. "Yeah?"

"I'm sorry I attacked you before."

"That's alright, Queenie. I can't imagine any of this has been easy for you." He reaches out and squeezes my knee. It's a moment of solidarity, of warmth, and I find myself leaning towards him before I catch myself, inhaling a sharp breath.

Because what the actual fuck am I doing?

He's a *biker*. Just because he quotes books and makes kickass food and is nice doesn't mean he's innately *good*. He can't be when he lives a life of crime. Riding on land and on waves to make the lives of others a hellish place.

One smile, one kind word from him, and it's like I'd forgotten all my inhibitions. Like I'd forgotten why I stay away from this side of the island. Like I'd forgotten that he's helping them keep me locked up in here.

I shouldn't mistake his niceties for something they're not. He's merely distracting me so I don't run away. He's trying to earn my trust and *fuck*, I hate that for a moment there it actually worked.

I wonder if this is what my mom ever felt like with her revolving door of guys. If this is how they reeled her in only to discard her in a heap of tears and a broken heart later. I always swore to myself I'd never be like her. What does it say about me that I was gravitating towards Slug with a fluttering in my chest, all because he showed me a bit of kindness and humor?

It's fucking pathetic.

It's fucking dangerous.

And I know I can't stay here. Not if this is going to be the risk.

"Slug, do you have a bathroom I can use?"

He smiles. "Sure do. Here, follow me."

Hopping off the counter, my feet bound after his quick footsteps. They lead me to what looks like a shared house bathroom. It's small and smells like lemon and bleach.

"I'll wait for you here in the hall," he says, then closes the door, leaving me alone.

He's cute, but he's kind of a dumbass.

I feel bad as soon as the thought takes place in my head, but I can't help it. I need to harden myself against these men and their tricks before I find myself falling. I scan the bathroom, noting that it has exactly what I came in here for. A window.

I shuffle around aimlessly for a bit, messing with the roll of toilet paper and turning on the faucet in the sink. Then I make my way over to the window and slide it open as quietly as I possibly can. It'll be tight, but I know I'll fit through.

Fucking amateur bikers.

Everyone knows if you live on the wrong side of the law, you should get better protection for your place. That means no windows at the compound. I know we live on an island and sometimes the sweltering heat makes ventilation necessary, but I'm sure they have enemies. Anyone could come in and shoot through their windows, killing everyone inside instantly.

Taking a breath, I grab onto the ledge and hoist myself up, angling my body so I can squeeze through the window. It takes a bit of sliding and quiet grunting on my part, but I finally fall on the other side in a crouch.

I'm outside now. The wind is whipping, and sheets of rain are pouring, but at least the ocean is nowhere near as tumultuous as it was when I got caught up in it before. I've swam in dangerous depths on occasion; that's nothing new. I might be wary about it doing it now, but I don't have any other choice. I have no money to call a cab.

No. I have to get out of here as quickly as possible. Fuck the Rogue Waves. Fuck this compound. Fuck the Krakens. I have a life to live.

And I'm nobody's fucking prisoner.

With that in mind, I run to the edge where the sand meets the shore, and as a wave rises up to kiss the earth, I dive in and let it take me away.

SLUG

The running of the tap and the muffled shuffling on the other side of the bathroom door become a soundtrack to my thoughts. More specifically, the woman on them. When Box first brought her in from the storm, she'd been all limp limbs in his arms, dripping wet with salt and rain and blood clinging to her skin.

There was something a bit grotesque about the image they made at first, until my mind registered the sight of the blood and everything inside me went as cold as the sheets of rain slicing from the heavens.

If there's one thing to get me riled up, it's the sight of a woman in pain. Trauma that comes deeply rooted from the seeds of my past, I'm sure. Who the fuck knows? All I know is that when I saw her, I knew I wanted to help her. To make her feel safe.

And when I walked in the room to guard her and saw the prospect lunging for her? Yeah, I lost my shit. It was a good thing he wasn't out in the hall when we emerged, or I would have kicked him in the nuts in passing. He'd probably been dragged off by a club honey like the trash he was. I make a mental note to bring the situation up with Rock to get the prospect booted from Kraken territory. It's the least he deserves.

Don't ever put your hands on a woman, a child, or an animal. I don't see how people can take joy out of torturing someone smaller and more fragile than them.

Not to say Naomi Queen—Queenie, I feel is more fitting—is fragile. Not with the way she came after me with that knife. It had caught me off guard, nearly gutting me in her ferocity. If I'd been Box, I would have probably let her cut me open. But he was... well, everyone called him crazy. I know differently. He just leans towards different proclivities that the rest of the guys don't.

He likes things wild and bloody and fast. He would have relished in being cut up by her.

Smirking at the thought, my eyes stray to the door. The water is still rushing on the other side. I frown at it then widen my eyes. Maybe she's taking a shit and doesn't want me to hear her. That would explain the water thing. I mean, I get it. If you gotta go, you gotta go. If I was in someone else's house, I don't think I'd want them listening in on all that either.

I wait a few more minutes that drag on and feel like hours. I frown at the door again. Is she constipated? I toe towards the door and reluctantly press my ear to it, trying to make out the noises from inside.

"The fuck you doin', creeper?"

I jump at the voice whispering in my ear, whirling to slap Box upside the head for pulling that shit. Again. Fuck. His manic laughter fills the space of the hallway, and his bright eyes dart to the door and back again.

"Is this your kink?" he asks, that already wide smile tilting further, making him look like some distorted, murderous clown. Which isn't so far from what he actually is. "Listening to people plop one out?" He *tsks*. "Here I thought I had all your desires *pegged*."

I flip him the finger, though a flush rises to my cheeks at the insinuation. Of course he knows my desires. He's pulled more orgasms out of me than I can count. I press my ear to the door again. When there's no sound but the running of water, I rap my knuckles against the surface, brows pulling together. "Queenie? You okay in there?"

Box snickers. "Or do you need Slug's help to lick your asshole clean?"

"Can you not right now?" My eyes roll to the back of my head at his antics. When there's still no response, I try to handle, but it's locked. "Son of a—"

"Alright, move aside Slug, my little Nug Nug." Lifting his booted foot, Box rams it into the center of the door. The force makes it cave in, breaking the lock. I move quickly, finding the bathroom empty and the window open.

"Fuck!"

Box whistles. "You done fucked up, Nug Nug."

"I hate it when you call me that," I groan. But I can't really seem to focus on his teasing when panic and dread settle in my stomach. Rock gave me the task of watching her and she escaped within moments.

This is so fucking bad.

I whirl and run to Rock's office, feeling Box prowling at my heels, his laughter trailing behind me like a cold ghost.

I bust in without knocking, breathing heavy, and catch Rock and Scorpion bent over his desk and looking at a map. They startle as they look up, a frown forming at Rock's brows as he takes in my distressed expression. He doesn't need to speak to command me to state my business.

I do it with dread weighing at the pit of my stomach.

"She escaped."

"What the fuck do you mean, she escaped?" Scorpion demands.

A clap on my back interrupts what I'm about to say as Box trails in behind me, his laughter grating on my nerves. "Our fish-out-of-water climbed out the bathroom window." I shoot him a glare, and he just flashes his teeth at me. "Gave Slug here the slip."

"Fuck, Slug." Scorpion frowns his disapproval, but it's really Rock's expression that makes my gut roil with the awful sensation of guilt and fear. He was counting on me to keep her safe and I let her get away. I let them down. I let myself down. I even let Queenie down.

Not that I really blame her for escaping. I can only imagine what she must be feeling. Cuffed, nearly assaulted by a prospect, and everything else she went through before landing here. She was afraid. I tried to ease it out of her with jokes and easy conversation. I thought for a moment it had worked, too.

Shouldn't be surprising she'd only faked it.

Everyone seemed to fake it.

I try pushing away those melancholy thoughts for more positive ones, but it's a difficult feat when I catch Rock's glare.

"Scorp, have Wire find out where she lives." Scorp nods and goes to obey the president, filing out of the room. "You two are going to go find her together."

Box slaps his palms together and rubs them like he's some sinister fucker from a movie or something. "Excellent," he purrs.

"And Slug?"

"Yeah, Pres?"

His glare is more terrifying than anything I've ever known. I feel it like the spectral image of a ghost ready to fuck my life six ways to Sunday. If glares could kill, I'd be dead. But more than the fear of his stare or his next words, I feel something heavy and unpleasant on my chest. Guilt tastes acrid and bitter on my tongue.

"If anything happens to her, it's on you."

NAOMI

The waves push me. My arms move with a single-minded purpose until I'm spit on the shores near my house. Shivering in my clothes and again at the cold winds, I walk up to the house and open the door, annoyed when I find it unlocked.

"Lourdes! How many times have I told you to lock the damn door?" I call out, glad to step back into my home and this piece of normalcy of my life. I can say goodbye to those asshole bikers, the wrong side of the island, and danger I don't want or need.

I can move on with my life, take a shower, put on clothes that actually fit, and go to work. But first, I need to get a new phone.

Lourdes comes bounding around the corner in a rush, slipping her arms into her jacket while struggling with her purse. The smile splaying across her face is unexpected and makes me pause. She's dolled up in a form fitting skirt that hugs her rounded hips. Long brown legs are clad in tall fuck-me boots, making her tower over me a good fraction. Her hair is in a natural do, the tight, black curls all but a cloud around her head. Her lips are painted, her makeup done with an expert hand.

My own filthy appearance must make her startle a bit too because she freezes for a brief moment before shuffling again.

"You look like a drowned cat," she supplies.

I try not to be miffed about the fact that she hasn't even noticed the bruises I'm surely sporting from my ordeal. Did she even notice I was gone?

"Anyway, I've gotta run."

My eyes narrow. "Where the hell are you going? It's pouring out."

"Dimas called." She squeals and does a little jump. Like I'm supposed to be happy that her douche of an ex called. He does this every time. He reels her in then cuts her loose just to get her hopes up and do it all over again. It's a pattern I see her repeat, one I'm all too familiar with. "He wants to talk."

Well, Dimas is an asshole.

The words can't seem to leave my tongue. It doesn't sit right with me to tell her something like that. I did it for my mom many times over and she gave fuck all about it. It's like I wasn't even there, like my warnings meant jack shit. I learned early on that women who let themselves be dragged along by men in that way rarely listen to anyone else's opinion because they're so blinded by love. One day, eventually, Lourdes might come to her senses.

In the meantime, I have to bite the urge to cuss him out every time.

"In this weather?" I try again, at least.

She sweeps past me, throwing the door open. "Yup! See you later! Or not! Don't wait up for me!"

The door slams and I'm left standing alone, shivering in our foyer.

Something tugs at my chest during this solitary moment. A bit of loneliness. Silly me to expect Lourdes to care that I was gone for fuck knows how long. I bet she was so hung up on her ex that she didn't even bother giving me a call.

With a sigh, I push those bitter thoughts away.

I can't put any blame on Lourdes. We're both roommates and grownups. We have our own lives and she's dealing with a lot right now. The truth is, it's not her job to babysit me just like it's not mine to babysit her. Besides, how could she have known what I'd gotten myself into?

She may be my best friend, but I know I can be closed off when it comes to certain things in my life. Call it childhood trauma. At least, I'm pretty sure that's what a therapist would say. It doesn't really feel surprising that no one really checked up on me.

I'm estranged from my family and am used to being alone besides. I've made it so that everyone is kept at arm's length. Both to protect myself and them from any trouble that might come our way.

I make my way up to my room and peel the wet clothes from my body before hopping in for a piping hot shower. The spray feels nice against my aching and bruised muscles. After rinsing the sand and grime off my body, I hop out and get dressed for comfort instead of style: black leggings I plan on wearing as pants—seriously, it's fucking comfortable—and a loose t-shirt and jacket with leather boots to adorn my feet.

I want to relax, sleep off the strain of the past few days and let my wound heal. But I can't. I need to go out, replace my phone, and then check in with the lab to report my equipment damaged at sea. Fucking bikers and their bullshit.

Who knows how the chain of command will react to me losing not only the camera but the boat and the other equipment? Not to mention, I never got those fucking water samples. We're already on a low budget and understaffed to boot. It's not like they'll fire me, but I still worry about how it could affect the work environment.

First things first.

I go out—locking the door behind me—and buy a new phone. As soon as I do, I sync to my cloud, regaining all my info and contacts I lost in the altercation. I change all my passwords, just in case, before I dial a number as I Uber my way to the lab.

He answers on the first ring.

"Got a new phone."

He grunts like I'm not stating the fucking obvious. "Remember our deal."

"Yeah, yeah. I gotta go, Julio. I'm at the lab. Got shit to do." I hang up before he can say goodbye and shove my phone into the zipper pocket of my jacket so I don't lose it. This back-and-forth dance is growing old, but I can't shake myself of it. It's too much of a predominant part in my life that, at this point, I'm not really sure I could live without it.

Once the Uber drops me off at the lab, I make my way inside. I even left my keys behind on that fucking boat and will have to order replacements, but thankfully the doors are unlocked.

The lab isn't really big. It's not a massive ten story building with scientists in lab coats running around. It is a fucking maze, though. It's three stories of white and steel sterile rooms, and materials in dire need of an upgrade. Flickering lights that need to be tightened.

Creaky boiler rooms that make the whole building shudder and groan.

Basically, it's some scary movie bullshit that annoys the fuck out of me every time I go inside.

Today is no different.

My booted feet squeak against tile, each step sounding more like a gunshot ringing because of how dead the place is. I try not to sigh at that. We are seriously understaffed and need better sponsors to fund our wildlife research projects. Sometimes a few of us stay and fill the halls with our laughter, but other times there's nothing but the deafening echo of silence. My own steady heartbeat. The sound of flickering lights. Sometimes, even, the turbulent thoughts running through my head.

I know Joel is supposed to be working today; we're the only ones scheduled. Today we should have been studying yesterday's water samples, but due to my lack of them and the hurricane besides, we'll probably be told to proof the lab to avoid damage over the equipment and go home.

I go up the stairs where Joel and I are supposed to be working, but I don't head directly to find him. First, I slip into an office and grab reports to fill out regarding the missing boat. We have free reign of the whole place and doors are hardly ever left locked for long.

Filling out the papers takes me only a few minutes. When I finish, I go to find Joel. He's usually working in our lab water tank at this hour. In the lab, though, things are eerily quiet.

"Joel?" My voice echoes against the cold metal and tile of the room, and I wince at the harshness of the sound. "Joel, you here?" He should be. The lab is opened, so who else would be here? "Joel..." My fingers graze against the water tank.

Made of thick glass, it holds sea water that we use to test for trash and toxicity levels and experiment with sometimes. It's tall, too. So tall that we need a ladder to climb up and get water samples from it.

My fingers slide along those thick panes while I stare ahead. It's a subconscious move. One I'm all too aware of when my fingers come across something slick and warm. I pull my fingers away and find them stained crimson with blood.

A gasp rips out of my throat at the sight. I turn, seeing blood dripping down the side of the tank in small rivulets. I follow the line upwards...

And I scream.

Bile rises in my throat, begging to be pushed out on the floor at my feet. I can't move though. I'm frozen, staring up at blood and gore.

I'm used to violence. I've seen a lot of shit in my life and have heard even more. You don't grow up the way I did and not know that shit like this exists. But I've never seen anything quite like it.

Joel's hanging half in, half out of the tank, his whole body wet like he'd been kept under for far too long. Water drips from wet fur. The half of his body that's submerged in the water is human in its entirety, but the upper half, the half that's hanging out and is all but mangled flesh and blood, is distorted into a wolf.

Sharp canines are pried open to reveal the tongue-less contents from within. Blood pools out, and his eyes, which are still human, are wide with what can only be fear.

I want to throw up at the sight so badly, but I force myself to get my shit together. Whatever did that to Joel, whatever killed him, because there's no doubt in my mind that this was a cold-blooded murder, could still be here.

Heart pounding up to my throat, I take a step back, my boots squeaking against the water. I curse when they do. I want to turn and flee. My shaking fingers reach to the pocket of my jacket, grazing along the zipper. I need to call the police. I need to call someone.

I never make it that far.

A man steps out from the shadows of the lab. Covered in water and wet leather, blood, and a manic smile, I know who he is immediately by the words on his cut.

The Rogue Waves.

I turn and run.

My chest heaves with every breath I take, and I can't seem to control them past my own furious need to get away. I can hear him laughing behind me, but he doesn't run. His steps are slow, sure. Like he's not bothered if I'm ahead of him. Like my capture is imminent, regardless.

I bound down the steps with that in mind. He has to know I'm running for the entrance. He has to know I'll call the police as soon as I can unless...

Unless he has others waiting to capture me outside.

The thought makes my breath hitch, and it's a struggle to stay upright. My knees threaten to buckle, but I keep them steady as I run. It doesn't matter. I need to escape, and I need to figure out how and fucking fast before they take me.

Fuck.

I hate that Daddy Kraken was right about them wanting me for what I witnessed, but how the fuck did they even find me? Did they get my boat out of a fucking hurricane and put the pieces together?

Thoughts whirling miles a minute, I don't see until it's too late. I crash into a body, my feet slipping against the ground. Arms wrap around me, and I struggle at first, until warm hands cradle my cheeks and tilt my face up.

"Queenie!"

I never thought I'd be happy to see those bright green eyes again.

"Slug!" My arms wrap around his waist and hold him tightly. I'm sure he can feel the pounding of my heart through all our layers and later, I might regret this brief moment of vulnerability, but all I can feel is relief. "He killed Joel."

Tears are burning behind my eyelids. Joel was a friend, as much as any of my other coworkers are. We were the seniors here, had worked in this place the longest and just like that, the poor wolf shifter is gone.

Because of me.

My body shudders to think about it.

"Ain't the two of you a pretty little picture?" a voice drawls. I pull away from Slug and find a man I don't recognize next to him.

He's wearing a cut, but somehow, he looks even more vicious than any other biker I've met so far, even the one upstairs bathed in Joel's blood. It might be on account of all his tattoos. They decorate every inch of his body, twining up his neck like overreaching vines, curling over his temples, and across the solid, sharp jut of his cheekbones. Head shaved on either side, a long blonde strip of hair is messy at the top. Piercings stick out of his face liberally, but it's the smile that really makes him look psychotic.

It's far too wide, far too chilling, despite how hot this guy is.

"Unfortunately, we don't have time for this shit. We got company." He reaches inside of his cut and pulls out a gun, aiming it in front of him.

A single shot fires out, making my ears buzz. It's preceded by the grunting curse of a man, and the sound of a body hitting the floor.

The man puts his weapon away and turns. "Well, look at the mess you dragged yourself into." He snickers. "It's time to go now."

Before I can protest or do anything else, the man is yanking me away from Slug and towards his own body. He bends in front of me, and I try not to think about the sight he makes on his knees before me. Like a god of mischief laying worship at my feet.

The thought is blown away when he wraps his arms around my thighs and hoists me up. A grunt leaves my lips as he all but tosses me against his shoulder, my head hanging, braids swaying down his back.

The surprise leaves me speechless until I start pounding my fists into his back. "You sonofabitch! Let me down!"

His hand slaps hard against my ass, and I feel the pain of it zing straight up my spine. He palms it and starts rubbing before slapping again.

"No can do, mate. We're getting you back to our compound if it's the last thing we do."

"B-but…" I feel surprised. No one has treated me with such blatant disrespect, or grabbed at my ass like that, in a long time. It shouldn't be arousing or thrilling. But it is. "There are more of them outside."

He slaps again and I squirm against the bastard, muttering profanities as he starts to walk away. "Cute of you to assume we haven't taken care of them yet."

Oh god.

Fighting at this point is useless. There's two of them and one of me. I'm wounded, they're stronger. And if there's one thing I know, it's that MCs have the stubborn determination of a thousand fucking donkeys, so they aren't going to let me go so easily.

I have nothing left to do right now except hold on and wait for them to deposit me back at their compound.

And when they do, they're going to wish they never fucked with me in the first place.

BOX

S he stops struggling against me, but I'm not a fucking idiot. I know what this momentary subservience means, and I'm so fucking ready for it. My dick gets hard just thinking about all the fun we're going to have when she tries to make her escape.

Stepping outside of the lab, we bypass the bloody bodies of the Rogue Wave assholes who were lying in wait for her to come out so they could nab her. Fucking dumbasses don't even know how to hide properly. We took care of them quickly, and I still wear their blood against my hands. Blood I'm now smearing against Queenie's round, delectable ass.

Fuuuuuck, that's good stuff.

We make our way to my bike. We're nearly on the other side of the island and it was easier to get here by water rather than by road. Mermen in MCs tend to ride both ways, but our preferred method is by waves. It's more dangerous since there's a storm, but this was an emergency.

Besides, we don't have witches enchant our bikes for no fucking reason. A few spells spoken over black chrome and steel, a bit of our own DNA to enhance its magic and voi-fucking-la. We got ourselves bikes that transform in the water just like we do.

The steel never rusts or breaks down. It uses the push of currents to its advantage, combined with hydraulic programming and a little bit of skill... we ride beneath the waves with a ferocity. Through currents, against sand, and with the rising crest of hurricanes.

I set the woman down on my bike in the same position I had her there the first time. She still doesn't move. She doesn't try to make a run for it. Her eyes look far away, but her lips are pressed into a thin line of fury. Oh, the pretty little thing is so full of rage, it fuels my own fucking cruelty.

I hop on my bike behind her, and our chests press together. She doesn't move away. I know she's wary of me, but she won't ever show it. I admire that kind of bravery in a person.

It makes them that much more fun to break.

I scoot forward so she can feel how hard my dick is for her through my wet jeans. She glares but doesn't move away. Like she knows this is a test. Like she knows I'm trying to rile her up and doesn't want to give me the satisfaction.

Awake, she's just so much prettier. She's all smooth, brown skin and a defiant tilt of her chin. Her clothes mold against the body I've been fantasizing about since I fished her out of the ocean. The shit I'd do to her...

I grip her by the hips and pull her closer so she's snug against me. "Hang tight, Queenie," I mock the name Slug gave her. The road name fits, I suppose. She is queenly with that hoity expression and rage that could bring down kingdoms. And I want to take the crown upon her head and shatter it before her eyes.

What can I say?

I like breaking shit.

She looks like she could break me equally good, if she dared.

"Shit is about to get bumpy."

I rev my bike and zoom out of the lot of the lab. Her body jolts and her arms wrap around me. She buries her face into the crook where my neck meets my shoulder, and I'm sure she can feel my shudder of arousal and my hard dick twitching against the heat between her legs. I speed through streets with Slug at my side until we arrive near the beach. My hips grind against hers, and her thighs tighten against me and my fat boy.

A holler of adrenaline leaves my lips as we slope down the sand and hit the water. The change overtakes us all. Gills open and breathe in salt water, our bodies hardening with scales beneath our clothes. Even our bikes take on new forms, and I'm fucking living for it.

Queenie's mouth gasps against my skin, but it's not in fear. No, I know it's not. Not when her hips press tightly against mine like she's sating an ache that's built up for her as much as it has for me. That's just what riding does. It's freedom. It's wild abandon.

It's a fucking craving.

We ride through the water at top speed, veering off in turns, dodging reefs and floating debris, until we make it to our side of the island, riding up the shores of our compound. I pull her off the bike with me, keeping her body tethered to mine. Her legs wrap around my waist, and she's not letting go. She's buzzing with something I can place deep in the threads of my own blood.

Kicking inside the compound, I set her down, already knowing what's coming as soon as her feet touch the floor.

She kicks out and I don't even try to dodge as her boot connects to my dick.

Pain splinters from my groin, all the way up to my spine. A gasp leaves my lips and that place where agony meets pleasure flares up inside my whole body. Pain is an addiction for me, and I'm always looking for my fix.

Laughter comes out of my throat that distorts into a groan of pleasure. I step closer to her, inhaling the sharp scent of her sudden fear at my approach. She's wondering why I haven't fallen to my knees, writhing.

The answer is simple.

I want her to fucking do it again.

I want her to hurt me, to destroy me. I want her to take those black leather boots and stomp all over my heart and fuck me up until I'm not the same when this started.

And I want to do the same to her.

"You call that a blow, Queenie?" I taunt. "That was shit. Hit me again. Hit me *harder*." I smile, flashing her a glimpse of my teeth. Others have called it feral, and I guess that's what I am. A feral fucking animal who cares about a few things only.

Eating. Killing.

And fucking.

"You're crazy," she snaps. "I've never seen someone look so gleeful for being kicked in the dick."

I hate that word. It's just a descriptor to use against people and things we don't understand. But I take the insult in stride just like I always do. People just don't understand my particular brand of pleasure. She will. Eventually.

Soon, when I break past those walls she's got around herself, she'll be begging me to wrap my fingers around her throat while I'm fucking her from behind.

Maybe she'll even choke me with her own braids.

Fuuuuck, that'd be nice.

"Maybe I am. But here's the thing, Queenie." I yank on the front of her jacket, pulling her close enough so she can feel my dick. "We just saved your fucking life."

"Box, let her go."

I want to groan at the interruption, but I knew it was coming. We've garnered ourselves quite the audience here in the compound. I reluctantly release her, prying my fingers away one by one. I let my touch linger. Let her feel my handprints like a fucking brand.

Maybe one day I'll brand her pretty flesh. I'll mark her with images of barbed wire and my name to claim her as my own. I may be "fucking crazy" but in a few seconds I've decided what I want and who I'll claim.

And that's her.

If she doesn't break first.

She backs away from me on shaking feet but doesn't take her eyes off me. Smart. She knows not to look away from a predator.

I do take my eyes off her, though, to look at Rock. My president is scowling at me, but I take it in stride. Not like Slug, who seems to be taking his reprimand way too hard. He's off to the side, standing quietly and looking on with a brooding expression. I know he's pissed at himself for letting her get away. I'd reassure him if I could, because the chase is part of the fun, but I know he won't listen, so I keep my mouth fucking shut.

"Status?" Rock asks.

"They were following her," Slug answers in a subdued tone. "They were looking to ambush her at her workplace."

Queenie makes a strangled sound. "They fucking killed Joel..."

"We took care of them." I flex my fingers. I can still feel their blood coating beneath my fingernails, while the rest was washed away with the ocean. There's no better sensation than the blood of enemies on your skin. Or riding in a hurricane. Or the sweet slide of pussy over cock.

"How many?"

"Five."

"Did anyone see you bring her back?"

"Can't be sure." But I fucking hope so. I know my smile conveys those words and it's what makes Rock roll his eyes before he swivels his gaze away from me to look at Queenie. A scowl forms. One that's made grown men cry, but only makes her tilt her chin up in defiance.

Fuuuuuuck. I want to fuck her so bad.

"You shouldn't have left," he admonishes. "I fucking told you they were after you. You aren't leaving again; we're going to keep you safe. You got that?"

A moment passes between them. I can't say I recognize it for what it is, because I don't, but I do recognize it as something. There's a shift in the air, a zing between them. It looks like Queenie wants to argue. Her mouth opens. Closes.

"You think they won't find out where you live?" Rock growls. "They found out where you work, they could easily go to your house and kill you in the middle of the night. Think about your friend Lourdes. Do you want something to happen to her because you're too fucking stubborn to accept our help?"

"How—"

"Wire found you in two minutes. You think the Rogue Waves don't have their own tech guy? That they won't find shit out as quickly as we did?"

This gives her pause. I can see the wheels of her mind turning through her eyes. I can see her begrudge this information. Just like I can see when she accepts. Bummer. I was almost hoping for a fight.

"Lourdes..."

"We'll send a brother to watch your place discreetly. But if I were you, I'd call her and tell her not to go home."

"My things—"

"Box and Slug here will go to your house to pack a bag with all your things."

Great. As punishment for Slug losing her, we get the boring job. At least it's not cleanup duty. Not that I mind getting my hands dirty, obviously, but I've been reprimanded for beating on corpses before and even I don't like getting on Rock's bad side.

Plus, I think this punishment is more for Slug than it is for me.

I'm pretty excited to go through her panty drawer. She's probably a boxer or thong kind of girl. Hmmm... I can't fucking wait to find out.

"I suggest you call that friend of yours before she heads home. And you two." Rock pierces us with one of his infamous glares. "Go. Now."

And just like that, the two of us are dismissed.

SCORPION

"**S**corp."

My gaze cuts to Rock, who stands as firm as his namesake. The glare he's piercing Naomi with would make a lesser man shrivel in on themselves, but she meets his glare with one of her own and fuck, if it isn't the hottest thing I've seen.

I push those baser instincts and thoughts aside though as worry sets in. I'm as pissed as Rock is that Slug lost her, but I won't voice it, and I didn't. Mainly because, taking one look at him, I already knew he was feeling like shit, and it isn't my job to add on to it. It's Rock's. I'm only VP, and while it's a big responsibility, it isn't as big as being president. I'm here to be a second opinion in case Rock ever needs it. I'm here to take the lead if he ever can't.

I'm here to clean up everyone else's fucking messes when he doesn't want to do it.

Thank fuck he's as strong and stubborn as he is, though. Because if it were me leading these fuck wads? It would make me tear my own fucking hair out more than I already do.

"Get Naomi settled," Rock says, never breaking eye contact with her once. But she breaks it for them, turning that penetrating gaze to me. Those whiskey-colored depths do something to me I can't explain. Yeah, they make my cock hard, much like they had the first time I saw her in Shark Mouth. But it's more than that.

I feel like she's seeing straight down to my soul and beyond. To the threads that make up my whole self. Past, present, and future.

It unnerves me as much as it intrigues me.

I swallow and hold out my hand to her. A gesture that goes ignored as she struts past me with an annoyed huff, storming into the halls. Rock heaves a sigh of annoyance and words of silent communication pass between us. We don't need words to speak sometimes, and I know what he wants me to do.

I follow after her petulant strides like she already knows where we're going and is upset about it. I really don't give a fuck. As long as she's protected and safe, she can throw all the tantrums she wants. I can't explain the fierce need to protect her. I like to think I'd do it for anyone under the Rogue Waves' radar, but that's the furthest thing from the fucking truth. If Box knew what I was thinking, he might laugh in my face.

I'm doing it for her.

I think we all are.

We just met her, but there's no denying she has a pull on us all already. That's why Box looked so gleeful when she kicked him in the dick. That's why Slug looks so guilty that he lost her, his past and history with women notwithstanding. We aren't immune to those dark eyes, the attitude, or the boots that could stomp all over us if we let her.

She marches up to Rock's door and throws it open, storming inside. I follow close behind, closing the door behind me with a soft click. I wait where I am, watching, assessing. She paces back and forth across the floor like a caged animal, her fingers reaching into her jacket pocket to grab her phone. She swipes the passcode, presses a few times, and brings it to her ear.

"Lourdes! Where are you?" She brings her thumb to her mouth and chews eagerly on her nail. "No, no, I need you to listen. Whatever you do, don't go back to the house. Wait... *listen*..." She pauses, lowering her hand, sighing, and staring up at the ceiling.

It looks like she wants to cry.

I hate tears, and I especially don't want to see them coming from her. It fucks with my heart, makes my chest ache.

"I'm happy for you. So, you'll be staying with Dimas for a while?" There's animated chatter on the other end and it makes my brows pull together. I'm only catching half of the conversation, but it seems whoever Lourdes is quickly changed the subject and disregarded the urgency in her voice. "That's great! I'm glad you made up, but—" She bites her lip as the chatting continues. "Yeah, but just don't go back to the house. It... it flooded. I called people in to fix it, but they can't due to the storm so it's going to be uninhabitable for a while." The lie falls off her lips so easily it makes my eyes narrow.

She's good at that. People who are usually good at lying have had a lot of practice. I wonder what else she likes to lie about. What other pretty untruths has she told?

"Great. Just, promise... yeah, yeah, I know. Okay. Love you, too. Bye." She hangs up the phone and shoves it back into her pocket. For a moment, it's like she forgets I'm there at all, but I look closer and know I'm wrong. From the way she rapidly blinks, I'd say she's willing the tears to go away because she doesn't want me to witness them.

Like she's balancing on a delicate edge of grief and heartache. I don't blame her. Her entire life has been flipped upside down within a matter of days. She was almost killed and is being forced to stay here when she clearly doesn't want to be here at all.

Not that we particularly care. We just want to keep her safe.

Still, I want to reach for her, but I figure it won't be welcome, so I keep my hands to myself.

Until she heaves out what sounds like a strangled sob and drops herself onto the edge of Rock's bed. Her usually rigid-straight spine crumples as she leans her forearms against her thighs. I startle at the soft, broken sound of her voice.

"They killed Joel." I hear the tears choking her voice. "They killed him because of me."

I can't stay still or silent any longer. I push myself away from where I'm standing and go to her. I don't think twice before I kneel in front of her, pushing my way between her spread thighs. She leans back, her breath catching with something that sounds like surprise at my proximity. Her pupils dilate with something that I analyze just a bit too closely and save in my mind for later.

My hands move, and suddenly I'm touching her warm, wet skin. Just like I wanted to do at Shark Mouth. If she would have given me the time of day, I would have taken her back to her place and spent the night buried between her thighs. And because my heart—and my cock—are intuitive, I know I would have run back, begging her for more.

"It wasn't your fault, pet. Get that thought out of your head right fuckin' now." Her eyes are wide, and I can see the uncertainty in them. She's going to keep blaming herself, and I may not know her, but I know which direction her thoughts are taking her to. That maybe if she hadn't been in the MC's sight, maybe if she'd stayed put, maybe if she'd never found them in the ocean in the first place. My grip tightens against her cheeks, and I pull her forward so our noses touch. "*Pet*," I growl. "If it's anyone's fault, it's the Rogue Waves'."

"I know that." Her breath fans against my lips. This close, I can see tears mingling with the salt of the ocean against her smooth, coppery skin. I lick my bottom lip in an attempt to avoid leaning forward to lick the salt from her skin. But we're so close, that my tongue grazes her lip.

She sucks in a breath, and I find myself freezing. We're too close. So close I can feel her heart beating against my own chest. So close I can feel her thighs squeeze around my waist from my kneeling position, like she's staving off desire, or maybe wanting to pull me closer.

I know I sure as fuck want to be that close.

Close enough where she can feel my dick grind into her hot pussy. Close enough that our hearts will beat in tandem like they're trying to break out of our chests and merge together. Making us one being. One heart. One soul.

The realization and contentedness that settles in my gut preceding the thought almost makes me rock back on my heels. My body twitches and it feels like she wraps herself around me tighter, pulling me closer.

Like she doesn't want me to go.

And I don't want to. But I know that if I cross a line now, if I kiss her, I won't stop there. Because I know and would swear my patch on it that Naomi Queen?

She's Old Lady material.

NAOMI

I don't know what's happening, and yet I do. Beyond the sorrow for what happened to Joel, beyond my anger, beyond everything that's fucked up in my life right now, there's him. His scent like salt and spice pervading my senses. His dry body pressing against my wet one, wedged between my opened legs like that's where he belongs.

For a moment, I pretend he does belong there. Like he's sliding home metaphorically. I know he realizes how close we are, and I see that he wants to give me space just as much as he likely wants to fuck me. That's the only reason my thighs tighten against him as he tries to pull away.

He gives pause, this beautiful biker with the smooth brown skin and thin twisted braids and bright, honey-colored eyes. For right now, I can forget he's wearing a patch. I can forget it has the name Scorpion stamped along the front along with the words: Vice President. I can forget everything except his beauty.

And right now, there's just a beautiful man and a woman drowning in too many emotions to think straight. And that's why she does what she does. It's why I do what I do.

I lean forward, and I kiss him.

It's slow and rough and deep. It's a tangle of lips and tongue and teeth. It's a maelstrom of hate and grief and need.

I couldn't stop the moan even if I tried. I don't try. Because this kiss? It lights a flame inside my belly, a flame that flicks lower between my legs in demanding force and makes me grind against his stomach with little finesse.

All with a fucking *kiss.*

Like he was born to give them. To flick his tongue against mine and draw out my cries of pleasure. His hands that had been momentarily gripping my cheeks now slide lower to my neck. He grips me there, his thumb trailing circles against my throat, while the other hand goes to my hip and squeezes.

I'd be lying if I said I didn't imagine this exact moment in Shark Mouth. When he smirked down at me and called me 'pet', a name that was somehow as endearing as it was insulting. I wanted him to whisper it between my thighs, which are now wet and slick with more than just ocean water.

His body slides up mine, but he doesn't once break the kiss as he looms over me. His hands slip beneath my thighs and he's tossing me. Only then do our mouths part, and a whimper of need and a surprised breath leaves me as I fall among the covers.

He prowls over me like a panther with eyes on his prey. His eyes flashing, his movements intense and purposeful. I can make out the muscles beneath his shirt, the veins moving, bunching with strain like he's trying to hold back a more feral side.

I reach for him again, my own movements unrestrained. I grab the front of his cut, the bitter reminder that this can be nothing more than what it is right now, a few simple kisses, and pull him against me. He falls against my body with a growl as his mouth takes mine again.

That fire alights over every inch of my chilled skin. Everywhere he touches sets me aflame. Our hips are aligned perfectly, and I feel his cock through his jeans. Hard, demanding like the rest of him. I grind against it, creating a delicious friction against my clit that makes me moan and pant into his mouth.

Teeth rake against my bottom lip then bite down hard until I taste the copper of my own blood. He laps up the bruise with tender care and those hands are everywhere at once. Slipping over my breasts to tease my nipples, up my abdomen, ever careful with my wound, slipping between the mattress and my back to run across my ass only to pull away again.

I groan in frustration, but a moment later I feel sated as his hand curls around my throat, his touch light, but with enough pressure to be arousing as he pins me against the mattress, pulling up. His strong thighs straddle my own and I can feel his hardness. Anticipate it.

His hips jerk, grinding against mine. I start to groan, but the sound is choked from me with the slightest press of his fingers against my skin. I inhale sharply, his delicious scent mingling into tobacco and caramel, the combination heady and arousing.

I gulp it in, the contrasting scents, while his hips slam and grind against mine. I don't even care that we aren't unclothed because this feels too fucking good to stop and bother with pulling off our garments. His hips slam faster and faster against my own, the friction rubbing, harder and more demanding. That fire builds, it bursts, it aches.

And then I'm exploding, crying out, fingers grasping for blankets like I can pull the scents together. Scorpion grunts from above me and I know my orgasm set his own off. It isn't until he's finished, his hips slowing their frantic movements, that I realize what the fuck I've done.

I got high off his scent and Rock's. Both of theirs.

Together.

It helped spiral me into orgasm, and it had felt good, but now it feels so wrong.

I know the regret must settle over my features, because I don't have to shove or scream at Scorpion to get off. His face registers the expression on my own and falls into that stoic mask before he pushes himself away. His clothes are damp from my own, but there's a cum stain on his jeans from what just happened.

He doesn't acknowledge that. He doesn't acknowledge this. He merely turns away. "Get some rest, pet," he orders before walking out.

I watch him go, my emotions crashing back down around me like a junkie coming down from their high. It's left me feeling empty. Hollow. I didn't want him to address what just happened and he didn't. I should be happy.

So why does it fucking hurt?

Sighing, I thrash my legs out in a small tantrum and sit up. I need girl talk. I just called Lourdes, and while her indifference to the panic in my voice had prompted me to lie, and I didn't want to disturb her while she was making up with Dimas, I needed someone to talk to about my conflicting emotions.

But when I reach my hand to my jacket pocket, I realize my phone isn't there.

I sit up in a flash and look against the covers, but it's not there. I search the floor, but it's not there either. Logically, I know it can't be under the covers, but I all but tear the bed apart in my search for it, but nothing.

My mind flashes back to Scorpion. To his hands slipping over my body. To his abrupt departure.

Motherfuck.

That bastard stole my fucking phone.

And he used seduction to get it.

"Fucking great, Naomi. I thought you were smarter than this."

Obviously, I'm not. The first quality-sized dick that comes my way and I'm blind to the cut and the criminal underneath. I let his pretty words and looks and my grief blind me to what he really is.

A criminal.

A bastard.

A fucking dead man.

DELFIN

P rospects. They get dumber every year. That's why I don't even bother to remember their names when they come waltzing into our compound, looking to be a part of our unit. Like it's just that easy. Like they can snap their fingers and their place will be secured.

No.

They have to earn their place in our family just like we all did. They have to prove that they're willing to get down and dirty and go the extra mile for us and for those under our protection.

Too bad this asshole couldn't even do that.

A giant bruise decorates his eye where Slug popped him in the face. Never would have known it was Slug if he hadn't told Rock right after he told him about the woman giving him the slip. Slug was usually peaceful, so it surprised Rock as well.

Rock had asked, "Why?"

And Slug looked prez in the eye and said, "He attacked Queenie."

That was the nail on the fucking coffin.

You don't ever assault a female. Certainly not one under our MC's fucking protection.

The words had Rock thundering through the compound until he found the prospect and where he'd slithered his worthless body off to. Once he saw the expression on the prez's face, he'd tried to run. With me stalking the shadows, he didn't get far.

Rock let him sprint towards the door where my hand shot out of the shadows to grab him by the neck. A choked squeak tore from his chest. I hauled him, kicking and screaming, behind our compound to the cellar that wasn't a cellar at all.

That's just what we called it.

It's where we tortured our enemies.

It's where we currently stand.

"I'm sorry!" he snivels, like the coward that he is.

"You're lucky it's us and not Box," Rock tells him darkly. "You see, he's taken a liking to her. If he knew you tried to hurt her, you know what he'd do to you?"

He whimpers and I see true fear flash through his eyes. He better fucking feel it. Box is one scary motherfucker when crossed. He delights in torture. I once witnessed him cut off a man's dick and shove it down his throat before he tied a wrap around the fucker's mouth and watched him choke to death.

Really puts things into perspective about cock sucking.

If he were here, I'm sure he'd do much, much worse than Rock or I ever could.

"Maybe I should wait for him to get back and let him have a go at you."

"No! Please!" The prospect jerks towards Rock like he wants to drop to his knees and beg. Too bad he is strung up by the arms, hanging by looping chains that attach to the ceiling.

Footsteps and the opening of the cellar door notify us of someone else's arrival. I turn and watch Scorpion step down. The Vice President's lips are pressed into a thin line of displeasure as he takes in the prospect.

"This asshole still alive?" he demands.

"For now." Rock dismisses the prospect by turning to Scorp. "Did you get it?"

Scorp reaches into his back pocket and pulls out a phone. I don't need to ask to know it belongs to the woman. Naomi Queen.

The one who made fun of my fucking road name.

"She'll probably figure out that I took it in a few minutes, so someone should be up there to calm her down. I know she's gonna rage." I swear he looks fucking guilty.

"She'll get over it. It's for her protection as much as ours. Get it to Wire. See if he can block it from being traced with his whiz techy shit."

"What about—"

"Delfin." Rock doesn't let Scorpion finish his sentence before he's turning to me and nodding. It seems my assignment is now out on the table. Teeth grinding together, I reach to the holster in my cut and pull out my gun. A knife is too messy, and I don't feel like staining my hands with his blood.

Staining my soul with his life is another story entirely.

I'm used to that shit. Used to the screams of the dying haunting me at night. I shouldn't let this particular asshole haunt my nightmares, but it isn't him per se. It's everything else. It's the bullets, the fallen comrades, the innocent cries, and everything in between.

Things in the present sometimes merge with the past until I can't differentiate between one or the other.

My finger squeezes the trigger, and the bullet blows between the prospect's eyes. Just like that. Gone.

But the shot is still there, ringing and echoing in my ears. My heart still pounds, my hands still shake, but I hide it well. I don't want Rock to know what's going on in my mind because I know he'd side-line me if he did. No more runs, no more heavy shit.

I should give it all up. But I can't.

I need the MC life like I need the next breath in my body, like I need the ocean against my skin. It's a part of me, and I have to suck it up.

"I'll go check on her," I tell Rock as I slide my piece back into hiding. He nods, oblivious to what's roiling inside my head. I shouldn't be anywhere near anyone else when I'm like this, when the past and present are colliding in my mind, but I'll say anything to get away quickly.

My legs are steady as I walk out of there, but the moment I'm inside the compound, my knees shake. My body collides against a wall, my hands grappling against the surface to keep me upright, the scratching of my nails helping to keep my focus. So I don't go back there again. Back to the death, to the war.

But my mind takes me there anyway. There I go, on a desert battlefield, with unrelenting sun beating down against my bloody body. Snaps ring out, echoing, buzzing. I groan, trying to dispel the image from my mind, but the groan sounds more like a roar of some beastly animal. I know what I probably look like. How pathetic I probably am.

Get your fucking shit together.

"Hey, you! Where the fuck is that small-dick, no good, motherfuck—"

My gaze snaps up, a sound of anguish pushing past my lips before I can choke it back in my throat.

No, no, no, no. She can't fucking see me like this. She'll tell Rock and he'll make me go to therapy or some shit. I got nothing against it. I know it helped him when he came back, but I'm not him and I don't want to sit on a fucking chair and talk about my problems for hours. It's bullshit. It makes me antsy.

My gaze barely focuses on her figure.

"You okay?"

Her voice does something to me. It pulls me out of it, and I focus on that. If I stare hard enough, the anxiety will go away. First, I focus on her face, on the way rage melts to confusion, her dark brows pulling together.

Focus.

Long slender neck, clad in a wet leather jacket, shirt, and tights that cling to her lithe, yet curvaceous frame. Black boots. Long, dark braids that trail down to her waist. Whiskey colored eyes. Plump mouth made for kissing.

"Hey, it's okay," she says, her voice calmer than before. "Listen to my voice, alright? Just focus on my voice, Delfin. Can you do that? Can you focus on my voice?"

A barely perceptible nod escapes me, but she notices it just the same.

"Good. Okay. Now I'm going to come near you, okay? You'll feel my body heat. Focus on that and on my voice. I'm stepping closer."

Her scent envelops me. The salty tang of the ocean and something else underlying that. Something sweet. Both floral and tasty.

"Okay. I'm here, Delfin. You can see me, right?"

I can. I can see the way the threads of fabric cling to her skin. I nod.

"I'm going to touch you now. Would that be okay? Would it be okay if I did that, Delfin? I'll touch your shoulders first."

I nod.

Then I feel her touch. That combined with the sight of her, the scent of her, the *sound* of her? It calms my racing heart.

"I'm going to touch your hair now, okay?"

"Yes."

She seems to startle at the grave sound of my voice, but her fingers dive into my locks just the same, pulling through the long strands.

"Can I touch your face, Delfin?"

"Yes."

Fingers cup my cheeks, and just like that, I'm back. Everything feels normal, if a little hollow, but even that is being filled up with the warmth and empathy that emanate from her eyes. They pulse and pour into me like that bright piece of her belongs within the darkest parts of me. She clears away the stains on my soul, bit by shining bit.

My own hand reaches out of its own volition to cup her cheek. A gasp pushes past her lips and I inhale the sound and every bit of her. Memorizing every line and curve. Every eye lash, every blink, even the tone of her skin.

I inhale her scent one last time before I compose myself and pull away.

"Thank you," I whisper, feeling my cheeks heat with embarrassment. I feel like a fucking fool, to have broken down in front of her. She already made fun of my fucking road name, and even though she helped me through this, I can't help but fear she'll make fun of this too. I clear my throat and run a hand through my long hair, letting the black strands fall over my face to hide my expression.

But the woman steps forward, and I tense as her fingers make the slow trek up towards my face, shoving my hair away. Her smile is radiant. "There," she whispers. "Don't hide your face."

Don't hide your face.

Amazing how something so simple can change everything within the span of a few moments and have the impact of a lifetime. Like a woman's kind words. Like a touch. Like her scent. Like her smile.

Like her light, chasing away the evil, darker shadows of my soul.

SLUG

Queenie's house is in a nice neighborhood. Not at all posh, but it's definitely not the kind of place you'd expect to find dirty bikers like me and Box. Yet here we are, packing a bag full of clothes and toiletries she might need for her stay.

At least, that's what I'm doing.

Box is rifling through her panty drawer.

"Can you not?" I sneer at him when he brings a scrap of lace to his nose and inhales deeply. "Stop being a pervert."

Box cackles, shoving the panties into his front pocket. "Says you, poop-peeker."

He's never going to fucking let me live that down, even though it wasn't even like that. Fuck. Can't do shit in front of Box because he's always twisting something really innocent into something gross. Like packing Queenie a bag.

He grabs another pair of panties, these made of silk and ribbons, inhales around the crotch area with a groan, eyes fluttering like he's fucking high or something. "Fuck, this is good." He shoves that into his pocket as well.

"Jesus, Box, are you going to take all her panties and make her fight you for them?"

His eyes light up and I know I fucked up and said the wrong thing.

"That's a great idea, my little Nug Nug." Then I watch with barely concealed horror as he grabs a handful of lace and silk and cotton and shoves them in the front of his jeans as if he doesn't have perfectly good pockets.

"Can you be fucking serious?" I snap, finding my patience wearing thin at the moment.

Box doesn't startle at my outburst. He just leans over the dresser on his elbows, smirking at me in a way that's all too condescending. "Aw. Tell Dr. Box what's on your mind, Nug Nug."

"Stop calling me that and hurry and help me pack." I grab a pair of jeans and shove them into the open duffel bag at my feet.

"Aaah, I see what this is about. It's about Queenie, our future Old Lady, isn't it? You done fucked up and now you feel bad so you're taking it out on me. It's okay, Sluggy. She's fine."

My jaw snaps together, grinding with irritation. I hate how on the mark he is, but I expect it. Because Box knows me. We've known one another for years and, despite our differences, we're closer than brothers. He's just saying shit to get me riled up and calm my racing thoughts.

Inhaling a deep breath, I know it works when the tension leaves me on the exhale. My eyes narrow.

"Our future Old Lady?" The words hurt leaving my throat, because I can taste the words 'Old Lady' and I crave when I know I shouldn't.

"Of course." Box straightens and slams the drawer closed after he's pilfered all the underwear. "Our. I'm not greedy enough to keep her from my brothers. Especially not you."

"She's not ours, Box," I point out patiently. "She's under our protection. Nothing more."

He cuts me a look. "You don't really think they'll keep it in their pants for long, do you? Not with the way they were all practically drooling over her at the compound." He bends and zips up the duffel, hauling it back up and slinging it over his shoulder. "We all want a taste of her cunt."

"Ugh, you're so vulgar." I push past him but can't bring myself to step out of her room, where the scent of her cloys through the air and my lungs. It doesn't ease any of my guilt. I should have listened to Rock. I shouldn't have let my guard down. But she was so open, so *nice* to me, and women rarely are unless they're club honeys who see my cut as a way into Old Lady status. Even women from the outside looking to slum it with bikers always gravitate towards the others before they gravitate towards me. I don't care. My self-confidence isn't shit. But something about Queenie makes me feel...

She makes me feel *seen*.

"You know you'll bury your face between her thighs the minute she invites you in." His hands stop me from leaving, trailing down the sides of my thighs.

The picture he paints is a tempting one, but I shove it aside with a fierce shake of my head. "She'd never." She doesn't seem to like any of us. I thought she liked me. It'd only been a ruse to get me to trust her enough so she could escape.

I don't like the feelings that left me with.

I sound like a damn pussy, but unlike others I'm not afraid of my own emotions. We've all got them and suppressing them is bad for the health. Gives gas, heartache, and fuck knows what else. But I do hate how whiney I sound. The truth is, I understand why she did it. She was afraid of us and what Rock threatened her with. Fuck, that asshole prospect attacked her right under our noses. No wonder she left the first chance she got.

It eats at me that I let it happen. That she could have gotten hurt, and it would have been my fault.

"She wouldn't invite me," I mumble low. But Box hears it.

"She will. You're a fucking snack, Sluggy. She'll be begging to bounce on your cock."

"Jesus." My eyes roll. "Have some fucking respect."

"I am being respectful," he argues. "That woman is going to be my Old Lady and I am going to worship her pussy, her body, her clit, her mind, all of it. And you and the others will be there to help me do it."

I try to ignore the words. More importantly, I try to ignore the feelings they invoke inside of me. Desire. Want. Desperation. A sudden image flashes through my mind, of Queenie riding my face, of me lapping up the juices from her folds as she trembles in orgasm. Just the thought of it makes my dick hard, and it's like Box can scent my arousal in the air.

He presses against my back forcefully, startling me into dropping Queenie's duffle on the floor. His body presses mine against the wall a fraction and he doesn't ease back. "You like that, Sluggy?" he whispers against my ear. His voice has dropped low, so low that for a second Queenie's image is blown away and replaced with Box's. And all the things that voice promises to do to me.

I force back the groan that wants to be unleashed, but Box knows me well and the hands that were trailing up my thighs, reach low to cup my dick through my jeans. His own groan is a force that trembles through my body, and he puts more pressure against me, rubbing against me through the material that separates us.

"So hard for our little Queen." Box nips the lobe of my ear and pulls me back.

Because I can't resist, my legs follow, ever obedient, until he switches our positions and pushes against my chest. I let myself fall against Queenie's mattress, groaning as I'm enveloped in her scent. It's like having her here with us, surrounded by her essence.

"There's no shame in desire," Box says darkly, his words low, seductive, and reassuring.

"I know," I reply tightly. It took me a long time to realize that. That I could fuck without feeling pain, that I could enjoy something as primal as Box's body moving against my own. It's only thanks to him that I realized that in the first place. He's so liberal, so free.

"Good." He looms over me, hands reaching for the buckle of my belt. With a few sharp tugs of his fingers, he undoes my belt, button, and zipper. The next thing I know, my boxers are shoved down and my dick is being held in his hand. He grips me tight, and I watch the rough movement of him jerking me up and down in quick strokes.

Moisture beads against the tip of my cock, and it makes Box smile just before he leans forward and laps up the smooth tip of me. My head falls back on a groan. He's fucking killing me.

"Imagine what she could do to us," he speaks against my dick, right before he tongues the underside of me. His movements are drawn out and teasing. "Imagine her sweet pussy hugging your cock." His mouth circles my head, and he sucks me inside, hollowing out his cheeks until my tip touches the back of his throat. He sucks on me hard, and my hips jerk up off the bed.

"Box..." Tightening my fists on the blankets, I try to catch my breath. "We can't. Not here."

He bobs his head up and down before he pulls away. I almost cry out at the lack of contact.

"Why not here?" he demands. My eyes flutter to his flushed face, the darkness in his gaze. "Because it's Queenie's bed?" A chuckle rumbles out of him. "Oh, Sluggy, that just makes it so much more enjoyable."

"But—"

"I think it's time you stop talking."

I blink and the next thing I know, he's shoving lace into my mouth, gagging me with a thin pair of Queenie's underwear. I can almost taste her in my mouth. And fuck, it's so wrong but feels so, so right.

"Nice and quiet, just how I like you," Box teases before he dives over me and takes my dick in his mouth.

This time, my cries are muffled behind the fabric. He works me up and down, relentless and demanding. His pace never slows, and he wraps around the base of me with his hand even though he can take me all the way without gagging. He plays with my dick, keeping me pinned down and at his mercy so I can't jerk up into him. Box does all the work, and he knows when I'm close because he takes me all the way until the tip of his nose touches my belly.

My scream is a gargled sound as I shoot my load into his mouth. He takes all of it. Every fucking drop, wringing me out until exhaustion settles over my bones. I'm breathing hard, taking in the hint of sex, of Queenie, and of Box.

He rises over me with a closed mouth smile. His fingers yank the panties from my mouth and leans down to take my mouth in a kiss. I open my mouth against his, gasping as liquid drips against my tongue, cum mingling with spit.

And I swallow that shit down without shame.

Box pulls away, his lips shining with arousal. "I want to fuck you against this bed," he whispers. "I want to leave my mark here so everyone knows who Queenie belongs to."

My face flushes with the image, and I'm not sure if I should feel embarrassed that we're using her scent to get off.

"But we don't have time for that right now." He stands and smooths out his cut with his palms, shoving the panties he gagged me with back into his pocket. "Later. I can fuck you while you fuck her, if you want."

I don't think she'll want to. I don't think she'll want me. Because if I had to choose between Box and myself, I know I would choose Box every time.

He must read the thoughts right off my face because he frowns. "Stop that shit or I won't make you come next time."

I take a breath and let it out before reaching to do up my pants. "Yes, master."

His eyes flare at the joke as he bends and yanks me to a stand. Our bodies press close, and I can feel his hard dick. I want to reciprocate the pleasure. Drop to my knees and let him cum all over my face like he likes to do, but he's right.

There's no time for that right now.

"Let's go."

We only pause to pick up her duffle, and then we're walking out of the house. On the porch, I scan the streets. Our bikes are parked in front of the house. Box's, with his black chrome and bright blue steel pipes, and my less-frivolous Harley in black and shining gray. They look strange here in this neighborhood, maybe a little suspicious.

What is even more suspicious is the motorcycle speeding away.

I give a shout, jumping down from her front steps and stepping into the street. Too late. Whoever is driving has already sped away and I couldn't make out jack shit.

"Did you see a cut?" I demand.

"Yeah. Fucking Rogue Wave cowards couldn't get close enough to try me." I hate how disappointed he sounds, but I have to admit I am, too.

I'm just glad we're here and not Queenie. And seeing that bike speed away just solidifies every protective instinct and nerve within me.

I am going to protect her.

No matter the cost.

NAOMI

Claws rake against my skin, splitting my flesh open and leave me to bleed out, half of my body submerged in a tank, mid-shift. There are gunshots that are drowned out beneath the water. The image of a camera flash. I'm swimming and I don't know where I'm going; I just know I have to get away. But it's like swimming through honey. I'm too slow. I can't outswim the knife as it plunges into my heart. I'm drifting, suspended through salt and sea, my eyes flickering. I'm barely alive and I pray for death, but it doesn't come. Headlights blind me and a motorcycle revs in the distance, riding the waves, crashing into me.

Then there's Joel's face. Twisted, mangled. There's blood, a feral smile, and a red, rogue wave crashing to shore to take me away.

I jolt, heart pounding furiously as the images from my nightmares chase me through wakefulness. A groan comes out of my throat. It all felt so real, so terrifying, and I hate that state of weakness dragging me under.

But underlying that acrid smell of fear, there's something infinitely warmer and enveloping. Hard arms wrap around my body, pulling me into the moment until I'm lucid again. Until I'm fully awake and see my surroundings. Darkness, but the comforting kind. A single light glows in the room, and it isn't the sights I focus on first but the scents. Tantalizing and unfamiliar, yet one I've come to recognize just the same. Tobacco and something sweeter, like chocolate mixed with caramel.

It's heady and comforting, and I lean towards it and the big body it seems to be wafting from. Arms tighten around my shoulders, lining our bodies flush together.

I want to argue. To ask Daddy Kraken what the fuck he thinks he's doing lying beside me? As if he thinks he has the fucking right to do so. I want to rage at him and rage at Scorpion for stealing my phone. But the vestiges of the nightmare still cling to my subconscious, and I allow myself a moment of weakness. He must have come to sleep after I left Delfin in the hall—this is his room, after all. And he's not completely mortifying.

I allow myself to be vulnerable for a single second in his arms, like I've never been with anyone else before.

His dark, thick lashes fan out against his cheeks. They're the kind of lashes females envy because of how pretty they look. Thick and long and...

My hands go to his cheeks, fingers sliding against his skin, his beard scraping with every pass. His breathing deepens, but he doesn't stir. The sensations rising inside me are foreign. I'm far from virginal, but I can't say I've ever spent the night with a man. I've never had a long-lasting relationship because I've never had a need of it. I like my space. I like being alone.

But I have to admit, waking up with warm arms wrapped around me feels... nice.

He's nothing to me. He's my captor, my jailor, a total asshole, but the shadows of nightmares still cling to me, and I want—no, I *need* —to feel something other than fear.

My fingers curl around his thick neck, just below his beard. That's when his eyes fly open, and I can't help but wonder if he'd even really been asleep at all. He watches me, his body stilling like a predator about to attack. The thought has my pussy clenching on empty air. What the fuck is wrong with me? Why am I fascinated with men who could attack me at any given moment? It's a primal need, probably stemming from our baser instincts.

I don't give a fuck.

I just know that I don't want to feel this panic anymore, and a good orgasm can help with that.

And Daddy Kraken is going to give it to me.

With slow, deliberate intent, my hand smooths a pathway down his bare chest. Every slow inch down has his nostrils flaring harder, faster. The hairs on his chest tickle my palm, and he doesn't speak until I reach the waistband of his boxers.

"Don't."

My fingers tease the band, tugging and snapping it lightly against his skin. "Why not?"

"I'm old enough to be your fuckin' father."

I still, thoughts invading my mind that shouldn't, before I give them a shove. My fingers resume playing, teasing. "Hmm," I hum. "*Daddy* Kraken does have a nice ring to it." A single finger slips into his boxers, grazing across the head of his cock.

"Naomi..."

I like the way he says my name, all angry and gruff. "Do you really want me to stop?" I will if he wants me to, but I can read over the rough lines of his features.

He *doesn't* want me to fucking stop.

"What do you want from me?" He answers a question with a question.

"Thought that was obvious." I graze the head of his cock once more and slip my hand out, bringing my finger up to my lips for a taste. "Mmm, delicious—"

My hands become shackled into an iron-clad grip. I'm flipped, my heart pounding, the breath whooshing from my lungs as my body is bent and twirled into a different angle. I'm no longer laying on my side but straddling Daddy Kraken's face.

My bare thighs are spread wide over him, his beard scraping against my skin. I can feel his breath, hot and rushed against my bare pussy.

I undressed before bed, ridding myself of my wet, pesky clothes and opted to wear one of his shirts instead. He pushes the hem up now, fingers gliding over my body smoothly until he reaches the undersides of my breasts. His thumbs flick against my nipples, the small, quick touch enough to have me slapping my palms back against his abs and arching into him. As I groan, my pussy glides against his face. The scrape of his beard against my clit causes an incredible friction and a jolt of pleasure has me seeking it again.

I grind over his lips and beard once more, my fingers digging into the skin of his abdomen. He doesn't seem bothered. In fact, his mouth opens, tongue darting out to lick from my clit, downwards.

"You want to come, Queenie?" he demands against my sex.

"Yes, *Daddy* Kraken. Make me come." Shamelessly, my hips grind against his tongue and mouth as I take my pleasure for myself, but he's not having it. His hands leave my nipples—I almost huff at the loss of his heat—and go to my hips.

"You asked for it," he growls before flipping me. My hands give out and I fall back, but he twists me around so my cheeks are pressed against his thighs. My ass is suddenly in the air, thighs straddling his shoulders. "You're gonna take my cock in your mouth, Queenie, while I suck your clit."

I moan, hands trembling as I lift myself up with one hand and reach inside his boxers for his cock with the other. I slide the black material down his legs until his erection springs free.

Holy fucking guacamole.

I've never seen a cock so thick.

I gulp as I stare at it, and I already know it's going to be a monster to get into my mouth. If my jaw breaks, it'll be so fucking worth it, though. I lean forward as Daddy Kraken leans up to taste me. My groan of pleasure is muffled as I take the head of him into my mouth. His hips jerk up into my mouth and I hollow my cheeks out as a single thrust has him in the back of my throat.

Warm and velvety, I suck, tracing my tongue along his length, sucking like I'm trying to swallow the marrow out of a fucking juicy rib-bone. And his fingers digging into my thighs? His beard scraping against my most sensitive areas? It has me ravenous with pleasure. I'm suddenly obsessed with giving and receiving in equal measure, so I ride his face, slamming my hips down against his reaching mouth.

His tongue laps up my juices, his lips suction against my pussy, and then his fingers are pushing deep inside me. So deep, I scream around his cock as the pleasure builds like a fucking storm, exploding into a surprise orgasm. I shudder against him, moving and prolonging my pleasure, taking him deeper into my mouth until he hits the very back of my throat.

I gag around him and that seems to set him off because not a moment later, hot spurts of cum are sliding down my throat, filling my mouth. I hurry and swallow, but cum still dribbles out the side of my mouth when he pulls out.

I'm still swallowing when he turns me around so I'm looking down at his face. His thumb comes up, wiping away the cum from my mouth, but before he pulls away, I take his thumb inside me, sucking at the pad of his skin and tasting him all over again.

"Fuck," he groans, pulling the digit from my lips. "Fuck!"

His hands go to my hips and lift me off him, settling me gently back down against the mattress. His movements are quick and efficient as he yanks his boxers up again and slides off the bed.

I'm too elated to care that he's obviously regretting what we just did, though I have to admit, it stings just a tiny bit. The taste of his cock is still in my mouth and my own juices coat my inner thighs.

At least my nightmares and the fear went away.

"Fuck, Queenie..." He runs a hand through his graying hair. "That was..."

"I know." I'm breathless, and I don't care.

His gaze cuts across my body, even in the darkness I can see the desire in his eyes. I know he wants to say something, but he's interrupted by the ringing of a phone.

It jolts me back to reality, that sound. Reminds me that I'm a fucking captive. Doesn't matter how good these men are at giving orgasms. They're holding me here against my will and they stole my fucking phone besides.

Sure, I got something out of this just now. An orgasm to rival all orgasms, except maybe Scorpion's. Really, they can't be compared. But I remind myself that these men are the enemy.

And I have a job to do now that I'm here.

And that's to make them regret ever fucking with me in the first place.

ROCK

I still taste her on my tongue, a sweet nectar that coats my lips and beard. It's an ambrosia, an aphrodisiac, and how fucked in the head am I to want more of her?

She's so fucking young. Too young for me. And yet she swallowed my cock like a seasoned honey but better. She made me see fucking stars, and for an instant, it didn't matter that I'm twice her age, or that she's under our protection.

All I cared about was getting her off. Giving her an orgasm that would make her forget anyone else that came before me.

For a second there, I think it did.

But the ringing of my fucking phone jolted us both back to reality. The hatred crept back into Queenie's face, and the regret crept through mine.

I shouldn't have fucking touched her.

I shouldn't want to do it again.

I yank my phone from my jeans pocket. "What?" I bark.

"Prez, I got something. You might wanna call Church for this."

I don't like the sound of that or the fucking tone in Wire's voice. It makes me feel uneasy. "Call Church," I tell him. "Be down in a few." I hang up without waiting to see what he says. I move quickly after that, yanking on my jeans and a t-shirt. When I'm finished getting dressed, I turn to look at Queenie and watch her staring at me warily.

"I've got Church," I explain stupidly, as if she hadn't fucking heard me speaking on the phone. "Try not to leave the compound." I reach into my pocket and pull out her phone and toss it to the bed. Her eyes widen as she takes it in. It didn't take Wire that long to make sure her signal was untraceable. She can use it, and she won't be found. I'd debated not giving it back to her at all, but she's not a prisoner here, no matter what she thinks. And I don't need that friend of hers calling the cops on us if she doesn't hear from Queenie.

If I expected her to be thankful that I was giving it back, I was fucking wrong. Instead of smiling, she frowns down at her phone then back up at me like I'm a fucking leper.

"And did you find everything you needed?" she sneers.

I don't have time for this shit. I know she's looking to argue because she thinks we're keeping her here against her will. When will she see that it's because we're trying to protect her from our enemies?

"We did," I tell her slowly, brows furrowing close together. "I'm not going to apologize for making Scorp take your phone. I'm the President of the Krakens, and that means my brothers' safety is my top priority. I had to know if you would jeopardize that."

"If you're worried about their safety, maybe you should have never brought me here."

The fire in her eyes is a fucking trip. It's also fucking infuriating.

"I already explained my reasons to you. I'm not going down this fucking road again with you. We're protecting you, and if you don't want it, then fucking leave and see how well you fare with the Waves." With that said, I turn and storm out.

I don't care how harsh I sounded, or the way her anger affects me. She is still acting like the Krakens are the bad guys in this scenario. As if we are the ones who stabbed her and left her for dead. As if we are the ones who killed her coworker and tried to kill her, too.

She's obviously holding a grudge, and I don't fucking know why. I want to say I don't fucking care, but the fact of the matter is that I do care.

Even when I know what a terrible fucking idea it is to do so.

"Talk to me, Wire."

Everyone sits around the table in Church. Box and Slug had arrived just on time before the meeting started, Slug with his sullen expression and Box with his feral grin.

Wire fiddles with his laptop, his fingers zipping across the keyboard with a fury. I know something is wrong based one his pale complexion and the thin line of his lips. "I got the video from Queenie's hard drive."

Everyone has taken to calling her Queenie. Road names are sacred, earned through blood, sweat, and tears. Slug all but baptized her and everyone goes along with it like she already belongs and is a part of our fold.

Before I can ask, Wire is already turning his laptop at an angle so we can all see the screen clearly. It's paused on a video, and with a single click it begins playing. My gaze narrows on it. At first, it's the image of water, of Queenie's blue-green fins at the edges of the video, though she's not in the frame. Her hands pass over the camera here and there as she prepares water samples. The video goes on until she swims into a sunken boat, weaving through halls.

My breath catches as I see what happens next.

It's so fast, but everything in the image is so clear.

From the two Rogue Waves holding a merman between them, to the third plunging his knife into his chest.

Into our brother's chest.

Raze.

A strangled feeling builds in my chest that's equal parts fury and sadness. I want to rage. I want to flip the table and destroy the laptop and the video on it. As if that can destroy what happened. The fact that our brother is fucking dead. As if destroying the technology can somehow make it untrue.

The video goes on as Queenie tries to get away from her attackers. My heart thunders in my chest as I watch. I know she got away. Her being in our compound is proof enough of that, but watching it feels like it's happening in present time. I want to reach through the screen and appear there to help her.

The shot breaks out of the water. I catch the sight of a boat before she's dragged back under. There's a scuffle beneath the water, and the camera catches sight of her attacker as she's whipped around. I memorize that face.

The face of the man I'm going to fucking kill.

His arm stabs out. I know that's the moment he plunged the knife into her. I fear for her life irrationally until a swarm of bubbles blurs the image. I know it's the storm pulling her away from that murderous son of a bitch.

Wire leans forward and presses another button. The video fast forwards and he presses play again. This time, we catch the image of chrome and steel zipping towards her right before the screen goes black.

Wire pulls the laptop back towards him. "She was telling the truth," he says grimly. "Those fuckers..."

"The scarred one is mine." Box cracks his knuckles. "I'm going to fuck him ten ways to Sunday and make him wish he'd never been born." The glee and rage are prominent things in his voice. He relishes in the violence, but beneath that I can sense he's as angry as the rest of us. Not just for Raze, but for Queenie.

"Fucking Rogue Waves," Cook spits venomously, though there are tears in his voice. "What's the plan, Prez?"

They're waiting for me to lead them, and this is probably the hardest part about being president of an MC. Knowing when to stay my hand, or when to ride out to war. No matter what I decide, I know they'll all have my back. The thing is, I've always been afraid about that. About making one wrong move and having their lives on my conscience.

Raze.

His life weighs on me. I'm the one who sent him out on patrol to guard our borders. The Rogue Waves must have gotten him then. Because I'd sent him away. He was our brother, and I've no doubt in my mind that he's dead. And I want revenge.

We all do.

"Rewind the video to Raze again and pause it." That's all the response I give. Wire does it quickly and turns the screen towards me.

I'd caught a glimpse earlier, but now I'm sure of what I saw.

"That's a treasure chest of fucking jewels."

Everyone leans in close to get a good look at it.

"Would ya look at that?" Box whistles low. "Think maybe Raze found where they stashed it? Maybe followed them or some shit?"

"That's the only explanation I can think of." I run a hand across my beard. "It's not like we've been actively at war with them. It's not like we were seeking them out for trouble. Maybe Raze saw something he shouldn't have. Was in the wrong place at the wrong time."

There's always been issues about territory. Our problems with other MCs as of late have been happening for years. Small skirmishes that are a result of living on a small island of criminals. Criminals who are always seeking more. We're always expanding, always garnering enemies. I should have predicted this.

"What are we going to do about it?" Scorp asks quietly.

The question settles oppressively around us like thick, black smoke. The decision is mine. It's always been mine. And it's not fucking easy to make. But I know what we have to do. I know what this video means.

"First, we're going to send our brother off." Murmurs of 'hell yes' ring around the room. "Then, we're going to fucking war."

NAOMI

After Rock leaves, Slug comes into the room, a duffel bag in hand. He doesn't look at me, doesn't say a single word. He just deposits the bag on the floor, gesturing from it back to me, before he leaves me alone.

I feel guilty and I hate that I do. I think I hurt Slug's feelings, and that doesn't quite sit right with me because he seemed so sincere when we were talking in the kitchen. I like him, but I slipped out on him and probably got him in trouble with Rock for it.

As soon as the door clicks closed behind him, though, I go to the duffel bag and find my toiletries inside. I fish out my toothbrush and toothpaste, then run to the bathroom and take a quick shower. Once I'm finished, I go out to get dressed.

A quick assessment of my bag, however, lets me know that I have no fucking panties.

"What the fuck?"

I want to curse Slug's name but hold back. Mainly because I don't think the sweet biker would do such a thing. This seems to have Box written all over it.

The bastard either stole my panties or didn't pack a single one.

If he thinks this is somehow a deterrent or something, he's fucked in his stupid head. I don't mind going commando, even if it is slightly uncomfortable.

I slip on a Nirvana t-shirt and some jean capris and a sensible pair of tennis shoes. I pocket my phone and slip towards the door, trying the handle. It opens with ease, and I'm surprised to find there's no big, surly biker waiting for me on the other side.

Confident, I walk out in the hall. I haven't seen all the compound, but I remember my way towards the kitchen. That's where I go, hearing voices wafting from within.

I stop in the threshold.

I haven't met everyone that lives here yet, but I'm familiar enough with the dynamics here to know that I've stumbled upon the club whores.

There's about five females in the kitchen, weaving around one another to make a meal. They stop when they see me, all of them freezing and taking me in. My whole body tenses, prepared for the cattiness, the ugly to come out.

But I recognize Sugar as she steps forward with a warm smile on her face. "Hey, girl. How you feeling?"

I scrutinize her tone, but all I get from it is genuine concern that makes me relax a fraction. "Honestly? Like I got run over by a truck."

She smirks. "Just a motorcycle. And a knife." At my wide-eyed look, she lifts her shoulder in a shrug. "People around here gossip. Ain't hard to put shit together. Now, let's meet everyone and then you can show me that wound of yours. Might have something for you." She doesn't wait for my permission and pulls me into the kitchen. "Everyone, this is Naomi, but everyone calls her Queenie." Sugar points at the girls around us. "That's Ritz."

The woman she points at has brown skin and bright pink hair tied up in twin buns. She has a punk look, with a purple, snake-skin mini skirt and a black halter top. Her bright red lips smile warmly at me, and she salutes in my direction with the spatula.

"Hey girl, welcome to the compound!" Her warmness has me relaxing even further.

"This here is Stef." Sugar points at another white woman clad in little more than a bikini, her long dark hair flowing in waves down her back. I have to say though, she rocks the look well.

"Hey, Queenie."

"The little one over there is Baby Gap."

Said little one peeks out from behind Ritz. The curls framing her small, round, coppery face make her look very young. When she smiles, it's to reveal a gap in the front of her teeth. Hence the name, I assume. She's adorable, though, and gives me a shy wave.

"And that's Eli." Sugar points at the last female. This one has my hackles rising again because of the way she blatantly sneers in my direction.

"Princess Eli," she corrects, tossing her bleached blond hair behind one shoulder.

Sugar rolls her eyes. "No one calls you that."

Her expression simmers into the cattiness I've been expecting. Her smile malicious and knowing. "Scorp does."

If the words are meant to freeze me in my tracks, they kind of do. Does she have a thing with Scorp? Knowing that makes me feel kind of... gross. Especially after what we did the previous night.

"Okay, gag, Eli, I don't need to know what the fuck my brother calls you in between pillow talk."

My head snaps to Sugar. "Scorp is your brother?"

She grimaces. "Unfortunately. He's my half-brother, though. Why else do you think I'm shacked up here?"

My face heats. I assumed what anyone would assume. That she was a club whore. I don't say that out loud though, but I don't need to. They can probably all read it from my face.

Eli snorts. "Fucking judgmental bitch."

"Eli!" Sugar reprimands.

I don't even feel bothered by it because it's true. I am being a judgy bitch and she has every right to call me out on it if she wants.

"Sorry," I mumble. "Internalized misogyny and all that."

Sugar waves off my words. "Don't worry about it, Queenie. I'm not a *honey*," she puts emphasis on the word, all but letting me know that's what the others call themselves, "but I know what it seems like looking in from the outside. I only live here because Scorp offered and it's safer than anywhere else. I'm lucky. We've only known each other for a couple of years and he's the best. Anyway, let's have a look at your wound, shall we?"

She leads me over to the island and I step up on the chair. A moment later, her fingers are lifting the hem and she's giving out a low whistle as she catches sight of the stitched-up wound.

"They should have let me know the moment they brought you in," she grumbles.

My brows raise. "You a doctor?"

Her smirk is mischievous. "No, but I am a witch." And then her palms hover over my wound and begin to glow. I watch in fascination as tendrils of light emanate from her palms, slivers of it tracing over my wound. Then I feel a twinge of pain as my flesh knits together from the inside out.

"That fucking stings."

Sugar smiles at me apologetically, pulling away as the last bit of flesh heals. "Sorry about that. I just sped up your healing process."

"Why the fuck didn't they ask you to do that sooner?" I grumble, lowering my shirt. "Would have saved supplies and shit..."

Sugar slaps her palm on my knee. "Right? That's what I said. This was stitched up by Rock, and Scorp doesn't like involving me in club business. Besides, it takes a lot of energy to heal wounds, and he's too protective to let me overuse my magic."

I scrutinize her. "Are you burnt out now?"

"Nah. Gave me a rush, but I'll crash hard at bedtime, for sure."

"Well, I appreciate it," I tell her genuinely. "I'm actually surprised you're here. I thought Merman MCs were exclusive for mer shifters only."

"They usually are, but because Scorp and I are half-siblings, I'm an exception—and honeys don't count as MC members. I got all my mother's gifts and none of my father's genes. Unfortunately, I can't shift in the water like you, you lucky bitch. Plus, I think they keep me around because I help enchant their bikes."

Ritz comes over to us, setting shot glasses along the bar and pouring tequila in each of them. Without a word, she slides each of us a glass and picks up her own. Her elbows lean against the bar as she openly listens into our conversation.

"So you're useful to them." I pick up the shot glass, cradling it between my hands.

Sugar does the same. "You could say that. The rest of the girls have a variety of gifts, too." She throws her head back along with the shot and downs it all. I'm surprised she doesn't even flinch at the taste.

"What are you?" I nod in Ritz's direction.

"Wolf shifter," she answers smugly, downing back her shot. She sets the glass back down then serves herself another drink. "They keep me around because of my sexual prowess. You know what they say about werewolves..." Her smile is all sharp teeth and mischief. "We have too much energy."

The other girls join in on our conversation. Soon, we start shooting the shit, and I learn a lot about them and why they're here. It's not the typical, territorial bullshit I'm used to with other women, save for Eli. They're all super nice and welcoming, and I find myself warming up to them and relaxing more than I ever have with Lourdes.

I learn that Stef and Baby Gap are mermaids and Eli is a witch. They all live at the compound and work part-time at the MC's underwater strip club.

It goes to say, the strip club intrigues me immensely.

Our conversation is interrupted by the arrival of the MC members. The energy in the air shifts. I can feel the intensity vibrating through the room like a current of electricity. Drinks are quickly poured as they make their way over to the bar, taking shots and downing them like water. Some girls are hauled into laps and kissed roughly. Music suddenly blares and I know that the party is about to begin.

Eli pushes her boobs up to her chin and shimmies over to an approaching Scorpion. She glides easily next to him, draping her body over his form. Seeing how close they are makes an ache of jealousy and discomfort build in my chest.

I've got no right to be jealous. Eli staked her claim, and if they're a couple, then Scorp is an asshole for cheating on her with me. But if she's just another club whore—*honey*, I correct myself—with delusions of becoming an Old Lady, then that's on her.

I know how these things go and what these men are like. They can't commit to a single girl and the girl? They're the ones who end up with broken hearts. Like my mom. Like Lourdes.

No fucking thanks.

But still, I hate myself a little bit for the feelings Scorpion and the rest of these assholes provoke inside of me. Like this burning jealousy igniting as Eli stands on the tips of her toes to press a kiss near the edge of Scorp's mouth.

Beside me, Sugar scoffs. "Scorpion hates kissing," she murmurs. "Yet Eli still tries."

With surprising firmness, Scorpion extricates Eli from his body and nudges her away with a shake of his head and narrowed eyes. His disapproval is suddenly obvious, and it gives me a jolt.

He hates kissing?

Never would've guessed with the way he tongue-fucked me in Rock's room before. If he hates kissing like she says, then why the fuck would he let me kiss him?

A mystery of the ages.

One that will have to wait because I'm still pissed at him for using me just so he could pilfer my phone from my pocket.

He approaches us slowly, his dark eyes wary as he takes me in. As he should be. The only reason I don't kick him in the dick right now is because I don't want Sugar to be mad at me for maiming her brother.

"Sugar," he greets.

"Big brother," she replies with disdain. "You leaving *Princess* Eli all by her lonesome?"

Scorpion's eyes roll. "Not even going to comment on that when you damn well know we aren't a fucking couple." He turns to me then. "How you doing, pet?"

My whole body bristles at the nickname even while my cheeks heat. I don't want him calling me that. He's got no right to give me a fucking nickname. Not after he used and stole from me.

"Like you care?" I retort.

His eyes darken and he steps close to me. I'm all too aware of his body heat, and all too aware of the memories of earlier assaulting me. They press between us, the memory of his lips, the taste of his tongue, the feel of him grinding against me. It's like a static buzzing between us, and the flush creeps up my face unbidden.

"Oh, I care, pet," he whispers, bending so his lips graze against mine. "I care a whole fucking lot."

Something flashes in his eyes. A flicker of something sad and dangerous. It doesn't belong in his eyes. An emotion that I never associated with Scorpion. He's dangerous, prowling, beautiful. That sadness doesn't belong there.

My eyes narrow. "What's wrong?"

He rocks back on his heels, giving us a few inches of space before his mouth twists into a semblance of a smile, though there's no joy in the gesture. When he bends down again, it's so his lips brush across my own in a sweet kiss. His fingers pinch my chin, holding me there before he pulls away.

"Do you care, pet?"

Yes.

But I can't say that aloud.

"Maybe..."

He smirks then tucks a stray braid behind my ear. "It's club business. But you've got nothing to worry about. We'll keep you safe."

Then he glides past me, going behind the bar to grab a bottle of rum by the neck. Then he disappears, pouring alcohol into his mouth as he walks away towards the living room, dropping onto the couch and staring at the ceiling.

"Wow," Sugar whispers.

I turn my flushed face in her direction. "What?"

She blinks, smile widening. "Scorp likes you."

"Oh, whatever."

"It's true. He kissed you. He never kisses anyone." Her expression shifts from humorous to wide-eyed surprise.

A moment later I know why.

I feel his presence behind me, and I'm enveloped in the sweet scents of tobacco and caramel. I don't turn because his face hovers near my cheek, beard scraping against my skin. "You flirting with Scorpion with the taste of my cock still in your mouth, Queenie?"

His words are spoken low enough to send shivers down my spine but loud enough for Sugar to make them out. Her eyes widen to comical proportions before she slowly flees away from us.

I whirl with a glare on my face. How fucking dare he? He's the one who ran away from me earlier. He's the one who regretted it as soon as his phone rang. He quickly got dressed and fled from the bed like it was on fucking fire.

"So what the fuck if I am?" I demand, pressing my palms against his chest, ready to shove him away from me.

His hands clamp down against me, holding me tightly as his lip quirks up into a smile. Fuck, I hate how good he looks when he smiles.

"Calm down," he orders with amusement. Then, his voice lowers until it's all but a purr. "I don't mind sharing you with my brothers..."

What the fuuuuuck...?

I stare at him like he's grown two heads. Did he just say what I think he said? Sharing? My gaze sweeps around the room to avoid looking into the intensity of his eyes and that's when I notice it. My mouth goes dry at the sight.

At the Kraken brothers with the club girls. Two or three mermen sharing a single girl between them. I watch as a brother I don't know palms Baby Gap's ass from behind while another brother is in front of her, tugging her shirt down to suckle on her nipples. A third kneels in front of her with his face up her skirt.

The fuck kind of world did I fall in?

This is new…

I know there are polyamorous groups and open relationships, I just never expected to see it within a fucking motorcycle club.

My tongue is tied in my mouth. All around me there are couples sharing and… fuck… is that some male-male action I see? Yup. Definitely. Those swords are definitely crossing. I swallow past the lump in my throat and try not to stare at this new development. At the new fucking views.

I'm saved from replying when my phone starts ringing in my pocket.

Saved by the motherfucking bell.

I take it out, holding up a finger to Daddy Kraken as I steal a glance at the caller ID. Fuck. I take a step away. I can feel my breathing going labored, and I fight to keep an impassive expression on my face. "I have to take this."

It'll be bad if I don't.

I walk away quickly, hurrying into the quiet of Rock's room before I answer the call and press the phone to my ear.

SCORPION

I watch as Queenie rushes away to answer a call. The speed in which she bounces out of here is fucking suspicious, as was her whole demeanor when she glanced at the phone. It has me pushing up to my feet and stalking towards Rock at the same time Box and Slug do.

Rock is staring at the path she took to leave, like she'd left a fucking trail behind her or something.

"The fuck was that?" I demand, tightening my grip around the bottle of rum I'm currently nursing.

Normally, I wouldn't give a fuck who leaves to answer their phone or looks for privacy to do so. But emotions are running high, what with the Rogue Wave assholes all but declaring war on us, Raze's death, and our mourning. Queenie's innocence was proven when we watched those videos, and her background is so fucking clean she couldn't possibly be involved with them. But something about it is *too* clean.

My gut is screaming at me. An instinct that says something is wrong. Why did she have to leave to answer? The music ain't that fucking loud, and the way she hurried, the way her face drained of color when she stared at the caller ID?

Fucking shady as fuck.

"She had to answer a call." Rock crosses his arms across his chest.

"She ran pretty damn fast to answer that call..." I take a swing of rum, relishing in the burn down my throat. "Anyone else find it fucking suspicious?"

"Wire said she was clean," Slug says softly. "Why would you think she has something to hide?"

"When she made a call from my office, she was quiet. Turned her back to me. Wire traced it, but said it was a burner phone she called..."

"That doesn't mean anything," Slug argues.

"Ain't you a fucking boy scout, Nug Nug," Box teases.

Slug rolls his eyes. "I think you're making a big deal out of nothing. Did you forget that they *stabbed* her?"

Rock rubs a hand cross his thick, graying beard. "Maybe so, but we have to be cautious. Her record was too fucking clean. Almost like it was forced or something. We have to be careful, especially with these Rogue Wave bastards pulling this shit... It could be a trap."

"You think she's a Rogue Wave spy?" I ask.

"Only one way to find out," Rock says.

Box bounces up and down on his toes and cracks his knuckles. Giddy and manic as shit. Like it's his time to fucking shine and he's ready for it.

A sliver of unease goes through me. I know what he's thinking, I know what he wants, but before I can object, he pushes past us.

"I'll get the truth out of her."

And then he's gone.

I take a swig of alcohol, knowing that none of this is fucking good. "Fuck."

NAOMI

"You good?"
  "Fucking fine, Julio."

He grunts and goes quiet. There's silence between the both of us. Like he's waiting for me to continue the conversation, but he damn well knows I've got nothing to say to him. Still, the stretch of silence is uncomfortable.

"Anything else?" I demand impatiently.

"You tell me."

Fuck.

I've always hated when he pulls this shit. Like he can see right fucking through me, even through the phone. He can't know what's going on with me. He won't like it if he knows where I'm at and who I'm with.

"Nothing to report," I answer with a blatant lie.

He grunts again. "Call you tomorrow."

The line goes dead, and I breathe a deep sigh of relief, slipping phone back into my pocket. That was a close one. I have to be careful what I give away when it comes to Julio. I don't doubt the time will come when he tries to track my phone or some shit. He's fucking done it before, the nosey, controlling, possessive bastard. And when he finds out where I'm at...

I turn around just as the door to Rock's room closes softly. My whole body freezes as I take in Box, standing by the doorway, licking his lips.

"And who is it you're reporting to, my delicious little creature?"

Fuck me.

I don't have time for this bullshit, and certainly not for his particular brand of crazy.

"None of your goddamn business, psycho." I step forward, leaving a good foot of space between us. "Now get out of my fucking way." I stare pointedly at the door. The last place I want to be is at that orgy fest, but I want to be alone with him even less.

But Box doesn't fucking move. Because of-fucking-course not. He makes an annoyed *tsk*-ing noise and pushes off the door, standing in front of it so he's blocking my view. "Here's the thing, my beautiful creature. I can't let you leave this fucking room." The way his voice purrs dangerously sends a slice of fear down my back. It's vicious and nerve-wracking, and I take a step back as he takes one forward. "Not until you answer a few questions for me."

The patch on his cut is suddenly that much more prominent. Like a neon sign blazing, tearing away the darkness and shrouding him in the vicious light of what he truly is. A criminal, with an Enforcer patch, and his crazy sights set on me.

My heart thunders up to my throat, and I try not to let my fear show. I should have locked the door when I came in, but I have a feeling Box would have weaseled his way in here anyway. There's no escaping him. I know it like I know the sun rises in the morning and the sea crashes to shore.

My arms cross against my chest to hide my trembling hands, but I think all the movement does is draw his attention to my chest.

His smirk is telling.

"Well?" I demand. "What do you want?"

"Oh, I want a lot of things, Queenie. But first, I want to know who you're reporting to." He steps forward as I step back. "Don't think we didn't notice that suspicious phone call."

I despair, something inside me steeling. I can't tell him. He can't ever know. Feeling braver than I probably should, I uncross my arms and step towards him. Our chests nearly bump. Even with inches of space separating us, I can feel his heat. He burns like a flame and standing too close with surely set me up in flames. But in a daring move, I do it anyway, standing on the tips of my toes so our eyes are meeting.

"What makes you think you have any fucking right to demand anything of me?" My saccharine sweet smile contrasts the venomous words.

But it doesn't compare to the smile Box gives me.

"I was so hoping you'd say that..."

I don't have time to blink, to react, before he's moving. My hands are caught in his vice-grip and he's pushing me backwards. My legs hit the edge of Rock's bed, and with a shove, I bounce against the mattress. The breath leaves my lungs. Fear pulses in my throat. Scrambling back, I try to turn, to let myself fall off the side and get away. But he's too fast. He's on me within moments, his heavy weight baring me down against the bed as he straddles my lap. His thighs squeeze on either side of my hips.

I struggle beneath him, bucking my hips wildly. My hands flail out, nails raking against the skin at his cheeks. All he does is laugh manically, gripping my wrists in his hands and pinning them above my head.

He leans down, his tongue flicking out against my lips. My mouth presses into a thin line, a growl rising in my throat. It does nothing but spur him on as laughter trickles out of him.

"Keep struggling, Queenie. All it does is make me hard." His hips grind against my center as if to prove his point.

I try to buck him off me, not caring that doing so only makes him grind harder against me. Guttural cries shriek from me as I kick out, trying to slip from his hold.

He laughs again. "Aaah, your screams are the sweetest music." Keeping my hands pinned with one hand, the other wrapped around my throat and squeezed enough to strangle the shrieking anger from me for a brief second. Then he pulls away.

"You fucking bastard." My breathing is ragged, my chest rising and falling with painful heaves.

"Name calling might as well be compliments to me, my beautiful creature." He tugs at my wrists, pulling one wide over my head while releasing the other. He reaches into his back pocket with one hand, but I'm not some docile captive. My nails scrape against him again and I begin to fight anew. He takes every blow with a groan of pleasure. The sounds are almost orgasmic, and with every hit against him, I can feel him growing harder between us, grinding tighter and faster.

And my body, treacherous fucking bitch she is, *likes* it. *Wants* it.

But I can't stop fighting. Even as every thrust of his hips sends a friction of pleasure jolting through my core, sending me higher and higher into something I shouldn't want, but my body is fighting to claim.

When Box pulls out a set of handcuffs from his back pocket, I know how fucked I am. Especially when the cold cuff slams closed around my wrist, choking my circulation. With cold, calculated precision, he slaps the other end of the cuff against the headboard. I yank on the restraint, the single moment of distraction has him slapping another pair of cuffs against my other wrist, restraining me against the headboard.

I'm helpless. My hands spread above me; I've never felt more vulnerable. Yet a fire rages inside me, a fury that I need to lash out with everything I have. My knee comes up, slipping beneath his heavy weight, and connects to his groin.

I don't know why I thought that'd work a second time.

He slips away from me but doesn't move to cup his precious jewels. His laughter is strained, pained, but delighted.

"Fuck, Queenie. You're on the right path to getting that Old Lady jacket and my brand on your pretty little skin." His thumb swipes against the pulse at my neck, which jumps under his touch.

The thought of being anybody's 'Old Lady' makes my stomach churn.

I snarl at him. "I'd rather die."

"So dramatic..." He digs his thumb into my pulse, making me gasp. "But I think I can change your mind."

"Never!"

"We will see."

There goes that feral grin again. It's a slow, curling thing that spreads across my skin like the slow glide of honey. Just as sweet, but with something underlying it that should frighten me. So why the fuck is it turning me on instead? I don't want it, this feeling spreading through my body as he takes the hem of my shirt and rips it up the middle.

He exposes my breasts to him, my turgid nipples peaking against the cold draft of the room. It's certainly that and nothing to do with the heated gaze that roves over my figure appreciatively, leaving heat over my body wherever his eyes touch it.

A flush rises up my neck and stains my cheeks. Why the fuck didn't I wear a bra today? It feels suddenly like a colossal mistake, with the way his tongue darts out against his lower lip, proceeded by his teeth pulling it into his mouth.

In a single, laconic sweep, his hands go over my skin, palming my breasts. The scrape of his calloused fingers causes goosebumps to rise over my exposed flesh. I fight back a shiver and lose.

"I have a few questions for you, Queenie," he says almost absently. But he's not even paying attention to me. His gaze is locked on his hands playing with my breasts. He kneads them, lifting and lowering them. They fit perfectly into his palms, and he seems to be enjoying it.

As if to pull away from his touch, I sink deeper into the mattress and squirm, but all that causes is for my hips to press against his dick, and my boobs to arch into his touch. My tongue feels leaden in my throat and my mouth opens. I want to respond to him, to tell him to go fuck himself, but the words are silent in my throat when he uses his thumb and forefinger to pinch my nipple.

No.

Fuck no.

I am *not* getting turned on by this. And yet, I am. Electric jolts of pleasure spread through me at the touch. It feels like my every nerve is bubbling, ready to burst at the slightest caress.

His fingers massage my nipple, like he's easing the ache of his pinch, or maybe, to ease the blow his next words bring. "Are you in league with the Rogue Waves?"

My head rears back against the pillows, my eyes widening. For a second, I forget all about the desire that was starting to build and my eyes narrow on those words. "Is that what the fuck this is about?" I jerk my hands, forgetting for a second that I can't reach out and slap him like I really want to. They're brought up short by the manacles he has me in, and the cold metal digs into my skin painfully. "You think I'm in cohorts with the fucking enemy?"

"Hmm..." Box's eyes flash on my face, but his hands never stop roaming against my body. He pauses at the edge of my pants, slipping his finger inside where the jean material meets my skin. He pulls away after a moment, tapping the patch on his cut. "I'm the club's Enforcer, Queenie." He leans down, close enough that I breathe in his breaths. "Do you know what that means?"

I jerk away from him, but there's no escaping this. "I'm not a fucking idiot," I spit. "I know what an enforcer does."

"Hm, not many people do..."

My eyes roll. "I've seen Sons of Anarchy, you stupid bastard. Just because I know you're the club's protector and torturer doesn't mean I'm involved in anything nefarious."

"That remains to be seen." He goes to my pants again, flicking open the button and sliding down the zipper.

Fuck, fuck, *fuck.*

I like this game way too much, and he knows it.

"Get off of me!" I try to buck him off, but all it does it make him try harder, his movements going rougher as he yanks my pants down my hips, leaving them just at the tops of my thighs.

His eyes widen as he takes in my naked pussy, a low whistle coming from his mouth. "Never seen a more beautiful sight than a woman going commando."

His attention on my lady bits makes me squirm even more. My face feels like it's on fire, and my pussy lips feel slippery with my treacherous wanting.

"That's because some asshole stole all my underwear!"

His eyes gleam with mischievous intent. Like a magician performing a trick, a silk pair of panties appears in his fingers in the blink of an eye. "You mean these panties?"

I glare at the garment in his hands. "I knew it. You fucking pervert."

He brings the silk to his nose and inhales deeply. A wide smile taints his mouth, and it's frightening and erotic and I don't know what the fuck is wrong with me. "I wonder if your pussy smells like this?"

A choked laugh bubbles out of me. "I can tell you that my pussy does not, in fact, smell like fucking laundry detergent."

He ignores my barb, reaching for his own button and zipper. "No," he agrees. "It probably smells sweeter."

"W-what the fuck are you doing?"

Instead of answering, he flicks open the button of his tight jeans and slides the zipper down. A shove of the waist, and he's exposed himself to me.

And holy mother of fuck...

I've never seen a cock more decorated than his.

If I assumed the ink trailing over his face, neck, arms, hands, and fingers were all he had done, I was so wrong. Ink trails like vines around the base of his cock, twining upwards. And the underside? A large metal rod is jammed through it.

Fuck me.

Lorum piercings have never looked so hot before. I'm so transfixed on it that I almost miss what's on the tip. Shining metal is pierced through the head of his bright, shining cock. Precum beads against the tip of him, glossing over that Prince Albert piercing.

His erect cock bobs against his stomach, and I can't pull my eyes away even though I want to. It sends a rush through my body, my pussy suddenly aching, as if demanding I put that beautiful thing inside me and let him pound me into oblivion. My breath catches as he suddenly brings my panties down, wrapping them and his palm around the base of his dick.

And he does the damndest thing.

He jerks off.

Rough, yet slow, flicks of his wrist against his shaft. I watch as he squeezes, grunting every time my panties close around the head of his dick. They slide up and down, his hips giving the slightest jerk above me. The noises he makes are musical, temptation incarnate.

"Your pussy would feel so much better," he whispers darkly. I still can't take my eyes off the mesmerizing sight of him jacking off with my underwear. "But bad girls don't get to come, do they?"

I lick my lips, my mouth suddenly dry, and I can't form a single coherent thought. My hands jerk like my body wants to reach out and touch him but is restrained.

"Are you in cohorts with the Rogue Waves?"

The question doesn't register. At least, not at first. Not when his other hand drops to my pussy and he grinds the heel of his hand into my clit. My hips jerk off the bed and deeper into his touch. The groan rips from my throat unbidden. I can't stop that single sound of pleasure even when I want to.

It brings Box too much satisfaction. His fingers slide from my clit, down to my pussy lips, not entering me, even as I clamp down on empty air, desperate for his touch to fill me.

"Are you?" He teases my entrance with a finger, and I want to cry out in frustration.

My mind swirls with a heady sensation, my thoughts barely hanging on. How can I even keep it together when he's jacking off above me and teasing me so deliciously with his hands?

"N-no."

"No?" His finger presses into me a fraction. My hips cant up, but he pulls away, not allowing me the friction I desperately need.

"No! I'm not. Why would I be involved with assholes who want to kill me?"

Seeming satisfied with my answer, his finger slips between my folds, moving in and out, the movement in time with the jerking of his own wrist.

A keeling groan comes from my throat. I don't recognize myself. I should be fighting him, I want to fight him, but instead my hips are angling upwards while his finger dives in and out of me.

"Who are you reporting to, Queenie?" His own voice is a guttural, barely put together sound. It washes over me, and the question chases away the heat in my body, replacing it with a heart that's not beating steadily enough and a coldness on my skin.

"N-no one."

He stops his movements, pulling his finger out of me. I almost despair at the lack of touch, but it's for the best. My skin is on the verge of bursting completely, and I try to stave off that sensation by counting down from ten.

Box's movements stop and he reaches for my hair, taking a few of my braids between his fingers. He observes them like they hold the mysteries of the world. "The problem with your answer, Queenie..." He wraps the thick cluster of braids around my throat and presses down. "...is that I don't fucking believe you."

My airway is cut off and I gasp for breath, the surprise of his actions making me suddenly desperate for air. If I had use of my hands, I'd scratch and claw at him. But I'm helpless. My legs flail, but he just presses harder onto my thighs and every movement I make is all but useless.

"I want the fucking truth, Queenie."

Stars dance behind my eyes. As he's choking me, his wrist begins pumping over his shaft once more, his grunts and my choking gasps echoing through the room.

"Fuck, you're so beautiful." He eases his touch and air pulls gratefully into my mouth, but he doesn't let up. As soon as I catch my breath, he's choking me again, harder. The pain of it is almost blinding and it's all I know.

Until his hips dip down and the head of his cock slides against my clit. Hot and wet, combined with the light scrape of the material of my panties and the cold, contrasting flick of his piercing, makes me want to cry out.

This is not a pleasurable experience.

Oh, but it is.

Shut up, slut.

The lack of oxygen is making me talk to myself.

"Like that, Queenie?" He thrusts against his hand, the head of his cock bumping against my clit. It sets my nerves alight. I find myself meeting his thrusts, wanting that brief bit of sporadic contact. But the moment I reciprocate the touch, he pulls away, leaving me on the edge of wanting. "Who are you reporting to, Queenie?"

I try to keep the groan of frustration off my lips, but it's there. I can't stop it. I glare up at him, my body tingling, and his satisfied fucking smirk makes anger surge through me.

Anger and realization. Because what the actual fuck am I doing? Letting him get to me like this? As far as methods of torture go, this one is new. I thought he'd cut off a finger or two, beat me with brass knuckles. Not this.

Sexual torture is the fucking worst.

Because to reach that orgasm, I'd give him anything. My social security number, my first born as a fucking sacrifice, the keys to my house...

And that realization is fucking pathetic.

I steel my resolve. I can't let him get to me, and I can't let him find out the truth under any circumstances. He doesn't deserve that from me, and the club doesn't deserve the wrath that would rain down on them from the asshole on the other end of the phone line.

"Who were you on the phone with, Queenie?"

I press my lips together.

"Not gonna answer?"

I glare.

"More fun for me."

He eases off my body, yanking my pants off the rest of the way. As soon as he gets them and my shoes and socks off, I kick out, my heel connecting to his nose. Blood drips down his lips and when he smiles, it taints his teeth, making him look even more feral than I thought him to be.

"Hit me again, beautiful creature."

I shouldn't take him up on that, but I do. My legs flail out in anger, connecting to his body. He's a fucking masochist, though, and he takes the blows while jerking off with my panties still. In. His. Fucking. Hand.

Frustration makes my movements even more wild. I kick out again, hitting him in the chin. The snap of his jaw closing painfully echoes through the room, and I feel a brief moment of satisfaction before he grapples for my legs, holding me by the ankles and yanking my legs open. He dives into the bed, landing between my spread legs.

I don't expect the kiss that comes after. His hot mouth against my center, or the way his tongue circles my clit in lapping, slow movements.

"Fuck!" My hips buck against his face, the rumbling of his laughter vibrating through me.

My legs burn from how far apart he's pushing them, but it only adds to the eroticism of the moment somehow. His teeth nip at my inner thighs, trailing languid wet kisses against my flesh. I'm dripping an embarrassing amount, but his tongue is there to lap up my desire.

Then he bites down on one of my folds, and the pain mingled with the pleasure has me screaming profanities at him. I don't know what I'm saying. I can't think beyond this moment. My head thrashes unpleasantly from side to side as I try to pull those sensations within me. Like I can bottle them up. I crave release.

And for the first time in my life, I crave this pain.

He bites the other fold, then bites down against my clit. It hurts as much as it feels good, nearly sending me spiraling into an orgasm that he once again doesn't let me reach. He leans up, slapping my pussy with his palm.

My body feels like liquid. I can barely move. Can barely speak past incoherent grumblings.

"You want to come, Queenie? All you have to do is tell me who you were on the phone with. Who you report to, and why your record is so suspiciously squeaky clean." He kisses my center like he's tongue-fucking my mouth. I groan, leaning into the touch, but he pulls away. "Just tell me those things and I'll give you what you want."

My eyes close and the sting of tears is almost too much. A single one slides out of the corner of my eye. It's embarrassing, but I know he can't see it, because the air is pervaded with little more than the sounds of his slapping flesh as he brutalizes his cock near me, bringing himself closer to orgasm while denying me that pleasure.

Fucking asshole.

"My record's clean because I'm not a fucking idiot who breaks the law." My voice shakes and I hate that it does.

He tongues my clit. "I believe you."

"Because I'm telling the fucking truth!"

"And what about the rest?" His kisses balance between being painful and being tender, the contrast of them sending my head reeling. "Who were you talking to?"

"No one."

He bites down on my inner thigh, making my whole body quiver. I don't know if I'm trying to move away from his ministrations at this point or towards them. Either is fine by me.

"Fucking liar." He bites again, his tongue flicking out against the wounds he makes. He has one palm pressed against my lower abdomen, keeping me locked firmly in place while he continues to assault my lower half with pleasure and pain.

I can feel my skin bursting open around my wrists from how hard I'm tugging at the confines, desperate to reach for him. To make him stop playing with me. I've never been denied an orgasm this long in my life, and I can't say I'm surprised at how desperate I am to get it from him.

"Fuck, Box, please, please..."

"Tell me, Queenie." His breath blows against my clit and his jerking movements become faster. He's enjoying my torture and pounding into his fist now. I angle my head for a glimpse at his cock, catching his fist moving faster and faster.

"Keep looking at me like you hate me," he orders gutturally. "Yeah, just like that." He works himself faster and my hips cant up on empty air, desperate for friction, for fucking anything.

And when he blows his load, a crazy, fucked-up part of me wishes it had been inside me. Crazy. Delusional. Horny...

Gah.

He doesn't pull away from me after his orgasm. He leans up, licking a line up from my pussy to my clit, keeping his tongue there.

He's teasing, he knows how close I am.

"Tell me," he orders.

I move. I want it so badly; I don't know what's going through my mind anymore. With a cry of irritation, I try to angle my hips against his mouth, to get him where I want him, but he pulls away each time.

"Tell me."

I thrash, my last desperate attempt to get what I need.

But it doesn't work. My resolve has burned away. I'm so fucking weak and pathetic.

"My father!" I cry out. "I was talking to my father. He checks in on me often because he lives so far away! Please, Box, please!"

My heart is beating too fast, I feel like it's going to crawl out of my throat. But I can feel his smile against my flesh, feel his murmured, "Good" right before his mouth closes around my clit and sends me flying over the edge.

BOX

H er orgasm is the sweetest sound I've ever heard. Like a choir of angels. No, fuck that, like the battle cries of Armageddon. It's guttural, loose, and angry. Just how I like it. My tongue slashes against her shaved folds, drinking in the taste of her.

She was right.

She doesn't taste like laundry detergent.

She tastes like sweetness and musk, and I want to rub my face all over her and walk out to the bar, wearing her scent like it belongs on me. Because it does.

She's still in denial about it, but we belong together. All of us.

And I've never had this much fun torturing someone for information. I didn't believe her at first, but I do now. I made her so desperate that she all but screamed the answers at me. Only then did I give her what she wanted.

And when her orgasm finishes, I lean up, my cock already aching for her again. My hands go beneath her thighs, all that expanse of smooth fucking skin. Lifting them, I settle her ankles against my shoulders, positioning my cock near her entrance.

In her languid state, she watches me from beneath lowered eyelids. She doesn't protest though, as the head of my pierced dick touches her entrance.

"You on the pill, Queenie?" I want to fuck her raw. I'm clean, and Wire's background check revealed she's clean and on the pill.

Asking is merely a courtesy. I'm taking her either fucking way because she wants me regardless.

"Yes, but..."

Before she can object or say stupid shit, I reach for her pair of panties, still sticky with my cum, and shove it into her mouth. There's a primal satisfaction knowing she can taste my desire for her on her tongue. Her eyes glare at me for doing that. I don't give a fuck.

"Glare at me all the fuck you want, you should know by now it just makes me hard for you." I push an inch inside of her. She groans around the material, gags as the taste of my cum touches her tongue. Then her nostrils flare and her glare becomes much more prominent. "You don't want me to stop, do you? We're just getting started." With a roll of my hips, I'm deeper inside her. Another inch.

Her eyes roll to the back of her head, and I know it's because of the barbell at the tip of my dick. The ladies love it. She will, too.

"You want me to fuck you, Queenie?"

She moans, nodding slowly.

"Good. Because I want you to fuck me like you're mad at me. Fuck me like you hate me." I lean down, pressing my tongue against her bottom lip, smelling myself on her mouth. "And then, I want you to fucking scream."

I push fully inside her, laughing out when her pussy hugs my cock, pulling me deeper, choking the soul right out of my fucking body.

Yes.

This. This is what I've been searching for. A hard, glorious fuck. Queenie's pussy wraps around me like a vice. It's all I've ever wanted and desired. Her. I've been waiting for *her*. My hips buck against hers. There's no finesse to my movements. If she wants to fuck prettily, slowly, she can fuck Scorp. I'm a beast, and I'll ruin her.

I yank the panties out of her mouth, and she sputters before I angle myself just right and rip a scream out of her throat. A scream I know everyone in the compound can hear.

Hell if it isn't the best fucking thing.

"Scream, Queenie!" My palms grab her tits, pinching those beautifully dark nipples, twisting until she's screaming with pleasure and pain in equal measure. I slap her ass, head turning to bite at her ankles. She can barely move, but I know she's trying, her hips jerking up. It's cute that she's trying, but I wouldn't fucking care even if she was little more than a pillow princess.

I grasp her hips, pounding her onto my cock. My balls tighten, and I know I'm not going to last with how tight she's squeezing me or how loud her screams are echoing.

"Box, oh my god, Box!"

My blunt nails dig into her skin, breaking it, drawing blood. It almost sends me over the edge. My thumb comes between our joining bodies, pressing down tightly against her clit, rubbing circles on her like I know she likes.

Her orgasm flutters through her. She jerks against me, pulling my own orgasm out of me. We jerk together, crying out, our screams mingling past the music, past the bullshit, past the problems. And nothing matters but this euphoric moment of us together. Of our rough joining. Of the fact that I know now she likes pain as much as I do.

And that's a good thing.

Because I plan on fucking ruining her and letting her do the same to me.

When we come down from our high, I wrap my fingers around her braids, tightening them in my fist. I claim her mouth in mine roughly before I reach for the key in my back pocket and release her from her bonds.

The moment I do, she rubs her wrists. They're red, bruised. The sight makes my dick twitch inside of her. I could stay like this forever, but my beautiful little creature has other ideas.

She shoves me away roughly. I slip out of her, cum and her juices sliding against her skin. I'm fucked up enough to want to lap it all up with my tongue like a panting dog. Queenie's already moving though, sliding her thighs off the side of the bed. Her footsteps are quiet, yet the tap of them on the floor are like gunshots echoing through the room.

Violent in nature.

She's pissed at me.

Only, I don't know what I did.

NAOMI

"You're a fucking asshole." The tears prick behind my eyelids. I don't let them fall. I can't. I don't want him to see the humiliation that spreads through me like a visceral disease, though it's probably obvious by the expression on my face.

He humiliated me. He used me for information.

And I'm not upset with him for sticking his cock inside my desperate, crying pussy. All of it was consensual. I'm embarrassed over the fact that I wanted it. Everything he gave me, every slap, every word, every pinch, the violence and pain mingled in with the rest of it? I wanted it as surely as I wanted my next breath.

The aftermath of that leaves me unsettled. Like there's a monster living inside my skin, and I don't know who she is. I've never been this reckless. Certainly never in my choice of men. I shouldn't have even let him touch me. Any of these bikers.

They'll ruin me for other men. Smart men, kind men, normal men.

They're criminals. All my life I've tried to avoid them and here I am, spreading my legs for them, with cum leaking out from between my thighs.

"I am sensing your anger. As hot as it makes me, I'm afraid I don't understand." Box shuffles around, pulling his pants up, not bothering to wipe off cum from his dick before he's zipping it into his jeans and smoothing out his cut.

"You used me!" My arms cover my breasts. Arguing with him naked and with his desire sliding down my skin gives me a touch of vulnerability that I'm forced to shove away. "You used me in this... sexual escapade of yours to torture information out of me!"

He reaches for me, but I step back. I can't deal with him touching me right now. I don't want or need it. I don't need to fall for his allure again. I need to get the fuck out of this compound.

"You enjoyed the torture." He smirks, and I want to punch it right off his smug face.

"That may be, but it shouldn't have happened in the first fucking place."

He makes a rude sound. "Regretting us already, my love? How unfortunate, because I want to do it again."

My lip pulls up, over my teeth in a snarl. "Never again."

"Oh, my beautiful creature." Box steps forward. I don't dare move from my spot, knowing I have to face him head-on if I'm to gain an ounce of respect. He stops, the cold leather of his cut grazing my still pointed nipples. He leans down, and I smell myself on his breath. "We are just getting started."

And then he laughs while I'm left stumbling away from him and his toxicity. I run to the bathroom, slamming the door closed. He doesn't follow, but I can still hear his laughter echoing around me like a violent song.

Like a violent promise.

One I know he means to keep.

I shower, scrubbing my skin raw until I can't feel a trace of him on my body anymore. A futile thing, I think, because I feel hollow between my legs where he filled me so well. I have the imprint of his hands on my body, and the beginnings of a bruise around my throat where he choked me. With my own damn hair, no less.

Not even burning water could take away the shame I feel at giving in so easily to his seductions. I should have just bit my lip, closed my eyes, and thought of London. Maybe then he would have left me the fuck alone, instead of leaving me wanting more.

Fucking bastard.

After drying off, I make my way slowly out into Rock's room with the towel wrapped around my body. Box is gone, but the space is occupied by someone else.

"Slug!"

He seems to startle at my appearance, even though he was facing the bathroom door as it opened. A bright flush rises to his cheeks, and he averts his eyes from my body. It's adorable, really. Just the sight of him makes me forget about Box's transgressions. Slug brings with him a calm disposition; one I inhale like weed because it's just too calming.

"Queenie. Hi, uh, I... Box left."

"Thank the lord for small favors." I walk into the room, oblivious to my almost nudity. Of all the men here, Slug is the least threatening of them all. Unlike the others, who make my nerves alight and sizzle in ways I don't want to contemplate, he makes me feel... safe.

I go to my duffel bag and begin pulling out a new outfit, along with a bra this time. When I glance up, Slug is still there, making it an obvious point not to glance at my bare skin.

"Slug, you okay?" The smile that touches my lips lets him know I'm teasing.

His big hand rubs across the back of his neck, his flush deepening. "Uh, I caught Box and... well... I..." He gestures at the bed where all my panties are neatly aligned.

"You're a panty savior!"

"Uh..." If I thought he couldn't get any brighter, I was wrong.

"How'd you get them back from him?"

"I might've... uh... punched him in the face and took them off of him by force."

I wince, knowing what a punch from Slug looks like, as I witnessed one before. I wonder if Box is out cold.

Like he could read the question from my face, Slug slowly shakes his head. "All it did was excite him."

Ugh. "Fucking pervert."

"That's what I said, too."

We share a terse smile between us. The air crackles in the space that separates us. Nerves flitter through me, and I'm all too aware of what I did to him and how tense it made him. How he had so much trouble looking me in the eye because I gave him the slip.

"Slug..."

"It's okay, Queenie," he says.

"It's not."

"But I understand why you did it. You don't trust us, and that's okay. If I was in your position, I'd be reluctant to trust us, too. I'm not mad at you or anything for what you did. I... I thought you'd be mad at me."

"The furthest thing from it," I say, my chest growing tight with emotion. This is the reason I feel safe with him. This precisely. Because he goes out of his way to make me feel better. Because he knows I shouldn't be apologizing. That doesn't mean I don't want to. "I'm still sorry. I'm sorry if what I did got you into trouble with Daddy Kraken."

His smile is rueful, and he waves off my words. "Whatever trouble I get in is my own fault." He goes quiet then, looking over my body as if assessing for damage. He sees my wrists and breathes out deeply. "I know Box," he whispers. "We are as close as..." He pauses, reluctant. "Brothers. I know he's never forced a woman before. He wouldn't. But I have to ask—"

"He didn't give me anything I didn't want." My face heats with awkwardness as I admit those words. I don't want him to know, but I fear everyone probably already does. They were listening to music, but I wasn't exactly quiet before. My throat feels rubbed raw from all that screaming.

His eyes still flash, even while his shoulders seem to ease with relief. "He still shouldn't have done it like that..."

"He shouldn't have," I agree. My hand goes to my wrist, rubbing the raw, red mark. "But like they say, it takes two to tango. I could have stopped him if I really wanted to." And I didn't. I liked the games he played. I liked pretending to be helpless, being dominated, even fighting gave me a thrill.

"Right."

Silence, as awkwardness permeates the air. I can't believe we're standing here talking about how I had sex with his club brother. My skin breaks out in goosebumps.

"I don't think it'll happen again, you know." I don't know why I feel the need to say that. My vagina almost cries out in protest at the thought of not having him inside me. That huge, pierced dick touched me in places not even the greatest toys could have. The way the cold metal of the piercings at his tip and base stretched my walls so fully... *Nrrrng*. But seriously? Why is my vagina being a greedy bitch? There's just too much hot dick in this compound, and I don't need to choke on them all.

Wanting to is another matter entirely.

"Why not?" He cocks his head to the side, his eyes bright with curiosity. After realizing what he asked, his cheeks flush. "I just mean, females don't usually complain, and they almost always beg to go again and..." He trails off with a sigh.

It's amusing and I can't help but tease him a bit. "I'm sure those women would count themselves lucky to jump onto his cock." Poor Slug looks like he wants the floor to open up and swallow him whole. Like he wants to be far, far away from this conversation. I didn't know he was so awkward about sex. It's endearing. "But I am not most women, Slug."

His eyes flick up, and the change is almost instantaneous. The shy expression fades into something else. Like when he punched that prospect and knocked him out cold. This isn't violent, but it's an expression clouded with something almost indescribable.

"Don't I know it," he whispers, so quietly I almost don't hear him.

"Slug..."

"Yeah?" He blinks slowly.

"I need to get dressed."

That flush rises again and just like that, the intensity is gone and he's an awkward baby bean again. "Right. I, uh, should..." Slowly, he turns around, giving me the privacy I need to get dressed. He's not leaving, and I know it's probably because Rock told him to keep an eye on me and he doesn't want me to slip past him a second time. That doesn't hit me with anger like it probably should.

"Slug?"

"Yeah?"

"Can you toss me some panties?"

His whole wide back tenses like I just asked him to chop off his own dick. His shoulders rise up to his ears and heartbeats pass before he moves. His fingers stumble on the bed to grab a simple cotton pair of panties as if he hadn't touched them to bring them into the room. Like touching them at all is taboo. Once his fingers grasp for a pair, he tosses them over his shoulder, and they land on my face.

"Thanks."

I quickly get dressed in my sweats, t-shirt, and fuzzy sweater. When I'm done, I walk quietly towards Slug. When my hand lifts to tap his shoulder, he turns and grabs my wrist. I startle, gasping and nearly falling back, but he pulls me close, his big hand spanning against my waist.

"Sorry." He winces. "Reflex."

My brows furrow. I don't want to know what causes a reflex like that because it probably can't be good, and his expression says he doesn't want to talk about it besides. That's okay. I don't mind.

Slug's eyes travel down my body, taking in my comfortable outfit. "Not going back out to the party?"

"No. I just want to sleep." I put space between us, space I think he probably needs to catch his breath. Or maybe it's me who needs to catch mine. The others make my body blaze, but Slug's more dangerous because he makes my heart flutter.

I've always thought best friends are easier to fall in love with rather than the bad boys. It's easy for lines to blur. It's easy to confide and fall and have a single person become your entire world. And for someone like me who pushes everyone away out of fear? To meet someone who has me opening up like I never have before, even to Lourdes? Slug is dangerous.

More dangerous than Box.

Because I can hate manic laughter and violence. But I can't hate sweet smiles and caring.

I tilt my head towards the door. "Do you want to go to the party?" I almost feel guilty because I know he's on babysitting duty, but I shrug it off.

"Nah, those parties get old and I'm not in the mood..." Sadness laces his words. I want to ask about it, but what comes out of my mouth is something else entirely.

"Netflix and chill?" Now it's my turn to blush at that suggestive tone and the breathy whisper in my voice. "I don't mean it like that," I correct quickly. "Just, would you rather lay down and watch a movie or something?"

"Um... Sure. I'd like that."

I go to the bed and realize it's still covered in the scent of sex with Box. Ew. With methodical, irritated movements, I start yanking the cover off and tossing it to the side. The simple sheets will do, I think. Besides, it's not all that cold.

Once the bed is clear of any evidence of mine and Box's joining, I go grab my phone and jump into the bed. I pat the side. "Come lay with me, Slug."

He does so slowly, kicking off his shoes and jumping into bed next to me. "So... what kind of movies do you like?" he asks as I lean towards him. It's natural that I gravitate towards him, relishing in his warmth.

My fingers click on the Netflix app on my phone. I share an account with my mom, so I click on the icon with my name on it and start scouring through the list of movies and shows. "I'll watch anything," I tell him. "But I'm partial to romantic comedies."

"I like a good rom com."

I tilt my head up to find Slug staring down at me. My breath threatens to catch, and I have to remind myself to breathe. "He cooks, he reads, and he likes rom coms? Damn Slug, you're every female's wet dream."

There goes that damn blush again. I wish it was something you could bottle up and save for special occasions. I don't know what special occasion would call for Slug's blush, but it warms me from the inside out. Being with him makes me feel like the bitterness inside settles somewhere far, far away.

Or like it doesn't live there at all.

"You'd be the only one to think that," he murmurs.

"What?"

"How about The Proposal?" He changes the subject quickly, pulling the phone from my fingers and pressing play.

Alright. I can take a hint. He doesn't want to talk about it, but that's a damn shame. I hope he isn't self-conscious because he's seriously a snack. I'd dip him in butter, grease, chocolate, sugar, and donuts and eat the fuck out of him all day long. That's how delicious he is. And sweet. Can't go wrong with a sweet tooth.

My thoughts are pushed away as the movie begins and soon, I'm immersed in Sandra Bullock and Ryan Reynolds. Slug's chuckles rumble against my body, and I find myself leaning closer towards him. His arm wraps around me and I fall asleep wrapped tightly, protectively, in his arms.

ROCK

"**W**ipe that fucking grin off your face," Scorp growls, shoving Box away. "We all know you got fucking laid."

Box chuckles in that maniac way of his before he takes a shot, pouring it back, then slamming the glass back against the bar.

"We all fucking heard you mutilating her in there."

"You call it mutilation; I call it stimulation."

I sigh deeply.

Children. I'm babysitting fucking children. Their conversation makes me feel two things.

One, old as shit.

Two, pissed off.

They banter with ease, the fucking shits, because they don't have the weight of an entire club on their shoulders. They don't have ghosts that weigh as heavily as mine. Now, I'm not comparing. We've all seen some shit, some of us more than most. And I know the lightheartedness in the air is to push away more melancholy thoughts of our fallen brother and the impending war with the Rogue Waves.

Still.

Fucking children.

And Box is boasting about fucking Queenie as if we didn't all fucking hear her shouts of pleasure over the music. And in my own fucking bed, too. It just reminded me of the feel of her tongue against my cock. And that pisses me off because I'm older than her. I could be her father. Why am I robbing the cradle when she could have her own pick of men her own age?

There's just something about her... It's the hardness, the rough angles within that soft little body. Beneath that whole façade, there's the slightest hint of vulnerability that has yet to shine through fully.

"Can we get to the fucking point?" I interrupt, before Box can go on a fucking rant like he's known for doing.

His bright eyes flick to me, still shining with mischief, but I'm not fooled. He can be as serious as the rest of us when he wants to be. He cares about the club and wouldn't put us at risk with his stupidity. He does that on his own time. The shiner he's sporting from where Slug cocked him is proof of that.

"She's not in league with the Rogue Waves," he replies casually, leaning his elbow against the bar. "Had her singing like a fuckin' canary, mate. Hmm..."

"Then who was she talking to?" Scorp demands. I can hear the jealousy in his tone.

Fuck. She's got him by the balls, too.

"Her dad." Box taps his fingers against his lips in thought. Like he's remembering what it felt like to have her beneath him. I know I'm sure as fuck thinking about what it felt like to have her mouth around my cock.

"You believe her?" I growl, trying to shove away that memory. It can't happen again. She has a way of making a man lose control. But besides that, she was in a vulnerable position. She wanted to feel something other than that nightmare and I obliged.

"No." At our incredulous expressions, he elaborates. "I mean, yes, I believe she was speaking with her father, but I think she's hiding something. We have to figure out what it is." He rubs his hands together. "Can't wait for that..."

"Keep it in your pants, asshole," Scorp demands. "We can have Wire dig into her."

"He already did and didn't find anything shady. She's as clean as a fuckin' whistle. Doesn't have social media and barely has an online fingerprint. He has access to her cloud but the only thing she has on there are a few pictures with Lourdes and one or two selfies. The rest is all marine biology shit." I hate how I have to point out the obvious to my VP. This woman obviously has him in knots. He needs to get his shit together. We all do.

"Maybe her life isn't that interesting." Box pours himself another shot. "Maybe she was one step away from becoming a cat lady before I rammed her with my fat boy." He pauses what he's doing to waggle his eyebrows suggestively in our direction. "And I'm not talking about my cock."

"Yeah, we got that, genius."

Box slams the liquor, some of it sloshing down the sides of his mouth. When he swallows, he smiles widely at us and announces, "I'm making her my Old Lady."

That gives us all pause.

"You're fucking crazy." Scorp tugs at the ends of his braids, a breath of laughter escaping him. "Like, seriously fucking crazy."

Something in my chest expands with an ache I didn't know was possible. The ease with which he declares it... the way he can say fuck it to just about anything... Sometimes I crave that freedom before I remember what a psychopathic child he is and then it passes. But the jealousy still burns inside me.

I got to taste her, but he got to fuck her.

"Sluggy and I are going to share her."

Scorp rolls his eyes. "Slug doesn't know his dick from a kitchen spoon."

The laugh crackles loud like a gunshot. Box's palm slams down against the bar over and over again. "But he wants her. And I know the rest of you fuckers want her, too." He sweeps his gaze over Scorp, over me, settling them on Delfin before coming back to me. "I'm a sharing man, Prez. The more the merrier..."

"Jesus fuck." I rub my temples to stave off the headache that's forming.

I can't deny his idea has merit, just like I can't deny that my body vibrates, and a primal, feral part of me wants to claim her as mine. I've never wanted an old lady before, but I can suddenly see Queenie wearing our jacket, the Kraken patch on her shoulder, a crown stitched on her back.

Property of...

I groan, knocking the raised shot glass from Box's hand. He doesn't even look surprised by the violent gesture. "Stop gossiping like old fucking women. We have a war to plan."

SLUG

The movie ends and she's still asleep. I press the lock button on her phone and push it away, but I don't move. She's been through a rough couple of days, and I know she could use the sleep. Maybe the selfish part of me just likes her in my arms. We fit together just like this even when I thought we wouldn't.

I shouldn't let illusions take over my common sense. I'm not Box. I don't dive head-first into situations. I'm not as cautious as Scorp and Rock, either. I'm somewhere in the middle of great men. I'm normal. And Queenie, she's...

Well, obviously she's a queen.

And I'm fine with idolizing her from afar in a tender moment like this. With her curled up against my body. Her arm is flung around my stomach, her cheek pressed tightly to my chest. She's adorable when she sleeps. Peaceful.

The door slams open, making her stir, but she doesn't wake.

The glare I shoot in Box's direction is murderous. "Ssh," I order.

He chuckles and prowls deeper into Rock's room. I'm sure the president will be pissed that we've taken possession of his space because Queenie's here, but for now he's too busy to bother. Until he does, it's ours to do with as we wish.

Box lowers his voice to a whisper. "You two make such a pretty picture." He stops at the edge of the bed, looking down at us like we're snacks he means to swallow whole. "Seeing you like this is giving me all sorts of ideas..." He trails off with a dreamy sigh that makes me roll my eyes. His gaze sharpens once more, and I don't like the look of it. "We can fuck her together, you know."

My body jolts at the sudden declaration. I'm glad I don't have anything in my mouth because what the fuck? I would have choked and seen the devil by now. That's the kind of shit you don't spring on someone like that. It just... it isn't.

"Jesus fuck, Box, have some respect."

"That's respectful, Sluggy. No greater sign of respect than DP. No greater form of love language, either."

"Christ." I pinch the bridge of my nose with my thumb and forefinger. "At least don't talk about her like she's not in the fucking room."

The bed dips as Box's knees meet the edge. He looks like a panther. Or more like the fucking fish he was named after. "What makes you think I wouldn't say this to her if she was awake, Slug?" His head tilts to the side. Soft tufts of blonde hair graze the edges of his darker lashes before he gives a toss of his head. He looks at her, and there's reverence in his expression. True reverence. Like she holds a thousand shooting stars beneath the surface of her skin, and he means to wish upon them all. He looks at her like she matters. And Box, he's never looked at a woman like that before. "I think she'd like that, you know. She'd like us together." His voice is soft, in a dream-like state.

I wonder just what he's imagining. What future is laced in the whisper of his words? What does he picture in his mind when he looks at her? I know what I see. When I look at her, I see home. I see life. I see storms and calm and laughter. I see sleepless nights, and I see...

I see love.

"You can take her pussy and I can take her ass."

The spit freezes on the way down my throat and I choke. A strangled sound comes out of me, though why I'm even surprised at this point is beyond me. Box is always saying stupid shit. This should be no surprise.

"Will you stop with your vulgarities? That is *not* happening. *Ever!*"

"Why not?"

Her sweet voice is a bucket of ice-cold water. The kind that's too stunning and leaves me hopelessly lost for a moment. All I can do is look down at her and watch that expression. The furrowed brows, the eyes flashing with hurt. Fuck. And what's worse, the only thing to break me out of my stupor is Box's cruel laughter.

"Yeah, Sluggy, why not?"

I fight the urge to flip him the finger and keep my sole focus on Queenie. Empty space between us echoes loudly as she pushes herself away from me. I hate the distance. It's inches that feels like miles. I want to reach for her, but I don't want to give her the illusion that something is going to happen when it's not.

"Because we can't," I say firmly. Then I decide to be honest. Or as honest as I can possibly be. "You don't want me."

"Slug." That delicate palm meets my stomach and crawls up my chest, moving in slow increments, stopping just over the rapid thumping of my heart. "Only I decide what I want... Not you."

NAOMI

I'd been awake for a while. Since Box burst into the room like a savage looking for a swift kick to the nuts for disturbing my sleep. Seriously, what the fuck kind of monster does such an insensitive thing, like wake a girl up from a power nap? But then he started speaking, and I didn't open my eyes because, I'll be honest, I'm a nosey bitch and wanted to know what they'd say.

Everything that came from Box's mouth was pure filth. That's no surprise. The trembling pulse of desire *was* a surprise, but that was easily replaced with confusion, then hurt, as Slug opened his mouth to claim that me and him were never, ever going to happen.

Why? The question burns in my throat, but I don't voice it. Not until I hear the passion in his voice and something I think is disgust.

"Why not?" My eyes fly open to watch his expression. The *oh, shit* face as he realizes I was indeed awake and listening to every single thing they said.

Box laughs. "Yeah, Sluggy, why not?"

I ignore him and focus my attention on Slug. On beautiful, honest, friendly Slug. Slug who makes me laugh and cooks like a dream. Slug who cuddles and watches rom coms and reads. Slug who treats me like a friend instead of a piece of ass, so at odds with his biker persona. Slug, who is so easy to fall for, even if it's within the span of a few hours, a few days.

I can see myself with him. I realize that in this moment. I wanted to avoid these bikers. To fuck out of this compound as soon as shit with the Rogue Waves calmed down. But after hearing him deny me, it snapped something inside my chest. It made me realize that I want him.

And Box, too; if not for his weird personality, then for his pretty dick and orgasms.

But to think that Slug doesn't want me in the same way... Well, it hurts my fucking ego. Makes me feel like there's something wrong with me. Am I ugly? I mean, I'm not blind and I know my ass looks good in jeans. I can be cute when I don't look beaten to shit by asshole bikers, a hurricane, and Box's stupid bike. Pretty sure Sugar fixed most of that with her magic, though.

"Because we can't. You don't want me."

I blink at the words, and before I know what's happening, my hand touches his stomach and drifts upwards. The hurt is replaced with anger. Who the fuck is he to decide what I want or not? I like him, he's nice, but that's just plain stupid to think. I know my own damn mind, and who gives a fuck if it changes every five minutes?

Right now, it's beating to the rhythm of Slug's name.

"Slug. Only I decide what I want... Not you."

The tone in my voice lets him know he fucked up because he stammers. "I know that, Queenie, it's just..."

"Just... what?" I don't move my hand. I want to feel the beating of his heart. It skips against my palm, a nervous pounding that would be endearing if I wasn't upset.

"Queenie," he groans, his palm bracing against my own. I know he wants to shove my hand away, but he just keeps it pressed tighter to his body.

"Explain it to me, Slug." This time the hurt does leak from my voice, and my lower lip wobbles. Strange how I don't mind showing weakness in front of him. Even if he's about to reject me and make me swear off men forever.

Because *seriously*.

"Queenie," he repeats firmly, gently sliding my palm down again.

"Do you not like me? Am I ugly or something?" The question is rhetorical. I'm fucking scrumptious, but maybe I'm just not his cup of tea.

His eyes widen. "No! Of course not!"

"Then what is it?"

"No one wants me, Queenie."

The confession rushes out of him like I pulled it from his soul. Following the words, I can see every insecurity fly over his face. Like I'm flaying him open without knowing and he has no choice but to confess what he would have otherwise kept hidden.

I feel suddenly ashamed of myself for pushing him, but at the same time I feel like he needed to say those words to me. To heal. Himself and whatever slow thing we've had building between us ever since I woke up and found him twerking in the kitchen.

People say it's impossible to fall for something within a single glance or within the span of a few seconds. With Slug, it feels like I did. I did fall for him because when we talk, my prejudice against bikers falls away. It's because of him. Because he's so fucking different from the rest.

"They take one look at me and the others and go for something better. I'm nobody's first choice. I'm not even anyone's second choice. I am nothing. And you, you are a queen, and you deserve..."

"What? What do I deserve?"

He swallows and lowers his gaze. "More than me."

"Slug..." I reach for his hand and hold it in my own. "You have to know that you were the first. The first to make me smile, the first to make me laugh. The first to protect me, the first to befriend me. You were the first person in this compound that I wanted. You *are* what I want."

I don't know who reaches for who first. Maybe we meet in the middle. All I know is that one moment, there's space between us and the next, we are desperate for one another. Our lips crash in an inelegant tangle, teeth jarring uncomfortably but even so we don't pull away. We pull closer.

The kiss is everything Slug is. It's sweet and patient, taking slow sips from my mouth like he has all the time in the world. His hands, in contrast, grasp at me with a desperation that makes me gasp. His big hands span around my waist, at the small inch of skin exposed, and that tiny touch makes me want more. Need it like I need my next breath.

We part, inhaling deep gulps of breath. His blonde-brown curls shade his eyes, and he looks sheepish. "You're sure?"

"Slug?"

He starts to pull away. "Yeah?"

I yank him back towards me. "Shut up and kiss me."

His relief flashes a second before we're at it again. He pulls me into his lap until I'm straddling him. Every inch of our bodies are pressed together and the intimacy clicks into place. This feels right. Me, grinding my hips against his dick to release the tension that's been building since he came into the room.

Slug makes me feel shameless. With Box, I was embarrassed, ashamed of my reactions. But with Slug it comes naturally, easily, and I'm desperate for more. I want his gentleness. I crave him. He's the type of man I've needed and wanted my whole life.

And I mean to have him.

My nails rake through his soft tresses of hair, scraping against his scalp. At the feel of my aggression, Slug groans into my lips, pulling my hips down against his erection. We break apart, a string of saliva connecting our lips. His tongue slides against his plump bottom lip, breaking the connection. It's completely messy and so, so erotic.

"Take your shirt off," he orders. His voice suddenly takes a tone, a dark tone. For a second, desire flares hotly in his pupils, and I see beneath the friendly person he is. I see the dangerous man who knocked out a prospect with a single punch. Like this double façade of a person lives inside of him.

I wanted gentle.

I don't think I'm getting a gentle Slug.

And I feel fine with that.

The sweater and shirt fly from my body, followed by my bra until I'm bare from the waist up. During this time, Slug's reached for his cut and slid it off his own shoulders. He pauses at his t-shirt a split second and that darkness is replaced with uncertainty. To take the feeling away from him, I slide the shirt up his body, pulling it off, and taking him in.

"Beautiful," I whisper. "You're beautiful, Slug."

A flush crawls up his cheeks. The warm touch of his thumbs against my nipples has me gasping and arching into him. The sounds I make don't sound human. Not entirely as he tweaks and teases, sending zings of pleasure through my body.

"So are you," he says with adoration.

Behind me, the bed dips and a presence crowds against me, bare chest brushing against my skin. Then Box's cheek is pressing against mine from over my shoulder. I'd almost forgotten he was even in the room at all.

As if reading my mind, his voice rasps against me. "Forget about me, Queenie?"

There's a pause in the room as both of them gauge my reaction. Slug, wanting to know if I'll accept Box in this, whatever this is, and Box, probably wondering if I'll push him away. The crazy thing is, I don't want to push him away.

Their contrasts against me feels so good, it sends a shiver of longing down the length of my spine. It crawls like spectral fingers, tickling over me until goosebumps rise along my arms. Slug, soft in front of me. Box, hard and dangerous behind me.

It's a heady combination and I find myself wanting both of them.

At the same time.

In answer, I arc back into Box, presenting my neck for his teeth. He chuckles, the sound reverberating through my body, before they graze along my pulse, biting down. The aggression has my hips shifting, bearing down against Slug's.

Slug's hands finger the waistband of my sweats, tugging them down a single inch. Tilting my hips up, I squirm and whimper. The need fills me quickly, the need to be touched by bare skin, to be thoroughly fucked and worshiped like I'm the queen they all say I am.

"Touch me," I order, not being able to stand the distance. Two separate sets of hands reach for me at once. Box's hands wrap around me to stroke my nipples while his mouth clings to my pulse, sucking, marking. Slug's hands tear at the sweats, yanking them off my legs. It's awkward to be handled between the two, but they manage to get me naked while fanning the flames of my desire.

Slug wrestles out of his own pants and pulls me back into his lap. Our thighs straddle together, and Box presses close behind me. He's already naked, his legs spread on either side of Slug's as he grinds the length of his erection against me. The hot tip presses against my lower back and I feel the beads of precum lubricate a line up my spine.

Muscular arms come around me once more. One hand cradles my heavy breast in his palm, squeezing and tugging, while the other slides down my flat stomach. He doesn't stop. Not that I expect him to. Box is both a considerate and inconsiderate lover. He knows my body already, and he's not going to warn me with the slow crawl of his hand. He has a destination, and he goes for it.

His fingers dive for my pussy. I cry out, bucking against him with a desperate cry as his thumb finds my clit. He plays me like he's tapping out the rhythm on a fucking guitar and I'm the one singing out the notes. Every breath, every cry, every whimper is a song that Box swallows with his mouth.

My head turns awkwardly to feel his tongue clash against mine at a deeper angle. All the while, Slug's hands are massaging my thighs, making my muscles languid and damn near pliable, ready for anything and everything they want me to do.

My orgasm is fast-approaching, but Box denies it to me even now. He takes his thumb off my clit and glides his fingers along my pussy lips, parting the folds open as wide as he can. Mouth tearing from mine, his breathing is harsh as he growls, "Fuck her, Slug." His chest pushes into my back, causing me to press closer to Slug. I'm trapped between them, with very little space to move. I can only feel and watch, eyes darting down as Box keeps my folds parted with one hand and takes the other to grip the base of Slug's thick cock. Not even Box's long fingers can wrap fully around his monster of a dick. I stare at the girth in wonder. While Box's is long and curved, Slug's is thick.

"Fuck," he curses when the head of his dick is pressed against my opening. Box is guiding him, playing the both of us like puppets. Because it feels so good, I don't care. I can only watch as Box's thumb flicks out against the head of Slug's glistening cock. His wrist moves, jerking him off in slow, teasing motions.

I bear down against them, taking Slug's dick and Box's thumb inside of my pussy. Inch by inch, he slides within me, Box stretching me with his thumb to accommodate Slug's girth. I feel too tight, too full. Too much.

"You're suffocating my cock, Queenie," Slug groans. The sound is ripped from somewhere deep in his chest. His soul. And that reverence shines in his eyes as he watches where we are joined, where he's still sliding in. Where Box's digits rest against the both of us.

Once I'm fully inside, my ass hitting against the tops of his thighs, Box slides his fingers out from inside me, keeping them against my lower lips, teasing the edges of my folds while he thumbs my clit.

And Slug begins to move and I'm gasping, blindly searching for an orgasm that threatens to slam into me like rapid fire. He pistons in and out of my body, slow and deep. I swear, I can feel him in my fucking throat. My groans become longer, louder.

Calloused fingers scrape along my skin, gripping the back of my neck and pushing me forward. My fingers scramble to grab at Slug's shoulders, nails digging in and breaking the skin. It only makes him thrust harder.

"Kiss him," Box orders. "Fuck his mouth with that pretty little tongue of yours."

The words are dirty and erotic. Our mouths meld together on his command, tongues clashing, seeking, wanting. I can't catch my breath. He swallows my every moan into his lungs only to push them back out.

Box pants against my neck, rubbing his free hand across my body while the other plays me like an instrument. His kisses pepper along my spine, his teeth raking against every sensitive nerve, biting on my pulse. He palms my ass, tracing figures against my cheeks. Every thrust of Slug's pushes me back against Box. His finger slides down the middle of my ass cheeks, stopping at my hole. He doesn't penetrate, instead teasing the tip of his fingers against me. Until one of Slug's particularly hard thrusts pushes me onto the digit and he slides in a fraction.

"Oh, fuck!" I scream from surprise and the lack of lube.

Box pulls his finger out with a *tsk*-ing noise. "See what you did, Sluggy? You're hurting our queen."

His thrusting stops. Firm hands grip my chin, tugging my gaze towards him. The concern in his eyes is evident. "I'm sorry, Queenie."

His hair falls over his eyes. He looks so boyish, my heart swells at the innocence. "It's okay," I whisper, feeling tears burn and my throat tighten.

The hand playing with my folds and clit slides up between Slug and I until Box's hand is level with Slug's mouth, breaking our silent connection. They ghost against Slug's lips, a quiet order followed by a verbal one.

"Taste," he groans. "Taste her."

And I watch with fascination as Slug's mouth opens and he sucks Box's fingers in all the way down to the knuckle. He groans around them like he's tasting a lollipop, lapping up my essence with fierce flicks of his tongue and suctioning of his lips. He licks all of me off

Box's fingers, and when Box finally pulls them free from his mouth, he makes a loud *pop* sound.

"How does she taste?" Box's question flutters over my body like molten darkness.

Slug's eyes never leave me own throughout it all, and I gush between my legs, onto his dick, and feel it leaking between us. "Like fucking heaven."

"Hear that, Queenie?" Box presses a kiss to the corner of my jaw. "You taste like fucking heaven." Then his fingers are wrapping around my throat, choking me slightly. I gasp for breath, the pain of his actions mingling with the pleasure of Slug's dick twitching inside me. A hand grasps my hip, pulling me up and down over his thick length. "Are you going to let Slug come inside you? Are you going to let me lap his cum from your pussy? Are you going to let me fuck you here?" His hand goes to my ass, palm slapping hard against my cheek.

Every word is punctuated with Slug's hips moving faster and faster. He pushes up into me, once gentle movements now out of control. I like this side of him. It makes me wild. My hips grind down to meet his, each time our flesh slaps, his body hits my clit. Jolts of pleasure lance through me at every touch, and my screams are muffled beneath Box's choking hold.

But the same fingers that were in Slug's mouth rise to press against my lip. I bite the tip of his calloused finger on impulse.

"Spit on my palm, Queenie." His voice rasps against my ear and the command doesn't register through the haze of my desire. When it does, I try to twist to look at him, but he holds me firmly in place by the throat.

"What?" Slug's hips cant up at the same time I ask the question, making it come out on a groan.

"Spit into my palm."

"Is that a kink of yours?" I taunt.

He growls, pretending to be frustrated with my stubbornness though I know, really, he's delighted that I talk back. But as punishment, his palm slaps down between me and Slug, right against my clit.

I spiral.

My orgasm crashes through me like the wave of a hurricane. I'm twirling through empty air, through darkness, and rising again.

Cresting a wave and falling to shore. My body jerks, pulsing and pulling Slug's cock deeper inside of me.

Even through the shocks of my orgasm, Box doesn't take mercy on me. His hand still chokes me, his thumb still thrumming my clit. Then his palm raises, and he orders once again, "Spit."

I obey.

He pulls away, loosening his fingers around my neck and turn to look over my shoulder, watching as he spreads the cheeks of my ass apart and slides his spit-covered palm over my center to lubricate me. He catches me watching and smirks that dangerous smirk of his.

"You ever taken it like this before?"

I gulp, but nod.

He glares, like he finds he doesn't exactly like the answer to that because he slaps me. Slug doesn't like the answer either, apparently, because he grinds harder into me, the movement almost punishing in its intensity.

"Who the fuck took this ass?" Box demands.

I roll my eyes and turn back to Slug, but he's paused, glaring at me. If I thought I'd find help in him, I'm surprised. "*Who*, Queenie?"

"You guys aren't killing my exes or hook-ups."

I scream as Box's finger pushes inside my back hole in retaliation. It's a surprising feeling, more surprising than painful. The pressure of being penetrated from both ends is almost too much. I sag onto Slug, breathing harshly into his neck.

"Wire will find out." He thrusts in and out of my backside, and another finger is ever so slowly inserted inside me, stretching the walls of my ass until I'm practically garbling onto Slug's neck. "Did they even make you come, at least?" he taunts. His fingers scissoring inside me. I feel the burn of the stretch and groan when Slug gives an experimental thrust.

I can't...

It's too...

Fuck.

Sweat beads against the back of my neck. My body heats. Goosebumps rise along my skin.

He inserts a third finger.

"Did he?"

"Mhnn...erggh..." My reply is muffled against Slug's skin.

"Sorry, what was that?" He stretches me, moving in torturous movements.

"Ugh... no..." I hate that the confession slips from me easily.

"Good girl." His lips press against my shoulder. "Only *we* get to make you come." His fingers disappear and my cry is of both relief and despair. With him gone, I feel empty, even if Slug's cock is more than enough. What can I say? I'm greedy. His presence leaves my back for a moment, and my limbs feel too tired to turn around and see what he's doing. I hear noises though, rustling.

Then I feel the slightly cold glide of liquid dropping between my ass cheeks. A shiver rumbles through me at the cold touch. Box's hand covers the lube, warming it up as he massages it between my ass, pushing a good amount against and within my hole.

I hear the squirt of more lube, hear the slippery slide of his hand and I know he's rubbing it against himself. A second later, the head of his cock is against the place where his fingers were moments before. The piercing teases my asshole with a dark promise. I gulp, biting against Slug's neck to keep from crying out. When he tenses, I smooth my tongue against the spot I battered and push up against his chest with my palms.

"Just you and Slug?" I ask teasingly, but in all actuality, it's a very serious question. For a second, I think of Scorpion, rubbing up against me and Rock's dick thrusting into my too-eager mouth.

There's a slight pause before he slides the head of his dick inside me. It burns, the tip of his piercing bordering just on the edge of painful.

"Any of us," Box answers. He makes tiny thrusts, pushing me against Slug as he slips centimeters inside of me. It feels like he takes forever before he's fully sheathed.

And my body is disintegrating in the best possible way.

"Me." He thrusts into my ass, pushing me against Slug. Slug catches me with his hands on my hips and begins thrusting in time to Box's movements. "Slug." He thrusts. As he retreats, Slug pushes up. It's a back-and-forth movement and neither of them are giving me a reprieve from feeling like I'm close to bursting. "Rock." They thrust. "Scorp." Thrust. "Delfin." Their thrusting becomes frenzied. I'm limp between them, but they control my body and, therefore, my pleasure.

My nipples are tweaked, mouths meet mine, tongues tangle, flesh burns. It's a blur of bodies and limbs to the point that I don't know where I begin and they end. We're connected, the three of us, and I've never felt closer to two people than I do in this moment.

I'm terrified at how much I want it.

And then someone takes my clit and pinches it between their fingers. My cries are swallowed by someone's eager mouth as the orgasm rushes over me. They move faster, their movements suddenly out of sync and out of control. I know they're close. The both of them. And when they cum simultaneously, I feel hot jets of their seed spill inside me.

Like a brand all on its own.

I won't even need a tattoo. Not when they've marked me in much more delicious ways.

We fall onto the mattress in a heap of limbs and harsh breaths. Cum pools out of me, staining my thighs. I should get up and clean myself off, but I can't bring myself to do it. Let their evidence touch my skin just a little bit longer. Because I know when I stand up and clean off, I might remember all the reasons I shouldn't be here in the first place.

Though one of them is already invading my mind, making my features twist into a mask of displeasure.

A thumb runs down the line between my brows.

"Regretting us already?" Box teases, but there's more to it. More hurt that he plays off with sarcasm. I wonder if that's his defense mechanism because he doesn't want to get hurt.

To think that I could hurt someone like him. I've always thought men like him had the power to destroy me with a single touch. It's why I've always avoided the dark and dangerous. But now I'm seeing a new side of them. A new side to bikers. Like Slug, and the undercurrent of hurt flashing in Box's eyes.

I smooth my expression and cuddle into his chest, reaching a hand blinding behind me to yank Slug against my back. I'm sandwiched between the two and it feels nice. Perfect, even.

"I'm just thinking about how I don't know any of your real names or anything about you."

Box's hands push away my braids. "If you want to know anything, you can always ask. My real name is Erwin Roberts."

"Erwin?" I snort. "Seriously?"

He pinches my chin with his thumb and forefinger. "Don't get any ideas. I like being called Box."

"Why do they call you that?"

He just smirks, flashing those dangerous looking teeth. "Because Box fish are the most dangerous in the whole fucking ocean."

I turn my head. "And you?"

Slug is tracing his fingers against my shoulder. It's lulling and threatens to drag me under. "My real name is Ethan Knight."

"Ethan... I like that. Why do they call you Slug?"

He shrugs. "Like a sea slug."

"That doesn't make any fucking sense."

"You can call him Slug. My little Nug Nug," Box interjects, reaching over my body to take Slug's nipple into his fingers and twist it.

Slug's abdomen contracts and he grunts, shoving Box's hand away. "Fuck right off."

"You love me." Box settles onto the pillows.

For some reason, watching this lighthearted banter is... it's cute between them. Almost as cute as Box gripping Slug's dick tightly in his hand or shoving his fingers in his mouth.

I blink, clear my throat. "Um... are you two... you know?"

"Are we what, Queenie?" Box's hand goes to my breast. The movement is slow and full of lazy leisure. Fingers flick across my nipple in a rhythm that's torturous, meant for slow-building desire. It's heady, and for a moment, I forget what I was going to say.

"Are you..." He caresses my other breast, tweaking and teasing my nipples.

"Yes?"

Bastard. He knows what the fuck he's doing to me. Distracting me on purpose so I can't get the question out.

"Arethetwoofyoubisexual?" The words leave my mouth in a single breath.

"Hmm... No," Box answers. "Pansexual? Yes."

Ah. Makes sense.

His hand dips to my stomach, tracing patterns along my unmarked skin.

I gulp. "And do the Krakens... do they..."

His hand tingles along my hips, sliding lower... lower, stopping just over the cleft of my pussy. "Do they?" Box prompts.

"Do they know about that?"

"Mhmm. In a polyamorous motorcycle club, do you really think they're going to give a fuck where we stick our cocks or with who?" The teasing, sudden touch of his hands against my clit have me arching into him, a gasp strangling out of me. "We're a brotherhood, Queenie," he goes on, sticking his fingers against my slick folds, sliding them through Slug's cum. "We look after each other." He scissors me, stealing the thoughts straight from my brain. "We protect each other." The cum slides out of me and onto the sheets. It's absolutely filthy, but Box's fingers lap up our mingled juices, spreading them over my pussy and clit like a lotion. "We won't judge." His fingers are inside me, pressing against my walls, and I'm squeezing down on him hotly. "We will always fucking have your back."

"Box..."

"You've asked enough questions for now, don't you think?" he teases as he lowers himself between my thighs. My legs widen as his shoulders fit between them. His breath hovers above my clit. I'm soaking all over again, wet with Slug and Box's cum and my own slick juices. And he leans over it and inhales.

My head drops back to the pillow. "Fuck."

"Not yet, but we'll get there, Queenie." The tip of his tongue flicks against my clit.

"I... I still have questions."

He lets out a sigh of exasperation. "So ask them."

I turn away from Box because I can't look at him right now. I can't see what he's doing to me and concentrate on everything I want to know about them. Maybe it's too fucking late to ask when I've already let them have me. But that doesn't stop me from wanting to know. Or maybe I'm trying to make myself feel better for breaking my own moral code and sleeping with men in a motorcycle club when I would never go that route.

"Can I call you Ethan?"

Slug's bright eyes widen as my full focus blazes on him. He looks sheepish, his face flushed, almost as if he was as distracted as I was with Box's face between my thighs.

"I actually prefer Slug."

His warm tongue touches me, and I nearly fly off the bed from surprise. He chuckles, the sound vibrating against my clit as he continues lapping up the cum from my body. "Told you I wanted to do this," he purrs. "Fucking delicious."

"Why?" I manage to ask, though my voice is breathless, and my nails grapple for the sheets.

"Because... uh... maybe I shouldn't..."

Box lifts his head enough to glare at Slug. I know, because I'm watching him out of my peripheral. Seriously. Can't fucking look away from his mesmerizing face, the dangerous tattoos stamped across his skin, or the feral expression he now wears.

"Answer the fucking question, Slug," he growls. "I've got her."

My brows furrow and I focus solely on Slug. At the discomfort he wears like a blanket. "You don't have to..."

"I want you to know everything about me. About us."

His words are followed by Box's fingers spearing inside me. I try to hold back my groan and concentrate. Seriously? This seems to be a serious fucking moment. I want to push Box away so I can listen intently to Slug. The only reason I don't is that I see the fear in his eyes. Besides, Slug and Box know each other very well. They're very good friends. Perhaps even more than that. I think having a part of me distracted with Box's touch helps ground him somehow.

So I don't push him away.

I wait.

"That's what my mother called me."

Box bites my clit and I cry out, reaching for Slug to hold on as he coaxes a fast orgasm out of my body so easily. I'm trembling, and he laps me up in the aftershocks. And I grip onto Slug while he caresses my braids and keeps talking.

"She was... abusive. Always drugged out. Had a constant stream of guys coming and going. I had a sister..." His voice is filled with sorrow. Through my breathlessness, I grasp his cheek.

"Sluggy..."

He clears his throat and like it was a call to action, Box begins torturing me once more. I let it happen. I give Slug the strength he needs to get through this story. If this is what it takes, so be it.

"Sarah and I were young and saw shit we should have never seen. And when we were old enough..." He blows out a breath. "The men paid my mother for our services."

Tears prick behind my eyes immediately. I try to imagine it, Sluggy so young and vulnerable and his sister, forced to...

"Oh, Sluggy..."

He clears his throat and Box rises over me, pressing the tip of his cock at my entrance. I shouldn't feel desire. Not in a moment like this. But I can see the pain, the torture in Slug's eyes. He needs to get through this story and this distraction is for him. So Box enters me, and I don't have to fake the pleasure. But my chest aches. My heart hurts. And I think Box knows this, because he leans over me and flicks his tongue across my chest like he can heal all my hurts.

My own fingers reach for Slug's. To hold onto him, to pull him closer. His body angles near mine and he inhales my scent in a deep breath.

"We had to deal with abuse for a long time. Until one of the men became too... violent. Too hard. He killed my sister."

"Sluggy—oh!"

Box bites against my skin, leaving a mark against my collarbone. He still hasn't thrust, but I can feel his dick twitching inside of me.

"That was the first time I took a life. And then I ran and ran... straight into—"

"Me," Box finishes for him. "I was little more than a fucking street rat crawling through dumpsters trying to find my next meal. We met and bonded. It's easier to survive the streets when you're not alone. My old man had just died, and I had nowhere else to go. Eventually, we took to the ocean and came here. Prospected when we were teens and have been here ever since."

"And your mother?" I didn't want to ask, but I had to. I had to know that devil of a woman had gotten what she deserved. I never thought I had a violent streak, but it's burning inside me now. Demanding retribution for a little girl and boy I didn't know.

And I hope that bitch is burning in hell.

"She overdosed." Slug pushes away my braids, cupping my neck. "It's a sad story, Queenie. But now you know. Why I can't deal with..."

With seeing someone being mistreated. With someone coming towards him just a little too fast like I did earlier. He'd reacted on instinct. A part of that little boy still lived inside him. Broken. Afraid. And suddenly, I understand their contrasts too well.

Why Slug is so sweet and respectful to women. Why Box is wild with abandon. They live their lives as if it's their last hour on this earth. It's why everything between us is happening so fast. They see an opportunity and they take what they want.

And what they want is me.

And now I have to decide if I'm going to give back. If I am going to give myself over to them as much as they're giving themselves to me.

The thought of opening up, of being vulnerable, is absolutely fucking terrifying. And I feel like a bitch for not sharing the broken, shameful parts of me like they do. But I'm not them. I don't live at the edge of danger. This is the scariest my life has ever been.

I can't open up.

Not now.

Not yet.

Maybe not ever.

"Enough questions." I lay back against the pillows, staring up at the two men who are fast-gripping my heart in their hands. "Make love to me this time. Slow and deep."

I only pray they don't break it.

"Your wish is our command." Box thrusts and Slug reaches for me, pressing soft, tender kisses against my neck and mouth.

"I want to hear you say it again, Queenie," he whispers.

Our eyes collide and I know what he means.

"You were the first," I tell him again while Box moves inside me. "The first I wanted. The first."

And then he kisses me.

And for hours, I lose myself in reckless abandon.

DELFIN

"Time to ride out!" Rock's order is met with hollers and cheers of excitement.

Today's the day. The day vengeance will be set in motion. And everyone is thrumming with anticipation. I should be too, but I'm filled with dread. There's no way that the night won't end in violence.

I should be used to it.

I am. I really am. I just don't like where it takes me. The dark spaces that invade my mind when I'm swallowed by it. It makes my stomach go tight and makes me feel like I'm weak.

A soft body bumps into mine, breaking me out of my thoughts. "Sorry." Fuck. Her voice is like soft honey and her perfume is a heady scent of... I don't fucking know. I can't place it. I just know it's addictive. Blueberries? It's fucking blueberries.

My gaze pulls down to the small figure. The woman. Naomi, or Queenie, as my brothers have taken to calling her for the past few days she's been sequestered with us. She's staring up at me. If I expected to see pity, there is none.

I meet her stare with a feral one of my own, but she doesn't cow down in fear. Why I thought she would, I don't know. If she could calm me the fuck down with nothing more than her touch, than she's not afraid of me when I'm "normal".

My mind flashes back to that moment when I lost control in the hall. To the way she pressed her palms against my cheeks, the soft touch of her hands against my beard and face. How she felt, all soft and malleable and fuckable.

Wait.

Fuckable?

What am I thinking? She belongs to Box and Slug. The two have made their little threesome obvious from the start. Box, most of all, is the loudest with his affections, and Queenie reciprocates with dick punches when he annoys her.

I admire her for that.

If anyone can confront Box, if anyone can confront *me*, they deserve respect.

Especially because she hadn't brought up what she saw to anyone. All because I'd asked her not to.

"Thank you," I'd whispered, the vestiges of my terror still clinging to my voice. "Go back to Rock's room and please, please don't say anything."

She'd looked at me with wide eyes, and I could tell she was worried for me at the time, but she respected my wishes. "I promise." And then she was gone, leaving me with a blank spot that I wanted her to fill all over again.

I had to force myself to shove those notions aside. She wasn't mine. She would never be mine. I was too fucked in the head. Sure, Box was as fucking mental as they came, but I'm different. I have monsters and nightmares.

Fucking pussy.

She deserves someone who could protect her, not someone who balks after the trigger is pulled.

"Delfin, hey." Her smile is a radiant thing on her face, even as she gifts it to me shyly. Her hand pushes braids behind the curve of her ear, but even as she does it, they fall back into place.

"Hey, Queenie." My words come out rough, too rough, but she doesn't flinch from them. She looks around both sides before stepping close. So close that her palms glide up my chest. I try to dare myself to step away from her touch. A stronger man would.

I never claimed to be strong.

"How are you doing?" she whispers, low enough so no one hears.

"Good. Thanks." I pull her hands away and walk past her. I hate to do it. To give her my back when every instinct in my body is urging me to stay and speak with her. I can't give into that temptation. One talk, one touch will have me craving more and more. And I won't jeopardize her. Won't put her in danger with my bullshit.

She's the only one who's been able to calm you down, asshole.

Fuck off.

I quiet the voice in my head as I mount my bike. I try not to follow her with my gaze, but it's so fucking hard. She's like a magnet and I'm her opposite end. I watch her mount behind Slug and wrap her arms around his middle. His smile is wider than I've ever seen it, and the way she leans her cheek against his back is... wholesome.

So fucking wholesome.

I'm surprised jealousy doesn't rip through me at the sight. Instead, my fucking chest *warms*. Jesus fuck, something is wrong with me. Tearing my gaze away from the happy couple, I rev my bike just as Rock gives the signal.

Sand tears behind us as we bust down along the shore. The bikes wobble initially, but once we get our momentum, we speed up, piercing past the water and diving down into the depths. Magic envelops our bikes and our bodies. Those who can't breathe underwater, like some of the honeys, are spelled with witch magic to remain safe. I can taste the crackling scent of it on my tongue. Behind me, Box screams a sound of joy and zips through the water ahead of him, hollering and popping wheelies and doing tricks.

The honeys laugh at his antics and among the laughter, I hear Queenie's. Husky. Loud. Free. It does something to my heart and to my cock. My cock is easier to ignore. But my heart?

You're so fucked.

Fuck you.

When we arrive at our destination, we crest up a shore, pulling out of the sand and onto a highway before pulling to a stop in the parking lot. We dismount and Queenie walks up beside me, cocking her head to the side as she looks up at the building.

She reads the bright sign aloud. "Sinful?"

She looks fucking amazing in those tight pants and leather vest. It shows off her midriff and pierced bellybutton, the zipper sliding down against the swell of her full breasts. Her braids flow loose around her body. She tosses them to the side, scrutinizing the building before us.

"It's a strip club," I supply.

She shoots me a teasing glance. "I know."

Of course she fucking does.

My eyes rake over her of their own volition. With her attire and the dark boots adorning her feet, she looks like she was made for this fucking lifestyle. Like she belongs right where she's at.

At our side. In our fold.

"I fucking love this place." Sugar comes up to stand beside Queenie, looping their arms together. "Very high class," she says. "Lots of eye candy. Lots of hotties we can fuck."

A growl rumbles through my chest at her words unbidden. Both women shoot me a glance. Queenie, with her brows raised, and Sugar with a knowing smile on her lips.

Fuck.

I silence myself and look away as Box comes up behind her, wrapping his arms around her shoulders. He bites against her earlobe. "The only men you're fucking are right here wearing Kraken cuts."

Queenie rolls her eyes and shakes him off her body. She throws him a saucy smile over her shoulder. "You don't get a say in who I fuck."

Before he can reply, Sugar pulls her away, the pair of them squealing with laughter. I can't help but be mesmerized by the blatant sway of her hips as she moves in those tight leather pants.

Box whistles low, clapping me on the back. "Ain't she something, brother?"

I give him a noncommittal grunt in response and push away and walk after her. She really is fucking something, but no one else needs to know my thoughts but me. No one else needs to know that I have a fucking crush on her like a fucking schoolboy.

No one else needs to know that I don't deserve her, because I know they'll try to convince me otherwise. Box will try and pull me into their fold, to their little unit, and I can't give myself up like that to anyone.

Least of all her.

Because if I hurt her, I'll never forgive myself.

<hr />

The inside of the club reverberates from the walls to the floors. The music is hard rock. Strobe lights bounce against darkness, illuminating the place in all its glory.

Sinful is a prestigious strip club that caters specifically to supernaturals. If you fancy getting a lap dance by a shifter with a fox tail or tentacle hands, this is where you come. With an array of creatures in all shapes and sizes, the ambiance is made for seduction. High end, beautiful females and males walk the place clad in scraps of material that barely hide a thing. Bills fly and smoke swirls above heads as soft drugs are ingested. The alcohol is of the highest quality, the pussy and drugs even better.

There's a reason we came here tonight, and it's not just so we can let loose. Sinful is set on neutral territory. Like Shark Mouth, this place is owned by the most ruthless sons of a bitches to ever walk the island. What they say is law, and even we Krakens respect neutral territory.

"Let's go over here!" Sugar pulls on Queenie's arm up ahead. All the honeys are huddled together up front, forming a unit of friendship. They lead the Krakens towards a nook at the center of the bar where a giant fish tank is erected. Four glass panes from floor to ceiling encase salt water. Inside, there's a pole smack in the middle of the tank, where a merman and mermaid twirl seductively around it in a sinuous dance.

They take their seats around the table and become enraptured with the performance. Soon, a waitress comes to take our orders and we fall into the routine of the moment. That doesn't mean we're fucking blind or stupid. Or that Rock didn't have a particularly good reason for bringing us here.

"Let's dance!" Sugar states, pulling Queenie to her feet. The girls all get up, following suit as they move and undulate to the music, mimicking the movements of the two in the fish tank, but with much more gravity and less gills involved.

I'm on edge, my eyes darting everywhere at once. I'm trying to capture so many bodies, anyone dangerous trying to come towards us. I know tonight is not going to remain as peaceful as it is now, and I can't let my guard down.

Even if Queenie looks sexy as fuck dancing over there, moving her hips like she's making love. A part of me wants to walk up to her and put my hands on her hips. It's been so long since I last danced to anything. I'd probably trip over my feet. But being close to Queenie would be worth it.

There's a small commotion feet away. I snap my attention immediately to a group pushing their way towards the girls. The growl leaves my lips in a warning and suddenly all my brothers are alert. We're on our feet in seconds, crowding towards them at the same time the Rogue Waves do.

The leader of the Rogue Waves is an ugly fucker they call Blood. His name is stamped right there by his President patch. He isn't as old as Rock, and certainly not as seasoned, but he's a sneaky fucker with a slimy grin. And his brothers aren't much better.

The energy in the place skyrockets. Tension presses around us from every inch, and the girls hide behind us. Except Sugar and Queenie. Though why I expected the two of them to be meek little witnesses to this, when they were the ones the Rogue Waves were walking forward to accost?

Beats me.

Rock takes the front of the line, calm as fucking ever. "Blood," he greets in a gravelly voice.

"Rock. Haven't seen you in a while." That greasy smile on Blood's lips goes wider. His eyes rake over the line of us and he all but sneers. "Looks like you're missin' a couple of members."

The heavy implication of his words sends a shiver of rage down my spine.

The fucking son of a bitch.

He's letting us know that he killed Raze. That he killed our brother in cold blood.

His eyes stop on Queenie, and I fight the urge to look in her direction, but I hear her suck in a breath. Like maybe she recognizes him. But I know he wasn't in the video she took.

Then I realize it's not him she's looking at. It's the bastard at his side.

His patch reads Vicious and he steps forward, a slow smile spreading on his lips as he takes in my—*our*—Queenie. "Fancy seeing you here, pretty lady."

It's the bastard who stabbed her.

A snarl rises in my throat, but I tamp it down before it can be unleashed. I know the others are feeling the same. The urge for violence. For death. For retribution. But we can't. Not here and not yet. Instead, we crowd just a bit closer to Queenie.

"A miracle, really," Queenie retorts sarcastically.

Vicious sneers and takes a step forward, disregarding Rock's big frame. He's cocky this one, I'll give him that. "A shame you left without waiting for me, pretty lady. I would have shown you a great time."

Just as Queenie's body tenses, Box sidles up next to her, tossing his arm around her shoulder. Though there's a smile on his face, I've learned to recognize the different *types* of smiles. And this one? It's the same one he wore that time he sawed through some asshole's stomach, pulled his guts out, and wrapped them around the fucker's neck.

"You eyeing my Old Lady?" His tone is accusatory and amused.

Vicious rocks back on his heels. "Old Lady?" Those eyes rake over her body. "She ain't wearing your cut."

"But she does wear my mark." Box's hand curves up Queenie's side. The move is sensual given the circumstances, and he stops just beneath the curve of her breast. I know for a fact she's not marked with his name, but the Rogue Waves don't know that.

I force myself to look away from the intimate touch and focus on the threat in front of us.

"You think some fucking ink is going to stop us?" The motherfucker steps closer, and I don't like his proximity. My body moves, a protective instinct rising inside me. I block him from reaching her. Silent and fast, he doesn't see me coming until he rams into my chest.

With a jerk back, Vicious all but growls at me.

"Look," Rock interrupts before he can say anything. He directs himself towards the Rogue Wave president. "You don't fucking come up to us and threaten a member's Old Lady and come out unscathed."

Blood's expression morphs. "You threatening me?"

Rock smirks in response. It's a chilling promise, and at the sight of it, they all lose their shit-eating expressions.

Simultaneously, their phones ring. It pulls their attention away from us long enough so that they look to one another in confusion, before pulling their phones out and staring at their screens. It's like the moment before a collision, before a storm hits. There's a calmness settling over them until the words on their phones register.

Chaos ensues.

Phones get shoved back into their pockets and Blood snarls, snapping his angry gaze up to Rock.

"Motherfucker—" He charges forward, his arm swinging up in a slashing motion.

I move on instinct, stepping in front of Rock with my arms up in a defensive position. I barely feel the pain of the knife as it slices through the skin on my forearm. Blood is warm as it trickles a slow trail down to my elbows.

I knew this was coming. Knew that what we did would make them react this way. Rock did, too; which is why my leader is wearing a smirk, and why the Rogue Waves stumble back because they know they've fucked up.

This is neutral territory, and they've just attacked us on it.

"You know the rules of my fucking club." He appears through a thicket of black smoke. One of the owners, summoned by blood and violence. Demon eyes glow red that mirror the flashing lights of the club, but there's something far more sinister behind them. His face is but a shadowy spectrum. He is darkness incarnate. The cold hand of death. Even without his brothers at his sides, he is frightening.

I could stare long enough and never truly make out his features. They blur when you stare too hard and incite fear even in the fearless. What I *can* make out is a form. Or the outline of one, anyway. Of a man in a suit, as he dusts off smoke from his cuffs.

"I should kill you right now for breaking the rules," the shadowy man continues. His voice is almost ethereal. *"But..."* The phantom of a head tilts to the side. *"I am feeling lenient tonight. Your problems outside of my territory are your own and you brought them in here. It's time for you to fuck off now."* Smoke billows around the Rogue Waves like it's a solid wall. It shoves them away. *"And never come back or you will face the consequences."* The smoke swallows them whole and a moment later, they vanish.

But not before their leader's voice trails through the air behind him. Menacing, a promise.

"I'll be seeing you again, Krakens."

"Don't bring your shit purposefully into my club ever again, Rock, or you'll find yourself suffering the same fate." The demonic form vanishes and with his disappearance, the music bumps back up, the dancers resume dancing, and I share a conspiratorial look with my brothers.

"What the fuck just happened?" Queenie demands.

"What happened is club business, babe," Rock responds.

This earns him a snort from her. "Club business," she mocks. "Fuck that. And fuck you, too." Even through the reverberations of the club, I can feel her body vibrating with anger.

She doesn't like to be in the dark. I can understand, but it's for her own protection. Besides, she doesn't need to know that Wire did some hacker shit and discovered what the fuck their club is up to. That they're moving illegal shipments of jewels and drugs through the waters and selling them in the black market, stashing that shit in sunken ships.

Our brother Raze likely caught on to them or witnessed it and they ended him for it. Naomi doesn't need to know any more than what she already does.

She snaps her attention away from Rock, dismissing him completely to look at me. Her gaze stays there for a long moment before she starts prowling towards me. I hold my breath, trying not to breathe her in as she stops in front of me. Her hands lift to cradle my arm, smearing blood against her fingertips. I want to jerk back so she's not tainting her flawless expanse of skin with my dirty blood, but as if she's reading what I'm about to do, her hand clamps down on me, holding me firmly in place.

"You're hurt," she whispers.

And fuck if that voice, the caring tone, doesn't go straight to my dick, my heart, and my head. In that order.

"I'm fine." I pull my arm away, putting distance between us. If I let her, she will try and nurture me. If I let her, she will worm her way inside my heart until I'm consumed with every inch of her. She will fuck with my dick, my heart, and my head.

And I'm weak enough to let her.

NAOMI

There's something about a big man taking a knife to the arm and barely flinch that makes you tremble between your legs. My clit's basically screaming like *la llorona*, demanding that fucker's kids. That's how I know I'm officially crazy. Officially *fucked.* When he walks away from me, and I still want him.

I tear my gaze away. The group of bikers have already spread out and taken their seats to watch the show and relax with the Rogue Waves gone. I want to know what the fuck went down with the Rogue Waves just now, but they obviously aren't telling me shit. I should be used to that, but I'm not. I've spent most of my life alone, and it's still never any easier to not be told the important things. In fact, it pisses me off.

I weave my way through tables to go sit next to the doors. I need a breather. I need space to think. But as I'm walking, a strong arm snags around my waist and pulls me into a lap. My ass hits a hard erection clad through jeans. I don't even need him to speak to know who it is.

"Let go of me, asshole."

Box purrs into the crook of my neck. "Where you going, Queenie?" His tongue darts out to lick a line against my skin, and I grit my teeth to avoid groaning.

Fuck no. I am not going to get turned on by this possessive asshole.

My elbow jams into his ribs and he barely grunts, but I can feel him getting harder beneath me. "I'm going to hang out with the girls."

His arm tightens around me, keeping me in place. "Stay with me. I want to spend time with my Ol' Lady."

I didn't miss the way he claimed me in front of everyone. Without my permission. Without even asking me if I want to be his Old Lady. He just fucking assumed. Like all these fucking bikers assume. They see something and they take it, regardless of the consequences. And I'm just another piece of fucking property to them. Not a person with real feelings and choices.

Box took my choice away from me and announced something that we never even came close to discussing. And I'm the stupid one for considering, for even thinking that they were unlike other bikers. But they're just criminals, and I'm not impressed.

"I'm not your Old Lady," I grit out. "Now let go of me."

"You are."

My blood boils and anger rises. "You don't get to fucking make that decision for me, Box."

His hands snake around me, his palms rising to cup beneath my breasts. Then his fingers are flicking my nipples through the tight leather corset. I feel his teeth graze the back of my neck, biting down, marking me. "You're mine," he whispers against my flesh. "I'm never fucking giving you up, Queenie. Even when the stars die, and the oceans become a vast desert. When mountains fall to their knees and the sun explodes in the fucking sky, you are mine."

The words are primal and I believe them. I believe he's telling the truth. That the rest of the world could end, and he would want me. That he would set off a nuclear bomb himself and destroy everything and everyone if I asked. He would do anything for me. Burn the world down. Kill anyone. And even never let me go.

But I'm not sure I want a love so destructive. I'm not sure I even want this life, a life I've fought so hard to leave. To avoid being used like my mom was used. To have the constant desperation of wanting to be loved. And of never getting it in return. Not the way I want to be loved. I don't want the violence. I don't want this...

I relax in his arms. And his arms go lax. Only then do I slam my head back against his face, hearing the resonating crack of his nose.

Then, I jump out of his arms and rush blindly through the club. I make my way towards the bathrooms, hoping he's not following.

I just need to fucking breathe. He's too much. He's making me question everything. What I want and what I need. My mother was always so desperate for love, that she was pushed away at every turn. I vowed I would never be like that, and so I'm pushing it away. But I believe Box when he says he wants me and will always want me. But I don't want him. Or this life.

Do I?

I feel like I'm gasping for breath as I rush through the quieter, dark hallway that leads to the bathrooms. I only come up short when I realize I'm not alone.

Scorp leans against the wall in the hallway, Eli in front of him. I'm about to turn back around and leave, thinking I've caught them in a compromising position but freeze. Scorp is holding a glass of some beverage, but it doesn't look quite right...

It appears to be... smoking?

My eyes dart up to Eli to find her glaring daggers at me. She mouths, "Go away."

Now, I don't like her. Not because she calls herself princess and seems narcissistic, not because she doesn't like me either. But because my gut is screaming at me, saying that something about this scene just isn't quite right.

"Scorp." I take a step forward. "Are you okay?"

"Of course he's okay. Go away. Can't you see we're busy?" Eli snaps.

I ignore her, eyes focused on Scorp. He appears sane enough, I guess. Maybe I just imagined the drink smoking. I'm not his caretaker, and it's obvious Eli is vying for the position of his Old Lady. I'm not new to these types of things, or women like her.

"I want to hear that from Scorp."

Eli's eyes flash and I feel an electric sizzle through the air. I can taste the crackling of magic around me, and I know she's about to pull some bullshit. Does she really want to fight me in this club? After seeing that fucking shadowy demon thing appear and whisk the Rogue Waves away? Is she really that stupid?

"Fuck off, Naomi."

Of all the girls, she's the only one who doesn't call me Queenie. I'm fine with that. I'm not calling her *Princess* Eli either.

I must not move as fast as she want me to, because the next moment, I feel something cold splash against my face. I gasp at the surprise of it, my mouth opening and catching drops of the sweet liquid. Thick dew coats my tongue. It tastes like tequila and something else, too. Something sweeter that invades my senses almost immediately.

I open my eyes to find Eli smirking at me like she's just won a battle. Behind her though, Scorp is glaring.

"Eli," he admonishes, "fuck off."

She whirls, and I imagine the surprise coloring her face. "What? Why? She interrupted us."

"Don't give a fuck. Get lost." When she doesn't move, his eyes narrow and his chest emits a rumbling growl that seems to put the fear in her step. She throws the glass she'd taken from Scorp down on her way past me. It shatters at my feet and when the liquid touches the ground, it flows up in wisps of smoke.

The fuck were they drinking?

Once she's gone, Scorp's head turns slowly, eyes regarding me lazily. He's leaning his upper body against the wall, one foot propped up to keep him steady.

"Something you need, pet?" He speaks as if that fiasco didn't just happen. As it is, I'm forgetting about it already. I don't know if it's the quiet part of the club, the tequila on my tongue, or his presence. It always feels suffocating.

"Just going to take a breath and get away. I feel..." I wave behind me in the general direction of where the men are. Box never followed me, and I wonder if I have Slug to thank for that. Probably. Which just shows how much of a gem that man is. Which just confuses me more. He's not like the others. Neither is Box—at least, not really. But I still don't really *know* them, and I'm not sure I want...

"Overwhelmed?" Scorp asks, reading my mind.

I sigh, my shoulders sagging. "A little."

"Hmm. It happens." He drops his head against the wall and looks up at the ceiling. It feels like a dismissal, so I start walking slowly towards the lady's room. Beyond, the door to the bathroom opens and a female walks out. I barely spare her a glance. Even as she slows to check out Scorp—he doesn't notice—and then looks at me. She mutters something under her breath and disappears in plumes of bright, purple smoke.

Scorp snickers. "Witches..." He waves the lingering smoke away with his hand.

I try not to cough as I inhale the remnants of her magic. "The fuck was that?"

"Fuck if I know. People around here are crazy." Scorp shrugs.

I want to walk away and get that breather I needed, but something about Scorp's blasé attitude is hypnotizing. And I feel like I'm being reeled in. Slowly, I walk over and lean against the wall next to him. Scorpion has a heady presence. It's addicting. I don't forget the way he used me to steal my phone. The way he seduced and distracted me for his own gain. It was deplorable and invasive. It should make me feel dirty. But all I feel when I'm near him is a steady beat of anger, and the desire to be used all over again.

"What are you doing here?" I shove my hands into the pockets of my leather pants.

"Hmmm... Taking a breath. Thinking."

I take a deep breath of my own. Something about the lazy consonant of his voice, about leaning here in the quieter part of the club, away from the noise is making my bones relax. "What are you thinking about?"

"The mess the club is in. Just... everything..." His hands fall at his sides, and I feel his fingers graze across my thigh. "About Raze's death." I lean into the touch. "About you." This emboldens him. His palm presses tighter into my thigh. There's nothing tentative about the touch, just something slow, like he's savoring the feel of me.

The firm pressure of him against me has me barely biting back my moan. And when he slides his hand up and down the length of my leg, easing towards my inner thigh until he's dangerously close to my center, a choked whimper escapes me.

I'm not sure what's happening right now. All I know is that it's heady. Something thick is in the air and it tastes like honeyed desire, dense on my tongue, making me dizzy. I wonder if Scorpion feels it too because his head *thunks* back against the wall and he lets out a groan.

"Fuck, pet." My stance widens as his touch travels higher and I give him access, letting him cup me between my legs. That firm pressure is all I need to release the sound trapped in my throat. The groan the comes out of me sounds inhuman in its desire. And it pushes Scorp into action.

He flicks away the button of my pants and slides the zipper down without looking. My own hands move to help him, pushing the pants and panties down my thighs. I don't know what's come over me, why there's a frenzy in the air, why my skin is itching for more. It burns through my veins, something demanding and cruel.

Scorp gasps as he shoves me harder against the wall, pushing my legs open as far as they will go with my pants down against my ankles. His thigh presses between my legs, sliding up against the wet folds of my pussy. I groan at the contact and gyrate my hips, rubbing myself against him for even the slightest bit of friction.

I hear the clink of a belt, the slide of a zipper, and then his cock is there replacing his thigh, the thick head teasing my swollen clit.

"Why are you here, Queenie?" he growls while nudging his cock head against my folds, though not penetrating.

"Here in this hallway with you or here on earth?" I gasp as he presses tighter against me. "I have to say I don't know why the fuck I'm here in the hallway, but if it's the latter you want to know, I'm a firm believer in a higher power."

His lips caress my cheek a split second before I feel a firm slap against my pussy. It makes my knees buckle and my eyes shoot open.

"You fucking smart ass," he growls against my skin. "Always have something smart to say. I oughta teach you a fucking lesson."

"Oooh, you're letting your inner Box come out," I tease. Inside I'm screaming. My pussy clamps on empty air, desperate to be filled at his words. I shouldn't want him. Not when he used me so callously before, but I can't bring myself to care about anything except this moment. The two of us, his skin against mine.

He trails bites along the edge of my neck, putting firm pressure and pain against me. He eases the pain of his bites with soft licks against me. The contrast of his teeth and tongue against my most sensitive areas is pure bliss. A tingling begins at the base of my spine and rises to my head until I'm dizzier by the second.

I need him.

Now.

"You know how it fucking sucks to pretend I don't want you?" His voice is guttural. When he breaks away from me, his eyes are wide and bright, pupils blown to impossible proportions. A smattering of scales starts covering his body. Like he's lost control of his ability to shift.

My skin itches at the sight of all that red and black against his beautiful brown skin. It shines like jewelry, and my trembling fingers reach for it.

"Then stop pretending," I say breathlessly. "Just take me."

A new urgency grips us both. He growls, the sound more animal than human. I feel the hard ridge of his cock again, but this time when I look down, I see that even that's shifted as well. Hard gleaming scales cover his dick like a condom. Every inch is glittering with red and black, his balls pulled tightly up against the base of him. Smooth. Hard. The tip gleaming. And when he spears into me, I feel every ridge. Every scale. It touches so deeply inside me that my head drops back against the wall and a groan tears from my throat.

My pussy pulls him in, just trembling at the ridged feel of him.

"It's like a fucking dildo." I've never been with a merman mid-shift. It's fucking glorious, how hard his cock is. When he's deep inside me, he drops his forehead against my shoulder with a groan.

"So...fucking...tight."

Lifting on my toes as best as I can, I swivel my hips to suck him in deeper. To feel him so deeply inside of me that I never want to go back to his regular dick again. If he was thick and long before, it feels twice as big now.

My words die in the back of my throat before they're even formed. When the hard press of his balls hits my spread pussy lips, we both cry out together.

"Fuck. Move," I demand.

Everything after my command is frenzied. Something unleashes within Scorpion. He starts thrusting, his movements punishing. There's nothing soft about our joining. It's as desperate as it is wild. Like he's trying to punish me with his cock.

Well, I've been a bad fucking girl.

"Punish me," I whimper.

"Yes."

The hallway grows loud with our echoes, guttural growls, and sighs. I can't control the volume of my words even if I wanted to, so I don't. I don't give a fuck who hears me, us, right now. I just want to feel. I want him crazy for me.

Every inch of him rams into me; he controls us both. He controls this pleasure between us. It rises, cresting like a wave and keeps me balanced right on the edge. More. I want more. He slams hard into me, the tip of his cock touching my g-spot. That, combined with the slap of his scaled skin against my clit?

I lose all control. I'm scratching, gripping him as I try to ride the waves of my orgasm. But he's relentless. Never stopping. Drawing it out of me until I'm cresting and falling all over again. The second orgasm hits faster, coming out of nowhere. My whole body feels like I've been electrocuted within the water of our passion. I'm twitching as I climb back down, and his hips are still thrusting. Like it's not enough. Like it'll never be enough. And when he comes, his whole body shudders as his fist rams into the wall beside my head.

"Fuck!"

Our chests press tightly together. Our breaths mingle as we try to come down from the high. Scorp doesn't kiss me. He doesn't offer words of reassurance for what we just did, and I'm glad for it. But his eyes are bright as he looks into my own.

Tonight is a night of confessions though, apparently. Of questions and honesty.

"We disgust you," he breathes near my mouth. "I can see it in your eyes every time you look at us."

The words pierce something in me I didn't think possible. I want to believe the Krakens are different, but the truth is, MCs aren't different from one another. They're bathed in violence. In blood. In the alphahole-ness that I've despised all my life.

Because I've seen it.

I know how this fucking story ends. It isn't with them proposing or us having children or me living happily ever after.

It's with them, ripping my heart in two.

"You're bad for me," I tell him honestly. Because of all of them, he's the one who would hear me the most. Box doesn't give a fuck about anyone but himself and his own pleasure. He would disregard my words as soon as I uttered them. Slug would get hurt, offended, if I told him that. Because in the end, he *is* a good guy and would hate to be trumped with the rest of them. Rock would tell me to fuck off, probably. Delfin would just stare.

If anyone would listen it was Scorpion, even if I thought he wouldn't understand.

QUEENIE AND THE KRAKENS

"I've seen this story a million times before," I tell him. "I've seen my mom get hurt by men like you over and over again. If I let you in, you're just going to break my heart."

"When the heart breaks, it means you opened yourself up to love, though." He slowly pulls out of me, and I almost miss his length. My feet drop to the floor, and he bends on his knees to pull my pants up again. His cum drenches over my thighs and I know it'll stick to the material, but Scorp doesn't seem to care as he sets everything back in place. Then he stands and does the same thing to himself.

Now, with distance between us, I feel my brain fog dissipating enough to realize what had happened.

"Those are fantasies, Scorp. Not all of us can afford to love and say fuck the consequences."

"Then that's not love."

My brows raise. "You know a thing about love?"

"I know love isn't for cowards. I know that when you love someone, you keep them, and you don't fucking let them go. You give it your all just to fucking be with them, fuck what happens and fuck other people."

"Then I guess by that logic, everyone who ever stepped out on my mom never really loved her at all." The words are sad but true. I wished she would have seen it instead of crying each and every time. She withered into something I didn't like. "I won't be her."

"Oh, Queenie." Scorp steps into my space and cradles my cheek with his hand. "Anyone who even dares to step out on you is an imbecile. And anyone who tries is going to get a bullet to the brain."

His words make my breath catch in my throat. The raw honesty of them have me feeling vulnerable. "I don't just want someone who will fight for me," I whisper, so low I wonder how he can even hear me. "I want honesty."

"Honesty." He tastes the word like he's forgotten the meaning of it. He leans forward and I barely breathe as his tongue starts lapping up the drying drink from my cheeks and lips. He savors the taste of it, his breath warm against me. "The honest truth is I'm not fucking okay. My brother is dead, Queenie." He pulls back, and for the first time, I see tears shining in his big honey-colored eyes.

It breaks the resolve inside me.

This is why I hate the violent lives they lead. Because it leads to this. To strong men breaking down. To lives being taken and innocents being pulled into the bullshit.

My hands reach for his cheeks, pulling him closer. "Hey," I whisper, bringing my lips up to his mouth. "It's going to be okay." I kiss him, lapping up the taste of the drink we both savored. Lapping up the feelings of this single moment. Giving him a distraction, an outlet for his grief. And he takes it gladly, stealing sips from my mouth and groaning as that taste explodes between the two of us.

"The fuck was in that drink?" he groans as he pulls away.

Fuck if I know. I can't speak the words though. I can only pull him closer. Sparks ignite between us all over again, and even though his cum is still drying against my pussy, I want him all over again.

"You make me forget," I manage to choke out. "You make me forget everything."

His body slams against mine. I've come to learn that I like the roughness. I like the way he handles me. The aggressive slam of his body versus the soft press of his hands. It's a contradiction. Hard and gentle in a way I never knew I needed.

"When I'm with you, I forget about the bullshit, Queenie." His lips nip the side of my neck. "I forget that the Rogue Waves started a war. I forget that they are transporting illegal shit through shipwrecked boats and that we just destroyed their shipment. I forget what it is to be Vice President."

His words register even while his hot lips slide up and down my neck. It all suddenly makes sense to me. The reason they all received text messages at the same time. Rock's smirk. Even the reason they were down in that shipwreck in the first place. I remember catching sight of jewels in a chest just before they came after me.

And if the Rogue Waves are using the water as their way of transporting illegal goods, then that explains the slow diminish of fish in the area.

Son of a bitch.

His confession clears my mind. Even though my body is tingling, nearly swaying where I stand, I manage to push him away.

"Wait."

He sucks in a breath and pulls away.

"Scorp..." I feel drunk. My tongue feels heavy. At first, my mind was clouded with the aphrodisiac of his presence. But that confession, it's sobering me up.

It's making me realize what's fucking going on.

"I think Eli drugged you." Us. Whatever concoction she brewed landed in my mouth. Minutes later, I was horny for Scorpion. I mean, I think I've always been horny for him since I saw him outside of Shark Mouth, but I won't admit that aloud because I never planned on acting on it.

His hazy vision clears up for a split second. His thick brows furrow. "What?"

"Eli," I repeat slowly. "I think she drugged you. How much of that drink did you take?" I knew I saw it smoking. I should have trusted my gut.

Realization seems to dawn over his lazy eyes. "Fuck," he curses. He storms over to where she tossed the glass at my feet, kicking the shards with his boot. Moving the liquid sticky on the ground causes plumes of smoke to rise up. "That bitch."

Normally I don't care for men who call women bitches, but in this case, it's warranted. Eli tried to drug him. Why? So he would be more pliable and willing to sleep with her? Rage swells in my chest and I shove past Scorpion, marching out of the hall and into the club where we're sitting. I can feel him following behind me, stoic, silently fuming.

At the table where we were sitting, I catch sight of Eli on one of the club member's laps. Her eyes widen as she sees me marching towards her. She tries to scramble off him, but it's too late. My fist is already cocked back and I'm aiming it straight towards her face.

She lets out a yelp as I pummel her with my fists. No one moves to stop us, though. I don't even care that smoke begins billowing around us, making goosebumps rise along my arms.

"You fucking bitch!" She falls from the guy's lap. Or maybe he pushes her, I don't know and I don't care. She tries to stand up and her arms flail at me. She gets in a few hits of her own, but my rage is fueling me, and I don't feel them. "Do you think it's cute to drug someone?" My fist meets the apple of her cheek. At this point, I know we've garnered attention, and I don't give a fuck. "If that had been a man drugging a woman to rape her, he'd get his balls cut off." I grab her hair, pulling her so her eyes are level with mine. "What should we do with a woman who tries to pull that shit?"

The shadowy, smoking form solidifies only slightly, and the same creature who'd appeared to dispel of the Rogue Waves appears. I can barely make out the figure of a man in a suit. He exudes power, danger. I'm not scared of much, but I find myself scared of him.

"A man who drugs a woman in such a way is a rapist piece of shit," that cool voice echoes like thunder around us. *"A woman who does the same to a man is also a rapist piece of shit."* There's a pair of red demon eyes staring at Eli with a hatred that makes my soul cold. *"Rapists get what they deserve."* His hand lifts, and before anyone can say anything, Eli's whole body explodes into blood and mist. It splatters against my face, and the hand that had been holding her head drops on empty air.

There's no longer anything in front of me. No Eli. No shadowy man.

Just blood, sprinkling down against the club's floor.

"Well," Rock cuts through the uncomfortable tension the demon left in his wake. "It's probably time for us to go."

I don't realize my breathing is heavy. Not until I feel Scorpion angle himself in front of me, his hand cupping my face. His honey eyes are warm on me. His touch is tender. There's still a small trace of the drug left in him, but I know this moment is all him.

And the softness of his voice threatens to melt me. "Maybe you do like us after all."

Maybe I do. And its nerve-wracking that they all seem to see it so well. That they know what I try so hard to hide. With every piece of armor they chip away, the more exposed and vulnerable I feel. The more I spend time with them, getting to know the stories of their pasts, seeing tears gloss over their eyes, hearing the tragedy they've gone through, I see them as people. Not just bikers.

It's not just about sex anymore. It's about something more. Something more primal. More frightening.

I know my walls are crumbling down.

Even if I don't want to admit it to myself.

SCORPION

I can see the moment her walls start crumbling around her. It's in her eyes. They're the most expressive piece of her. They really do hold the key to her soul. To the very essence of what makes her Queenie. That anger, the guarded, stiff body, mind, and heart? It all stems from somewhere.

Her mom. But I feel like there's more to it than that. And while I want to bring it all tumbling to the ground, there's no time for that now.

It's not like we were just kicked out of Sinful, but the owners are a band of demon brothers, and their magic surpasses anything I've ever seen before. We've already pissed them off once tonight by bringing our shit with the Rogue Waves into their place of business. Add that to the fact that fucking Eli's body matter is sprinkled all over the floor?

It's best if we go.

My fingers intertwine through Queenie's. She tenses and tries to pull away, but I hold strong. I don't want her to let go. I was just inside her only a few moments ago, but this still feels more intimate than that, and I suddenly find myself craving it like never before.

Sure, I've wanted her since the moment I set my eyes on her at Shark Mouth, but this is different. Maybe I should feel violated. Fuck, maybe the both of us should after drinking whatever the fuck Eli gave us. I'm a dumb ass for accepting the drink she'd readily offered, but I was riding the highs of my own sorrow. My mind was heavy with thoughts of Raze. I kept seeing his body, the knife plunging into it over and over before he slumped through the water.

My fucking brother. Dead because of those bastards.

So, yeah, when she sultrily slid her body next to mine and handed me a drink, I accepted. Through my sorrow I couldn't even pick my way out of the haze that clouded my mind. I couldn't realize that anything was wrong.

And then I saw Queenie.

The flashing lights of the club backdropped against the curves of her curvy body and my mouth watered. I didn't know anything beyond my pain and beyond seeing her figure. The woman who brought the truth of my brother back to me. The woman who suffered at the hands of the Rogue Waves. The woman who wanted absolutely nothing to do with me.

And yet I wanted to call her mine.

"Let's go." I tug her hand and she follows, a reluctance light in her step. We have to address what happened between us, but right now I can tell the only thing she want is to get out of the club. To dip into the ocean and wash away the blood from her face.

We step out into the night, a warm salty breeze pressing against my warmer face. I don't realize I'm sweating until it hits me.

Fucking Eli and her bullshit.

I tug Queenie towards my bike and hop on first, though I don't release her. She stands off the side, and it's the most unsure I've ever seen her.

"Hey." I jerk lightly on her hand, drawing her towards me. Her thighs press against my knee and the chrome of my bike. There's too much space between us. Not just fragments of an inch or two, but her emotions are drawing away from me and I don't fucking like it. "You regrettin' me, pet?"

She bites the bottom of her lip, and I want to take her mouth in mine. Soothe her hurts with my tongue.

"We were drugged. You more than me."

I swipe my fingers across her bruised knuckles. Her skin shouldn't be marred like this, but seeing her fighting for me against Eli? Seeing her defend me like only my brothers have ever defended me before? I needed to see that. Needed to live it, experience it.

"Still wanted you, pet. Even after this shit completely fades, I'll still want you. I've craved you since the first time I saw you and that hasn't changed. You're the only woman I'll ever kiss, the only woman I'll ever want. The only one I'll ever fuckin' claim as mine."

Those whiskey fucking eyes. They gloss over and even in the darkness I can see the unshed tears. I don't want her to cry, though. I want her to believe that I'm not like those pieces of shit that walked out on her mom. If I say I'm in, I'm in. She's my only, and that's what she needs to start believing.

Slowly, I lift her hand to my mouth and press a kiss to the backs of her knuckles.

"Never had someone defend me as fiercely as you did, Queenie. I'm not gonna take you for granted. And I'll do anything in my power to prove it to you. We still have shit to talk about, things we can hash out later."

She wants to speak, but I've rendered her speechless. Her mouth drops open and closes in rapid succession. I just smile at her. Let her gather her thoughts, and if she tries to build up those pesky walls again, I'll tear them to the fucking ground. Every single time.

"Want you on the back of my bike," I tell her. "But this shit is still in my system, and I ain't gonna put you in danger like that. Go hop on with Slug, pet."

"Can you drive like this?"

My teeth flash. "I've driven in states way worse than this back when I was young and stupid."

At this, she snorts and the air feels lighter. "You're still stupid."

I laugh as she starts to pull away. "Only for you, Queenie. Only for you."

NAOMI

Slug doesn't say a word as I climb on behind him and hold my hands lightly at his waist. Maybe a few hours ago, I would have wrapped myself around him like a koala, hanging on as he zipped through the streets and towards a shoreline.

Eli ruined that for me.

I can't help but feel dirty. Like there's something tainted crawling over my skin that won't be washed off. It's not just specks of her blood that still stain my face. It's the creepy-crawly sensation. I know the drink was never meant for me, but it landed in my mouth regardless. It made me dizzy, but it still hadn't been as much as what Scorpion ingested. And I'd known something was wrong, but I hadn't listened to my instinct and in our drugged haze, we'd done something irreversible.

I can't help but feel like I'd taken advantage of him somehow. That doesn't settle right in my stomach. It makes it churn with discomfort. It makes me want to wash off the evidence of what we did from between my thighs.

Then Scorp has to go and say all that shit.

He's still drugged. That's the only fucking explanation. But when I turn my head slightly to the side, I see him riding steady on his bike. There's no wobble, no danger.

I turn back forward, giving in to the urge to bury my face in the back of Slug's cut. My sighs are drowned out by the rumbling of their motorcycles. Why is it so hard to believe that Scorpion wants me? I mean, I know he's wanted to fuck me, but that's primal. It's different from actually claiming a woman. And claiming someone in the MC world is as serious as signing your name at the altar.

Maybe it's because he used me for my phone. Maybe it's still my inhibitions making me second guess everything.

All I know is that he's right. We do have a lot of shit to talk about. A lot of unresolved tension we need to hash out. And I need to fucking decide what I'm doing. Because the more time I spend with these men, the deeper I'm falling.

I shouldn't. Fuck, I know I shouldn't. But they're an addicting, hypnotic force that I can't seem to pull away from. They're sinking their hooks into me as the hours go by, and it's going to make it harder to walk away in the end.

And I will be walking away...

Won't I?

"Fuck!"

The bike beneath me swerves and the air around us is penetrated with shots fired. My hands scramble to grab ahold of Slug, arms wrapping around him as his bike teeters. He fights to steady the bike, and once he gets it under control, his hand grasps for me as if in reassurance.

I'm not sure anything can reassure me when bullets are fucking flying at us.

They ping off chrome, and the girls that are on the backs of the brothers' bikes cry out. I want to turn and glimpse at what's happening, but my heart pounds against Slug's back like a sledgehammer.

"Rogue Waves!" Rock shouts.

Fuck.

They were just lying in wait for us to leave the club. The revving of motorcycles arriving almost drowns out the banging sound of bullets. Slug tries to swerve as best as he can. Sparks fly as they hit and as one, the Krakens break into a formation that seems practiced. The biker in front of us pulls out a gun from the waistband of his pants and turns, retaliating with his own shots.

My cheek presses against Slug's back. Turning, I catch sigh of Scorpion trying to keep control of his bike with one hand and dodging, while a free hand searches for a gun I know he's keeping on him.

I wonder if they all have guns.

Slowly, I unwrap my hands from around Slug's middle and search his waist. His body is tense under mine, vibrating. I wonder if it's that hidden rage coming out to play. Those thoughts scatter when I find a gun strapped at his waist.

Quickly, I pull it out, tightening my thighs around the bike so I can blindly push at the safety. I hear Slug cry out for me, but the words are far away. My heart is pounding in my ears with adrenaline. I'm drowning out everything else but the violence of the moment.

These bastards have been fucking up my life at every turn and now they're shooting at us?

Not to-fucking-day, bitches.

The gun is cocked and in my hand as I turn my body. One hand holds tightly to Slug and the other sets off a vengeance against the mermen riding behind us with splotches of red on their vests. The patches with waves of blood that probably signify all the lives they've taken.

It's for that spot I aim and pull the trigger. My shots hit true, and the Rogue Waves go down, skidding across the pavement.

"Woohoo, motherfuckers!" Box hollers his delight out into the night, his own gun firing off. He doesn't aim to kill, but to maim. I want to look at him and his savagery, but at that moment, the Rogue biker I'm aiming for moves faster than me.

I hear the shot of the bullet.

Then comes the pain.

I cry out in surprise, the gun nearly falling from my hand. I manage to get a grip on it, even as my arm is pounding. The warmth of blood trickles down my arm, staining my wrist and fingers. I turn back around, burying my face into Slug's back with a grunt.

"Fuck, Queenie!"

I pat him on the stomach to reassure him. The last thing we need right now is Slug getting distracted and causing us to wreck. Already, I can see the shoreline past his shoulder. It's not a solution in the slightest. There's just more open space out there for us to get hit.

This is a cluster fuck, and I'm not sure what the fuck is going on. How we're going to get out of this alive.

Just as the thought takes residence in my mind, we veer to the left sharply, just as the rise of the waves meet the shoreline. Every Kraken does this, waiting until the last possible moment to jerk away and turn with a sharp precision that can't be anything but practiced.

As we turn away, the Rogues plunge into the ocean with shouts of protest. Another sharp turn and we're riding up the slope of sand, leaving them behind. The speed picks up and we put distance between ourselves and the Rogues.

They were caught off guard, so convinced we were going to go into the water. So they followed and the change overtook them and their bikes. By the time they get control and rear back, it'll be too late. We're already going too fast for them to catch up.

"Fuck yeah!" Box shouts from somewhere near me. "We got ourselves a live one, boys!"

Slug doesn't slow, but some of the others do. I turn, watching as they stop near a fallen Rogue Wave member and hoist him up on the back of their bikes. Slug speeds up, and I force myself to turn back around and breathe deeply through the pain.

I don't want to think about what it means to know they captured a member of the MC that killed their brother. I don't want to think about the pain in my arm. I just want to get back. To get out of this fucking traffic and the police lights that are shouting off in the distance.

So when we make it to the compound after that, I sag in relief against Slug before he parks. I get off the bike, my knees nearly buckling beneath me. The only thing keeping me upright is the fact that Slug jumps up, grasping my arms in his hands.

"Thanks." I try to smile at him, but it's wobbly. The hand still holding the gun shakes and he pulls it from my grasp, flicking the safety on it before shoving it back in his pants.

I'm not going to fucking cry over this, but I feel suddenly exhausted. I feel banged to hell and pissed off, my anger threatening to aim in too many directions. This night has been complete and utter shit.

"You're hurt." Slug's eyes darken and for a moment, I'm reminded of when he knocked that prospect out. The danger that made him morph into another person entirely. A being of violence and blood. Something similar to Box, but silent and deadly. A creature on his own spectrum.

I wouldn't want to be on the receiving end of his wrath.

We're interrupted when the rest of the members pull up. I step away from Slug to rush towards Sugar. Her arms wrap around me in a hug of comfort, and I can smell the salt of her tears.

"Girl, you scared the shit out of me!" Sugar looks down and sees the blood dripping down my arm. She can't hide her wince. "I'll fix that up for you."

I'm grateful. I don't think I can go through another round of stitches. A part of me just wants to go in and pass out. To sleep for a year or two and wake up when all the bullshit is over.

Unfortunately, at that moment Box hauls the Rogue Wave member over his shoulder. He stops in front of me, eyes glossing over me.

"If I wasn't carrying this piece of shit, I'd lift you up by that ass and wrap you all over me." He doesn't exactly whisper the words or hide the desire lacing through them. "The way you handled that gun out there?" He whistles low. "Nothing sexier than a woman who has the ability to shoot you in the heart."

I can't help the eye roll he elicits out of me. "You *would* think that."

"I do." He smiles wide and stops when his eyes snag on the wound on my arm. Then they darken, almost as much as Slug's did. But with Box, there's a hint of manic delight. Funny how I can read everything on his expression so clearly. How he's turned on by what I did, but pissed that I got harmed in the line of fire. And I see the glee there, too. There's absolute joy.

And I know he's going to make this fucker pay for my wound, even if he wasn't the one to shoot me.

"You gonna take care of my Old Lady, Sugar?" he asks on a low drawl.

"I'll get it sorted."

"You're a gem." He hoists the man up higher and marches up to the compound.

"Hey!" I call out, not liking how easily he dismissed me. "Where are you going?"

"That's club business, babe!"

Pft. I snort. "I'm not a fucking dumbass, Box. I know you aren't going to sing him lullabies."

Box's laughter chortles behind him, but he doesn't reply. He keeps going, his boots stomping with single-minded purpose until he disappears into the compound.

"Come on, let's get inside." Sugar guides me inside and once we step in, the other girls follow. They murmur over me, their voices low, kind and caring. It makes a lump rise in my throat. I don't know how to respond to this type of affection. I've never had it before. Yes, with Lourdes, but never in a bigger group. And certainly not after I played a part in Eli's demise today.

Shouldn't they be seething? Shouldn't they hate me because I helped rid of one of their own?

Any other women would treat me with animosity. They'd hate me. Feel like I'm encroaching on their territory. Moving in on their men. But not these girls. They're kind to me, and I know it's genuine and not fake just because the men are watching the exchange.

They pull me into the compound and set me down. Baby Gap pulls my braids back, pulling a hair tie off her own wrist to tie my hair away from my face so Sugar can take a look at my arm.

"Just a graze," she murmurs.

"Yeah well, this graze hurts like a bitch." My whole arm feels like it's on fire. Like I dipped it into a pit of fire just for the fuck of it.

"I'll take care of it quickly," Sugar assures.

While she gets to work, I look up. Members of the club are dispersing around the compound. Some have already disappeared. Others have taken up positions near entrances and exits with their guns drawn. And Rock... He's standing a few feet away, watching while Sugar hums over my arm. Her magic is a tingling sensation down my nerves. It zaps through me and the pain in my skin turns itchy. I resist the urge to scratch as she heals me. And when it's done, Rock storms over to me.

I stand on my own, meeting him in the middle. It's like I was pulled in his direction and once I'm there, I can't look away. There's a storm in his eyes, and they're hard and cold like steel. I'm lost in the moment of his gaze just like he seems to be lost in mine.

I ruin it with my next words. "You're going to kill him."

His big arm wrapping around my waist catches me off guard. I gasp as he pulls my body close, left breathless at the proximity of him and the heady scent of tobacco and caramel. It drowns out everything else around me. Until I'm aware of him. Only him.

And when he bends down so his nose tickles my own, his lips a scant few centimeters from my own, I don't have the strength in me to push him away.

Just like I don't have the strength from stopping the kiss that renders me speechless. He takes me in his mouth in front of everyone, not caring in the moment that he's older, that he's got responsibilities. It's only us right then and the taste, texture, and feel of him consuming me.

But it's over all too soon.

"No one fucking hurts you and lives," he whispers against my lips. "No one."

He leaves me with those words. They travel through my body, sending shivers over my system. They were primal. Beastly. And he said them with so much conviction, I could image him standing before that scumbag and pulling the trigger himself. On my behalf. Because of the blood sticky against my flesh.

I shouldn't find violence so erotic, but I do. Maybe I'm broken. I've tried so hard all my life to get away from that kind of thing, only to be drawn towards it like a moth to flame.

Fuck, maybe violence is my legacy and I have nothing left to do but bathe in it.

"Damn, girl." Ritz whistles from behind me.

"You've got these men whipped."

I turn and meet Sugar's laughing eyes. There's a teasing hint to her mouth and on the other girls' mouth that makes heat creepy up my face.

I fidget where I stand, unsure of how to act now that the high of the chase is running out of my body. "You guys aren't mad at me?" Alright, not the most eloquent way to phrase a question, but certainly not the worst. I could be a bigger dipshit than I already am, so at least I have that going for me.

"What do you mean?" Baby Gap bites her bottom lip, her sweet voice tender with confusion.

"What happened with Eli... If I hadn't realized what had happened, she wouldn't have been..." My fingers waggle in the air and I make a poofing sound out of my lips. Speckles of her blood probably still coat my face unless Sugar got rid of that with her magic. I don't want to ask or bring myself to look into a mirror, though I do feel cleaner.

"Man, fuck Eli." Sugar scowls. "Ratchet bitch. Who the fuck tries to drug someone to get laid?"

The other girls echo their disgust.

"It just doesn't make sense to me," Baby Gap adds. "We can have our pick of any of the guys here. We aren't Old Ladies... not like you," she amends shyly. "But we all know our roles here. We know who we're with, who wants us and who doesn't. We have protection from anything that would harm us. Why would she risk that?"

"Who knows why ambitious people do the things they do?" Sugar shrugs. "She wanted to be an Old Lady, but she couldn't take no for an answer so she was doing whatever she could to get Trinidad's attention." At my blank stare, she amends, "Scorpion's. Sorry, I forgot not everyone knows his real name."

"And it cost her life." Ritz shudders. "But yeah, we don't blame you, Queenie. Any one of us would have outed her if we'd known she was so sneaky. I'm glad you did. She always gave me bad vibes, but what she did was unforgiveable. Like that demon said, what if it had been the other way around and a man drugged a girl at the club? It goes both ways."

"Far as I see it, you were just doing a good thing," Sugar concludes. "Now get over here. I think we all deserve a drink." With a swish of her fingers, magic sparks to life and suddenly, a bottle of wine is zooming into her open palm. "Tonight was some crazy shit." She uncaps it and takes a swig before handing it off to me.

"Take a drink, girl, and come relax. You deserve a break. Swear you have such weird luck. At least you're getting a good dicking out of all this bullshit, right?"

My face heats and I pull in a long drink to prepare myself for the interrogation I know is sure to come.

"Now, I know a lot of you bitches have already fucked almost all of these guys, but I haven't and I'm curious... what's Box like in the sack?"

I groan as the other women cackle with laughter. The sound of the joviality just reminds me of Lourdes, and it makes me miss her something fierce. I haven't called her, and I feel bad. With everything going on, there's no excuse for why I haven't given her a ring. I told her I didn't want to interrupt her time with Dimas, but knowing that asshole, he could have dropped her like a fucking hat at any time. I know Rock says he has a prospect guarding our house. Surely if she would have returned, they would have told me.

At least, I hope they would.

As if I conjured her from thin air, I hear her voice.

"Let me through, motherfucker!"

I pause, sure I've just imagined it.

"Get off me, you big oaf!"

Wait... what the fuck?

It's at this point I realize we've all gone quiet and turned in the direction of the front of the compound. A member is standing near the door, and he draws his gun up higher, pointing at it just as it bursts open and another MC member comes in...

...dragging my best friend behind him.

ROCK

"You're singin' a tune I don't know the words to, mate." Box bends on his knees, uncaring that they soak through with the blood of the Rogue Wave strung up in our torture room.

The bastard awoke the moment Box nearly dropped him on his head and started screaming when he was strung up by chains up on the wall.

I arrived in the thick of the bastard's beating, my council brothers standing around him with their arms crossed against their chests.

Delfin stands back from the others, his fists at his sides. I can see the look of torture on his face, and I wonder if this is painful for him. We serviced together for a while, but I know that some of the shit he's seen is heavier than what I ever lived through. When he came back from the army, he just wasn't the same. Never has been.

He's not quick to pull triggers anymore, and when he does, I see the way his body shakes afterwards. I never thought about it before, but I wonder if the violence takes a toll on him.

When I came back, my mind was fucked up. I had to go in to see a psychologist several times a week before I felt like I could even function. When Delfin came back, I wanted to do the same thing for him, but he'd growled at me when I brought it up, so I let the whole subject drop.

I could force him. As President of the club, I could make any one of them dance in any way I pleased. But I'm not that kind of a leader. They deserve a fair shot. He deserves to figure shit out for himself. And when he does, I'll be here waiting for him with the name of the psychologist on hand and an appointment waiting.

Until then, I clap my hand against his shoulder, giving him a squeeze that's meant to be reassuring, but his body is as stiff as a board.

Scorpion watches the events unfold. Usually, he's the one in control of his emotions among us. In my absence, he should curb Box's desire for destruction. For blood and vengeance. He doesn't seem to want to, though, and I wonder if it's whatever fucking drugged up magic is still in his system or if he's doing this for Naomi.

Fuck, my own rage is riding an all-time high, and I want to strangle the bastard for what he did. He hurt Queenie. He hurt what's ours.

And for that, he can't fucking live.

But first, information.

Another cry permeates the room and I step forward, stopping Box just before he pulls the knife out of the bastard.

"Leave it in," I order. It'll keep him alive longer.

Box smirks and pulls back. Already, his face is splattered with blood. As the club's Enforcer, he's in charge of these beatings. Of making sure we get information easily and quickly.

I'll let him work the bastard over. Get a few shots of my own in there. I know we're all itching to watch him fucking struggle. Somehow, we've all claimed Queenie for ourselves. She's *ours*. The motherfucking Kraken Queen.

And they'll pay for hurting her.

He trembles in the face of us, as he should. But I know Box scares him the most. My Enforcer slaps his palm against the Rogue's face.

"Don't cry, you little bitch." He shakes his head, turning in our direction. "I swear, the men I play with seem to get weaker every fuckin' month." He looks back at the guy. "My Old Lady got shot at and she didn't bitch as much as you're doing."

"Fuck you, man. I didn't shoot at your fucking woman." The guy's teeth chatter and blood sprays against Box. He doesn't wipe it off. He relishes in that bit of gore.

"I don't give a fuck if it was your mother who shot her, I'm still going to fucking kill you. And that's nothing compared to what my man Slug the Nug Nug is going to do to you."

The man in question takes a prowling step forward. It's difficult to see this dark side of Slug. It scarcely comes out, and when it does, it's fucking terrifying. Add in the fact that the one hurt in the crossfire was Queenie, and on the back of his bike?

My brother looks like a demon has swallowed his body, taken possession of him. His eyes are blown wide, the pupils expanding with unbridled rage.

Box chuckles as the hanging man flinches away from Slug's presence.

"Ah, that shit gets me hard every time. You see, little Rogue Wave, once we're finished with you here, I might fuck Slug over your corpse. Might even let my cum drizzle all in your mouth. Would you like that?"

He yanks on his chains. "Fuck, man, just kill me already!"

Box scoffs. "Where would be the fun in that? You see, I don't want to lie to you. You're going to die regardless. But it's up to you how painless it will go." He stands up, Box's body lithe and graceful. I know him well enough to recognize the movements as sexual. His body leans close to the future dead man's like a promise. "Don't give us information? The more painful this shit is gonna be. Be honest? Well, a bullet to the brain quick enough for you?" When the man is silent, Box holds up a finger. "Tick tock, mate."

"I'll tell you whatever the fuck you want to know!"

This has Box grumbling. "Weak ass bitch."

I step forward before he rages out like he's known to do. "You killed our club brother."

Those fearful eyes are drawn in my direction. He looks at me pleadingly. As if I would ever have any fucking sympathy for the bastards that stabbed Raze in cold blood. Like Box said, I don't give a fuck if it was your fucking mother, sister, or dog.

My brother is gone.

And I feel no pity for those who brought this upon themselves.

"That wasn't me!"

"It was your club," I interrupt impatiently. "You represent your club. You are an extension of them. *You* killed my club brother and I want to know why."

And just like that, he starts singing.

"He was in the wrong place at the wrong time. Came on our stash of jewels and drugs down in the ocean. Blood couldn't let him live after that. Said he'd just take our secrets back to you. But then that little bitch got in the way—"

He's silenced with a blow to the face, courtesy of Slug. The blow is so hard, it knocks the guy out cold.

Fuck.

"Sluggy, my man, you know it turns me on to see you take charge like that."

My eyes roll as Box wraps his bloody arms around Slug, sliding his palm down to cup his dick through his jeans. He rubs against him, and Slug doesn't push him away.

I interrupt before they start fucking each other here and now. "We needed information from him, Slug," I admonish. But I don't think he can even hear me anymore at this point.

I know about his past, just like I know about his strange relationship with Box. I can't imagine what he endured as a child, and I know these situations always take him back there. Back to that place when he was a young boy, scared and abused. He's not scared and abused anymore. He can hold his own when he wants to. But that darkness still overtakes him, and it's hard to get through to him when it does.

Only Box seems to be able to do that.

And that's the only way he seems to snap out of it.

Except now's not the time to watch my brothers fuck each other in front of that asshole's limp body.

"Scorp."

Because my VP can read me so well, I don't need to speak what I want. He goes to one of the drawers we have set up down here and pulls out a vial of smelling salts. He uncorks it near the asshole's nose and waves it underneath.

He comes to with a jerk and a gasp. His eye is already swelling shut.

"You were about to tell me where my brother's body is."

He trembles, keeping his good eye on Slug and Box. Box smirks at him, all while running the heel of his hand across Slug's dick.

Jesus fuck.

"The body!" I snap, my patience already fraying. "Where the fuck is Raze's body?"

This pulls his attention back to me again. I know he knows what I'm talking about. I can see it in his fucking eyes.

"They didn't do anything with the body," he confesses. "It was left to rot in the sea."

A sigh leaves me through my nose. I feel suddenly a thousand years older, sadder. We won't even be able to find our brother's body. Not with the hurricane that happened that day. Not when the waves are so volatile. We won't be able to give him a proper burial, but it doesn't matter anymore.

At least now I know he's dead and not their prisoner.

At least now I know that my brother's at peace in the sea.

Without blinking, I pull the gun from my holster and aim it at the bastard. I should let them have their way with him. I should let them torture him some more for the fuck of it. For Raze. For Queenie. But I'm done and I have more important things to worry about.

So when the bullet sounds around us and his blood spills against the tiles, I do nothing but shove my gun back away.

"It's done," I whisper. "And now it's time to officially put our brother to rest."

NAOMI

"**S**on of a bitch whore! Let go of my arm this instant!" Lourdes yanks at the biker holding onto her and before he can blink, her hand shoots out, palm smacking against his face.

I have to blink very hard to make sure I'm not dreaming. That I'm not fucking hallucinating as some weird aftereffect of Eli's fucked up magic. But by the silence of those around me, I know this is fucking real.

"In all my life, I've *never* been disrespected so badly."

She almost seems like a mirage, though. But I know she's not. Clad in tight jeans and a sparkly shirt, her hair puffs out around her. She's a vision as always. Perfectly put together, beautiful with her ebony skin shining beneath the light. And so, so pissed.

"Lourdes?"

Her dark gaze snaps straight to me, her perfectly groomed brows snapping together in a furrowed expression of anger.

"Girl, why didn't you *tell* me what was going on?" She marches forward, hands on her ample hips in a pose that is impatient. But I know her well enough. She's angry. Worried.

And I'm just confused as fuck.

"Lourdes, what are you doing here?"

She doesn't appear to have any visible wounds, and she looks far too good and not heartbroken, so that's good. But I know how much a person can hide beneath the surface. Except... Not Lourdes.

She's never been able to hide anything from me. She wears her heart on her sleeve and is so easy to hurt for it.

"What am I doing here, she asks." Lourdes rolls her eyes. "Ungrateful bitch. I came to rescue you!" She takes me in and her lip curls. "But it doesn't look like you need rescuing at all."

"Lourdes, *what* are you talking about?"

"I *saw* you, Naomi." She waves a hand in front of her face, just beneath her eyes. In response, the dark color of them flash a smoky white before blinking back to normal. "Aw, fuck." She sways in place, and I reach for her before she falls down.

"Here, come sit down." I guide her towards the couch, and the other girls make room for her to plop down on. Once she regains her breath, I lower my voice. "Did you have a vision?"

Lourdes is a witch gifted with the ability to see the future. She can't do magic like Sugar or anyone else we know. Her powers are a bit rare on the island, but she has a difficult time controlling them because, unlike us shifters, she wasn't born with her magic. It was gifted to her by the witch of her bloodline who had it before her. Once that witch passed, the magic moved on to Lourdes. And when Lourdes passes, the magic will move on to someone else.

While she grew up knowing she had witch blood, her powers never manifested. Some witches were unlucky like that. Born of powerful lines, but human through and through. Then one day, she just began sensing future events. Seeing them like they were happening right in front of her.

She hasn't had an episode in months. I thought her powers were all but dormant.

"I saw you being manhandled by some psycho kangaroo fucker with tattoos and a huge dick."

I blink at her and the worry in her voice.

Beside me, Sugar busts out laughing.

"Lourdes..."

"I thought I was getting a sneak peek into your sex life and tried to shut it off because, okay, I love you, but I don't want to see your coochie, even if the guy was hot. But then I saw the blood on him, and you were resisting. I couldn't just ignore it, Naomi. We have to get you out of here, protect you."

"Honey, you gotta calm down and take a breath for a second," Sugar says. Her voice is soothing. At least, to me it is. Lourdes' hackles only seem to rise. I've seen her like this before. When someone doesn't believe in her visions or claims she misinterpreted them, she gets pissed.

"Naomi, please!"

"I think the man in your vision was Box." It had to be. What other manhandling psychos do I know, the men in this compound notwithstanding. Box is the only one who would fuck me with blood on his body. That particular scenario hasn't happened yet, and my thighs squeeze together as I picture what I have to look forward to in the future.

"I don't care if it was a fucking bag. We need to get you out of here—"

Her tirade is interrupted as the compound suddenly fills with voices and bodies. Her eyes widen as she takes each and every one of them in, stopping on a blood-covered Box as he prowls in our direction.

"That's him," she squeaks. "Naomi, *that's him*!"

Box is indeed covered in blood. It drenches his knees like he knelt in it, and it's splattered against his face. When he smiles at me, it's manic, and I know what Lourdes must be seeing. How it must frighten her.

And all it does is turn me on.

"Miss me, my beautiful little creature?" The hand that reaches for me is covered in blood too. Lithe fingers wrap tightly around my neck, briefly cutting off my airway as he pulls me close to the edge of the couch and leans in for a kiss.

It's sensual, erotic, and not meant to be witnessed. But the fucks that Box gives could fit within a microcell. He relishes in the audience and chuckles against my lips when Lourdes gasps aloud beside me.

Right before her fist strikes out and hits him on the side of the face.

He jerks away from me, letting me gain my breath. The blow barely fazes him, but he does turn slowly in Lourdes' direction like a predator.

"Let go of her, you big-dicked, kangaroo bastard!"

Oh, shit.

"Lourdes..."

"What will you do to me if I don't?"

Lourdes tilts her chin up a fraction. She's putting on a brave face. I know she's afraid, but she's always been stubborn. That's one of the things I love about her. Her fierce loyalty and protective instincts over those she loves. Because when she loves, she gives it her fucking all.

"I will fuck you up."

Box throws his head back then and laughs. And when his fist draws in her direction, she tries not to flinch away, but all he does is chuck her beneath the chin.

"You're funny," he says.

When he pulls away again, Lourdes stares at him with way more confusion than when he first came in. And when she next speaks, her voice rises to a screech. "Can someone tell me what the fuck is going on here?"

"Babe, this big-dicked kangaroo is the Kraken Motorcycle Club's Enforcer," Sugar says helpfully. "That's why he's covered in blood."

Lourdes stares at Sugar like she's crazy then turns back to me. "You better start fucking explaining, coño."

I take a breath. This is the part I dreaded. I wanted to keep the truth from her. I wanted her to live a normal life without getting sucked into my bullshit. Where the thing she had to worry about was if Dimas was going to cheat on her again instead of fighting for her fucking life against an MC.

So when I explain to her, I'm reluctant. But I don't lie to Lourdes. Ever. Not because I'm afraid she'll find out the truth with her magic eventually, but because she's my friend. She's always been honest with me, even when I've been guarded with her sometimes. But guarded doesn't mean I've lied. Some things I have withheld.

I don't hold anything back now.

I tell her what happened when I went to get the samples and how it all led me here. I don't tell her about falling into bed with the men. I don't have to, because fucking Sugar and big-dick kangaroo over here take the liberty of doing it for me.

Lourdes just takes it all in and remains silent even after I've finished.

"So let me get this straight..." Her voice is strained and I'm not sure what emotion she's trying to conceal. "You have been here this whole time—after you lied about our house being flooded, mind you—having a fucking *cock-fest* and you thought your best friend

199

didn't need to know that?" Her eyes leave me to rake over the other bikers. All of whom have found our conversation incredibly interesting. "Are you fucking them all?"

I almost choke on my spit.

What the fuck, Lourdes?

Warn a girl before you ruin her lunch.

"Hell no," Box answers mutinously. "Just the council members."

"Jesus Christ, Box, can you shut the fuck up?" My face is flaming at all this information they're putting out there.

I really want to hide my depravity from Lourdes and they just go and blast it for everyone and their fucking mothers to hear. Why don't they wake up the ghosts while they're at it?

She's always been so innately *good.* I think that's why I was drawn to her as a friend in the first place. Because she grew up in a way I could never understand. With a stable family and parents who loved her and each other. She's been faithful to Dimas, even while he was an asshole who doesn't deserve her.

What will she think of me if she knows I've been rolling around in bed with a bunch of bikers?

"Okay, okay. So you're fucking him?" Lourdes points in Box's direction.

I sigh. "Only when I'm suffering the aftereffects of a concussion so I don't have to remember it."

Box snorts. "You love my cock."

True.

I love that piercing most of all, even when I know I shouldn't.

"Okay, okay, who else?" Lourdes' eyes are wide with curiosity. "Who else are you fucking, Queenie?"

Jesus Christ. I think Lourdes has finally lost it. RIP. Rest in paradise. Send me a postcard from the other side. Cause of death? Too much dickformation.

"Well, there's Sluggy over here." Box stalks to where Slug is sitting and plops himself in his lap. Hard. Then rubs his ass all over Slug's dick.

I bite back my groan at the sight of that.

So far I've only seen Box dominate the bedroom. What would it be like for Slug to be the one in charge? Hmm, my mouth waters just thinking about it.

"Who else?" Lourdes demands.

"She fucked my brother."

"Sugar!" The betrayal!

She gives me an unapologetic shrug. "Don't think we didn't fucking notice, girl."

Great. Everyone knows I've been around.

"Who else?" This time, Lourdes directs the question at me. I can lie to her face, especially when I know that everyone is listening in on our conversation. The MC members are chuckling, chugging back beers and watching us like we're a fucking TV show.

This isn't Keeping up with the Kardashians, Caribbean Version. This is my fucking life they're putting on blast here.

Can we not?

But, I can't lie to her. Ugh.

"Daddy Kraken."

There's a collective silence from everyone around me as they seem to process this information. I quickly have to amend, "We haven't fucked, though."

I just took his cock down my throat and guzzled his cum. Nothing major to see here. No, sir.

"Daddy Kraken?" Lourdes' eyes bug out. "You're fucking with the leader of this lot?" A laugh, hands slapping against her thighs. "Okay, before he gets naked, please tell me you command him to '*RELEASE THE KRAKEN*'? Because if you don't, I gotta say that's a wasted opportunity."

Rambunctious laughs echo through the room as Lourdes starts spouting out her kraken jokes. And just like that, my best friend has been accepted into the fold of the MC. I want to sigh and despair, but this was probably inevitable. Being friends with me is dangerous, and she doesn't know just how much. But right now, it's not looking so dangerous as they hand her a beer and pull her into conversation. She's molded herself so easily into the situation. Lourdes was always like that. Always able to fit in anywhere no matter what and where she was.

But all that laughter and chatter dies down the moment Daddy Kraken walks into the room. His face is set in grave lines, graver than I've ever seen. I can see the distress marring his features. I can see the weight of the world balanced on his shoulders.

Something in me aches at the sight of that. I want to walk up to him and wrap my arms around his waist. Let him lean into me so I can unshoulder whatever burdens he carries. I'm surprised I even want to, but I know what a toll being the president must take. Especially on the cusp of war.

"Brothers," Rock announces to the room. "Tonight, we've learned that our brother Raze was murdered, his body lost at sea." His voice is thick with emotion. "Tomorrow, we celebrate our fallen member, and we'll throw a party to remember him by. It's what he would have wanted."

The mood turns somber. Even Lourdes is looking on with a sorrowful expression.

"We will put his soul to rest back where it belongs. At sea."

"At sea!" everyone echoes, lifting their drinks in salute.

"Party hard, brothers," Rock says, but his eyes find mine and stay there. "We only live once."

Funerals were somber occasions, and for an MC, that was no exception. The air is thick with sorrow, drifting across the wind like ash. Not even the sea breeze can shift it away from us as we stand at the edge of the ocean, just where the waves meet the shore. The place of our births. The place between land and sea. Our feet touch both, connected by more than just ourselves. Our lives. A part of us. A part of life.

And a part of death.

Rock asked me to stand beside him while he put his brother to rest before we came out here. Looking at the sorrow in his steel eyes, how could I bring myself to say no? Not that I would have. I want to be here for him. For all of them.

I didn't know Raze, but I watched him die. I watched the knife glide savagely into his body, and that single action connects us. It's a different connection than the one he shared with his brothers, but a connection just the same. I'll always remember that moment. I'll remember the fear I felt. I'll remember he went silently. He didn't cry out, beg for mercy.

There's strength in knowing what's coming and accepting it.

There's no body for them to send off to the sea. Raze is already one with it. So the Krakens, the honeys, and even Lourdes stand at the edge of the shoreline and stare off at the horizon.

So far, Rock hasn't said a word. No one has. I know we're all waiting for the Kraken President to give his words of farewell, whatever they may be.

Through my peripheral, I can make out the severe lines of his features. The clenched jaw, the thick brows lowered over heavy lids, and eyes that are glossed over, glittering brightly like the surface of the ocean before us.

I reach for his hand. It's an instinct to comfort, to lend whatever strength is in me and give it to him. Later, I'll second guess every choice I've made since I've met them. Maybe I'll even try to convince myself that I shouldn't have done this. Shouldn't have reached out. Because when you give men like this a single inch, they'll ask for a mile. More and more until they consume you whole.

Is it bad that I want that sometimes?

Rock looks at me, his calloused hand squeezing my own. He lets out a shuddering breath, one only I and the wind can hear. The sea breeze lifts his peppered hair a fraction, and it's like he's been reborn.

"Today, we lay one of our own to rest." His voice carries out down the line of leathered and tattooed Krakens. "We've got no body, but we know he's in the place he should be." His eyes stay on the sea before him, his lips a hard line. "He's home, at sea, where he rode like a fierce motherfucker beside us. He was loyal to the club, to us, until the end. And for that alone, we know that he's going to be fine on the other side." He pauses. The whole world does, like the ocean itself is listening to the soft dirge of Rock's voice. "Goodbye, brother," he whispers. "Rest in paradise."

It isn't a grand speech. It wasn't long or particularly eloquent, and yet tears prickle my own eyes at the words. There's a realness in them that hit something in my soul. I hold onto his hand tighter, and he responds with a squeeze of his own. There are always words spoken between silences, between touches. And in this, our intentions are as loud as if they'd have been shouted.

I am here.

You are not alone.

And in a time of epic sorrow, perhaps that's all that the silence needs to whisper to us. Sometimes that's all we need. A little reassurance, a little squeeze of the hand.

So that we know, for certain, we aren't all alone in the world.

—————

Another party precedes the funeral. This one isn't like the rest. This one is as somber as the ocean. Even with the music loud, voices are muffled. But with each drink downed, they gradually get rowdier. At first, they mourned Raze's death.

Now, they're all celebrating his life.

Well, almost all of them.

Rock isn't out here with the others. He's not shooting the shit with Box or consoling a brooding Scorpion, who sits alone, nursing a bottle of rum. The honeys are quietly checking in on everyone, playing waitresses. Even Lourdes—who stayed the night—has taken it upon herself to help.

Something isn't settling right in my chest as I watch the revelry go on. Not because they're starting to party, but because their president isn't among them at all.

I slowly make my way to Rock's office, trying to go unnoticed. I don't knock, but the door is thankfully unlocked, so I slip inside, closing it behind me. The noises aren't drowned out but muffled a fraction.

And just like I knew he would be, Rock sits behind his desk, a tumbler of whiskey held in his massive hand. He barely glances up when I step forward, my thighs pressing against the edge of his desk. My palms meet the surface and slide forward. He's watching my fingers move, inching towards his, but he doesn't respond. Not even as I pull the tumbler from his hand and take my own swallow.

He doesn't even comment on the fact that I don't cough it up. Yes, the whiskey burns on the way down, but I've been drinking this shit my whole life. When I take a generous amount in my mouth, I place the drink back in Rock's hand.

He still hasn't said anything.

"Daddy Kraken..."

"Not right now, Naomi."

Naomi. Not Queenie. I don't know why the use of my first name fucking hurts, but it does. Not me—I'm not going to take this personally. No, I hurt for him. For what he has to endure.

To try and gather my own thoughts, I look around the room. I've only been in here twice before. Once after I'd tried to make my escape and a second time to make a call. I hadn't really focused much on the images on the walls. Biker paraphernalia, expensive-looking models of motorcycles on shelves, photographs, framed pictures of older models, and a framed picture of motorcycle club logos.

One of a ship splintered apart in the water catches my eye.

Rock notices where my attention is and breaks the silence. "The Shipwreckers MC," he supplies. "One of the strongest and oldest MCs in the Caribbean." He takes a swig.

"Hmm..." I turn my attention back to him. "How are you *really* feeling right now, Rock?"

He scoffs and sets his drink down with a clang against the surface of his desk. I don't flinch away. Then he's standing, his presence looming and intimidating. It charges the air with currents of electricity that I feel against my arms and the back of my neck.

"Do you want the truth or a lie?"

I meet his gaze, my tongue feeling thick in my mouth. "The truth," I say. "Always the truth."

His arm reaches across the space that separates us. I still don't flinch. Not as his paw wraps around my braids and tugs me forward until I'm all but half-hanging off the desk.

"I'm pissed off," he says darkly, breath blowing against my mouth. "And I don't know if I should go out there and kill someone or..." He stops himself.

"Or what?" My voice is husky with arousal.

His steel eyes flash at the daring in my tone. I can't hide my smirk. This is a dangerous game. We both know it. He's already claimed that we can't happen again, not after that first time. But I know he wants me, and I want him. And this moment is precarious. Filled with sadness, anger, and the need to unleash it all.

And I can help with that. I want to be the vessel between mourning and healing. I want to embrace the danger because it feels like it's all I have to maintain control, and it's all he needs to heal.

"Or fuck you over this desk."

I smile, knowing he means every word, even if he had to force them out from between gritted teeth. He *does* want me. And just the words have slick arousal coating at the lips of my pussy. My clit thrums with anticipation. Wanting. Waiting.

Needing.

"Yes." The word comes out more groan than anything.

Rock's pupils expand, his nostrils flare. Then his other hand is cupping my cheek softly. So at contrast with the hand gripping my hair, holding me closer to him. I live for the contrasts of touch. Of calloused fingers and soft mouths, of a rough hand against my skin but a gentle caress against my clit.

"Be sure, Queenie," he growls. "Because once I fuck you, I won't be able to stop. Once I have you, I'm going to make you mine."

Forever.

The word underlines the tone of the sentence. I should balk. Turn away. Forever is too long of a commitment, considering I don't even know what the fuck I want. But I can't bring myself to push him away.

Take note, it's not only guys who think with their dicks. Women think with their clits, too.

And damn the consequences. Damn the day after.

"We only live once." I echo the very words he said yesterday. Just like that, the dam between us is broken, and I'm hauled the rest of the way over the desk. It all happens in a blur. The moment my feet hit the floor on the other side of the desk and I'm in front of him, he's turning me by the hips, his palm shoving against the middle of my back until I'm splayed out across his desk. Papers and his tumbler go flying, but it doesn't seem to matter as he crowds behind me, grinding his dick against my ass.

"Then hold tight to the edge, Queenie."

I obey.

"*Daddy* Kraken is going to show you how it's done."

ROCK

Her thick curves press softly against my every hard edge. The moment her hands reach up on the desk to grasp the edge, her knuckles paling with the force of her hold, I smooth my palm down the arched curve of her spine, stopping over her ass to give her a pat.

"Good girl," I praise.

Her entire body shudders and I make note. My queen likes to be praised. I wonder what else I can discover about her. There will be plenty of time to explore that later. Later, there will be time to roam my hands over every inch of her body. Tenderly. Slowly. For now...

I dig my fingers into her hips, hiking them above the desk a single fraction, just enough so my hand can skate between the smooth wood of my desk and her body. When my fingers find the button of her jeans, I tear at it and the zipper, loosening the tight material. I yank it down the length of her thighs, shoving it just past her knees.

"Don't let go of the desk," I order.

Her sigh lets me know she heard me, and I drop to my knees behind her, tugging her pants off the rest of the way. I get her boots off, leaving her skin bare to me in nothing but lacey, black boy shorts.

My hard cock weeps at the sight of her ass in that material. The globes curve out, begging to be touched. To be kissed.

To be fucked.

I palm the heavy globes in my hands, letting my fingers tease the edges of lace. They slip inside, my calloused fingers meeting the edge of her wet pussy. I love how drenched she is, and we haven't even gotten fucking started.

Her ass wiggles against my fingertips, her pussy lips searching for friction. I give her what she's looking for, teasing the edges before slicking them against her wetness. She moans, the sound echoing through the room. I want that and more. I want everything.

With a growl, I fist her panties and yank. The material gives, tearing off and leaving marks against her smooth skin. Then I bury my face into her pussy from behind, yanking apart her thighs with a rough movement. My tongue dives in to taste her slick sweetness. Lapping up her juices and biting each fold in between my teeth, every flick makes her moan louder until she's thrusting her backside against my face. My mouth is coated in her arousal and my dick is straining against my pants.

I can't take it anymore.

I need to be inside her.

I stand, gliding my beard against her skin as I go until I'm hovering over her. I kick aside her ankles, spreading her legs as wide as they can go. With one hand, I keep her pressed to the surface of the table while the other unbuckles my belt in a hurry, shoving my boxers down a fraction so I can pull my aching cock out.

Giving it a squeeze that I feel at the base of my spine, I watch the small bead of cum wet the tip before I glide it in between her ass cheeks. I poise myself just at the entrance of her pussy. Her body tenses, and I know she's trying to forcibly suck me in.

My palm meets her ass, the sound resonating through the room. "Hold still," I order.

She whimpers, her breathing erratic. I wish I could see her face right now. To see her lips purse as she begs, "*Please*, Daddy Kraken."

Fuuuuuck.

My dick twitches against her folds and my hips flex, causing me to slide the tip in. And that simple touch feels so fucking *good*...

"Call me that again."

I've liked it since the first time she uttered those syllables to me.

"*Daddy* Kraken."

The words unleash a beast inside me. I've gone as slow as I can possibly go and now, I want to unleash this fucking rage. So I plunge to the hilt inside her and she screams my name, her pussy clamping down on me, choking my cock inside. Her hot, wet folds contract and I begin to move.

There's no finesse to this. There's just rage and a bit of sorrow. And Queenie, precious fucking Queenie, letting me use her to fuck it out of my system. So I take advantage of that fact, my hips slamming in short thrusts against her. With every slam that goes faster, her breaths wheeze out of her until I make out a chant that makes me fucking dizzy.

"Daddy Kraken. Daddy Kraken. Daddy Kraken."

My chest falls against her back, my hands lifting her by the hips to find that perfect angle inside her. Each thrust brings me closer. My balls draw tight up behind my cock. And with every push forward against her, I make sure her clit rubs against the edge of the table, giving her the friction she craves.

She doesn't need to tell me she's coming for me to know that her orgasm is close. I can feel it in the way she squeezes around me, tighter and tighter. I relish in it, my hands pushing her hips harder against the desk. There will be bruises on her skin after this and I'll kiss them for her later. Right now, I'm rubbing her against the wood while my dick impales her, faster and faster until I feel her body start to contract.

"Yes, Daddy Kraken, right there, please. Yes!" Her palms slap down against the desk as the orgasm drowns her. I let it milk me, setting an unrelenting, rough pace until she's climbing down from the high. Until her clit is too sensitive and she's all but begging me to slow down. To give her a second.

Her braids wrap around my hand, and I tug her up. She's all weak limbs and a pliable body, so she goes without complaint. At this angle, I can feel her all the way down to my spine and my thrusts can't slow. And it's only when I feel myself getting to that edge that I pull out of her heat and flip her around so she's facing me.

"Get on your fucking knees." My voice is a growl not my own. It's savage.

And she obeys.

A queen bowing before her king.

She slides down to the floor in front of me, staring up with eyes hooded with desire. On her knees, her face is level with my cock. I palm the underside of it, bringing the tip an inch away from her mouth.

"Open those pretty lips."

Her mouth opens and I have to hold back my groan at the sight she makes. Ready for me. Allowing me to take my pleasure in whatever way I see fit.

"You're going to take my cock in your mouth and you're going to swallow every fucking inch of me."

In response, her mouth opens wider, so I push myself inside her.

And holy fuck.

Her warm, wet tongue swirls against my tip first, before she opens wider and sucks me in. She doesn't gag but takes me to the back of her throat. Hollowing out her cheeks, she begins to suck.

"Fuck me with your mouth," I order, my voice guttural and unrecognizable.

She works faster against me, swallowing me down deep. I can't sit still for long. My hips start slamming into her mouth, making her gasp through her nose. She takes all of me, and I make her choke. Spit pools out of the corner of her mouth, sliding down her chin.

She makes a pretty sight on her knees, but I fucking want more.

"Shove your shirt down."

Her low-cut top is pushed over her pert little breasts, baring her dark nipples to the air. I reach out, pinching them between my fingers. It makes her scream around my cock, and it almost makes me cum. I have to pull away and hold her head steady, controlling the movements, pushing her up and down my cock just the way *I* like it.

"Play with your tits."

I want to watch. I want to take this memory with me to my fucking grave. When her dainty little hands start pinching and tugging at her nipples, wringing pleasure out of her own body while I use it for mine.

It's the sight of that, of her obedient and wanton, that has me pumping inside her faster and faster. I don't care how harsh her breathing is getting, because she pulls me closer to her by one hand, daring me to give it all to her. And I do. That feeling of euphoria climbs up my spine and pools low in my belly. I feel it coming and when I finally do, I explode in her mouth.

Jets of cum shoot out over and over again. I've never cum so fucking much at one time, but I make Queenie take it. I make her fucking choke on it until she's gagging and can't take anymore. My hips pull back and cum leaks from between her soft lips, sliding down the sharp jut of her chin and along the length of her slender neck. It mingles with her spit, and she swallows what she has in her mouth already.

It's fucking filthy.

I don't give a fuck.

I press the sensitive head of my cock against her cheeks, gliding it along the cum she wasn't able to take. I lap my dick with it, bringing it to her mouth and shoving it past her lips.

"You'll lick every fucking drop."

She sucks on me, licking me like a fucking lollipop. My body trembles with each swipe of her tongue. It's too sensitive, but I still lap it up with the cum on her face and make her clean every bit of it. Until there's no more liquid on her face, but damp, sticky evidence left behind.

My thumb finds her bottom lip, pressing against it. "Good girl," I praise.

Her body trembles and her lips curl into the softest of smiles. For a brief second, there's a hint of vulnerability in her expression. She probably isn't used to taking orders so readily. But I know she did it for me. To pull me out of my own head. Out of that space where anger and sorrow were taking over. And I took from her.

Now it's my turn to give.

I haul her up by the arms and place her on the edge of the desk then step between her legs.

"Queenie..." My throat feels thick with emotion in a way I've never felt before. It makes me drop my forehead to hers and breathe her in. If she's feeling vulnerable, so am I. I've never let anyone see my weaknesses, but she came and offered an outlet for them. Was it selfish of me to take? Maybe.

But I needed it.

I need her like I need air and sea.

Her arms wrap around me, pulling me close. We stay like this for a few moments, breathing each other in. She smells like something fruity and creamy both, dessert packed in this little package. I breathe it in deeply. Memorizing it down to the last bit.

"I shouldn't want you," I mumble against her hair. The words make her stiffen and I feel her try to pull away from me, but I don't let her go. "I shouldn't want you because you're younger. I shouldn't tie you down to someone like me. Someone in this life, but I'm selfish." I pull away to stare into that whiskey gaze. "Life is too short, Queenie. We could die today or tomorrow. Who the fuck knows? All I know is I don't wanna waste whatever time I got left bein' a fuckin' dick. I want you. I want you to be my—"

I don't get the rest out. Shots blast through the windows and wood of the compound. Papers scatter, glass breaks. Queenie lets out a scream of surprise. I react on instinct at the sounds, grabbing her and pulling her off the desk and under it, plastering her body to the floor.

I hear my brothers beyond my office crying out. I hear them returning fire. I have to be out there with them. Fuck.

My hand presses Queenie's face against the floor. "Stay here," I order in her ear.

Her nails scrape against the ground. "Lourdes," she gasps. I can hear the tears in her eyes, and I'll kill the bastards shooting at us for that alone.

"I'll protect her, but you have to fucking stay here!"

She doesn't say anything, and I take it as her ascent. Within moments, I'm moving, standing and fixing myself with rapid flicks of my wrists and fingers before I reach for the gun in my chest holster. I rush out of the office, slamming and taking a quick moment to lock Queenie inside.

Just in case.

And then I'm rushing into the chaos.

NAOMI

"That fucking son of a bitch." I wrestle into my pants, cursing the Kraken President to hell and back for that bullshit he pulled. "*Stay*," I grumble. Like I'm a fucking dog or something.

Shit, right now I wish I was so I could take a whole ass piss all over his desk in retaliation. I mean, I can still do that, but I don't want to squat over cherrywood. Seems criminal.

Shots are still ringing out as I struggle to get my boots on. I'm rolling around the floor and when it's finally securely on my feet, I crouch and frog-march across the room towards the door. There's aren't any more shots aimed this way; they're all focused towards the other areas of the compound. I can hear the wood and glass splintering.

Fucking knew they were too complacent with this shit.

My hand fumbles for the doorknob, shaking as I turn it. I'm trying to keep an air of calm, but my heart is pounding up to my throat. Lourdes was out there. Lourdes, Sugar, Baby Gap, Stef, and Ritz. What if they're hurt? What if they're—

I can't afford to think that way.

If they're hurt, I make a vow then and there to fuck over any and every Rogue Wave I ever see.

Determined, I yank on the door, but the fucker doesn't budge.

"No." Frantic, I try again. And again. And again. "That motherfucker!!!"

Daddy Kraken locked me inside of his office. The rat bastard.

I stand and run to his desk, yanking open drawers and searching inside for anything I can use to pick the lock. I smirk when I reach in for a letter opener, but before I can make my way back to the door, a window in the office shatters. I duck on instinct, barely registering the sound of boots kicking through the windowpane. Of a grunt and of them landing down and shaking the floor I'm currently huddled on.

"Well, well, well..."

I turn, my fists tightening around what I now know I'll be using as a makeshift weapon to get out of this. Really, it shouldn't be such a surprise to see the bastard in here considering his club has been fucking up my life at every fucking turn.

"Vicious," I greet breathlessly, like we're old friends and like I've just run a marathon. Really, I'm calculating my chances of survival right now. Considering the fucker is pointing a gun in my general direction and I'm armed with nothing but a letter opener, I would say they're pretty slim.

But I've got speed. I've got the skills of a man who didn't want me to be defenseless out in the world. I can use anything to my advantage here in this room. A chair. A book.

Heh. Death by book.

Slug would laugh.

"This place was way too easy to break into," he says conversationally.

I make a note that, if I get out of this alive, I'm telling Rock to redecorate because this is bullshit.

"Now, you're going to stand up nice and slowly, and you're not gonna fucking scream as you come with me to my compound."

The man with the scar slashed down his eye, the Rogue Wave fucker who stabbed me, is staring at me like I'm a snack he means to devour.

Yeah, not today, asshole.

"Go on, now. Stand up."

I do as he says, pushing to my feet, hiding the letter opener in my palm as I do it. I need to be very careful with the next few moments. They determine if I live or if I die. And because I prefer to live, these moments are precarious.

"You're gonna come towards me. Slowly, bitch."

My lip pulls back against my teeth in a snarl, to show him just what it is I think about his foul mouth. Bastard. My grip on the letter opener tightens as my feet crawl in slow increments in his direction.

He's sneering. Staring at me like a prize he's longed for and I'm finally within his grasp.

"The fuck do you guys want from me?" I stall for time, hoping he's as much of a talker as he looks.

"You're fucking delusional if you think this is about you, bitch. Now shut up and keep moving."

There's not a lot of space that separates us, so I rush through my words, unable to keep quiet. I just want him talking. I just want to buy time. "It obviously is about me if you're going through this much trouble."

"Maybe it was about you at first. Can't leave no witnesses behind. *Now*? It's about them."

The Krakens. He wants to get to them through me.

Who said bad guys were original? Oldest shit in the book, swear to God.

But what the books never wrote about were the females they liked to kidnap. Fairytales have always portrayed us as weak things. As crying, fumbling women who lay helplessly in wait for men to come save us. What they don't know is how fucking *vicious* we can truly be.

Shots are still firing in the compound and I'm in front of him. I'm out of time now, so there's nothing left to do in this moment except strike.

My legs and arms are steady as the hand fisting the letter opener jabs once, twice, each blow a quick succession against his chest. The surprise has him stumbling. A shot whizzes past my ear, deafening me momentarily. But I don't give him a moment of reprieve. I remember the moves I was taught from a young age, my fists striking out against wrists, against his neck.

He gasps and grunts in pain, but he's stronger than he looks and doesn't relinquish his hold on the weapon. Instead, he retaliates, jabbing out at me, clocking me on the face with the gun. I see stars and I try not to let them hinder me, but he's advancing, whipping the gun at me again. I duck the second blow, dropping quickly to the ground and with all the strength I can muster, I jam the letter opener into his thigh.

He screams a curse. A shot goes off. Then he's falling to the floor, grasping at the letter opener still lodged into his leg.

My heart beats a frantic rhythm in my chest. The door to the office is locked, I'm alone in an enclosed space with an enemy who is physically stronger than me. I have two options. I can take him out or I can escape out the window and hide.

Fuck!

I make a run for the broken window. My hands reach up, grasping at the windowpane. Glass digs into my palms, and I cry out as I haul my body up.

There's the clank of the letter opener falling, and as quickly as I hoisted myself up, I'm gripped by the waist and thrown backwards. The wind knocks out of my lungs. I scramble back as he advances but he drops low, grabbing my ankle. I kick out with my feet, trying to dislodge his hold. It feels useless when it's a vice grip. I do manage a kick to the nose. The crunch of cartilage breaking is only satisfying a moment before he lands on me, pressing the barrel of the gun to my head.

I stare into his smug, bleeding face defiantly. "You aren't going to shoot me." He would have done so already. I'm betting he has orders to bring me in alive. "They told you to keep me alive."

"No," he admits, his hand wrapping around the braids splayed out on the floor. "But alive doesn't mean *unharmed*."

I fight against his hold, striking my fists out against his most vulnerable spots. The wound on his thigh. His dick.

That has him howling. He drops my braids and I kick out one more time, my foot connecting to the soft flesh of his inner thigh.

"Bitch!" He shoots the gun blindly in my direction, aiming true. The bullet grazes against my arm, the painful impact and surprise making me stagger backwards. That fraction of a second distraction is all he needs.

I can't dodge the blow he aims at my face this time or the way my knees buckle beneath me, sending me sprawling. The gun whips against my face so hard, my vision blurs around the edges.

A gasp tears from my throat as he tangles his fist into the roots of my braids and brings my head slamming down against the floor.

And it's lights out for me.

DELFIN

The moment bullets start flying, my mind races back to a different time, blurring until the compound and my brothers all but disappear and I'm standing in the midst of a desert. Geysers of sand and limbs explode around me. The sounds and shouts are deafening, becoming nothing but white noise as chaos rains down.

A growl tears through my throat. My gun is in my hand, firing back against the oncoming enemies. Even as my comrades begin dropping around me. One by one, they fall, and I know that I'm next. I should care, but I don't. I don't care because I don't want to go back home without them. I don't want to go back to dream about the lifeless eyes staring at me accusingly from beneath blood and sand.

A bullet sends me blasting backwards. I fall, expecting to be cushioned by a pillow of gold and await my demise. But when I hit the ground, it's hard, the wind knocked out of my lungs.

It's what wakes me up from the nightmare I was trapped in.

Sound comes alive. Bullets are blazing, hitting glass, shattering it and splintering the wood of our compound. I try to take deep breaths as I realize where I am. Not in the desert. Not in the war. I'm here, surrounded by my brothers. And just like then, we're being attacked *now*.

I sit up, pushing through my own disorientation. I make out the screams of the honeys. Frightened, they hide behind whatever they can find, though the open space of the compound doesn't provide much protection. They're huddled together on my left behind the couch.

"Delfin!" Sugar's hands are over her ears, her eyes wide as she takes me in.

There's a fierce burn on my shoulder where I know I just got fucking shot.

"Stay hidden," I manage to growl. I push myself to a standing position, grabbing the gun I'd dropped on the way.

But even as my brothers are firing out of the shattered windows, we're useless. We're blind, unsure of where the enemy is at. They're not shooting with any finesse themselves. It's nothing but chaos and a fierce anger exploding.

And as quickly as the melee began, it ends. One by one, the enemy stops shooting. We hear motorcycles, but by the time some of our brothers rush to peek out, I know it's already too late.

They're gone.

My hand trembles, but I can't bring myself to lower the gun. I keep a firm grip, just in case, and take a look around at the destruction left behind. Everything is upturned. The couch flipped to hide the honeys; glass shattered in every crevice so that the floor fucking glitters. Wood and debris are scattered through the room.

I look for dead bodies among the destruction, but my brothers on the floor groan and get up, pressing hands to bleeding wounds. I assess them with quick glances. None of them look fatal.

My attention turns when Rock kicks through the mess. His every breath is heavy, and he's scanning the floors. "Lourdes!" he calls out.

A whimper comes from behind the couch where the honeys are huddled. Then slowly they stand, shaking glass from their hair and shoulders.

Lourdes, Queenie's friend, stands last. She swipes away tears from her cheeks, hiccupping as she looks to Rock.

Our Prez seems to breathe a sigh of relief at the sight of her unharmed. I know it's because of Queenie. She and I are nothing, yet I still feel relief at seeing her best friend okay.

But I don't see Queenie anywhere. I know she went into Rock's office before the shooting started. She's okay, I'm sure, or else Rock wouldn't be standing out here. But something curls in my gut. It hits me, as fast as that fucking bullet did. Instinct. Something I've always had. Something I've always fucking listened to.

"Rock." My nostrils flare. My voice draws his attention. The urgency in the single word. But no one knows me more than him. There is something we share that the others don't. It's the ability to know when something is wrong and communicating with a single look. "Where's Queenie?"

"In my office."

My feet take me in that direction quickly. My gun is still drawn, the feeling in my gut growing as I lift my booted foot and slam it into his office door. It splinters inwards and I burst through the wood, eyes scanning, but I already know what I'll find.

Gone.

Queenie's gone.

"Fuck!"

Rock is already looking at the blasted window of his office. It's big enough to fit someone through, and it's currently missing all its glass. He tears through the room, grabbing the edge of his desk and flipping it until it flies against the wall.

I watch it all happen with a sense of quiet dread.

And when Scorpion, Box, and Slug quietly walk into the room, their expressions matching in severity, I know that this has gone beyond war now. They've surpassed it. The Rogue Waves shot up our compound as a distraction so they could get the one who has been their real target all along.

Queenie.

Once Rock calms, he turns to us all. We're all watching him. Waiting for him. For our leader to go and get back our queen.

Yes. Our. I'm not even surprised by the turn my thoughts have taken. I may not have something with her like the others, but I won't deny the pull she has or the hold she has over me. I won't deny it. Not again. And she's an innocent. She doesn't deserve this.

If the Rogue Waves wanted to be decimated by the Krakens, they've just assured that not a single one of them is going to make it out alive tonight.

"Wire," Rock snaps. His voice is hoarse, like he's holding back a growl of emotion. "Can you track them?"

"I can try."

"Fucking do it then. Find her. Find my Old Lady."

I grit my teeth at the words, silently correcting them in my head. *Our* Old Lady.

SLUG

"They're not even trying to fucking hide," Wire grumbles. Hovered over his computer screen, he's frowning at it like it's a puzzle he's trying to solve.

Meanwhile I'm trying to solve the puzzle of how the Rogue Waves had the balls to shoot up our compound and take one of our own. As Sergeant at Arms, it's my job to make sure plans go through without a hitch. On land and on sea. To make sure that we're all prepared for shit to go down.

We were ill prepared for this.

The thing is, I should have expected it. But we were all riding the high of Raze's funeral. We were all lost in our own thoughts, confident that we were going to have at least another day before the war started, never mind the fact that we'd recently killed one of their members and outsmarted them on the road.

They were thirsty for revenge.

And they are going to use Queenie to get it.

Helpless, innocent Queenie.

The thought of her suffering has taken me back to the one place I hate more than others. To another time when I was young and afraid, my hand clasped tightly to my sister's just before she was yanked from my arms. Beaten. Raped. Abused. All in exchange for a little slip of powder in the palm of my mother's hand.

It was then I vowed I'd never let another innocent suffer again. That if I saw an injustice being done, I would stop it.

So I killed the fucker that day and I've killed several fuckers since then with no remorse to be had at all. I've done it with darkness taking over my soul because that darkness grounds me. I'm one with it.

It's my friend now, keeping me company as I sit silently, and I wait... and wait.

We're all stuck on a waiting game as Wire searches through his programming, trying to find where the Rogue Waves are holed up at. Rock and Delfin stand by with their arms crossed. Scorp paces the length of the room. I'm just sitting here, my imagination running wild with all the things I plan to do to the bastards who took her. And Box...

"I'm going to rip their guts from their bodies and string em up by the balls!" He's raging around the room. Too much energy vibrates out of him. Too much energy he could be using for something else and could be putting to better use.

Instead, he's jumping on the balls of his feet, and while his mouth wears a grin, it doesn't light up his eyes. He's just as worried about Queenie as the rest of us and this is how he shows it. In screaming promises of violence.

I can't even take his hand in mine to calm him down. Not when I'm feeling the same violence thrum through my blood like a song, begging to be belted out. I want to enact every thought spinning through my head.

But to do that, first we need Wire to stop staring at the screen and give us the fucking answers we need.

"Have you found her yet?" Lourdes bursts into the room. Rock has already kicked her out twice already, but she keeps coming back, demanding answers that we are all as desperate for as her.

"That's the thing I can't figure out," Wire grumbles again. "They're all at their fucking compound."

"What?"

"Then what the fuck are we waiting for?" Box pulls his gun out and cocks it. "Let's go get her back." He starts towards the door but stops when Scorp steps in front of him.

"Stop," the VP orders.

"Get the fuck out of my way."

This isn't going to end well. I know from experience that when Box doesn't get what he wants, he will fight to the death until he has it. I've seen it before when we roamed the streets as children. He always had to be better, faster, mightier than his adversaries. And telling him he couldn't have something was like dangling a raw carcass in front of a shark who hasn't fed in weeks.

"Box," I cut in before he can do something he will regret, like punch Scorpion in the face. There's a lot of his personality that they tolerate, but I know that's the one transgression they wouldn't stand for. "We can't go after her."

He whirls on me just like I knew he would. His fingers curl into fists, but he doesn't lash out at me. Not like he would to them. Not now.

For as much as Box likes to be violent, for as much as he likes to hurt and be hurt, he won't hurt me. Not like this. Not out of anger. But his eyes reflect a wildness that he holds within. He's a beast caged that needs release. He needs to hunt. He needs his prey.

"Slug..." His nostrils flare and I can't hold back from him anymore. I go to him, pulling his cheeks with my palms so our noses touch. I feel his skin vibrating with the strength of his rage. I will him to look in my eyes.

"I want her back as much as you do, but we *can't*."

He snarls, gnashing his teeth. His hands grip my wrists as if he means to yank my touch away, but he doesn't. There are a lot of things Box can bear, but losing my touch isn't one of them. So he keeps me tethered to him, even while his fingers flex and demand to push me away.

"We can't go after her because it's a trap."

A rumbling sound erupts from his throat. "I don't give a fuck."

Of course he doesn't. He would walk into that compound alone if he had the chance, guns blazing, not caring how many bullets could rip through his body. When he had a goal in mind, he was singular and obsessive about it. He didn't stop to think or plan. It was impulsive, violent, and enraged.

"Queenie could die."

That makes him freeze. It makes everyone freeze. There's a heavy silence in the room, penetrated with nothing but the click of Wire's fingers across the keyboard.

And then the ringing of a phone.

I release Box slowly only after he's calmed down and turn to see Lourdes pulling a phone out of her pocket. It's Queenie's. She stares at the screen, silences it, then pockets it again. Only then does she speak. "So they want to lure you to their compound."

"They have a trap set up for us, most likely," Rock whispers.

"Lourdes, can you see anything?" Scorpion all but begs. His eyes are wide and pained, desperate for any good news he can grasp onto in the hopes that Queenie is alive.

Lourdes' eyes fill to the brim with tears. "You don't think I've fucking tried, asshole?!" She pushes aside her curls, tangling them in her fingers. "I can't control my fucking magic. I have no idea what I'm doing or how to—"

The phone rings again and with a frustrated shout, she pulls it out, silences it, then pockets it.

"Naomi is my best friend," she whispers. "She's important to me. If I could help, I would. If my magic were at all enough..."

"We'll get her back," Rock says with determination. "They have her at their compound, demanding we come and get her. We know it's a trap, a set-up, so we'll be prepared to storm their fucking compound and get our Old Lady back."

I watch Box's transformation at Rock's words. He shakes off his sadness and desperation, and in its place is something else instead. That violence that shone in his eyes only moments ago brightens until it's burning like a fire.

He turns and looks at me, and I feel an echo of what he shows in his eyes in my own heart.

"We'll get her back," he promises, and I feel the words down in my own soul. Because I feel just as murderous, just as vengeful as they do.

If not more.

"We will," I agree, standing straighter. "We'll tear their fucking compound to the ground." My eyes meet Box's. My lover's. My friend's. We're connected by so much pain and sadness from our pasts, but now, with Queenie, there's so much more between us. "We'll tear it down if it's the last thing we fucking do."

SCORPION

I can't concentrate. I can't focus. I can't shake the worry and rage that's taken up space inside my body. All I can think about is Queenie. Her smile, the cute furrow of her brows, the anger, and most of all, her fearful expression.

What must she be suffering right now at the hands of our enemies?

They've already tried to kill her once. I wonder if, now that they know she's tied to us, they'll want to take their time? Will they want to make her suffer first? I know how vicious the Rogue Waves are. They didn't get their name for nothing. They're bathed in as much blood as we are, if not more.

It's on their fucking crest for god's sakes.

And we know where she is. Or so we assume. She could be at the compound, or at another location entirely. While Wire double checks, we're all tasked with patrolling the streets. With finding the motherfuckers that wear a red wave on the breast of their cuts and bringing them in for questioning.

So that's what me and Delfin are doing.

I know nothing but the sound of Queenie's husky laughter and the wind and waves in my ears. I know nothing but my worry and anger at the thought of losing her before we could even begin. If I could go back, I would fuck her properly. I would say all the words she needed to hear to know that this is as real for me as the sun in the sky and the sea on the ground.

It wasn't just Eli's fucked up magic in my system that had me confessing.

I've wanted her since the first moment I saw her.

Now that our future might be wiped away, I'm scrambling to find her before it can come to that. And when we find the assholes, I know nothing but her laughter, the wind and the waves, and their cries for mercy. But I'm not God, and I don't mean to grant them shit but pain.

My knuckles split open and bleed. I'm raging and I don't notice until Delfin is forced to pull me off their bodies. But none of them talk.

So we keep searching. We keep finding.

And I keep beating, repeating the same mantra over and over again, willing it to the wind, to the seas.

We have to find her.

We have to.

ROCK

I should have never locked her up in that fucking room.

I can't even look at my office without wanting to destroy it. I can't look at the busted door without wanting to obliterate it entirely. And I can't fucking stand the sight of blood on the floor, knowing it's my fault she shed it.

I wanted to protect her. Instead, I ended up harming her. I should have known it was a trap. As president of this fucking club, I have to think of every outcome. Any other day, I would have. But my head has been too meddled. With thoughts of Raze and having just spent myself within Queenie's body, I wasn't fucking thinking straight.

That's on me.

Anything that happens to her is on me. And I'll never forgive myself for it.

NAOMI

The pounding of my head wakes me up from unconsciousness. It takes me a moment to orient myself, to push past the grogginess in my mind for me to take in my situation. Through each pulse of my brain screaming, I register something new. *Pulse.* The coldness beneath my cheek. *Pulse.* The scent of salt water. *Pulse.* It's soaking through my hair. *Pulse.* Dimness surrounding me. *Pulse.* Blood, crusted against my nose, upper lip, and arm.

And of course, there's the pain.

It radiates up my face and forehead, making my entire head pound. I wince, and even that hurts. My palms slip against the floor as I push myself up to a sitting position. Groans rumble through my throat. I try to think past the pain in my face and arm to assess the damage in my body. I'm fully clothed and nothing else hurts except above my neck and where the bullet grazed me.

Good. That's good. It means they haven't touched me. Yet.

Fear threatens to slice through my body, but I force myself to replace the sensation with a rigid, burning anger. I fucked up before in Rock's office. I was too cocky, confident in my win. It was my downfall. But I was taught to fight. Taught to shoot and defend myself. I can get out of this.

"You're a bitch, but that don't mean you're weak."

I channel those words. I know I can get out of this, but I can't let fear overtake me. I can't feel sorry for myself. I have to focus. So that's what I do. After assessing my injuries, I notice a heavy weight against my ankle. A single look down shows me I'm shackled with a chain and padlock.

Motherfuckers.

I follow the length of the chain and see it's drilled into the wall with steel bolts. Difficult, but not impossible. It'll hinder me for sure. But I'm not going to let it stop me.

I take in the rest of the room. It's a dank thing, with dripping water pooling on the cold ground. I can't hear anything but the echo of the water drops at first. When I strain, I can almost make out a groaning sound, one I recognize all too well. When I hone my eyes into the dimness and observe once again, I realize that I'm on a boat.

I wonder if this is the Rogues Waves' compound. I don't give a fuck where they settle, but it'd be nice to know where I am.

Beyond that, I don't hear voices. And the complicated thing is there's only one door for escape. My situation keeps getting more complicated by the second.

With an experimental tug on the chain, it digs into my ankle. The only way out is with a key, obviously. It's bolted in too securely and brute strength won't get me out of it. Cunning will.

I huff a breath and groan at the pain it causes against my face. Fuck. My nose. I let my hands wander gently up to it. My head was slammed against the floor, and while I've suffered similar injuries before, this one is a bitch. I prod at the space around my nose and realize that it's fucking broken.

Great.

No wonder my breaths are coming out wheezing.

I scoot along the ground, pressing myself against the wall to brace myself. My heartrate accelerates and I grind my teeth as I reach for my nose. When I set it, I swear I black out for a second. My vision darkens. I don't cry out, but my body lolls to the side momentarily. Tears burn my eyes and slide down my cheeks.

"Fuccckkk..."

I can't even brace myself before I hear footsteps and a door being pushed open, though my ears do pick up the little fact that it's not locked. Better for me, I guess.

Then a light strikes, and I'm blinking away the tears as a couple of Rogue Waves step into the room with me. I recognize them from the club. Their sneers pull their features into lines of hatred.

I glare at them defiantly even through my pain, while at the same time pressing myself harder against the wall. It's better if they think me weak and afraid. While I might be the latter, I am not the former.

"Finally awake," Blood says. The president of the Rogue Waves is as unimpressive as he's always been, so unimpressive that I don't bother taking in his features too deeply. Black hair, ugly mug, crazy eyes. He's basically a storybook villain.

Also, points for stating the obvious, captain dipshit.

"You're the bitch that's caused me so much trouble." He steps forward and the slow sound of his footsteps against the floor make me wince. He mistakes it for fear and smiles maliciously. It's not the same type of smile I've come to recognize from Box.

Box is a cruel adversary. But he would never hurt me. He would never not give me what I want.

This man means to end me. I can tell.

"And now you're shacked up with the Krakens." He stops a foot away from me and lowers himself so we're at eye level. His eyes rake over me. Assessing. Leering. It makes the hairs on my arms stand on end. "They seem pretty taken with you." His hand reaches out, touching my knee. I try to jerk away from him, but I'm pressed tightly to the wall. "Makes me wonder how good that pussy tastes." His hand slides up to my thigh. I can't move. I'm frozen even if I want to lash out at him. I wait like cornered prey. He moves to my inner thigh, stopping close to where I don't want him to be. He smirks at my fear as if he can smell it. I know he's doing this, not because he wants me, but because he wants to make me squirm. "Your men will come to save you, and when they do, they'll find themselves six feet under."

I breathe my relief when he steps away from me. The other men at his sides look on in disappointment. Like maybe those assholes were hoping for a show that was denied them. Fuck that, and fuck them, their mothers, and their whole family.

Yeah, that's probably very petty bitch of me, but I don't give a fuck. Next time don't raise assholes.

"Sit tight in here, princess," Blood says. "Your men will come trying to save you in no time. Maybe I'll let you say goodbye before I blast their brains out. Maybe I'll send them off in style and let them watch my men fuck you before I kill them. Whatever mood I'm in later."

Bile rises in the back of my throat, but I shove it back down. With a few more leering comments and sneers, they leave. I listen intently, but no lock slides into place.

Only when they're gone do I slump in relief. It lasts a second before I straighten. This whole thing is a trap for the Krakens. That's not surprising, but dread fills my gut. Once they find out where I am, and I have no doubt Wire will find out, they'll come for me. And if it's indeed a trap...

Box never thinks about the consequences of his actions. I don't doubt he'll try to rush in, guns blazing. It will only get him killed.

And that can't fucking happen.

None of them are going to die because of the Rogue Waves. None of them are going to die because I'm locked in this shithole.

Determination fueling my movements, I reach into my hair, digging into my braids for the clips and bobby pins I keep secured there for this very reason.

My father didn't raise no fucking fool.

And their mistake was thinking I'm some helpless female when the reality is that I'm so much fucking more than that.

With a smile curling my lips, I start to work on my locks.

In movies, lock picking always takes a few seconds. Minutes, at the most. In reality, it takes so much longer than that. By the time I hear the click and the padlock snaps open, sweat beads my face in rivulets. I don't wipe it off until I shove the chain off my ankle and stand. My legs are wobbly and my head is pounding, but there's a fire burning inside me. A need and determination to get the fuck out of here before the Krakens try to show up and get hurt.

So I rush over to the door, slowly opening it so that it doesn't squeak. I'm not sure if there's anyone on the other side, but I doubt it. And when I realize that they left me alone, I cackle internally.

Fucking idiots.

Villains are so dumb outside of movies. It doesn't disappoint me, though. Better for me to face stupid fools instead of smart ones. It'll make it that much easier to escape. Keeping my body plastered against the wall, I tip-toe down the hall, my ears straining. Outside of that room, the boat groans and creaks. It's filled with haunting sounds, the echoing ricochet of arrogant laughter, bounding off steel walls. Are they getting drunk?

Dumbasses.

A split second of fury grips me. They really think I'm so weak that I need no guard, that they could hold me and threaten me and make me watch as they killed the men I'd come to care about?

Big fucking mistake.

A new rage grips me.

"Bitches are always looked down on."

Those words have lived with me my whole life.

"Bitches ain't shit in this world. So you gotta prove you're different."

For the first time in my life, I find myself thanking him for his teachings. For showing me how to live. I've hated him all my life, but for this I can be grateful for.

Because I don't know the layout of the boat, I find myself wandering aimlessly for several twists and turns, hitting dead ends or doors where voices echo behind them. I quickly backtrack, my heart pounding up to my throat. My need to get out intensifies; I try not to let it make me clumsy, but soon I'm rushing and my feet are echoing on the floor.

And when I run into a Rogue Wave member, I don't give myself time to think, *I'm fucked.*

He gives out a shout of surprise at the sight of me. His hand fumbles for the gun holstered at his side. While he's fumbling, I move, rushing towards him with a silent cry. He is barely able to whip out the weapon before I'm on him. My fist strikes, sure and true, until my knuckles sing with the pain of that one blow. But it hits home, cracking his jaw to keep him silent. I'm sure it's broken. I pride myself in my aim, but he's relentless and tries to point the gun at me. I dodge, weaving under his arm, grabbing it and snapping his wrist. The gun falls and shoots at a wall.

Fuck.

Others will come running at the sound.

My time is almost up.

We grapple. My aching body makes me slower than usual, but so does his broken jaw and wrist. He flails aimlessly, getting a few lucky shots in that have me gasping. My vision blinks in and out of focus, energy already waning, but I hold strong.

His fingers wrap around the ends of my braids as I dive for the gun. He yanks me back and my cry echoes off the walls. I fall onto my ass, taking a knee to the back. The breath leaves me in a *whoosh,* and I gasp for breath.

He grunts in anger, and I can only imagine what he's trying to say to me. My fingers grasp for his ankles, like I'm scrambling to get away. He just pulls harder and my eyes water at the force. I slip my fingers up his jeans, nails digging into his skin...

His fingers dig into the roots of my hair...

And he doesn't see it coming when I yank the gun from the holster at his ankle and shoot him in the foot.

With a guttural cry, he jerks away from me, falling back. His hold releases and I turn around. I show no mercy because he would have shown none to me. With a single bullet between his eyes, I end his life. Bile crawls up my throat, but I force it back down. Now's not the time. Not when I hear the pounding of footsteps coming for me. Shouting as they realize I'm not where they left me.

Quickly, I pick up the discarded gun, shoving both of them into the waist of my pants before I make a break for it. I can hear their footsteps and it's like their heavy breaths are hot on the back of my neck, making my feet move faster around their maze of a compound. They're close. I can feel it. Hear it. It's like fear itself chases at my feet, making me jump, nearly tripping me up. My palms slam into a metal door and my shaking hands grip the handle, praying it's unlocked.

It is.

I stumble inside the dimness, closing it quietly behind me. I lean against the frame, struggling to contain my breaths. Outside, I hear the commotion as they try to look for me. I can make out words in chopped succession.

"She's outside!"

"Fucking find her!"

They think I've made a run for the outside. Good. While they disperse to try and find me, I can take a few minutes to catch my breath. I only give myself a few seconds to pull air into my lungs before I glance around the new room I've found myself in.

Boxes pile over one another like towers. Some stragglers sit off to the side with missing lids. The thought that they could be weapons propel me to go and check. I won't survive here with a single gun I stole from that asshole amongst all those MC members, or whoever is still out there. I need a way to protect myself.

The first open box I encounter isn't filled with weapons. But chests that are flipped open and filled to the brim with jewels. Gold glitters from the top of the chest, rubies and sapphires winking in the dim room.

Fuuuck.

This was the shit they had hidden in that abandoned boat I caught them in the first time. They probably moved all their product when they realized I was with the Krakens. I ought to pocket some of this out of spite, but I think of all the people they've killed because of this shit. How many have died in their thirst for jewels and drugs?

I don't want anything to do with it.

Teeth clanging together, I move on to the next box. The lid is half-off, so I shove it the rest of the way quietly and peek inside.

What I see makes the breath in my throat catch.

"The fuck..."

I don't even reach in to grab what's there. I step back, my breath quickening at the red sticks and pile of wire within.

Bombs. The Rogue Waves have fucking bombs in their compound.

What the fuck? Do they all have some sort of death wish? A single spark could make this shit blow sky high. They can't possibly be that stupid, can they?

Check the wires.

That voice urges me to think, to calm down and get a closer look at what's in the box instead of trusting a first glance. I lean into the box, my eyes following the maze of different colored wires. They're wrapped up, but not connected to the sticks of dynamite. Bravely, I reach for one, examining it closely. There's no starting powder here, either. They're blanks.

Okay, so maybe the Rogue Waves aren't as fucking stupid as they look.

But suddenly, an idea begins to form in my head. Quickly, I look through the rest of the boxes, finding an array of things like jewels, drugs, guns, and finally what I need.

Gun powder.

A slow smile curls on my lips as I run my hands through the grains. It's been so long since I've actually touched something like this, but my body remembers and my mind rushes through it.

I hurry through the process, being as meticulous as possible. Sweat runs down my forehead and between my shoulder blades, and my heartrate kicks up as I hear noises outside of the door. I'm running out of time, but I need to hurry. I need to make as many as possible...

I'm not sure how much time passes, but I work like I have death over my shoulder, slowly reaching out to grab me and pull me into the afterlife. Once I start the process, it becomes as easy as breathing. But eventually, I run out of time.

The door clangs and I gasp, sliding myself and my projects behind a pile of crates as it opens. I try to angle my body in a way that allows me to see, but with the way the towers of crates are positioned, I can barely see beyond the wood and to the person who entered the room.

Boot steps clank on the ground, and I can imagine whoever it is looking for me.

Fuck.

I pull the gun from the back of my pants and hold it in my palm. It's a bad idea to have a gun fight in a room that contains all this powder. Unless I have a death wish, which I fucking don't.

I am so thoroughly fucked. Unless I can fight hand to hand. Realistically, these men are taller and stronger than I am. I've always had to rely on speed and skill, but sometimes even that isn't enough to get out of sticky situations.

It will have to be.

I have to make sure it is.

The merman is still in the room with me and approaching closer. Fuck. I shove the gun back into my pants as an idea forms. I'll need to be quick and stealthy if I want to get out of this alive. Grabbing my projects under one arm, I grab a fistful of powder in another and as I start to back away, leave a trail of it on the ground as I go. I try to envision myself as light as possible to make as little noise as I can. I see the shadow of a body peeking behind crates, grumbling to himself. I left a mess, and I'm sure it's only a matter of time before he sees my workspace and realizes that I'm in here with him.

I hurry and, in that hurry, I fucking trip like a dumbass.

Because why wouldn't I royally fuck up so close to freedom?

A crate topples over behind me, narrowly missing my head. I yelp from surprise and curse myself for the sound. For a second after it falls, the world stills. And then I hear a voice growling.

"Come out, bitch. You can't escape."

"Like fuck I can't."

I'm already caught, so there's no use crab walking backwards towards my exit. I shoot to my feet and catch sight of him over a couple of low crates. His smile is feral, and he starts to make his way towards me. But I'm already running, dropping the grains of powder as I go. He shouts and as I rush past crates, I bump into them purposefully. It slows me down, but sends them flying to the ground, blocking his path towards me.

I reach the door, throwing it open. He shouts for backup. I'm sure they've heard him, but at this point I don't care. Freedom is so close, I can taste it. I turn, whipping out the gun from my pants and aiming it in the direction of the trail I left.

His eyes widen as he realizes what I'm about to do.

"No! You fucking bitch! Don't!"

The last thing he sees before I pull the trigger is my own feral smile.

―――*ee*―――

I run before the explosion shakes at full force, but even so it blasts me back against the wall. Searing heat rushes in my direction, air and soot choking me as I gasp for breath. My back aches from where I slam into the wall, and as smoke rushes towards me, seizing up in my lungs, I roll onto the floor and try to crawl away.

The fire is spreading. The explosion tore a hole in the boat of their compound. It rocked it, and I'm sure it left a gaping, melting hole in the metal. As we speak, I'm sure water is spilling into the space. I'm sure others are realizing what the fuck happened and are trying to find me.

It won't be long. It isn't long. As I crawl along the ground away from the danger of the smoke, my hands meet booted feet. I look up to meet the dangerous, pissed off gaze of the Rogue Waves president.

I don't see the blow coming, but his foot meets my face, sending me backwards. My vision fades into unconsciousness, and when I blink and can see again, I think I only blacked out for a few seconds.

Blood reaches down and grabs a fistful of my braids, yanking me up. I cry out, dropping my project. He doesn't even seem to notice that I had it in my hands. His rage blurs across my vision as he pulls me up at eye level, my feet dangling beneath him. My neck feels like it's going to snap off, my vision swims in and out, darkness and light.

Then all I see is his sneering, angry face.

"You fucking bitch."

His fist connects to my cheek.

I've never known a pain this great before. It blinds me and I cry out, my nails scraping against his wrists to try and get him to release me. It doesn't work.

"You destroyed my product, my money, and killed my brothers with that little fucking stunt."

Good.

The smile that curls my lips, even through my pain, makes me feel victorious.

He shakes me by the hair. "You think that shit's funny?!"

"Hilarious," I croak. The smoke has coated my lungs and throat, making my voice hoarse. The sarcasm still gets through.

"Fucking cunt." He drops me to the floor and the pain that hits my stomach with his steel-toed boot has me struggling for breath. Saliva pools out of my mouth, leaving me gasping like a fish on land.

I need to get out of this position. It's dangerous. It's...

"You Kraken whore." Another blow, this one harder than the last. It flips me onto my back, where the gun in my pants digs into my spine. If only I could reach it...

I try to force myself up, but Blood is there again. His blows don't relent. I know he wants me unconscious, but I force myself to stay awake. I won't let myself pass out. I won't let him get the better of me. So I try to keep my hands up to protect my face. It works for a moment, but his rage is a fucking force.

"I was going to keep you alive until those bastards came for you." He grabs me by the neck and lifts me in the air like I weigh nothing. "But I think I'll just kill you now."

I don't fight even as his hands squeezes my throat, cutting off my airway. My hand reaches behind me, feeling for the gun. When I grab it, I whip it out. There's a manic expression in his eyes, a sadistic glee as he watches the life slowly leave me.

But I'm not a dead bitch yet.

And it takes a moment for him to feel the barrel of the gun against his stomach. By the time he does, it's too late. The trigger is pulled. Once, twice, three times. He drops me and I roll, standing on shaking legs even as I'm coughing for breath. Even with the smoke clouding around us. He's fallen to the ground, fingers grasping at his bleeding wound, but still alive.

Bastard.

I don't give the President of the Rogue Waves a moment to recuperate. I don't torture him the way he tortured me and would have done worse. I just point the gun at his head and pull the trigger, watching brain matter and blood splat across the ground beneath him.

Dead.

I just killed an MC president. I'll think about that more later when I'm safe. For now, I turn, trying my best not to faint from the blows he aimed my way and I bend, picking up the project I'd dropped.

I stumble the rest of my way through the compound, trying to be as careful as I possibly can be. But there's chaos, I'm sure. Everyone is probably scrambling to put out the fire. To stop their compound from sinking. To find their president. They probably aren't worried about me at all. I barely see anyone and those I do see all wear prospect patches and are running for their lives as fire coats their cuts.

I see a light at the end of the hallway. Bright, blinding sunlight.

With a breath of relief, I make my way towards it, soaking in the sun as I take a step outside. The breeze caresses my wounds, and freedom is a single gasp away.

I drop the stick of dynamite and wire I made at the entrance and walk down the ramp and onto a dock. Motorcycles are tethered to the side, floating like little boats. I grab one at random, pulling it with aching muscles up onto the wood and straddle it, ready to ride off back to Kraken territory.

Before I do, I take a look back at the compound of the Rogue Waves. I was right. It is a boat, though a chunk of it is blown to bits, fire licking out of the hole and spreading onto the water. My heart breaks for the sea creatures I've likely just harmed, but I vow on my life that I'll make it up to them somehow, in some way. It might not be enough, it might not ever be enough, but I'll fucking do it.

I see members of the MC inside, trying to help get one another out. Whatever they might have been, at least they're loyal to each other.

And for that, they'll all have to die.

"I'm sorry," I whisper as I aim the gun at the entrance of the boat. I'm not sure if I'm talking to the ocean, the boat, or the MC. Maybe it's a lament for all of them, for what I have to do. But they are criminals. They've driven away the fish from our waters, they tortured me, killed people.

And for this, I won't feel remorse.

So I pull the trigger and watch as the bullet hits the bomb I made. It blows, setting off a chain reaction in their death trap. Steel explodes. Heat and debris hit me, but I can't look away. It's like staring at the sun, blazing, colorful, and tragic.

And when the licks of fire start to touch the sky, I rev the engine of the motorcycle and leave that destruction behind.

DELFIN

The past few hours have been nothing but torture. It didn't seem to matter the amount of bloody knuckles we got, it didn't matter the amount of times I pulled the trigger as soon as information left their lips. We weren't any closer to finding Queenie.

Every single scrap of information given to us has been a series of conflicting things. Torture from Box hardly helped clear it up. It's almost as if the president gave them all different sets of stories in case they were caught by us, just to drag this out for as long as possible.

We're all going crazy, and I don't even feel the shadows of the past threatening to drag me under, despite how many lives I've taken today. It just doesn't matter. Not when Queenie's life is on the line.

"Fuck this bullshit." Box's seat flies to the wall, splintering into pieces. It startles everyone out of their current argument. Tensions are high, and members—those involved with Queenie—are screaming at Wire to get his shit together and find her.

"Box, sit the fuck down!" Rock orders.

"No!" he snaps. "Fuck this shit. You all might be happy sitting on your asses, but I'm going out to find Queenie right the fuck now."

I've never seen Box directly disobey an order. Is it treacherous of me to agree with him? Even more treacherous that my legs act of their own volition, standing and following after him as he storms outside.

"Fuck!" Rock yells.

Soon, they're all following Box as he pushes his way out of the compound.

"Box!"

He flips everyone the finger. The agitation he feels is contagious. I'm ready to snap myself, only holding my shit together for Queenie's sake. But the thought of her suffering, of whatever she could be going through, fucking kills me.

I've lived through war. I've seen my brothers taken by enemies only to come back scarred to shit, if they even came back at all. And they were all trained to fight, to survive that shit. What would happen to Queenie who isn't a part of this life? The damage they could do to her body, her mind...

She helped me out of my own head. Her voice is the light that pulled me from my own darkness. I've stayed away from her, too afraid to taint her with the stain on my soul, my hands. She's too good, too precious. I can't deny there's something about her. Siren's call. It's the goodness in her heart that makes her a beacon of light for me. For all of us. I know that's why they're attracted to her. To her strength and sass, to her kindness and resilience.

And I want it, even if I don't deserve it. I want her. I think I have since the moment her palms caressed my cheeks and she pulled me from the past. But now she's gone.

Lost.

And we have to get her back.

"Box, I gave you a fucking order."

Box ignores Rock as he straddles his bike. "I'm going to storm their fucking compound and tear through the whole place to bring her back if that's what it takes."

"Box!" Slug grabs Box's shoulder, giving it a squeeze. They stare at one another and silent words of communication pass between the two before Slug nods, his eyes closing in acceptance.

He steps back just as Box's bike comes to life.

Rock lets out a curse just as the waves in front of us rise. We've been riding long enough to know what the movement means, and what the sounds accompanying it indicates. Within moments, guns are in our hands and pointed at the spot as a bike crests the beach and stops a few feet in front of us.

The rider is all but slumped over the handlebars, dripping in the salt of the ocean. I'd recognize those braids anywhere. They curtain her whole face, and it isn't until she looks up that we realize the state Queenie is in.

"Fuck!"

Box drops his bike, but he isn't fast enough. I am. My own feet swallow up the distance, catching her as she slumps over the side of the bike. I catch her in my arms, hefting her up and standing. She sags in my arms, her whole body shuddering before she lets out a sigh of relief.

I assess her injuries, unable to look away from the bruising forming along her throat and swelled face. The sea washed away the blood, but I know she had it at one point. There are still smears of soot along her forehead, and I catch a whiff of gunpowder, fire, and salt.

"Queenie," I whisper.

Her eyes flutter open and she gifts me with a weak smile. My knees go weak at the sight of it. Here she is, broken in my arms and fucking smiling.

"Blew it sky-high," she whispers. "Fucked 'em up."

"What'd she say?" We're suddenly crowded, and Box is hovering. The manic look in his eyes still bright as he takes in her every injury. Even Slug looks ready to commit mass murder in retaliation for every bruise she suffered.

"Sky-high." She sighs the words out just before her body goes limp against mine. I pull her close and turn to take her inside. Rock could patch her up. I know he'd want to. But Sugar can work magic faster. I know it'll take a lot of energy from her, but Queenie needs to be okay. She has to be.

Because when she wakes up, I am going to pull my head out of my ass.

I am going to make her mine.

NAOMI

I awake to zero pain and a barrage of memories. I sit up with a gasp, only to find the whole of the Kraken MC surrounding me. Kind of eerie, if I'm going to be honest. No one likes to wake up to find a bunch of eyes on you.

"Am I naked?" I groan. "The only way you all staring at me while I'm sleeping would be acceptable is if I'm naked right now."

"Jesus fuck, Queenie," someone groans. "What the fuck happened?"

I close my eyes and lean back. It's only then that I realize I'm not laying down on the couch. A hard body is beneath me, warmth emanating against my backside. I shift against the big body beneath me, ass wiggling against a thick lap. Turning, my face scrapes against a stubbled jaw, and I meet the tortured eyes of Delfin.

His thick brows are pulled together in a frown as he takes me in, looking over my face like he's searching for something.

"I probably look like shit." I'm breathless. Mostly because I'm surprised I'm even in his lap in the first place. Rock's, maybe. Slug's or Box's, sure. Even Scorp's. Delfin has been avoiding me ever since I saw his episode in the hallway. I understand feeling embarrassment over something like that. Maybe I don't know a damn thing about PTSD, but I know pride, and I know I wouldn't want anyone else to witness it either.

So why is he holding me? Why are we so perfectly aligned, hips to hips, my thighs spread open outside of his? His heart beats a rhythm against my back that's almost erratic and feral. His palms hold me reverently, carefully, like I might break at any given moment.

"You're beautiful," he whispers, low so only I can hear. But he says the words with such a grave expression, I'm not even sure if I believe him or not.

"Queenie." Rock's voice draws my attention away from Delfin to the front where the men are aligned, each with several varying degrees of severity marring their expressions. Particularly Slug's. My heart aches at the sight of him. What must he have gone through knowing I was taken by the enemy? It couldn't have been easy for him. How much of his past came to the front of his mind while I was away?

How much internal pain does he have right now?

"Queenie, what happened?" Rock asks. "Before you passed out you said something about them being sky-high. We need to know everything that happened. From the moment they took you to how you escaped. Where did they hold you? What did they do to you?"

"Christ, Rock, let her catch her breath," Scorpion grumbles. When my attention sways to him, he gives me a rueful sort of smile. "Hey, pet. How you feeling?"

I take a moment before I answer, assessing my own body for injuries. I know I should feel like shit. I took a beating, after all. But I don't feel anything. All the pains and aches are gone, only a remnant of a phantom brokenness left behind. Like the memory of being hurt should be there, but it just isn't. I don't even feel tired anymore.

"I feel fine." I look around. We aren't alone at the Kraken compound. Every member is here, as are the honeys. I catch sight of Sugar, nearly slumped over the bar but being held up by Baby Gap. I suppose I have her to thank for curing my injuries, though it obviously took a toll on her energy, and she's all but passed out. I also see Lourdes a little ways behind the men in front of me, twiddling her thumbs and tears glossing over her eyes.

I give my friend a weak wave and she breaks down in tears, shoving past the group of men and dropping to her knees in front of me. "You stupid bitch," she whines between sobs. "I was so worried. I thought—I thought—" She can't get the rest of her sentence out, but she doesn't need to.

I may have been a cold friend. I may not ever express my emotions or be what she always needs. Sometimes she might live too often in the clouds instead of firmly on the ground, but this is proof that we love one another. My heart aches seeing her like this. Knowing anything could have happened...

I grasp her sticky cheeks with my hands, lifting her face to meet my gaze. "No more tears," I tell her. "I'm fine."

"Good." I don't see the punch against my arm coming. It hurts and I flinch back against Delfin's chest.

"Ow!" I cry out. "What the fuck was that for?"

"For scaring the shit out of me, you dumb bitch!"

I rub the spot, but a smile touches my lips. "Won't happen again."

"Of course it fucking won't," Box growls. "Because we're going to go fucking kill every last Rogue Wave unfortunate enough to wear that piss-ugly cut!"

I blink and Lourdes stands, stepping away so Box can drop next to me. He doesn't seem to give a fuck that I'm still sitting in Delfin's lap as he pulls me forward in a firm yet gentle manner and sears me with a kiss. I don't think he's ever been this gentle with me before. His touch is soft, holding me close so our fronts are touching. He doesn't handle me roughly like he usually would. It's his kiss that's aggressive, though. His tongue fences against mine, dominating and caressing at the same time.

I lean into the kiss, attempting to devour him on my own. I wasn't sure how much I missed this until his tongue started plunging into my mouth. It's then I realize what I could have lost. Despite my inhibitions about this lifestyle, I *have* come to care about them all. Especially Box's particular brand of crazy. I crave it, even when I say I don't.

When Box pulls a moan from my throat, I shift against Delfin's lap, feeling the sudden rigid hardness probing at my ass. It has me tearing my mouth from Box's with a gasp and shifting...

"Alright, there's time for that later," Rock grumbles. "For now, we need to know what happened to plan a fucking war."

It takes me a moment to catch my breath and to pull away from the distraction Box makes as he begins caressing my skin in tender movements.

"Um..." I push his hand away. "That won't be necessary."

Rock growls. "The fuck it won't."

"Calm down and don't growl at me," I snap. That shuts him up immediately. "It won't be necessary because the Rogue Waves are already dead."

My declaration is met with silence. Box pauses his ministrations against my body, his bright eyes widening. "Come again?" he asks.

I groan and lean back against Delfin's chest. Sensing my shift of mood, the gentle giant holds me closer. Gentle, being what I need him to be. Kind of like I was what he needed in the hallway. He's grounding me, because I have to relive that abuse as I unload it all onto them.

I start by telling them how they took me from Rock's office. I tell them everything, every fucking detail I suffered and everything Vicious said to me. I'm met with growls and low curses, but no one dares interrupt the story. Not even when I tell them how I picked the locks on my chains, how I got free, stole a gun, killed one of them, then made a bomb out of the materials they had stashed away in that room. When I talk about Blood and what he did, I feel the tension in the room. The murder drifting through like a gust of wind. Then I tell them about shooting him, and then using the bomb to blow up their compound, and finally how I stole a bike and made my way back here.

I'm met with silence at the end of the story. A shocked silence that becomes so uncomfortable, I start shifting against Delfin, but he's holding me a bit tighter, keeping me tethered firmly against him.

"I'm sorry, I thought I misheard you." Rock strokes his beard. "I thought you said you killed an MC president and its members by blowing up their compound with a homemade bomb."

I smirk. "No, I did say that."

I don't think I've ever seen Daddy Kraken look so shocked before. Or any of them for that matter. But Daddy Kraken looks especially stricken. I try not to feel offense at their shock. After all, I've hid who I really am for a long time now. What I can really do, the abilities I have.

"How in the fuck did you manage that?" Scorp demands. I don't mistake the twinge of awe in his voice.

I just shrug my shoulders in response.

"No, seriously, what the fuck—" Before he can finish his questioning, the wooden walls of the compound explode around us and the world erupts into chaos. Bullets pierce through the doors and everyone drops to the ground to protect themselves.

Within seconds, I feel my body flying over the couch and Delfin's heavy weight landing on top of me. The breath leaves my lungs and I groan, my fingers scrambling on the ground to try and pull myself out from under him, but he keeps me pinned.

"Stay down, love," he orders in my ear.

I don't have time to think about the endearment he just uttered because he's standing. I can hear the Krakens readying their weapons from my place on the floor just as the doors to the compound burst open.

There's a brief moment of collective silence and then a growled, "Where the fuck is she?"

Ah, fuck.

I push myself to my feet and peek over the edge of the couch to find a line of leather-clad assholes pointing their weapons at the Krakens.

NAOMI

F uck, fuck, fuck!

"Stay down!" Delfin tries to shove me back against the floor, but my gaze is riveted on the line of men in cuts. Bearded and tattooed, it's just another MC group come to wreak havoc on the Krakens, but in reality, I know they're so much more than that.

And if I stay hidden, I know exactly what they'll do.

I dodge Delfin's outstretched hand and start forward to dive in the middle of the stand-off. But as I'm sweeping past, a strong arm wraps around my waist and Box is pulling me towards his chest. "Where you going, sweetheart?" he demands, nibbling the lobe of my ear.

"Let go of me." I claw at his arm, but it does nothing except make him laugh in that manic way of his.

"Where the fuck you think you're going?"

I kick out my legs, struggling to get forward. I must make some sort of noise, or I must cuss Box out, because the leader of those leather-clad assholes turns his attention towards me, even while his gun is steadily pointed in Rock's direction.

I don't need to look at the image on his cut to know who the fuck he is. I'd recognize him anywhere. From that dark skin to the graying stubble along his jawline. And even if I did look down at his patches, I'd already know what they say.

Julio Cortazar.

President.

And just beneath that, the image of a ship being blown to bits.

"Stop!" I call out to him. "Just hold on a fucking minute!"

Of course, no one fucking listens to me, though I'm not sure why I'm even surprised at this point.

Men never do.

Julio's eyes narrow on my thrashing figure and on Box's possessive arm wrapped around me, not letting me go. I see the flare of rage and anger, hidden behind a cold mask.

"Let go of her," Julio demands.

"You came to shoot up my fucking compound and are now making demands?" Rock cocks his gun like he's prepared to shoot.

"Don't!" My plea likely falls on deaf ears.

"Who the fuck are you?" Rock demands.

Julio barely looks his way, and that in and of itself is an insult, from one president to another. "I think the better question here is what the fuck you all think you're doing by holding my daughter hostage, asshole."

I stop moving and groan.

Fuck.

Looks like the cat's out of the bag.

Rock

This fucking motherfucker has the audacity to come into my compound making demands? Hell no. I take him in everything from his leather boots up to the gun pointed in my direction and to his cut. There's an emblem there. One I recognize from my office.

The Shipwreckers MC.

What the fuck could the Shipwreckers possibly want with us? While there are a shit ton of MCs in the Caribbean, the Shipwreckers home base is a few hours away from our own. We've never crossed paths before. Never even been on one another's radar. They take care of their shit, and we take care of ours. That's the way it's always been. That's the way it should be.

So why are they here now?

"I think the better question here is what the fuck you all think you're doing by holding my daughter hostage, asshole."

The words register, and just like that everything seems to fall into place within moments. All of it, it all makes so much fucking sense now.

The cryptic fucking phone calls that are untraceable. Queenie's clean as fuck record. Her ability to fight and survive. To shoot. To make a homemade fucking bomb.

I never would have guessed. Never would have even fucking known if not for this.

Naomi Queen is a motorcycle club princess.

A sense of betrayal washes over me right after the realization hits. She kept this part of herself a secret. Everything we shared with her, and she hid from us the most important part of herself: who her fucking father is.

MC worlds are fucking dangerous. They always have been. And there are rules, laws that each of us must abide by. The Rogue Waves fucked up and pulled our woman into their bullshit, breaking the rules we've had established for years. We don't involve families, and we don't involve Old Ladies. There's another rule, too.

The rule that says not to fuck with a president's daughter.

Some MCs are archaic; they send their daughters off to marriage with other MCs to join forces. Women in some worlds are little more than commodities made to make the clubs stronger.

And what is Queenie?

She's ours.

She is.

I don't plan on giving her up. Even if she lied to us.

I watch, dumbfounded, as the president of the Shipwreckers aims his gun in another direction. This one at Box. The fucker just smirks in response. The president—Julio—doesn't seem to like that. He prowls forward, closer and closer. I tense. What's to say he won't shoot my club brother right then? I have a feeling the bastard could, but Queenie is right there. If he came through all this trouble to find her, he isn't going to put her in harm's way. That, I have confidence in. My instinct tells me I can be sure of it.

Fuck.

The Shipwreckers MC.

My brain wraps around that fact. Their club is fucking legendary in our circles. I recall mentioning them to Queenie just before the compound got shot at. Just before I fucked her over my desk while the logo of her father looked on.

And she didn't say a fucking thing.

Anger grips me and I cock my gun in her father's direction. The rest of his MC points their weapons in my direction. The thing is, I don't even give a fuck if they shoot at me right now. I'm too pissed. Too fucking livid at the fact that Queenie lied to us. I always knew she was keeping secrets, but something to this extent? Why would she think we didn't deserve to know? That we'd have a legendary MC breathing down our necks if anything happened to her.

She lied.
My queen lied to me—to us—and for that, she will pay dearly.

NAOMI

T he barrel of Julio's gun presses against Box's forehead after his slow prowl in our direction. It indents into his skin. The metal and gunpowder smell of it threaten to choke me, but behind me, I can feel Box release that feral smile of his as Julio digs it in hard.

"Don't bother threatening this one," I tell him. "He's into that freaky shit." Then I elbow Box hard in the gut, making him grunt. "Box, get your hands off of me."

I can feel his reluctance, but he finally does what I say. As soon as he does, I shove Julio's arm away. He puts up little resistance, but then drops his arm and turns that glare on me. I recognize it well enough by now.

I've lived with it my entire life, when he deigned to be in it, anyway.

So I know there's a lecture coming. Sure enough, he doesn't disappoint.

"We had a fucking deal, kid."

The growl he aims in my direction seems to set Box off. Within seconds, his own gun is against Julio's forehead and he's leaning into it. "Is it the deal where I blow your fucking brains out right here?" he asks.

"Box, fucking stop it." He doesn't listen, so my hands snap out against his wrist. With a few quick maneuvers, I pull the gun from him. My fingers flash across the weapon, pulling the casings of bullets out and dismembering it, dropping the pieces onto the floor. "I said fucking stop! All of you, put your fucking guns down."

Box growls, pulling me close with his hands on my hips. He nips my ear, his hands sliding over my body in a suggestive manner.

Holy fucking shit.

Mortification must shine in my eyes. I elbow him. What the fuck is he doing in front of Julio? Gross.

"I didn't know you had so many talents, Queenie."

Julio snorts at Box's words, but that humor is replaced immediately as he glares at me. "We had a fuckin' deal," he repeats.

"I know we had a fucking deal, Julio."

We stare at one another. That fucking deal has been the bane of my existence since I was a fucking kid.

"The rest of us must be missing something here." Rock's voice is low and dangerous. It sends shivers down my spine and makes me almost afraid to turn and look at him. He's pissed. I can sense it in the space that surrounds us. "What deal are you fucking talking about?"

My heart pumps up to my chest. I know what he's thinking. That I really am a spy. That I have been this whole time and I've betrayed them, but it has nothing to do with them. This deal has been one that Julio has hung over my head for as long as I can remember.

It's Julio who answers, as though reminding me of words I could never forget. "I don't care where you are. I don't care who you're with. You could be in the middle of fucking and I don't give a shit. When I call, you. Fucking. Answer."

The words seem to register around the room. Somewhere, Lourdes pipes up, "Is that why your phone has been blowing up for fucking hours?"

I close my eyes. I've kept Julio a separate part of my life for as long as I can remember. The only time we ever speak is in those moments when he's ringing me up to make sure I'm okay. I've kept him a secret from everyone, because I never wanted other to know that my fucking father is the president of a motorcycle club.

"Julio and I have a deal," I explain, my voice tight. "My sperm donor here wouldn't let me move away from home unless I agreed to his terms and conditions. One of them being I answer his phone calls no matter where I'm at, what I'm doing, or who I'm with. If I don't, he assumes the worst and tracks me down just to make my life hell." I make sure he can hear the disdain dripping from every word in my voice.

"If you're gonna move hours away from me without the club's protection, you'd better be damn sure I'm monitoring your every fucking move, Naomi. I've got too many enemies to let you out of my sight."

My eyes roll with anger and irritation. "I don't recall you ever being this fatherly when I was a kid."

It's a fucking joke, really. He never gave a shit about me growing up. If anything, my mother and I were a nuisance to him. Had I been born a man, he would have initiated me into the club. Instead, I was a hindrance he was forced to protect. In the end, I was still blood even when he didn't want me at all. Me or my mother.

"I have a question," Wire pipes up from somewhere, his voice curious. "*How* did you track her? I monitored her phone..."

Julio's jaw ticks, but it's me who answers. "Part of the deal was that he gets to know my whereabouts at all times." I pierce Julio with a glare. "Bastard had a witch put a blood tracking spell on me."

That spell has been the bane of my existence since he put it on me. I have no privacy because he is always watching. Always calling. Always there. It makes relationships hard, knowing that at any moment he can call and knows where I am all the time.

There's a collective silence as the Krakens try and process the information I've just given. I dare a glance around my gaze stopping on Rock. I regret it immediately. The look of pure betrayal that mars his features gut me. It's betrayal and anger both prominent between the crease of his brows, the sneer of his mouth, and the disdain in his eyes. He looks at me like he doesn't know who I am. I suppose he doesn't. None of them do. They never did.

See, I'm not just Naomi Queen, the girl they fished out of the ocean. I'm also Naomi Queen, the daughter of a motorcycle club president.

"Can you all just put your guns down, please?" I ask.

Another moment of silence precedes my words. It makes me want to rip my hair out, the way they're still staring at each other with distrust. I mean, I get it, it's a small room filled with a bunch of shady motherfuckers. They're so used to getting stabbed in the back, to being betrayed, that I know they won't put their weapons down easily.

"Put the guns down!" I snap. "You can have a dick measuring contest later."

"Not until I know what's going on," Julio says.

"I could say the same thing," Rock adds, glaring at me from beneath gray lashes. "How is he your father? His name wasn't on your birth certificate."

At this, Julio snorts. I want to mimic the sound.

"Fake documents."

I know they want a deeper explanation than that, but to tell them the story of my life is like ripping open parts of my flesh and stabbing at all the vulnerable places within me. But if I want everyone in this room to come out unscathed, I am going to have to reveal pieces of me that I always kept hidden.

"My mother was a club whore—honey." The words feel vile leaving my mouth. Dirty. Like they don't belong on my tongue. But I have to say them. Because they are the truth.

Not every MC respects the women that are there to please them. My mother was one of those women. Desperate for attention, desperate to become an Old Lady. I'm not sure what she was like before I came along, though I can almost guarantee that she got pregnant with me on purpose to tie Julio down. It hadn't worked as he wanted nothing to do with my mother. Hell, he hardly wanted anything to do with me.

It wasn't until I was old enough to understand that I realized what my mom was. I watched as she jumped from member to member of the MC, though none of them actually took her seriously. She was always so desperate for their attention, and I wonder now if it was really love she was after and if so why mine was never enough.

"She didn't add Julio to my birth certificate," I continue as a barrage of memories hit me from every angle. "No one knows he's my dad, and I don't go around announcing it either."

Besides, my mom left that life behind her. She no longer actively seeks the attention of the MC. She's alone. And unhappy. And every time I see her that way, I wonder if it's because she regrets me, if she regrets the fact that I wasn't enough to keep Julio tethered to her.

But if there's one thing I've come to realize, it's that Julio does whatever the fuck he wants.

"Now it's my turn to ask questions," Julio snarls. His eyes rove over my body, and I wonder if I have the remnants of bruises from my altercation with the Rogue Waves. I keep the anxiety I feel from his assessment at bay and let him look me over. I don't know what it is he sees, but I can tell it makes him angry. "What happened to you?" he demands. "I swear if these men hurt you, I'm going to burn their compound to the ground and watch as them scream within the flames."

"Geez. Dramatic, much?"

He ignores my retort, staring me down, waiting—no, *demanding* —an answer.

I have no other choice but to tell him the truth because I know if I don't, he'll kill them all anyway and I can't let that happen.

So I tell him. I tell him that the Rogue Waves were out to get me because of what I witnessed. I tell him about the storm about ramming into Box's bike, about being trapped in the compound against my will at first, of them protecting me, of the Rogue Waves catching up to me, and finally of my escape.

Julio listens to my story patiently, but throughout the whole thing I can see the way his jaw works. I know he's holding back his anger just like I know he will explode within moments. I hold my breath and wait for it because there's no stopping it. There's no stopping his anger or the words I know he'll throw at me for hiding all this from him.

Slowly, I watch as Julio lowers his gun and shoves it back in the back of his pants. He takes a deep breath, stares at me, flicks his fingers causing the rest of his club members to copy his movement lowering and putting away their weapons. It makes the Krakens do the same albeit warily.

"The only reason," he begins, "that I let you move down here without MC protection is because I'm not on your birth certificate and it's extremely hard for anyone to trace you back to me. But I told you if you fell into trouble to call me and you didn't." He glares and I feel it down to my bones. "You should have called, kid. We could have protected you."

Rock emanates a low growl. "We can protect her. We *protected* her."

Julio snorts out a mocking laugh. "Some protection you offered." He gives a pointed look at my body, as if he can see the bruises that are no longer visible on my skin.

This makes Rock bristle with offense, but surprisingly, he doesn't respond in anger. "We fucked up," he admits. "But the Rogue Waves are gone now."

I wonder how much that hurts him to admit.

"Thanks to my daughter."

The tension in the room can be cut with a knife. I hate that I'm in the middle of this. I hate that they all look like they're ready to go for each other's throats.

This is why I wanted to keep this part of my life a secret. It's why I didn't want any of the Krakens to know who my father is.

And when I stare at Rock, my eyes apologetic for the situation, he just glares back at me. I gulp past the sudden lump in my throat, and the fury burning in his eyes lets me know that I'm well and truly fucked.

SCORPION

The Shipwreckers MC.

I never would have thought a legendary MC would find themselves standing in the middle of our compound glaring at us, threatening us.

Especially not over a woman.

Come to think of it, it makes sense. How cagey she is, her cryptic phone calls, the way she knows how to handle herself against us. She never balked at being in the clubhouse, never balked at the women, at our language. She gave as good as she got, and she was able to leave the Rogue Waves compound, blowing it to bits behind her.

The truth is Naomi Queen was never an ordinary woman. She is so much more than that, and now I know why.

The problem is she lied to us in the beginning about who and what she is. Now we're facing the consequences of her actions. The truth is I want to be angry with her, but I can't bring myself to feel it wholly. If we would have known, maybe it would have saved us a lot of shit that we've dealt with since the beginning, but right now there's only tension between two different clubs who aren't rivals but are acting like it in the moment.

I know Rock wants to assert his dominance, and this is his territory so he has every right to blow out her father's brains for the blatant disrespect, but at the same time... It's her *father*. How could he do that? Julio is a legend. We're at an impasse and if I know Rock, which I do, I know he wants to reach a hand out in solidarity, but he doesn't know how. He's stoic, but I'm not and as the VP of the club, it's up to me.

"Look," I say stepping forward. "Shit got out of hand. The important thing is Queenie safe now. Everything's okay, the threat is gone, and we can now relax. Baby Gap, how about you serve our guests a drink?"

It takes a moment, but the honeys rush to do as I ask.

"Someone turn on the music!" I call out, then I step forward once the music is playing, offering my hand to the Shipwreckers MC president. Julio. Queenie's father. He stares at it a moment, and the ease with which my smile appears on my face is almost disarming.

"Scorpion," I introduce myself. "VP."

It takes only a moment, but the promise of food, drink, and music has him reaching his hand out and shaking mine. It's as much a show of solidarity as we'll get, I think. But I'll take it. And just like that, the tension in the room eases and everyone visibly relaxes.

Rock steps forward, offering his own hand. Two MC presidents size each other up and I hold my breath, watching it happen until Julio reaches for Rock. They shake, smiles on both of their faces.

"Now that you're here and everything's fine, how about a little party?" Rock offers.

We deserve it. We've been through shit the past few days, Queenie especially, and now that the Rogue Waves are gone, now that we know what happened to our brother, it's time to move forward.

As much as we can move forward. I won't deny that there's a part of me that's pissed off because Queenie lied about who she is. But confronting her will come later. That I promise in the silence of my stare and smile as I turn to look at her. She's watching us, and when her gaze snags on mine, my lips curl wider and wider, and I visibly see her gulp as the panic settles in.

She's fucked and she knows it.

NAOMI

Typical men.

They don't hold grudges like females do. One moment they're waving guns in each other's faces and the next they're partying together like they've been friends for a lifetime.

Seriously who the fuck understands them?

I watch from my place at the bar as Krakens and Shipwreckers alike mingle together. They cuddle up to the honeys, they drink and shoot the shit, music pounding through the speakers vibrating along the compound floor. It's peaceful. You wouldn't even believe that only hours ago I came out of an enemy compound, fighting for my life, zipping away on a motorcycle and leaving flames and destruction behind me.

I hate admitting it, but I am my father's daughter after all.

Speaking of, he sidles up, silently taking the seat next to me. There's a moment of quiet as we stare at the party going on. This has always been a dance between us. It's always been some kind of game. He tells me what to do and I ignore it. He lectures me and I ignore it. He calls to check in on me and I never call him 'dad'. I pretend to be annoyed, and while I am, at the same time I don't know if I should be touched or angry. The latter always wins because I feel he only protects me because I'm his blood and not because he really cares about me. I don't think he ever did. I'm just a means to an end. What end, I can't be sure. I never was, but like I said, it's a dance between us.

He pretends to care, and I pretend not to give a fuck.

"Their compound is shit." Julio finally breaks the silence between us. "Too easy for an enemy to get in."

"I know," I reply. "It's one of the first things I noticed when they brought me here."

"They're going to have to fix it up."

"Yup. Wouldn't want bullet holes decorating the walls. It frightens guests."

Julio snorts and I swear it's laughter.

Another moment of silence passes us by. "They claimin' you?"

I almost slide off the stool I'm sitting on at the question. Gross! I'm not talking to my dad about this shit. Besides why does he care who I shack up with?

My sneer and my quiet seems to be answer enough for him. He looks at me, shaking his head back and forth.

"What?" I demand.

"It just seems to me like you have this entire MC wrapped around your little finger."

My whole body bristles at the insinuation. "I don't have them wrapped around my little anything."

He picks up his glass and takes a sip. "You keep telling yourself that."

"Look..." I'm annoyed at the direction of this conversation. "I don't wanna be anyone's Old Lady." I spit the words out, saying them with so much vehemence that Julio stares at me, his eyes slowly widening as if with realization.

"Whatever," he says finally.

Good. I won't have to have this conversation with him, but as always, my father finds ways to disappoint me.

"I didn't do right by your mom."

I freeze, completely floored by the topic. I want to tell him he has no right to talk about my mother. He treated her like shit. He passed her along between his club brothers, and then when she got pregnant, he completely ignored her. He ignored me up to a point. I was only ever on his radar when he wanted to lecture me about safety, but when I needed a father figure, he was hardly there.

Sure, he showed me the skills to defend myself and that's what saved my life today, but when I wanted someone to teach me how to ride a bike, when I wanted someone to hold me at night, when I wanted someone to just be there, he wasn't. A part of me blames him for what my mom had to go through. He never paid any attention to her after she had me, and whatever attention he gave was only to toss money in her direction. Other than that, he left her alone. Because of that, she bounced between club members, hoping that she could find someone who would want her just as she was. She gave so much of herself for so long, and I was forced to watch the tears. I was forced to drive them away. I was forced to grow up before my time because she never would.

So yeah, I blame Julio. I blame his MC. I even blame my mother. Thanks to them, I got this view on life that love doesn't really exist. That no one can ever really care about another person, especially not criminals who always put their brotherhood above anyone else... Even their own family.

"You and I both know your mom wasn't Old Lady material," he continues.

This declaration should anger me, but it doesn't because it's the truth. She tried too hard to fit into the MC lifestyle, but it wasn't for her. Instead of pining after them, she should have left to find her own happiness, but she was so stuck on being a part of the MC life that she couldn't see beyond.

"You know you aren't your mom, right?"

"I know that."

Because I've tried so hard in my life *not* to be like her. I don't think I've ever hid it, and Julio can see right through me. I feel like he's always been able to do that. He seems to know what my deepest fear is; that I'll be just like her, that I'll beg and beg for a love that will never belong to me. That I'll be discarded, used, and no one will ever truly care. Maybe that's why I've been keeping everyone at bay. No —I know that's why I've kept everyone at bay. Even Lourdes.

"You ain't me, either," he says, taking another swig of alcohol. He hisses after he swallows and sets his glass down on the bar. He reaches for me, giving my shoulder a squeeze. It's as much fatherly love as I've ever gotten in years, if that's what it could even be called. Then quietly, so quietly, he leans forward and whispers in my ear, "You're better than both of us, kid."

Tears accumulate behind my eyes, but I shove them away, far away with all the other issues I keep deeply buried. With all the other fucked up things that are wrong with my life.

QUEENIE AND THE KRAKENS

He doesn't need to see how much his words affect me. I won't let him because I still hate him.

"See you, kid." He stands up, not bothering to wait for me to reply. Like he knows it'll never come. We are both so used to this dance that I know what his next words will be as he walks away. "Answer when I call."

"Whatever, Julio."

I watch his back as he walks away. A single whistle draws the Shipwreckers attention. A jerk of his head lets them know it's time to leave.

I watch as they all say their goodbyes. The Shipwreckers nod at me on their way out. Respect for the Motorcycle Club Princess.

Ugh. That fucking title.

They all file out, and as they do, the room suddenly feels smaller, more confined. Especially as the Krakens get up and crowd me one by one.

Rock. Scorpion. Delfin. Box. Slug.

I tilt my chin up, taking them all in. The anger that's shining in their eyes intensifies now that it's trained directly on me, but I don't fear it.

I don't fear them.

"A motorcycle club princess," Box drawls, those bright eyes shining with manic glee.

I make a sound of disgust in the back of my throat. "That fucking title is so demeaning," I growl.

"And inaccurate," Box adds. "You aren't a princess." He bends and the tip of his tongue slides against the side of my face. Sensual and warm, it sends a shiver down my spine. "You're a fucking Kraken Queen."

"He's right," Rock adds. "And what happens to a queen who lies to her kings?"

I keep my mouth shut, knowing damn well it's a trap.

Box giggles with glee. "She gets punished?"

Rock isn't smiling, though. None of them are except for Box. "That's right," Rock says. "She gets punished."

Box pushes into my space, his hands claiming my hips, fingers digging into my skin. Its possessive like everything else he does.

I hold my breath as his face presses closer to mine. Close until our noses squish together, and I taste the whiskey on his lips.

"This," he purrs, "is going to be so fun."

And then he jerks me to my feet, and I'm being lifted and thrown over his shoulder.

I don't fight back as he marches me down the hall. I have an inkling of an idea what's in store for me.

And just what my punishment could be.

BOX

"**N**aughty, naughty girl." My hand slaps against the curve of that luscious ass, making Queenie yelp and jerk against me.

I'm almost disappointed she isn't fighting back. A well-placed kick to my balls would only heighten the eroticism of the moment, to be honest.

Alas, she seems resigned to her fate. Dare I think it, *excited?*

A shiver crawls down my back and my balls pull up behind my hard dick. It's been weeping for her for hours, and now it'll finally get a taste of that sweet pussy.

I can feel the others following at my back, and I know they're just as eager as I am. I make my way down the hall, heading straight for my room. I'd go to Rock's, but mine has all the fun toys in it. I'm not saying the Prez is vanilla, but compared to me, he's probably a fucking saint. Given, I'm not completely aware of the sexual proclivities of the others, but at this point I don't care. I just want a taste of Queenie and Slug together. Right fucking now.

The others can watch for all I care. They want to punish Queenie just as much as I do for the lies and deceit.

If I'm honest with myself, I'm not really bothered by all that. I knew she was hiding something since the beginning. Now I know what it is. To be honest, it makes her all that much more interesting to know my Old Lady can fuck shit up when she needs to, that she's just as bloodthirsty and violent as I am. That she'll do what needs to be done, like blow up an entire compound if someone tries to fuck her over. There's something especially seductive about a woman who can handle her own.

I want to bring that side of her out. I crave the violence that she emits. I crave what she hides just beneath the surface. I want that push and pull between us. More than I want my next breath. I want to hold her down. I want her to buck against me. I want the roughness of her joining, brutal and chaotic, just like we are. When we clash together like an explosion, I want everything she has to offer me and more.

I kick open the door to my bedroom with the heel of my booted foot. The inside is dimly lit, the light bulb casting dim shades of red and blue across the walls and floor. I aim for the bed—only then does she struggle as I toss her down onto the mattress. It's fun to watch her try and squirm away from me, but before she can get very far, I drop to the bed on top of her, straddling her hips with my thighs.

"Going somewhere?" I smirk down at her, flashing my teeth. Queenie growls up at me, though the action feels halfhearted, and before she can bring her fists up to hit me where I know she's going to try, I grab her wrists, pulling them up to my headboard. I keep a pair of manacles clasped there precisely for moments like this. Usually it's Slug I keep chained up in here so I can roughly fuck his ass and suck on his cock when I want. Now, I'm using them on Queenie.

She yanks against the bindings as I close them around her wrists tightly.

"What the fuck are you doing, Box?" she demands. I note a hint of breathlessness in her voice, her chest rising and falling rapidly.

I smirk. The panes of her face are cast in light shadows, and she looks so, so beautiful. "Teaching you a lesson about honesty."

She gives a halfhearted tug to the manacles. "Let me go," she demands, though she sounds resigned to her fate.

I don't like the defeat in her eyes. I want the woman who fights back, the one who gives as much as she gets. The woman who kicked me in the dick because I pissed her off.

Pressing my hips down against hers, letting her feel the rigid hardness of my erection, I lean down into her until the tips of our noses touch. She holds her breath at my proximity, and I smirk, bending down so my tongue trails against the softest part of her neck. I trace figures against her skin over and over again until she lets out a soft sigh and her tense body relaxes a fraction. Only when it does do I sink my teeth into her, biting down hard, tasting a slight coppery tinge of blood on my tongue.

She gasps then cries out, a curse falling from her lips like it's a prayer, and I eat it up like it's me she's worshipping. She may as well be because it doesn't matter if she calls up to God.

He's not here.

But *I* am.

And I'm going to make her pay her penance.

I pull away, licking the wound clean but leaving my mark behind. She shivers again, trembling beneath me, and I look down at her with smirk. It only seems to anger her because she struggles against her bindings in earnest now. The satisfaction I feel of seeing the spitfire come out from within her is indescribable.

"That's it," I whisper. "Fight back."

She yanks hard, but all she does is dig her wrists deeper into the manacles. I like to see her squirm. It makes me harder by the second. I bear down on her with my hips, letting her feel the promise of what's to come.

Behind me, I hear the others get into place. I throw a small glance over my shoulder, watching as Rock sits on the high back chair that's perched in the middle of the room. He sits with his elbows along the armrests, leaning back, watching with his brows pulled together. Scorpion takes his own seat next to Rock while Delfin hides in the shadows of the corner of the room.

As brothers, we live on the wild side. We fuck the club honeys openly in the middle of the compound for everyone to see. I've seen everyone's dicks and they've all seen mine, so I'm not shy about them watching me now. Slug, however, is a little bit more modest, but when our eyes meet there's no hesitation in them. There's only anger, betrayal, as he stares down at Queenie beneath me.

"Come here, Sluggy," I whisper. It's like a promise, my voice low and seductive. When he and I are together, I'm the one in charge. When the both of us are with Queenie, we fight to take over. We dominate her and she has no choice but to give in.

Slug crawls up the bed behind me, constricting my view of the others, but I don't need to watch them now. All they need to do is watch us, watch me and Slug as we punish her for everything she's hidden.

Slug looks over my shoulder and we both stare down at Queenie. He's silent and her eyes are pleading at him to let her go, even as she fights the manacles, even as she tries and is unable to get away from us. I make a *tsk*-ing noise at the back my throat.

"Now, Queenie, are you going to take your punishment like a good little girl?"

She growls, snapping her teeth up at me. It's feral and vicious and I love every second of it.

"Let go of me!" she snarls.

"I don't think so. In fact, I think I'll keep you here for a good long while so that you think about what you've done."

"What exactly did I do?" Her hips snap up against mine as she tries to buck me off her, but all it does is make me bear down harder. Even Slug behind me pushes my hips down to pin her against the mattress.

From behind me Rock growls, "You lied." His voice is dark with menace and the promise of pain to come. Pain and pleasure both. The two always went hand in hand for me, and the darkness in his voice makes me shiver. Who knew our daddy could be so sexy?

"Lied about what?"

As if she doesn't know. I pierce her with a look, one eyebrow raising up to my hairline. It makes her sigh, but that expression of defiance never once flickers from her face.

"My life is my business," she snaps. "I don't have to tell you guys jack shit."

"On the contrary... You're my Old Lady. Anything that happens to you *is* my business."

"Jesus Christ." She exhales with exasperation. "I am not your Old Lady. I'm not anyone's Old Lady."

The denial spurs a shiver through me and now I know it's really going to begin.

"Not my Old Lady? We'll see about that."

Then my hands are moving slowly, steadily creeping across her body. I'm tempting her with every light caress and fierce press. First, I go down to the hem of her shirt. With all the strength I have, I grasp it, yanking and tearing it up the middle, baring her beautiful tits before me.

Her nipples are pebbled and hard, staring up angrily at the ceiling. They move up and down with every harsh breath she takes. I let my fingers hover over them, the promise of a touch building up her anticipation. Despite her saying she doesn't want this, I know that she does because her body tries to lean up towards my touch, but I hover just out of reach. Eroticism lies in the foreplay of the game, and I'm a fucking expert.

I blow a warm breath onto her nipples. The sensation alone is enough to leave her wanting... Just a whispering promise of a touch against her skin and she's trembling, wanting more, wanting what I won't give. When she lets out a sound of frustration, my fingers go to her waist, snapping at the button of her jeans.

Soon the only sounds that fill the room are her desperate panting and the slide of the zipper going down. The flaps pop open, revealing the lace edge of her panties. My mouth waters at the sight.

"Box..." Her voice is a low warning, one which I don't heed. I dip two of my fingers at the waistband of her panties, sliding my fingers in so they touch both cloth and skin. Her skin warms and I decide to tease a little more by dipping my fingers lower until my whole hand fits into her panties. Trapped beneath her jeans and silk, I run my fingertips over the coarse hairs of her pussy, sliding down the slit. I tease the edges, finding her already wet and aching for my cock. I don't dip my fingers inside even as she squirms against me, hoping that I'll take pity on her and give her a thorough exploration.

"That's my naughty Old Lady," I whisper. The words make her still just like I thought they would, and with a chuckle, I release my hand from the confines of her clothes and push back against Slug.

We move in tandem, angling our bodies so that we can yank the jeans down her legs together in a swift flowing movement. Once she's naked from the waist down, I stand at the end of the bed beside Slug, watching her legs kick out. She's surprisingly silent, but her gaze says it all. It's glaring between Slug and I. They stop briefly on Slug, *pleading.* I want to laugh and tell her that the expression she currently wears will get her nowhere. He's just as mad as the rest of them, and she'll find no solace with the most tenderhearted of the Krakens.

"Slug..." Her voice is practically a plea. She knows just as well as I that he's the one out of all of us who won't be able to stay mad at her. Hell, I can't even stay mad at her, but I also know how he feels. If she would have simply told us who her father was, everything would have gone a lot differently.

We could have joined forces with her father from the very beginning. At least, that's probably what everyone else is thinking. Personally, I would have liked to burn their entire compound to the ground from the start.

Fuck the rules.

And fuck that washed out MC.

"What to do to you first?" I swipe my tongue along my bottom lip right before I take it between my teeth. The possibilities are endless, and I make sure to put on an extra fancy show just because I know the others are watching.

I have to make this memorable, not only for me and them, but for her as well.

I have to make sure she's pleasured so thoroughly that she admits to being our Old Lady and that she'll never lie to us ever again.

Slowly I dip my thumbs into the waist of my own jeans sliding them down over my thighs. Because I'm commando, my cock springs free almost immediately, the pierced tip red and weeping for her.

That draws her attention back to me instead of Slug, who's remained silent this whole time. Shoving my jeans down past my knees I palm the underside of my dick rubbing it up and down.

The action is a promise, as are my next words.

"Here's what's going to happen," I whisper. "We're going to pleasure you, but we're not going to let you come. We're going to pleasure you so badly that you'll be begging us for release. Slug and I are going to take turns fucking *you*. We are going to fuck *each other,* and when we finish, we are going to come all over your beautiful skin. I'm going to claim every fucking inch of you, from the tips of your braids down to the tips of your toes until you're screaming and begging. I'm going to make you mine until you have no choice but to accept the fact that you're my Old Lady. That you belong to *us* and no one else."

Her breathing picks up with every word I say. I smirk at her, knowing she can't resist the allure of what I'm promising.

And just like that the torture begins.

My cock is rock hard in my hand. I tug it up and down, giving it a firm jerk. One that would seem painful to others but is perfect to me. I kick off my boots and bend to yank the rest of my pants down over my legs. Beside me, Slug does the same, pulling his clothes off in slow, drawn-out movements.

Once we're both naked, I dive in first, my knees pressing deep into the mattress of my bed. I hover over her, enjoying the view. I use my hands to press her thighs down to keep her from kicking out at me. Once she's well and truly restricted, I lean down, face hovering over her pussy. I lick a stripe up her slit, over the hairs, up to her waistline. She packs an intoxicating scent, and her body stills like she's trying so hard not to give in to the pleasure that she's knows I'm bound to give her.

That makes the challenge more fun. She should know me well enough by now to know just what I'm like.

I like a fucking challenge.

So without wasting anymore fucking time, I dive in, my tongue slipping between her folds and tasting the ecstasy and essence that is my queen.

NAOMI

I know it's coming, but my hips still lift off the bed when Box tongues the inside of me.

The warmth of his tongue explores my inner walls. It's demanding and violent and he's nowhere near my clit, and yet it still feels good just the same. I bite my lips to keep from calling out, but all I taste is blood. I avoid his gaze, knowing those sinister eyes are going to be watching my every move, in tune to my every reaction. Instead, I look up and glance at Slug who stands at the end of the bed, glaring down at us with his arms crossed against his wide chest. I know the others are behind him, but they're encased in shadows and so silent it's like they're not even there at all.

So my attention focuses only on the two who are in my line of sight.

My hips press down into the mattress, trying to get away from him, but Box's tongue is punishing. Every fierce lick is preceded by the squeeze of his fingers digging into my thighs. The rough sensation has me trembling, my clit quivering, crying out and demanding attention. Attention he doesn't give to the one place I want him to be. Instead, he focuses on the inside of my walls, leaving me breathless with his tongue. He draws one fold into his mouth, pulling on it and releasing only to do the same to the other side.

He's an expert at teasing and driving me up, just at the edge of a cliff, making me want to reach out for something that's just not quite there yet.

I try to keep my own emotions in check. I know he wants me to give in, to say that I'm his. That I'm *theirs* but I'm not. I never have been. I'm my own person and I don't belong to anyone. I didn't belong to my father back then, I don't belong to him now, and I didn't jump from freedom just to fall into the fiery pan of their own hierarchy.

I don't want to be controlled and I know they'll try to control me just like my dad has controlled me my whole life. I don't want to have to watch my every move because I'm associated with them. Just look at what happened because they dared bring me into their compound to try and protect me. It ended in chaos and death... With blood on my hands and the secret of my father revealed.

This is all reason enough to run, but Box has me trapped between him and the mattress, and all my thoughts are flying out the window with each pass of his tongue against my skin.

I try to cling on to that hesitation I've had since the beginning. I cling onto it with every scrap of strength I have left, but Box is pulling me closer and closer to their side. It's like a game of tug of war between us and I'm failing. My knees are giving out and he's tugging me harder and harder towards him, towards their side. The Kraken side where they want me to be their queen.

And when I feel myself tripping, Box eases back and just like that, I'm pushed back to my senses, nearly falling to the ground. I've held in my pants, but I can't any longer. My breathing speeds up as he hovers above me, and that alone makes my whole body tremble. He's not touching me, but my body is shaking, desperate for it. It felt like I was going to give in for a moment, but I can't. I have to be strong.

"Have something to say?" he purrs.

I hate the cockiness in his voice... like he thinks he has me. Maybe he did and I'm ashamed of myself for it, so I jerk up against my bonds, snapping my teeth, growling at him like a beast.

"I have *nothing* to say to you."

"I didn't think you would." He eases back and takes the warmth with him. He stands, clapping Slug on the shoulder. "I was just getting started," he adds, lightly shoving Slug forward.

Slug's knees hit the end of the mattress, and my neck is curved as I strain to look up at them. I tug at my bonds, but a part of me relaxes because I know Slug won't be as brutal as Box, despite the expression on his face.

I know Box would never hurt me, of course, but he gets a thrill out of these sick games. I know I can stop them at any time I want, but a part of me doesn't want to. Maybe a part of me believes that I *should* be punished. Maybe I can take this as my last memory before I leave them for good.

Slug straddles my thighs. His fat cock presses against my entrance, the tip stretching me, teasing me as it slowly slides in a single inch. My attention is pulled from him as Box loudly makes his way to the bedside rummaging through drawers.

"What the hell are you doing?" I demand.

He's looking for something, and a sick feeling seizes down my spine.

He smirks. "You should be paying more attention to Slug."

After the words are spoken, I feel a sharp slap against the side of my ass. I gasp, jerking, lifting my hips; that single movement makes Slug press deeper into me. He stretches my walls, and even though I'm wet, it still burns.

He's only seated halfway into me, making me pant heavily. I turn to Box in time to see him pull straps of leather from the drawer at his bedside. My eyes widen as I watch. The crisscrossing straps are connected to something else something long and ridged.

"Oh, fuck." The words leave me on a groan as I realize what it is.

I can do nothing but watch as he dangles it from his fingers near me. "You like this?" he asks.

I've never used a strap-on before. Never had one used on me either. I wonder what his intention is. I bite my lip to keep from blurting out my own curiosity.

I don't even get the chance to do that because Slug suddenly starts moving his hips, snapping them in rapid fire movements against mine. He slides my body up the mattress, and I'm curled against the headboard, trying to hang onto the bonds for dear life as he stretches me to max capacity.

I'm groaning, even as I try so hard to beat the noises back. Slug is brutal. Though I knew he would be, this seems to have a little bit more aggression to it. I meet him with my own, chasing my own release, trying to get there before it's denied me.

I'm vaguely aware of Box rounding the bed. There's a thump as he tosses the strap-on to the mattress beside me, and then I see his tall frame appear behind Slug. He stares down at me over Slug's shoulder

I hear the noise of a cap popping followed by a squirting, and then Slug grunts. His balls slap my flesh where he has me split open, pressing me down tightly against the mattress and pinning me there as Box grips his hips. I can't see it, but I know when it happens. When Box enters Slug in a single stroke.

Then the real fun begins.

I'm caught beneath the heavy weight of sloppy desire. It burns against my bones and scorches my veins. Box fans that fire, igniting the three of us with the brutal snapping of his hips against Slug's ass.

I'm completely stretched out, filled to the brim. The three of us work in tandem; Box pushing Slug into me, me rising up to meet the aggressive thrusts with everything I have, taking him deeper as if I could pull him into my soul.

I start screaming the moment they begin moving faster. Licks of fire crawl over my skin, ready to combust. I want to explode. I reach for the orgasm that wants to claim me, but it's still so far out of reach. Even as Slug runs his hands across my body, pinching and squeezing my nipples, raising and dropping my breasts, bending to lick all over my skin to bite softly. I just can't reach it.

Everything about this joining feels desperate. Slug's hands tantalize over me while Box grips Slug by the back of the head and pounds into him with fiercer snaps. I cry out when Slug reaches between the space where we are joined and thumbs my clit, circling the little nub in a variety of different pressures. Hard. Soft. Rough. Gentle. The contrast of sensations makes me want to cry. Just when I feel like I'm teetering along the edge and I'm going to snap, Slug groans and pulls out of me.

Jets of cum ribbon across my skin, warming my already fevered body. They fly up, landing against my chin and my lips, and my cry has me opening my mouth to taste him.

Behind him Box chuckles and I hear a slap as his palm cracks across Slug's ass.

"Are you finished already?" he teases.

Slug grunts in response, and it's followed by the slippery sound of Box pulling out.

"Take a break, my little Nug Nug."

Slug flops to the side of me, letting Box take over in front of me. I expect him to enter me as quickly as he did Slug, but instead he leans over me, his hands reaching running his fingers through the come.

Pebbled all over my stomach and body, he smears it into my skin like a lotion, scooping some up on his fingers bringing them to his lips. He groans in ecstasy like it's the best taste in the world and smears more on himself, bringing his fingers to my mouth. I keep my lips closed and he smirks, pressing his thumb to my lips.

It's a dare.

One I can't back away from.

So the tip of my tongue darts out to taste, and he shoves his whole thumb inside my mouth. I close my mouth over him, groaning at the flavor.

From beside me I feel Slug's hand on my thigh squeezing. It's a supportive gesture, and I know his anger has dissipated and I can breathe an easy sigh of relief.

"How does he taste?" Box asks. He pulls his thumb away with a pop. "Like sin?"

I purse my lips and reply, "Salty."

To my surprise, he tosses his head back and laughs, the sound echoing through the room. For a second, I'm lost in the sound. For second I can almost forget why we're here and what we're doing. But that second is all I get before he reaches for the straps that he previously tossed to my side and holds them up, dangling the strap-on above my body.

"I'm going to put this on you now," he promises.

I swear he's waiting for me to protest. I should protest. I shouldn't want any part of this. Now that the trouble is gone, I should get up and leave with Lourdes and not come back. But if this is the last time we're all going to be together, then I want this. Even if he's trying to get me to make a promise I can't afford. Even if he thinks he's going to get it out of me, he won't, but I want to give him this in return. If I can't give him anything else.

He smiles as he bends, and I help by lifting my hips up while he begins strapping the leather around me. It goes around my hips, the heavy dildo flopping cold against my fervent skin.

"What are you doing?" I ask once everything is strapped in place.

Box climbs over me, straddling me backwards. "It's your turn to fuck me, queen," he says over his shoulder.

While I want that—the very thought has my pussy leaking—I have no idea how we're going to go about it. Not with me tied up.

He must see the confusion in my eyes because he chuckles. "Slug is going to help you." The words are like a silent command because a second later Slug's hand comes between us. Box's ass hovers above me, and I watch in fascination as Slug's fingers press into Box's hole, smearing lube into the tight ring of muscles. He grips the dildo, smothering that in lube as well. He holds it upright, gripping it from the ridged base.

"Ready?" Box asks, as if *I'm* the one about to take it up the ass.

Before I can reply, his fingers dig deep inside of my folds, stretching my tight channel while his thumb works circles around my clit.

With Slug keeping a firm hold on the base of the textured dick, my hips jerk up, and just like that the tip slips into the rim of Box's ass.

He doesn't seem to need stimulation or much foreplay for this. He bears down on it, and I watch as the thick length stretches his muscles, pushing inside with the help of the lube. Slug pulls away just before the end of the whole dildo slips into his ass.

With every thrust of his fingers inside me, my own hips rise to meet him. He bounces above me, our flesh slamming together. He doesn't cry out every time we meet, instead choosing to cackle his joy into the room. I can only hold on for the ride, letting myself feel every sensation like a dangerous ache of sin.

He's above me. Inside me. I'm tied up, moving my hips into him with brutal thrusts, and yet it seems he's still the one dominating me.

I cry out, the sound muffled by Slug's mouth closing over mine. His tongue pushes past the seam of my lips while his hand encircles my neck. He squeezes, but it's not hard enough to bruise or hurt.

The domineering action coming from him is a surprise. It's both beautiful and threatening, gentle and demanding. And when he pulls away, he whispers across the skin of my cheek, "Will you be our Old Lady?"

SLUG

I t's a low blow to ask her like this. I know it. She knows it because she pulls away and moans. *"That's not fair."*

Her eyes are full of hurt but also desire. Box brings her to the brink only to pull her down again with each thrust of his fingers and movement of his hips bearing down against hers, but I can't help that the question pops out of my mouth. I shouldn't have asked, but I needed to.

Box would force her to stay here. If he could, he would keep her tied up forever, saying he was protecting her, saying she wants it. I know that maybe a part of her does, if what I'm reading in her eyes is correct. I can see that she cares for us, but when you care about something you don't lock it away. You don't keep it trapped, and if we forced Queenie to stay here, she'd grow to resent us. That's not caring, and it's certainly not love.

Yes... *Love.* Because I've grown to love and care about Queenie. It'd be a lie if I said I wasn't hurt that she didn't trust us enough to tell us her truth, especially when I bared my own so openly. At the same time, I understand when we didn't start off on the best of terms.

And all the anger at the lies is blown away by the relief I feel. The relief that she's okay and that the Rogue Waves didn't harm her like they could have.

This feels like a fresh start. Like we can finally move forward without that MC looming over us. I know Box is doing this because he wants to prove a point and make her lose all her inhibitions. He wants to hear that she will give us a chance, even now that she doesn't need our protection anymore.

But Queenie doesn't see it that way. After getting to know her story, I can comprehend why she doesn't want to trust us. She doesn't want to become a statistic—to become like her mother. I respect that, but I want to shake her and say, "We aren't like him. We aren't like your father. We're not going to discard you like he did your mother. You can trust us..."

I know instinctively she won't believe those words, and I don't know what it's going to take to convince her to stay. To convince her that we would adore her and not step out on her. Not even Box who, despite his fucking insanity, would be loyal to her forever.

"I know," I whisper against her skin, feeling my heart breaking piece by tiny piece.

Drawn back into the moment at hand, with Box torturing her body slowly, I give her another kiss, pouring all my love and affection into the single action. I help bring her to heights of pleasure, flicking my fingers over her pebbled nipples, squeezing and pulling.

Her flesh is soft beneath my hands. Delicate, but she's not the hopeless woman that everyone thought she was when she arrived. She's so much more than that. She's a true Kraken Queen, and I know just how much we all want her.

Rock, Scorpion, and Delfin are silent in the background, the only hint that they're there at all is the harsh panting that occasionally escapes their lips. I know Box calculated this position perfectly, giving them an unobstructed view of her body. He's giving them a show, opening her pussy lips up so they can see him fuck her like she deserves to be fucked.

I know Queenie is about to come because she cries out. Only, Box pulls back at the last moment. She lets out a frustrated groan against my mouth, biting the bottom of my lip, drawing blood. I pull away slowly, my own dick hardening. I turn towards the source of her irritation. Box leaves her on the edge so he can grip his own cock. He jerks it like he's brutalizing himself, pleasure going hand in hand with the pain.

Suddenly, Rock and Scorpion move in unison, like hearing her cry out was the last straw for them both. They stand, prowling over to where we're at just as Box finishes pulling the dildo from his ass. He turns at the last moment, still jerking his hard cock in his palm, and he comes, squirting jets of it out on her face and opened mouth.

He bends, slapping a hand over her lips. She moans, and that sinfully low voice of his echoes through the room. "Swallow me," he orders.

Her eyes stare defiantly back at him, but all he does is smirk.

I know why he wants her to. His body vibrates as they stare at one another, all but daring.

Box is desperate. He's wild and free. He's shown me what it is to want without inhibitions, to take what I deserve because the world is cruel and no one gives anything for free. That we have to rely on our own strength sometimes and to not be ashamed.

But Queenie's different.

He can try and take as much as he wants, but even beneath the façade, he's unsure of what the result will be. He wants her to stay, but like the others, he has no idea if she will. So he makes her swallow every last drop because it's his way of giving her a piece of him. Of putting a bit of himself within her to keep their souls tethered together somehow.

The thought of it makes me sad, and I want to say something, but I bite my tongue because I won't dim his own hope with the darkness that invades my thoughts. The thought that maybe, after all this is done, Queenie doesn't want to be kept.

And she doesn't want to stay.

NAOMI

The taste of Box is sharp on my tongue, and yet I swallow it down. Every last drop of it. It's only when I do that he removes his hand from my mouth, and it's only then that Slug reaches tenderly, wiping at my skin with a discarded shirt.

Box slides away, both him and Slug making room for Rock and Scorpion. When they approached, I can't be sure. But they loom over me like shadows. Like danger. It does something to my insides, makes them melt into goo.

The Kraken President glares at me. If I could hear emotion within a single gaze, my ears would be thrumming with the sound of anger. And if looks could kill, I'd be dead twice over.

The tattoos are stark against his skin even in the dimness of the room. The graying of his hair rimmed around his head like a halo, angelic and contrasting the expression he currently wears.

I can't even tear my own gaze away to glance at Scorpion. Not when fear and Daddy Kraken hold me entranced.

Rock doesn't speak, and he tears his gaze away from me as if I burned him. That hurts. It shouldn't, but it does, and the conspiratorial look that he shares with Scorpion makes me shudder. They speak without words. Within moments, Scorpion is grabbing my ankles, twisting my body so that I'm face down on the mattress. My arms scream out in protest at the twisted position, and I start squirming, struggling, kicking out at Scorpion to let me go.

As if he ever would.

As if I even want him to.

Not when I want my own release so badly.

My curses muffle against the bedsheets. Those curses become garbled screams as a palm suddenly strikes down on my ass. The surprise of the sting makes me freeze, and I curse when another one lands, finally reacting by thrashing my body.

Daddy Kraken's voice stops me cold. "You lied."

"I didn't lie!" I spit out, the pain on my ass traveling up to my hips and wrapping around me, tickling my clit. I shouldn't find being smacked arousing, but I do.

"No," he agrees. "You just kept the truth from us and that's the same thing." His voice is a growl in the darkness.

A part of me wishes I can turn around and look at the expression on his face. Another part of me remembers how terrified I am of what I might find there. Something that might crumble my walls and keep me tethered to them forever.

I know I'll find disappointment in that stare. Disappointing others has never bothered me before, but I find now it does, and I don't like it.

I don't say any of this, though. I don't rip my chest open and show them every vulnerability that lives beneath my skin. I've done enough of that today, and right now I only want to be fucked. I want to be punished. I want to receive whatever it is they have to give me, and then I want to leave.

I want to leave and never look back.

"How do you think you would have reacted if you'd have known the truth about me? Would you have rejoiced? Would you have called my fucking father and told him to come down and take me off your hands?"

His silence is answer enough. He's the club president, and while his pride would have told him that he could handle the situation with the Rogue Waves, if he would have known even for a second who I really was, he would have called my father.

He idolizes the Shipwrecker MC. That much is obvious from all the posters on his wall. He would have felt like it was his duty to turn in the Shipwrecker Princess back to her kingdom.

And just like that I would have been locked up all over again.

If Julio would have known what was going on here, he would have come down an instant, and I would have had to say goodbye to my entire life. All because of Rock and his misplaced sense of duty.

"You would have betrayed me," I whisper into the blankets, but he hears me.

A moment later another slap resonates through the room, this one on my left ass cheek. I squirm, pressing my pelvis down into the blankets. The friction it causes against my clit is just a brief reprieve. His palm cracks out, slapping me on the other one. He repeats the movement several times until my ass is screaming and probably bruising at this point.

"Box is right," Rock says in between pauses. I'm gasping, biting down on the sheets so I don't give him the satisfaction of crying. "You're going to be punished."

I feel hands on my waist lifting my body. I'm amazed I still have strength to leave my ass up even after the hands disappear.

The position is really uncomfortable. My arms twisted, my ass in the air...

Hands that I know are Scorpion's shove my braids away from my face, twisting them into a coil over my shoulder. He's gentle with me, and the unobstructed view I get from my peripheral is of him, taking his bottom lip between his teeth and an expression that breaks my heart.

The thought flies away when Rock's hand slaps down against my pussy this time. I jerk forward, my arms twisting. I bite into the sheets.

"This is for lying," he says. Another slap echoes. And another, and another. He doesn't tell me what each hit is for, leaving me to guess, but all I'm thinking about is the pleasure that's dripping down my inner thighs each time his hand connects to my skin, alternating between my ass and pussy.

The sharp sting of pain reverberates up my clit. It nearly causes me to come right then and there, but Rock pulls back. His big hands massage the globes of my ass.

Thick digits dive in between my folds. Rock's. He doesn't take his time with me, and he's not gentle, shoving his fingers inside, stretching me to my fullest capacity. I moan, hips jerking and gyrating in search of the pressure I desperately need against my clit.

His fingers leave me, and I despair at the lack of contact.

"Are you our Old Lady or not?" he demands.

"No."

A slap makes me jump.

"Are you our Old Lady?"

I'm panting when I answer, "No."

Another slap.

"Are you?" he demands, his voice guttural.

He wants to break me, but he's really fucking foolish if he thinks he can tear me apart.

"Daddy, I am unbreakable."

He growls at that, and with a vicious command to Box, I suddenly find myself free from the confines of the handcuffs. I fall into the mattress, my shoulders aching. I don't get a moment of reprieve before I'm being flipped around, twisted this way and that.

When I'm face to face with Rock, he snarls. I can almost taste the whiskey on his breath. "Are you," he repeats slowly, carefully, "our Old Lady?"

I stare him in the eyes. I'm fearful but also wet with anticipation as I dare to reply, "I am not."

"Then what am I to you?"

My lips twist up into a sultry smile. "You're my Daddy Kraken."

The steel in his eyes flares to life like the barrel of a gun.

"Then you'll beg your *daddy* for forgiveness," he growls and flips me. I fall on to all fours and Rock crowds behind me. There's a slap on my ass, but at this point I don't feel the pain anymore. I hear the sliding of a zipper, the rustle of jeans, and then I feel Daddy Kraken's cock against my opening. He teases me, sliding the tip of himself between my folds.

I try to lean towards him, but he keeps me steady, digging his hands into my waist.

"Stay where you are," he orders.

There's another moment of silence, more wrestling, and then Scorpion is climbing onto the bed in front of me, kneeling. Naked.

I didn't get to see him fully naked back at the bar, but *fuuuuck*. I *knew* he was packing a prize-worthy eggplant cock beneath his jeans.

I know what that monster feels like inside me. I know the sounds he makes when he comes, but seeing him like this is nothing short of glorious.

Of all of them, Scorpion is the prettiest. The barbed wire tattoos look like the vines of roses, thorny and imperfect, as they climb up the side of his face, all the way down his arms and chest. There are other images as well. Of waves, of a Kraken, of bleeding roses and grim reapers, all woven against his skin like a tapestry.

They're all beautiful in their own right.

But there's something special about Scorpion's gleaming, honey eyes and the texture of his beard and the callouses of his hands.

Scorpion takes my chin in the palm of his hand. Lifting my head, he looks me in the eye. His expression is tender, hurt, and filled with thousands of emotions I don't want any to name.

"Hey, pet," he greets. The name is enough to make me want to move, but I stiffen because the head of Rock's dick pushes inside me, spreading me wide. He slowly drags out the movements, inserting inside me inch by inch.

"Pet." Scorpion draws my attention back to him.

"Yes?" I ask breathlessly.

"You're gonna put my whole dick in your mouth." The words are a command. The VP is authoritative, a side of him I haven't seen before. So when he swipes his thumb across my bottom lip, pulling it down and almost daring me to open my mouth, I follow his command like it's instinct. "Good pet," he praises, and I groan because being praised for sucking cock is a turn-on.

Who knew?

My mouth opens and he tilts his pelvis forward, the mushroom head of his dick kissing my lips. He pushes it past my lips, forcing my mouth open wide. I pull the length of him inside while Daddy Kraken pushes further into me from behind. He starts thrusting without preamble, every movement rough. Hairs from his chest tickle my backside, and every movement pushes me to take Scorpion deeper.

I can only take half of him before I start feeling him in the back of my throat. His palm cradles the underside of my chin softly. Every touch is a tender encouragement and like Box and Slug, I'm very aware of the contrasts between the two men on either side of me. Brutal and aggressive, tentative and soft.

When the tip of his dick starts pushing towards the back of my throat, I pull away, only to be stopped by Scorpion's grip tightening on my chin. My eyes flick up to him.

"You can take it all, pet."

My heart stumbles in my chest. He says the words like he's so sure I can do it. Like he fucking believes in me. It's not a dare that makes me want to fight against him, but something that makes me want to prove myself to him.

When he sees the submission in my eyes, he pushes deeper down my throat. I relax my jaw, flicking my tongue against the underside of him. Velvety and smooth, yet thick and long, I start gagging against him. I try to breathe through my nose, to control that reflex, but my eyes begin to water.

From behind me, Rock pushes deep inside me, shoving me against Scorpion until the tip of my nose touches his stomach. I groan around his length. Holy fuck, they're both so deep inside me that the three of us take pause, waiting a single moment to breathe through the intensity of our joining. Then we move in tandem.

I hollow my cheeks and begin bobbing up and down against him. I try to keep my own pace, but with Rock's thrusts, I move just as brutally. Scorpion holds my braids away from my face, his hips moving in sync with me. He rotates his hips like he's dancing, and eventually my eyes stop watering as I get used to the pace they've set.

My body is on fire. I'm warmed over every inch and filled to the brim in every crevice. My pussy clenches tightly down on Rock, spasms of electricity sliding across my hips and clit. It quivers, ready and desperate for release that he doesn't give me. But he chases his own. I know it's close and I try to reach mine as well, simultaneously pulling it out of Scorpion, flicking my tongue faster and faster against him.

Their grunts become a soundtrack around me, so I know the exact moment when it's going to happen. Scorpion doesn't pull his eyes from me as he comes, shooting jets of come down the back of my throat. I almost choke before he pulls out, closing my mouth firmly with the palm of his hand and forcing me to swallow.

I can hardly even do that. Cum drips out from the sides of my lips, and I struggle for breath while Rock is still pounding into me from behind. He slows his pace, though, giving me time enough to swallow and take a breath.

The charged air changes a fraction. I'm panting, my entire body aching, still on that precipice but with no end in sight. I can barely move myself, my body languid and drugged as Scorpion moves me, lifting me with Rock still deep inside me. He pushes me back, leaning me against Rock's chest. I'm all but draped over the President, his whiskey-filled breath fanning harshly against my fervent skin.

His big palms grip my inner thighs, pushing them open until my hips are screaming. A hand trails over my skin. It feels like he's bringing me down from my high all while torturing me back to that desperate place. Especially when his fingers meet the place where we're joined together. His dick pulses hotly inside of me, and he grazes the edges of my open pussy lips. Then his fingers flick higher, right against the nub of my desire.

He presses down and I groan, my limp body jerking. I try to pull away from the contact, squirming against his body because my own is just too sensitive. They've played me too long that my body either wants to be granted what it's been teased with or to be left alone.

"Stay still," Rock orders against my ear.

"I—I can't—! I need—"

"What do you need?" he rasps.

"I need to come."

In front of me, Scorpion chuckles. "Think we should let her?"

The bed dips on either side of Scorp, and Slug and Box appear in my line of vision. "I don't know," Box says, sliding his tongue along his bottom lip. "Will you be our Old Lady, Queenie?"

"You—bastards—"

Rock pinches my clit between his fingers, causing me to scream out.

"Wrong answer." Box smiles down at me, but it's Scorp who moves. He leans down and I watch through hooded lids as he levels his mouth where Rock's hands are.

"Hold tight then, Queenie," Scorp whispers while Rock removes his hand.

Scorpion licks over my clit at the same time Rock surges his hips upward.

And then I'm lost in oblivion.

SCORPION

Sniffling wakes me in the middle of the night. My body rolls, coming into contact with Queenie's warm frame. I crack my eyes open and am greeted with the sight of her tears glistening in the darkness. It makes me instantly alert.

"Queenie?"

She shifts on the bed, the chains on her wrists clanking with the movement. At some point last night, Box put them on her again. We all had our fun, taking turns with her over and over again, edging her and not giving her release. Box kept her tethered to his bed to prevent her from giving herself release.

His form of emotional manipulation, probably.

Now that I'm faced with the sight of her tears, a sick feeling coils in my gut.

I've seen Queenie cry once. It was over her coworker. I don't want to see her cry again. Not while she's in bed with us.

"What's wrong?" I press close to her, draping my body over her side. The bed is big enough for all of us to fit, however the only ones here are Box and Slug. Rock and Delfin left at some point in the night, but I couldn't bring myself to do the same.

I needed to be next to her like I needed to breathe.

"Like you care?" she snaps. Her voice isn't loud, though it makes Box stir a fraction before he falls back into a deep slumber, cuddling close to Slug.

I drop my voice low. "Contrary to your belief, I do give a fuck about you." Then to prove the point, I reach for the manacles, unclasping them from her wrists. That position can't possibly be comfortable.

Once she's free, she slumps against the mattress and turns her tear-stained face to me. The glare in her eyes pierces my chest in a way that makes sure I don't dare reach for her.

"Queenie..."

She groans, dropping back to the mattress. Her hands move down her completely naked body where she grips herself between her legs. "Scorp..." She moans my name like a prayer. "Please... please let me come."

Wet noises of her touching herself fill the room. It's sloppy and without rhythm, punctuated by the soft sound of her sobs.

"Stop." My hand clasps against her wrist, stopping the movements. Before she can protest or jerk against me, I push her flat against the mattress and climb over her.

The relief I see in her eyes threatens to melt me. "We went too far," I whisper.

"Scorp..."

"I'll make it better, pet." I nudge my cock against her entrance. "I promise." I press inside her and she clamps around me, pulling my cock into her warm heat. We groan together at the feel.

"Please, Scorp. Please." She begins chanting the words like a prayer.

"I've got you, pet." I thrust forward again and again. Rolling my hips, rubbing up against her sweet spot. She mewls, her nails clawing at the skin on my back as she rises to meet me.

It only takes a few movements, only a few thrusts for her to cry out. Her orgasm comes, hard and fast. One on top of the other, as if they had been built up this entire time. Her body squeezes mine, her cunt milking my dick and ripping the orgasm out of me without warning.

We shudder together, panting and inhaling one another's breaths.

Our foreheads touch as we come back down from the pleasure. Her eyes are sealed tightly closed, the tears still sticky against her cheeks.

"You know we'd never do anything you didn't want us to do..."

Her eyes open at my words. "I know," she whispers.

"Did we hurt you?"

Her bottom lip wobbles. "My pride is bruised, but I wanted it. I feel better now, thank you."

"My pleasure."

We're silent for a moment, and suddenly the weight of our own reality is pressing between us. The fact that it's probably almost sunrise. The fact that I can still see the truth in her eyes that she wants to leave.

I sigh. "If you want to leave, we will let you go."

Her eyes tear up all over again. "I don't know what I want, Scorp."

Emotion clogs my throat. She says that, but I'm not sure she has it in her to stay. I press a soft kiss to her lips. "Let's go to sleep, pet."

And I hope that when I wake, she'll still be lying in my arms.

Though that's a dream that seems too far away.

DELFIN

It's early morning when Queenie sneaks out with Lourdes in tow. They both freeze at the sight of me sitting on the couch, like they were both caught doing something wrong. Queenie offers her friend a nod, and Lourdes stalks out of the compound quietly.

Leaving me alone with an approaching Queenie.

My mind flashes back to everything I witnessed done to her the night before. It'd been like a gift to witness. While I wanted to join in and touch, my body remained frozen in the shadowy corners of the room, and all I could do was watch them pleasure her.

My own cock remained hard as hell beneath my pants. It wept for her touch. For her mouth. Her hand. Hell, even for her eyes to give it a little glimpse.

But I wasn't like my brothers. I wasn't comfortable with fucking openly. Oh, I could watch, but I wouldn't let them see me. I never have and I won't.

It's not just because of the scars that mar my body. I have my reasons...

"Delfin..." Queenie looks over me. I wonder if she's waiting for me to stop her. I won't. She's free to come and go as she pleases now that the threat on her life has been eliminated.

"You should hurry," I tell her. "Before Box wakes up."

The fucker will probably try and tie her to the bed again.

She's quiet a moment. "You aren't going to try and stop me?"

I look up at her, strings of hair webbing across my vision. "Why would I stop you?"

Something flashes across her eyes, but I've no idea what it is. "I thought after last night—"

A growl cuts her short. "After I watched you get fucked?"

I don't know why those words escape me, or why I'm being so crass towards her. I'm not bitter that she's leaving. Fuck, I expected it. I think I'm more irritated with myself, and I'm taking it out on her. I'm a bastard. A real bastard.

Taking a breath, I settle a calm gaze on her, though inside I'm a storm. I try to shove all emotion down. It'll hurt less when she inevitably walks out the fucking door.

"Sorry," I apologize. "I shouldn't have said that."

She gives me a rueful smile. "You're right, though."

There's another beat of silence in which the anxiety tries to grapple with me.

"Why didn't you join?"

I jolt at the question. "What do you mean?"

"Why didn't you join us?"

A strangled laugh comes out of me. "That's what you want to know?"

She blinks and crosses her arms across her chest. Her skin is covered in bruises and love bites from last night. And she looks so beautiful.

"It doesn't matter."

"Delfin." Her cutting voice is an order.

"Jesus..." I can't say no to her. And she knows it. She's a shining star and I'm the fool addicted to her light. "I didn't join because I have a monster inside me, Queenie. You've seen it."

It's a suffocating force. One that pulls me under and drowns me despite being able to breathe underwater. The way I lose myself with the sounds of gunshots and violence...

"Delfin..."

"I don't want to hurt you, Queenie. I don't know if that monster would emerge and what it would do."

She steps forward until our knees are touching. I want to flinch away from the touch like I've been doing since I met her, but I hold steady, trying not to be a fucking coward. But then she climbs on me, lifting one leg and another, draping herself over my body.

Her firm hand takes hold of my face, keeping our eyes tethered. "I know you wouldn't hurt me."

"No, you don't."

She pauses a moment. "When you were... When you were having your panic attack in the hallway, how did you break out of it?"

I blink slowly. "I heard your voice."

She smiles knowingly. "Exactly. If my voice pulled you out, then why would you think you'd hurt me? Have you hurt anyone else before?"

I want to gasp on the pain that suddenly wants to rise. "Not women. Just... bad people. Men. Our rivals. To protect the club."

She nods as if she understands. "So why do you think you would do anything to me?"

God this woman. She was too fucking precious for words. "I—I don't know."

She shoves aside long strands of hair. "I wouldn't do anything that makes you uncomfortable..."

My dick tightens at those words alone. She feels fucking incredible above me, her body like a dream. But I still can't bring myself to touch her. Not unless she knows...

"I killed men," I confess. "Hundreds... I've shot them point blank. I've blown them up and I—" I swallow. "I've lost just as many as I've killed."

Her fingers pass over my scars, tender kisses of her skin against mine. Every touch feels like she's healing pieces of me, putting my fucked up self back together again. She doesn't ask me how I got them, but I think it's self-explanatory.

War. That's what happened.

And it took away bits of me until I became unrecognizable and hated myself. But Queenie doesn't hate who I am.

And maybe that's enough...

"I've killed men, too," she whispers.

Because we couldn't protect her.

"I hate that for you." My hands finally move, grasping her wide hips.

She smiles. "I hate that for you, too."

I don't know who moves first. We meet somewhere in the middle. Our lips come together, a clash of teeth and tongue. Of a desperate need for connection.

My fingers tangle within her braids, my touch gentle despite my want. She grinds down against me, my hips rising to meet hers.

"Delfin," she moans when we pull away. "I need you."

She has got to be sore from the night before, but she's grinding down against me hard.

Slowly she pries away from me, standing in between my legs. We stare at one another. Silent, seeking permission.

Do I want to take this step? The question is burning in her eyes. In answer, I reach for the hem of her shirt.

"Yes..." I whisper.

I tug at the shirt, pulling it from her body. I gently toss it to the ground then reach for her pants. We wrestle with her button as she kicks off her boots. Once she's bare before me, her hands reach for my own pants. I lift my hips as she yanks them down to my thighs.

Then she's climbing on top of me, pressing her wet folds against my weeping dick. I groan as she rubs herself against me.

She's taken control and I let her. She keeps me focused, and her warm skin calls to me. My lips meet her neck, nipping and biting against her pulse.

I take my cues from her panting breaths and from what I witnessed last night. I know what she likes from observing her with the others, but I'm gentler, letting her set the pace she wants.

She sinks her way down onto me, pulling my dick inside her until her bottom touches my thighs. I groan, biting a bit harder onto her neck and making her arch into me.

"Jesus..."

She chuckles and then begins to move. She bounces on my cock; every time she comes back down, her flesh slaps down onto mine.

She sets the pace, moving fast then slow, and I'm along for the ride. And I fucking love it. I love her taking control, love how she's giving me what I need. What we need from one another.

"Fuck." I tug on her braids, making her gasp. I swallow the sound with my own lips, pulling a piece of her into my body.

I start moving, meeting her thrust for thrust. The moment is moving too quickly, and I mean to savor every moment. I mean to savor the feel of her and cherish it for the rest of my fucking life.

We groan as we rise and fall together, and the crest of the waves come. I feel it in the base of my spine, in the tightening of my balls.

She squeezes me harder as her orgasm approaches. And together, we fall.

Our groans are captured against each other's mouths. I kiss her deeply.

Because I know this is the last chance I'm ever going to get.

I feel the finality of it as we catch our breaths. As she pulls away. It takes a moment for her to extricate herself from me. She stands, my release and hers glistening at her thighs.

Without a word, she pulls herself back together, and once she's dressed, she reaches for me.

Our lips whisper a kiss. And she pulls away, her eyes glistening.

"Goodbye, Delfin."

I say nothing as she walks away, the door to the compound closing behind her. That click is finality, and as soon as she's gone, there's a hollow echo in my chest.

"Goodbye, Queenie."

NAOMI

Days pass and eventually they become weeks. I fall back into my routine exactly the way it had been before the Krakens ever came barreling into my life. Eventually, things become so routine that I could have forgotten that the Krakens even ever existed at all. That I never got to know them.

That I was never hit by Box's bike.

That I was never wooed by Slug's twerking.

That I'd never called Rock 'Daddy Kraken.'

That I never witnessed Delfin's flashback.

That Scorpion never called me 'Pet'.

I try to pretend they are easy to forget. That I can erase them from my mind. I even tried to forget those first few days. Determined to be happy with my decision to abandon the compound and them, I throw myself back into work.

With the hurricane gone, the waters and seas calm, work proceeds as normal. Or as normal as can be. I step into the halls and imagine the blood staining the glass, of my friend's half-shifted body hanging from a tank of sea water.

I close my eyes against the memory the moment it hits and force myself to push forward.

It doesn't work.

Not when my phone rings and rings. I ignore it out of habit that first time, and when it begins ringing a second, I pick it up.

"What?"

"Kid, we had a deal."

Usually, I would respond to Julio's assholeness with my own, but at this moment I can't bring myself to do it. I just grunt into the receiver, and he pauses. The silence stretches on for minutes, and all he can hear is my breathing.

"Kid," he mutters finally.

"What?"

"Give them a chance."

I suck in a breath the moment he says it, but before I can retort, he hangs up, and I'm stuck right back where I started.

Trying to move on from what had happened to me while every thought was bombarded with the past and my own feelings.

I'm not the type of woman to wallow. Fucking ever. If someone didn't want to be in my life, then they could fuck their way right out the door. But the thing is, I am the one who always turns away before anyone can do that to me.

Because I refuse to be like my mother. I refuse to let others stomp all over my heart. To use me. I refuse to become the type of woman who is too desperate for love that I eventually forget the most important thing of all.

That I need to love myself more than anyone else could ever love me.

And it's only with that in my heart that I'm able to move forward.

No matter how badly it hurts.

SCORPION

I'm drowning myself in booze at Shark Mouth when Sugar finds me.

"Jesus, Trinidad, what the fuck?"

I ignore her, pulling a swig of whisky into my mouth. The burn has long since passed, and I'm so numb I don't know what reality is anymore. I only remember what once was. What it felt like weeks ago before now, when I wasn't a sad sack of shit pining after a woman who wants nothing to do with me or my club.

Every drink I take feels like another mark of her on my mind.

I easily remember what she felt like in those last few moments we had together. I remember the feel of her legs wrapped around my waist, pulling me deeper into her with every slide in and out. The way she was putty in my hands. In that moment, I felt I could have molded her into anything and everything I wanted. I could have gotten her to agree to anything.

Except, apparently, to stay.

I want to throw the bottle across the bar and watch it shatter. I want to start a fight. I want my knuckles to bleed so I can focus on the pain instead of her expression as we came together. The expression of a woman who was going to leave me.

"Scorpion!"

Fingers snap in front of my face, and I pull the bottle away from my mouth with a growl.

"The fuck do you want, Sugar?"

My sister is glaring at me with her hands on her hips. Her lips are pinched together, her brows pulled in anger. She's been trying to get through to me for days, but I grew sick of her constant nagging so decided to lose myself here in the bar.

"You're a fucking mess, dude," she says. "Come back to the compound."

"Nah." Too many memories.

I'm not sure if I say those words aloud because her eyes soften around the edges and she looks... pitying. Fuck.

"You really think it's better here at the bar where you first met her?"

It's not. Nothing is. Nothing will get rid of this sensation in my chest like there's a huge piece of me missing. I don't know what to do with the emptiness, so I fill it with the alcohol because that's all I can do. Because if she's not here, I'm fucking lost.

"Oh, little brother..." Sugar sighs.

And I know I said those words aloud, and because I don't want to open myself up any more than necessary, I turn back to the bottle. This time, instead of trying to convince me to leave, Sugar takes a seat next to me and orders herself a glass.

ROCK

I'm a fucking dumbass.

I am the President of a fucking Motorcycle Club and I'm wallowing around in self-pity like the rest of my members. Instead of going out and riding on the waves of the sea like an actual member of the club, I'm sitting behind the new door of my office, a glass in hand, drowning myself in alcohol like a dumb ass.

I shouldn't be doing this.

I'm the fucking leader of one of the most feared clubs in the Caribbean.

If I want something, all I have to do is take it. And what I want is Queenie.

But I tried. We all did. We all tried to fucking keep her here with us and it didn't work. I'm not going to fucking grovel.

Fuck that.

We can have whoever the fuck we want. We have club honeys in abundance. Women trip over themselves to get to us. I don't need her. We don't need her.

Fuuuuck, who am I even kidding?

With a sigh, I take another swig of my drink and slam the glass down. For days I've been lying to myself. I've been trying to purge Queenie from my system by drowning myself in paperwork and the many legitimate businesses the club has going. I've even given the members free reign to do whatever the fuck they want.

I admit I'm not at my best. I'm like a fucking love-sick teenager who got his heart broken for the first time. It's pathetic... and yet I can't shake the depression that's consumed my bones like a layer of skin. But that's just what Queenie is. She's a clinging force that I can't just claw off, no matter how badly I want to.

I've tried putting her out of my mind by drinking myself stupid, working, and even using club honeys. The latter failed completely because my treacherous dick couldn't get it up and the club honeys want nothing to do with me.

It's like they know Queenie's the one in my heart.

That or they blame me for her leaving.

But I can't keep her here against her will. I did it once and she hated us for it. It made her leave and not look back.

If I did it a second time, I know just how much it would make her hate me. Us. More than she probably already does.

More than once I've had Wire track the location of her phone. She hasn't been hiding from us. More like she just picked up her life right where it left off.

Like we'd never been a part of it in the first place.

With a groan, I slam the glass back down against the table, only this time it cracks, splintering and leaking whisky down against the surface.

I just watch each drop pool into a wider pool until my glass is empty. Just like the hollow echoes inside my own chest.

The empty hollows where Queenie should have been.

SLUG

"Where the fuck are you going?"

Box doesn't break his stride. Instead, my words seem to make him that much more determined to continue stomping towards his motorcycle. He doesn't even look at me until he hops on, straddling it with his strong thighs.

"Mind your business, Nug Nug."

Weariness presses down against my bones. The past few weeks have been their own special brand of hell. Ever since Queenie walked out of our lives, things around the compound have been tense. I never expected them to be happy, but I didn't think this would happen.

I, more than anyone, knew what effect Queenie had on Box as well as the rest of the club members. But particularly with Box. Others probably thought it was a passing fancy, something he could easily distract himself with until something new and better came along.

I know the truth.

"You can't kidnap her." I move to stand in front of his bike, and he freezes with his hand on the key, ready to start it up.

The scowl forms on his face. There's no smile, just unbridled rage he's having a hard time containing. "Get the fuck out of my way, Slug."

I cross my arms across my chest. "I know what you're up to," I accuse. "I won't let you do it."

"She belongs with us."

"Not if that isn't what she wants."

Box starts his motorcycle, his answering snarl drowned out by the reverberations of his beast. He can barrel me down with his fucking bike if he wants to, but I'm not moving from my spot.

Box reads this from my expression and revs the engine. "Get. Out. Of. My. Way."

"Why? So you can go stalk her? Bring her back against her will?"

"Fuck! Don't you understand, Slug? I will do whatever it takes to get Queenie back. Whatever it fucking takes."

And I have to hit him with a hard truth, one I know he isn't going to want to hear. "She will hate you. Really hate you. It won't be just pretend this time." His eyes flash at those words because he knows they're true. He knows what the consequences of his actions will bring. I push on. "You'll drag her back against everyone's wishes, and when you lock her up, she will dream about the day she gets to leave. She will plot her escape every minute of every day. She will try to get away from us, and where she once loved us, there will be nothing but loathing instead."

"Shut the fuck up, Slug." He pushes himself off his bike and prowls towards me until we're toe to toe. His nostrils are flaring, taking me in. I see the way his fists clench and wonder if he's going to take a swing at me. He's never done it before, but I'm not afraid of him.

I'd give my life for him, just like he'd give his life for mine. We owe each other that and so much more.

"She'll hate us, Box. More importantly, she will hate you."

"Shut up!"

"You can't make someone love you, Box. Life doesn't work like that."

We'd spent almost our entire lives on the streets. We've had to fight and scrape for every fucking thing we've ever owned. It's no surprise that Box thinks he can earn her love by force. I want Queenie's love as much as he does, but he can't take away her right to choose.

"What if she doesn't choose us?" His voice gets small and so unlike Box that my heart breaks even more.

What I don't tell him is just how much the question threatens to break me, too. Truthfully, it's not even an outcome I want to fathom, and yet those words bring the reality crashing down around me.

What *if* she doesn't choose us? We can't chase after her for the rest of our lives. We can't pine and wait. She'll move on eventually and we'll—

"Then that's just something we're going to have to learn to live with."

DELFIN

Queenie lives rent-free in my mind. I think about her more than I should. My brothers are pissed at me. At least, Box and Rock seem to be. They know I watched her leave and did nothing to stop her.

But what could I have done? Tied her down? Forced her here?

No.

At least I got those last few moments with her. We all got a last moment with her.

And I've been stealing more for myself.

Maybe I like the suffering. Maybe I can't live my life without it, but I spend my days driving through town, passing by her place and her work. To catch a glimpse of her.

Not to bring her back like Box would have done, but just to... to make sure she's okay.

At first glance, it seems like she's moved on. But I know her. Fuck, I've observed her often enough to know what truth lies behind her eyes.

She's as miserable as we are.

And it shouldn't bring me joy, but it does. Because when I see that expression I know.

For the first time, I'm positive and hopeful.

Hopeful for what the future might bring.

BOX

S lug was fucking right.

It doesn't matter how much I want Queenie for myself, and it's quite a fucking lot, I can't force her to want me. I'm used to taking everything I want, but it's Slug who makes me realize that a heart isn't something you can steal, and love isn't something you can force.

Sometimes it just isn't meant to be.

But I refuse to believe that Queenie doesn't think about us, that she doesn't want us just as fervently as we all want her back in our lives. I believe she will be back. I fucking know she will. It's only a matter of time before she comes to her senses.

I'm not a complete fucking saint.

Even if I'm going to listen to Slug and give Queenie her space to realize what it is she's missing, I'm still going to watch her from a distance. Whether he thinks it's a good fucking idea or not. I don't give a fuck.

I'm a masochist, always fucking have been. So I'm going to torture myself with glimpses of her, as many glimpses as I can as many times as I can.

Because I need her like an ache. I need her like a need a kick to the fucking balls to get an erection. I need her back because let's face the truth, without her, Slug and I aren't complete. Without her, we will never be complete.

So I spy.

I watch from the shadows as she goes about her life, and I smirk to myself while it happens as the days go by. Everyone else thinks it's over. That she was able to get over us that quickly, but watching her is how I know the truth.

She can keep on pretending, keep on going about her life as if we were never fucking in it in the first place, but the truth is she misses us. The Kraken MC is imprinted on every little fucking thing she does. We're there even when she tries to drown us out.

Poor little Queenie, I want to laugh.

She's so fucked.

Just like we're fucked.

And I'll just wait for her to realize that she can't live without us.

NAOMI

"Earth to Naomi."

I'm pulled out of my fucking daydreams with the sound of Lourdes' fingers snapping in front of my face. I blink, coming slowly out of my reverie.

"Huh?"

"Coño, Naomi, I've been talking to you for five minutes straight. Where's your mind at?"

It's with the fucking Kraken MC, much to my own dismay. Fucking ridiculous, really. I spent all but a week with them and already they consume every waking thought. I knew this would fucking happen; it's why I wanted out before feelings could set in. Before they could invade my mind and soul.

Sometimes I feel like the only thing that's been keeping me going has been my personal mantra.

You are not your mother.

You are not.

I've said it so often that I'm starting to believe it. She never would have been strong enough to leave.

Speaking of...

"Sorry," I murmur, pulling myself back to the present. "I'm just surprised you found the time to hang out with me today. Dimas finally let you off his leash?"

Lourdes sits back in her chair. We're hanging out at a coffee shop. The sun is shining brightly overhead, heating our dark skin. Whisps of sea air push back my braids and tug at Lourdes' curls.

She taps her nails against the surface of the table, looking at me with a soft expression. "Dimas and I broke up."

"Oh."

"For good."

My eyes widen. "Oh."

She sighs and leans forward again, resting her forearms on the table and pushing away her latte. "I know we've been through this before and you probably don't believe me. Hell, I've been back and forth with him so fucking often and have gone through so many ups and downs with that asshole that I realize now what a terrible friend I've been."

I'm struck dumb by her confession. Things I've only ever thought of her when wiping her tears, words that are probably better left unsaid because I know the response that comes after they're muttered like the back of my hands.

I know, because she's like my mother.

Or so I've thought...

"Lourdes—"

"No, let me finish. I feel like if I'd been less obsessed with the idea of Dimas, then I would have paid more attention to what was going on with you. Friends are supposed to be there for each other and I've been lacking lately. For that, I'm sorry."

I reach across the space that separates us and take her hand. "Lourdes, no. If anyone's sorry, it's me."

Her eyebrow raises in that sassy gesture I love.

"I mean, it is pretty fucked up that you never told me who your father was after how many years of knowing one another, but I'm pretty forgiving."

We chuckle and pull away. I look her over, looking for anything to indicate that she's unwell. That she's going to burst into tears at any given moment. But... what's usually there after a breakup is there no longer. She doesn't seem to have puffy, red shot eyes. She doesn't look haggard.

In fact, she looks very well put together.

At least more put together than me.

Fuck, I look like shit compared to her. I should be ashamed but I'm not ashamed about my appearance. More about the fact that I didn't notice her either in the past few weeks.

"You really left him," I whisper.

She smiles, and it's full of sadness and quite a bit of hope. "I did."

"Why?"

She reaches for her cup, her finger tracing the rim. "Because I realized that I loved him more than he loved me." She sighs. "And I deserve more than someone's half-assed love. I deserve someone who will burn down the world to be with me."

Her words have my mind flashing back to Box. To Scorp and Slug. Rock and Delfin. To all the Kraken members. They would have burned the world down for me. They would have done that and so much more for me, and I...

"So I've decided I'm going to just relax and have fun." She downs the rest of her drink and stands, obviously finished with the depressing conversation and ready to move on. "Speaking of, there's a new lingerie store that I want to go to down the—Woah!" As she speaks, a body bumps into her from the side, nearly knocking her back down onto the chair. An arm shoots out to steady her, pulling her up before she can fall.

I watch, a little bewildered myself, as she collides, chest-to-chest with a tall man. For a second, Lourdes is stunned and both of them freeze, staring into one another's eyes. For a second, it seems like the rest of the world falls away around them. Slowly, her hands smooth up the lapels of his suit jacket.

"S-sorry."

The man flashes a smile at her, and I have to do a double take of it. It had flashed something vicious within a fraction of a second, only to blur a second later. Fire seems to burn within those dark eyes and I blink, but when I open my eyes a second time, his features seem to alter into something I can't quite discern, erasing from my mind as soon as I catch a glimpse until I don't even know what I'm looking at anymore.

"The fault is mine," the man replies, his voice deep and lilted with the hint of an accent.

For a second, Lourdes seems frozen where she stands. "Erm..."

Slowly, he extricates himself from her hold, gifting her with a bow that seems straight out of a historical romance movie.

"Have fun," he drawls, lips twitching up into a smile, "at the lingerie store."

And then he's gone, whisking past us as quickly as he ran into her. And when Lourdes finally turns to me, her eyes are wide, almost frightful.

"You okay?"

"Huh? Oh, yeah. Yeah, sure. Let's go, slow poke."

I stand with a smile on my face. "Yeah, let's go."

We walk to the store in question and begin trying on sets of lingerie. We laugh and joke and it feels like old times, however my mind is on other things. On how happy Lourdes looks, how it's been so long since I've seen her look like that.

And it was there, in a changing room, with a studded leather vest hugging my breasts, that it hits me.

Lourdes *left* Dimas.

Lourdes, the woman who I've often compared to my mother, had the strength to leave a man who wasn't good for her. Those words she said echo in my mind.

"He wouldn't burn down the world for me."

I've always said I wouldn't be with men from an MC because they'd toss me around and not give me what I wanted or needed. But as I stand here, I realize that I may have already found men who *would* give me the world, if I only asked.

Men who would burn down another MC for me.

Slug sucker punched a man who hurt me. Box pulled me from the ocean. Since the beginning, the Krakens have tried protecting me, and I was just too stubborn to accept that that's what they were doing.

They were protecting me all along. And despite my own reservations, I fell for them in the time that they had me trapped in their compound. I stayed because deep down I wanted to. I wanted what only they could give, and when things got too real, when my feelings threatened to overwhelm me, I took the coward's way out and walked away.

Because it's easier to walk away and deny feelings rather than stay and get hurt like my mom did, like Lourdes did. But the thing is, the Krakens are nothing like my father. The Krakens are nothing like Dimas. They're good men; on the wrong side of the law, but good men just the same. They push me to be stronger, to accept my feelings that I'd otherwise keep hidden.

Without them I've been wandering in limbo, and before they came into my life it was much of the same thing. I realize now that they bring something to my life that I've always wanted but pretended I didn't.

Excitement.

Passion.

And the one thing I swore I'd never have.

Love.

I pull the garments off my body and quickly exit the dressing room.

"Lourdes."

"What's wrong?" She comes out of her dressing room clad in a soft green negligee. "Is everything okay?"

"I messed up, Lourdes."

She looks at me and seems to see everything I'm not saying. She gives me a soft smile and a single nod of her head, and her eyes glow with the mischief of someone who knew that this would happen all along.

"You bitch!"

She cackles.

"You knew?"

The accusation doesn't seem to faze her. "I had a vision the minute we left the compound. It was of you going back to them."

I grumble at her, which only makes her laugh harder. In between her fits of giggles, I feel suddenly very nervous. She had a vision let me going back to the Kraken compound.

But would they take me back? I've been gone for so long, and despite everything we've been through and the fact that they wanted me to stay, they still have their pride. Will I still fit in with them even if I go back?

Lourdes is laughing like she can see the doubts on my face. "I can't tell you what else I saw," she says.

"Well, why the hell not? You do every other time."

"Because every other time, my visions weren't about you. If I tell you, it might change the course of your actions." She smiles ruefully. "Besides, it took you long enough to realize your feelings. You need to be brave and face them."

"But what if I get hurt?"

"That's the point of love, Queenie. Sometimes it hurts and that's only because it means you had the guts to love at all."

And that's my problem. It's always been my problem. All my relationships have been flings. I've kept everyone at arm's length, even friends. Not because I'm brave, not because I'm avoiding becoming like someone else. It's because I'm a coward, and it only took me this moment to realize that Lourdes is braver than I could be. Maybe she got her heart stomped on many times, but in the end she put herself out there even knowing what the result could be.

And I'm such a dumbass for doing her such a disservice as to compare her to my mother. Maybe I've even been doing my own mother a disservice. Maybe I've been doing myself a disservice for only now realizing the bravest of all of us in this life are the ones who dare; who dare to smile, who dare to dream, and who dare to love.

"Go," Lourdes orders. "Go get your Krakens."

I smile at her. "I will."

"You better, and then call me afterwards 'cause I want the tea." She raises her arms and flops them around, her version of imitating a Kraken bursting past the surface of the ocean. "Release the Kraken!" she screams, drawing all eyes to towards us in the store.

I laugh and wave her off. "I'm going."

And with my heart pumping up a beat in my throat, I run out of the store and towards the Kraken motorcycle club.

I've been staring up at their compound for twenty minutes and can't bring myself to walk up.

Queenie, you fucking coward.

Taking a fortifying breath, I give myself a pep talk.

Come on, bitch. Grow some ovaries, get up there, and walk in...

Fuuuck, why is love so scary?

I feel like I'm on the verge of an anxiety attack. My chest begins heaving, my hands shaking. I'm being ridiculous. I can face down mermen trying to kill me, shoot them point blank, make a fucking bomb, but I can't go up the slope of sand and into the compound.

Queenie, what are you waiting for? Just go!

"Queenie?"

I yelp as my soul tries to yeet itself out of my body, and I whirl to find Scorpion behind me, standing on the edge where the sand meets the ocean. He's drenched in water, waves crashing against his back. He doesn't seem to notice them.

He's staring at me so intently I feel like I can melt on the spot.

But seeing him also gives me a wave of strength.

"Scorpion..."

"What are you doing here, Naomi?"

He doesn't sound angry or sad. Just... resigned.

I hate that. I hate that maybe I'm the one who did that to him. Sweet Scorpion.

"I came to see you."

"Well, you saw me." He starts making his way upwards, walking right past me and towards the compound. That bit of rejection hurts. It makes me want to curl into myself and give up on this entirely. But as soon as the thought forms, I imagine Lourdes there, slapping me upside the head and telling me to stop being a pussy.

"Scorpion!"

He freezes but doesn't turn around. I hate that he won't look at me. Have I so thoroughly ruined what we have here?

I want to hope that there's still a chance.

"I'm sorry," I blurt out.

He finally turns, slowly, but there's no particular expression on his face other than boredom. "For what?"

I take a breath. "For leaving."

"I knew you were going to leave, Naomi. You didn't really keep it a secret."

I refused to be called their Old Lady. Maybe I'd given away more than I should have. Maybe Delfin told them about our conversation.

"Well, I'm back now."

He scoffs. "Back now? What does that even mean? Are you here for a little while to come in, use us right before you leave us high and dry all over again?"

The words feel like a slap in the face, and they instantly piss me off. All of my earlier fear is gone, and in its place is instant rage. I march up the slope towards him and my palms meet his chest, shoving him backwards a step.

"How dare you?" I demand. "How dare you flip the situation and make it seem like I left you?"

I mean, I did leave, but that's besides the point.

"You guys kidnapped me. You guys held me here against my will and then get mad when I seek freedom? Way to gaslight me, asshole."

Scorpion rolls his eyes. "Please. You know that if you wanted to leave, you would have left. You blew up a compound, Naomi, and killed everyone inside it. I find it hard to believe that you were so helpless when it came to us."

He has a point.

"You and I both know you stayed because you wanted to until you didn't want to anymore." There's hurt in his voice. He doesn't disguise it this time and it cleaves through me.

"I left because I thought I had to."

"Make all the excuses you want," he says. "It doesn't change the fact that you left."

"Can you really blame me for leaving?" I step closer until we're toe-to-toe.

All he does is look at me sadly. "Why are you back, Naomi?"

What can I say? That I was a dumbass? That I realized all too late that I was a coward desperate for love but too afraid to reach out for it? That I was terrified of making my mother's mistakes and that I'd be left alone and heartbroken? That they were too much, too soon and I wasn't ready for what they could give me?

I'm not sure if there is anything I can say that will make me leaving better, because I hurt them. And I hurt myself, too.

I guess the only path here is one of honesty.

"Because I love you."

Scorpion blinks and his eyes widen, his mouth drops opened. He looks flabbergasted and I step forward, raising my hands to cup either cheek.

"What did you say?"

"I said I love—"

He drops down to claim my mouth in his. The kiss is tender but no less intense. His mouth claims mine with deep strokes of the tongue. It's all-consuming, and we press together tightly. His hands smooth down my body, cupping my ass, and in one swift movement, he's lifting me up. My legs wrap around his waist, and we pull away, panting as he turns and marches me straight up the slope and towards the compound.

He kicks the door open, and my heart is hammering against his chest from nerves and anticipation. Scorpion wants me. Maybe there's hope that the rest of the guys will as well.

"I'm glad you're back, pet," he whispers against my lips as he steps through the door. He takes another kiss from me, stopping in the middle of the room. The music that blasted seconds ago from the speakers dims and the chattering stops, but it doesn't matter that we're being watched.

All that matters is... I feel home.

When a fist wraps into my braids and yanks tenderly, pulling me away from Scorpion, I gasp as I'm met with Box's menacing stare. He smiles, licking his lips as he looks down on me and takes me in.

"Thought that was you," he purrs. "What are you doing here, Queenie?"

I gulp, but somehow end up bringing a smile to my face. Scorpion squeezes my ass, whispering, "Tell him."

"Planning on it."

"Tell me what?"

"I love you."

"Ha." He tugs my braids tighter, pulling me towards him so our lips are touching. "You think I don't fucking know that?"

And then he claims my mouth in his.

It's brutal and violent, and it's everything I love and miss about Box. He dominates me, and when he pulls away, Scorpion slides me down his body and turns me, keeping his big hands on my hips. Like he's holding me steady or keeping me from fleeing again.

"I knew you'd be back," Box says.

I frown. "Don't make me kick you in the dick."

"Oh, I'd love that." He cackles gleefully.

"God, please kick him in the dick. They've all been fucking ridiculous since you've left."

Suddenly we're surrounded and Sugar's the one who spoke. She shoulders Box aside daringly and pulls me into a hug.

"Missed you, Naomi," she whispers. "But don't ever break my brother's heart again."

When she pulls away, we communicate silently, me promising it'll never happen again and telling her she has the right to be a big sister and punch me if that's what she wants. Her eyes shine with humor before she steps to the side, revealing Slug and Delfin.

Delfin approaches me first and my heart swells with affection. He's silent as he stops in front of me.

"You good?" he asks, his voice all but a growl.

I smile shyly. "I'm good."

He nods before he bends and presses a quick kiss to my cheek. That's as much affection as he'll show publicly and I respect it. It means everything to me. He didn't offer an explanation because he knows why I did what I did, and I can't help but wonder if he, like Box, knew I'd be back eventually.

Then Slug approaches me, his gait shy and uncertain. I'm the one who reaches out first, taking his hands in mine. "Slug..."

"Are you really back?" he whispers.

"Yeah, Slug. I'm really back."

"I'd hoped."

Even after I hurt them and walked away, they'd still hoped. It was selfish of me. Well, maybe not selfish. Maybe I needed that time to realize that what I really want in the world is them.

The men crowd around me and I feel full, my heart near bursting with joy. But there's still one puzzle piece of me missing.

"Where's—"

Rock.

Everyone parts in dramatic fashion to reveal him. He strides over, intensity around him like a palpable aura. He swells with it, and it makes me gulp. This, this is what he looked like the last time I'd seen him. Filled with rage and desire, but he looks different, too. Haggard. His eyes are rimmed red, and he flicks his eyes up and down, assessing me like he did the first time we met.

"What do you want?"

I know that with him it's going to be different. He's not just going to open his arms and welcome me back to the compound. He wants more. Rock has always wanted more from me, demanded it. He's tried to force me to act like a queen, as if he knew all along that I had it in me the whole time. Something I didn't even know myself.

"I came back for you."

His eyebrows raise and his arms cross against his chest, highlighting the contours of his muscles body.

"Fuck, you're gonna make me say it. I fucked up, okay? I was too much of a coward to stay and fight for you. But I realized something while I was gone. I realized that all I did was push you all away even though part of me deep down knew I always wanted to stay. Because I want you. All of you. Not just for today and tomorrow, but for the rest of my life. I love this compound. I love the club, the honeys. I love riding on the back of your bike. But mostly I love you, and I came back here to tell you guys that... that..."

"To tell us what, Queenie?"

I take a deep breath. "That I want to be your Old Lady."

There's a beat of silence. Two. Three. It stretches for miles until Rock uncrosses his arms and steps into my space. He bends so low that our noses are touching, and he smirks.

"It's about goddamn time."

And he kisses me, just as tenderly as Scorpion and as possessive as Box. It makes my toes curl and finally, finally I feel like I'm where I'm meant to be, surrounded by who I'm meant to be with.

"So you finally admit it."

"Yes. I want to be your Old Lady."

"Good," Box says. "Because we already bought you the fucking jacket."

Tears prickle at the back of my eyes when one of the honeys procures it. Leather and long-sleeved, with a logo patched over the breast in a symbol that has come to mean so much to me.

And just beneath the kraken tearing through the sea?

Queenie.

Kraken Queen.

Rock takes it and holds it out, an invitation for me to step into it. I do, placing one arm in the sleeve and then the other. I look down at it, at this big step I've just taken, and I'm not terrified anymore.

"Welcome home," Rock says with a smile.

Yes. That's exactly what they are, what this place is to me.

Home.

The End

If you enjoyed the Caribbean's paranormal, criminal underbelly and want more, please consider joining my Patreon for a special bonus scene from Lourdes's point of view!

ABOUT THE AUTHOR

Aleera Anaya Ceres is the International Bestselling author of several series including the Origins of the Six series and the Daughter of Triton series. Like most introverts, Aleera prefers to curl up with a good book, listen to music, paint, read tarot cards, and snack on the tears and heartbreak of her readers. A proud Mexican-American from the state of Kansas, Aleera currently resides in Tlaxcala, Mexico with her husband and children.

You can find/contact her here:
aleeraceres@aacbooks.com
Facebook.com/AleeraAnayaCeres

ALSO BY ALEERA ANAYA CERES

Adult Fantasy Series

Fae Elementals

A Dance With Fire

A Sword of Ice

A Shield of Water

The Dark Waters series

Riptide

Reverse Harem Series

Royal Secrets

Secrets Among the Tides

Whispers Beneath the Deep

Caresses Between the Sand

Death Beyond the Waves

<u>Royal Lies</u>

Slave to Ice & Shadows

Princess in Frost Castles

Queen of Frozen War

<u>Origins of the Six series</u>

Academy of Six

Control of Five

Destruction of Two

Wrath of One

<u>A Daughter of Triton series</u>

Triton's Academy

Triton's Prophecy

Triton's Legacy

A Daughter of Triton Box set

<u>Dr. Hyde's Prison for the Rare</u>

Escaping Hallow Hill Academy

Surviving Hallow Hill

Reverse Harem Standalone

Queenie & the Krakens

Paranormal Romance Series

<u>Deep Sea Chronicles</u>

Fall in Deep

Siren Queen

<u>The Blood Novels</u>

Love Bites

Blood Drug

My Master

Last Hope

Young Adult standalone

The Last Mermaid

Made in United States
North Haven, CT
27 August 2022

23339111R00200